Pra
IN THE VEIN~

"A provocative dark fantasy with all the alluring qualities of siren song. Sensuous and lushly romantic, *In the Veins of the Drowning* ensorcelled me from the very first page."

— Ava Reid, #1 *New York Times* bestselling author of *A Study in Drowning*

"An absolute riptide of a book. It draws you in, pulls you under. Atmospheric and evocative, Cassidy's writing sews adventure, romance, and political intrigue together while maintaining its ominous tenor. Monsters lurk, and danger knows your name. I was completely swept away."

— Rachel Gillig, *New York Times* bestselling author of *One Dark Window*

"Cassidy has written your new favorite romantasy couple: a king tormented by his honor and a siren grappling with her monstrosity, each of them walking the knife's edge of duty and desire. Sensual, gripping, and resonant as siren song, *In the Veins of the Drowning* will sink its lure into you and leave you breathless."

— Allison Saft, #1 *New York Times* bestselling author of *A Dark and Drowning Tide*

"Perilous stakes underscore a defiant, hate-to-love affair that's as vulnerable as it is sexy. *In the Veins of the Drowning* is a sprawling, incandescent debut that emerges with talons and teeth."

— Isa Agajanian, author of *Modern Divination*

"As glittering as the sea and lush as its foamy waves, *In the Veins of the Drowning* will lure you in like a siren's call with its mysterious lore and fierce, yet tender romance. Imogen and Theo are perfect reflections of each other and I have no doubt they will ensnare the hearts of readers the way they've ensnared mine. Devastatingly atmospheric and utterly captivating."

— Maddie Martinez, author of *The Maiden and Her Monster*

"Rich with atmosphere and lore, this lush fantasy is like the sea that roars at its heart: fierce and dangerous; darkly glittering. The ferocious tide of Imogen and Theo's irresistible romance will sweep you off your feet, but it is Imogen herself — grappling with her power and what it means to be a monster — who will steal your heart. A gorgeous, spellbinding debut."

— Claire Legrand, *New York Times* bestselling author of *Furyborn*

"*In the Veins of the Drowning* is a seductive study of the monstrous, weaving a rich tapestry of prose and emotion in which beauty has talons, memories hold magic, and blood runs deep."

— Maggie Rapier, author of *Soulgazer*

"Consider me drowning and gasping for air. *In the Veins of the Drowning* is as seductive as a siren's song and as haunting as the sea itself. Don't miss sinking into this gorgeous debut!"

— Brittney Arena, author of *A Dance of Lies*

IN THE
VEINS
OF THE
DROWNING

IN THE
VEINS
OF THE
DROWNING

BOOK ONE OF THE SIREN MAGE

KALIE CASSIDY

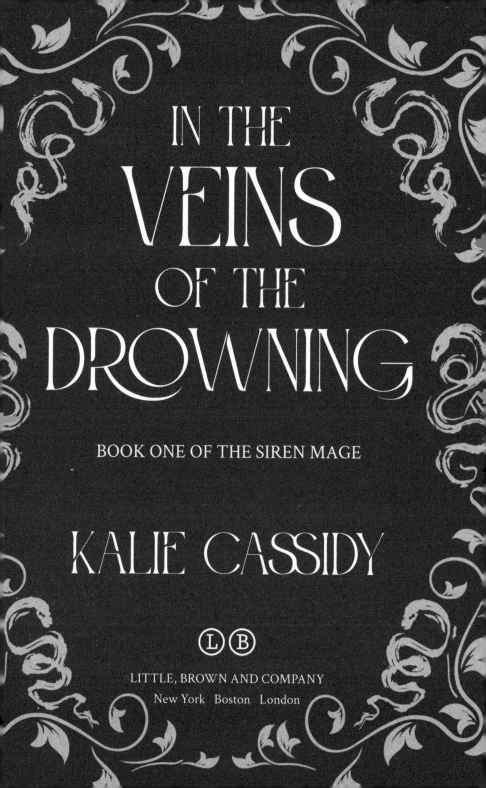

Ⓛ Ⓑ

LITTLE, BROWN AND COMPANY
New York Boston London

The characters and events in this book are fictitious. Any similarity to real persons, living or dead, is coincidental and not intended by the author.

Copyright © 2025 by Kalie Cassidy

Excerpt from *In the Wake of the Ruined* copyright © 2025 by Kalie Cassidy

Hachette Book Group supports the right to free expression and the value of copyright. The purpose of copyright is to encourage writers and artists to produce the creative works that enrich our culture.

The scanning, uploading, and distribution of this book without permission is a theft of the author's intellectual property. If you would like permission to use material from the book (other than for review purposes), please contact permissions@hbgusa.com. Thank you for your support of the author's rights.

Little, Brown and Company
Hachette Book Group
1290 Avenue of the Americas, New York, NY 10104
littlebrown.com

First Edition: July 2025

Little, Brown and Company is a division of Hachette Book Group, Inc. The Little, Brown name and logo are trademarks of Hachette Book Group, Inc.

The publisher is not responsible for websites (or their content) that are not owned by the publisher.

The Hachette Speakers Bureau provides a wide range of authors for speaking events. To find out more, go to hachettespeakersbureau.com or email hachettespeakers@hbgusa.com.

Little, Brown and Company books may be purchased in bulk for business, educational, or promotional use. For information, please contact your local bookseller or the Hachette Book Group Special Markets Department at special.markets@hbgusa.com.

Print book interior design by Taylor Navis

ISBN 9780316587600

LCCN is available at the Library of Congress.

Printing 1, 2025

LSC-C

Printed in the United States of America

For those who seek a home.
May you find it, and when you do, may it be sturdy and warm.

AUTHOR'S NOTE

In the Veins of the Drowning is a story about belonging, love, and identity. While it explores the lighter side of those themes, this story also contains darker imagery that might be difficult for some readers, including body horror and abuse. A full list of content warnings can be found on my author website.

IN THE
VEINS
OF THE
DROWNING

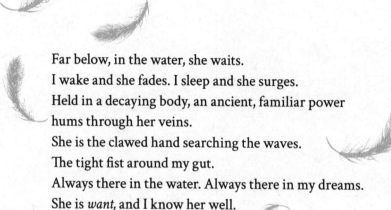

Far below, in the water, she waits.
I wake and she fades. I sleep and she surges.
Held in a decaying body, an ancient, familiar power
hums through her veins.
She is the clawed hand searching the waves.
The tight fist around my gut.
Always there in the water. Always there in my dreams.
She is *want,* and I know her well.

PART I

THE MOUNTAIN

1

The air had grown heavy with the scent of the sea. I could nearly taste it, curling through the warm throne room like a tentacle.

It filled me with an upending sort of dread.

Guests poured in from the entry hall, their tittering and chatter pinging off the marble, but I clung to the outer edges, closer to the bone-white walls. I'd done so well keeping away. I'd spent my life ignoring the lure of the sea, only for it to slink past Fort Linum's defenses on the silks and fine wools of the long-traveled guests like an insidious stowaway.

"Imogen?" Agatha came to my side, studying me with sharp, worried eyes. She looked much the same as she had when she had been my teenage governess and I had been a girl of six. Impossibly youthful, warm brown skin, curls as shiny and dark as the ink in a pot. Soft lines did not even crease the high edges of her cheekbones, but I supposed one must smile often to earn them. "What's wrong? You're pale."

"It's the dress." I set a hand to my sternum, where a deep fluttering had started. "It's too damn tight. Will you loosen the laces?"

Her look turned raw with frustration. "They're not long enough. I don't understand why you agreed to wear this awful thing." She adjusted the ruffle at my shoulder, shaking her head. "How you agreed to marry a man whose job it is to hunt and kill —"

"Agatha, please." I kept my attention on the room — the food-laden tables, the flickering candles, the cups filled with wine. "Not now."

"Then when? The wedding is in two days."

"I'm aware." When I met her gaze, there was a desperation in it that twisted my insides. "You know that I wasn't given a choice."

Tense, she scanned the throne room, then leaned in close. "We could leave," she whispered. "We should have left years ago. There might be a way —"

I grabbed her by the hand and dragged her around the head table, into a tight, shadowed alcove. "Agatha, enough." Her brown eyes were wide and searching, as faceted as polished wood. "Please. I beg you to stop condemning me for trying to make the best of this situation. I've done well keeping myself safe here, haven't I? I will continue to. I must."

Disappointment stooped her shoulders, but her voice filled with a cutting edge. "If this marriage, and the misery it will bring you, doesn't make you see that you do not belong here... I have little hope that anything will."

I wanted to tip back my chin so I might appear sure. So that she might think me as brave and hardy as she was. But I was no such thing. "That's unfair of you." I sounded ground down and soft. "Where would I go?"

She threw up her hands, exasperated. "Well, I suppose we'll never know now, will we?"

An awful pit grew in my stomach. It was still early in the afternoon. The engagement feast wouldn't be fully underway for a while yet. I searched the room for my fiancé, but he was nowhere to be seen. Nor was King Nemea. More gossiping revelers slowly crept through the towering throne room doors. More and more salt air slithered in with them. My breaths turned rapid and shallow. "I'll be right back."

Agatha reached for my hand and held it tight. "I'm sorry. I just want you —"

I shook my head. "I know. I'm all right. I just need some air."

"I'm coming with you."

Even in the dim, I could see how Agatha's petite body had gone taut with vexation and the pit in my middle only widened. There were so many ways in which I was powerless, but it hurt me most to know that what I lacked caused Agatha so much pain.

"No." I gave her hand a squeeze. "Come up with an excuse if someone notices I'm gone. I won't be long."

I whisked away from her before she could protest further, through the tall oaken doors and the clog of visitors. I couldn't remember the last time Fort Linum had been so full, but I shouldered my way to the courtyard and up the winding narrow path that led to the fort's parapets. The air outside was cool and clear. Blessedly empty of brine.

The fluttering in my chest instantly ceased.

My too-wide skirt scraped the walls, snagging some of the beads, but I trudged ahead. My favorite spot in all of Fort Linum, the one with the grandest view of the sea, was at the end of the battlements, and up a steep run of stairs. I was gasping by the time I reached the secluded spot.

Tugging at my bodice, I traced the thin gray edge of the northern beach in the distance. On a map, the Isle of Seraf looked like a beastly jaw protruding from the waters of Leucosia. It was all jagged peaks and ravenous valleys, and upon its highest summit, King Nemea had built his fort. He'd forced it into existence, carving it from the rock, cramming it into the crooked teeth of the island like a stuck piece of gristle.

I tried to purge my anxieties with an exhale, only to have my eyes sting. It was inexplicable, how both terror and anticipation over my wedding filled me in equal measure. How I both feared what might come of it and hoped for the best. I struck the wall with my palm. "Bloody fucking Gods."

"Has the party already started, then?"

The deep, smoky voice made me jump. I whirled toward the far end of the curved lookout to see a brooding figure — dark and tall — leaning against the fort wall. He wore a white shirt, tucked neatly into his trousers. His black boots were polished to an absurd shine. No doubt he was one of the many newly arrived guests who now swarmed the fort, thrilled by a rare invitation to gawk. To see what the Isle of Seraf and its hateful, reclusive king had become over the last many decades.

I adjusted my skirt and glowered. "The gentlemanly thing to do would have been to announce yourself when I arrived."

He gave a conceding nod. Brow pinched, his gaze fell over the abundance of red silk ruffles at my low neckline, the heavy glass beading in the precise color of blood — the king's color — stitched onto my bodice. The dress was gaudy and unfashionable, and as he stared at it a sardonic half smile curled his mouth. "Unbelievably, I didn't notice you right away."

My mood was tenuous, and I wanted to see the smug tilt of his lips fall. I gave a scoff. "How dare you laugh at me, sir."

His eyes rounded with indignation. "I was not —"

"Oh please," I said. "I had wished to be alone, but every inch of this place is crawling with ill-mannered people — this parapet included."

His mouth opened, then shut. For a long moment, he simply stared at me, stupefied. "Well..." He crossed closer, narrowed his eyes to a scowl. "Seeing as how we had both hoped to be alone, perhaps we could be alone together. Though I see that you might not be in the mood to share."

I held his stare. He reminded me of summer. Skin a golden brown, eyes the color of dark leaves. The wind tousled his inky hair so that it hung over his creased brow. He was regal, towering and straight, well-built and graceful, but it was the way he looked at me down the length of his ever-so-slightly crooked nose that made me certain he was of noble birth. I yearned to tell him *no* simply because he seemed unaccustomed to hearing it, but something in me clamped down on the impulse. "We can share," I finally said, "but only if you promise not to laugh at this ludicrous dress again."

A breath. Another. Then his scowl melted into a full smile that dimpled his left cheek. "A tall ask."

My jaw unhinged in amused outrage.

"Forgive me." He raised his hands in surrender, face serious once more. "I'm simply relieved to know you're aware that it's . . . noticeable."

"Of course." I gave my skirt a deprecating flounce. "I'm impossible to miss."

He gave another dimpled smile as he rested his elbows on the crenellated wall and stared at the vista.

A long silence sat between us. "And why," I asked, "are you seeking refuge from the party? Strange to travel all this way, only to hide."

He flexed his jaw. "This fort . . . It's not a pleasant place." His low voice had turned somber, ill at ease. He forced a flat smile. "And the wine is terrible. And you?"

I eyed the strong lines of his profile. There was something inviting about him, something that made me want to tell him the truth. "I'm most certainly avoiding the wine," I said, instead. "Expect to wake with a headache and a burning stomach if you drink too much."

"You couldn't pay me."

We stood side by side, staring over the mountain peaks and old twisted cypresses, out to the glittering band of sea.

"Quite a view," he said, quietly.

"It is." It was endless and sweeping and made me feel immeasurably small. "I don't think that's why Nemea built this fort so high up, though."

He gave a disgruntled sound deep in his chest at my mention of King Nemea. Mood suddenly sullen, he turned and rested his back against the parapet wall.

"You don't like him, do you?" I asked. There were not many who did.

His sidelong glance was fleeting. "I've heard rumors this fort was built this high so that he could pitch people from the windows and be certain they would die."

I gave a dark laugh, then gasped in a shallow breath. Nemea was far more inventive in his cruelty than to simply throw subjects from fort windows. "That's quite the rumor. And do you believe it?"

The way his attention bore down on me made me still. He studied me, as if he were cataloging my every feature, as if he searched for something in them. Finally, in a voice that rolled through his chest like the storms over the valley, he said, "I think the only reason anyone would reside this high up — this far from the rest of the world — is because they either have something to fear or something to hide."

My breath snagged. I looked toward the sea again, blinking against the returned sting in my eyes, feeling stripped bare. "Oh."

"Have I upset you?"

"Not at all." I fisted my skirt and started toward the stairs. "Excuse me."

"Wait." He took a tight step closer, a gentle hand raised up in offering. "May I be of assistance?"

The earnest crease in his brow made me want to spit. "Do I look like I need it?"

"You do," he said, commandingly, wholly unfazed by my turn of emotion. "There are tears in your eyes."

He looked at me again with that incisive stare, like I was made of water he could see straight through. I opened my mouth — to say what, I wasn't sure — when he cut me off.

"The entryway and halls are full of guests eager for gossip. As we've established, you're quite . . ." His gaze darted down the front of my body. ". . . conspicuous in that gown. It would be wise to take a moment before you descend."

His fastidious caution stunned me. There was something about him that made me want to relent. Perhaps it was that I could sense no malice in him, no lack of patience. I could feel his steadiness, a rooted, immovable quality that made me want to linger. We stood, gazes locked, at the top of the stairs.

A strong gust boomed up the wall below us. It howled around the fort's corners and ran through our hair. I took a step back. "Thank you for the conversation," I said, curtly. "Enjoy gaping at Seraf's horrors, my lord." I started down the stairs. "They're as endless as the cheap wine."

When I returned to the throne room it was close to bursting. It brimmed with beating music, bodies, and more of that unfamiliar salt air.

Agatha stood at my side, arm looped with mine. She took a deep breath and gave a shiver. "I suppose it's best you can't breathe."

I grunted at that, unamused. The conversation from the parapet played over in my mind, and that odd plucking feeling in my chest had returned. "I need some wine."

"It's worse than usual." She took a sip of her own half-empty glass and grimaced.

"Then I'll drink it quickly." I wound us through groups of whispering guests, toward where the drink table sat. I downed a quick glass, then tried to pull in a breath, which earned me her scowl.

"Nemea ordered the dress to be made that tight on purpose, you know." Her mood hadn't improved in the least.

I took another gulp. "Yes, I know." I'd already surmised that Nemea had wanted my gown to be as heavy and pinching as a fetter. Expensive and garish, so that visitors would see his ward, would look closely, and I would be tasked with hiding my pain. He wanted me to remember that even in marriage, I would still be his to control. "I hope you find someone to dance with," I said in a gentle voice, trying to change the subject. "I know how you love it. The music shouldn't be ruined by my circumstances."

"They're hard to ignore," she said. I watched the first of the dancers twist and spin, letting the vibrations of the drum and lute stifle that feeling in my chest. "And how was dinner with your adoring captain last night?" Agatha asked, the question dripping with sarcasm. "Was your husband-to-be what we'd expected?"

We'd expected him to be dull and harsh, but to my surprise, he'd been anything but. I'd been surprised by his wit. He'd shown manners and offered thoughtful conversation. He'd kissed me softly when he left, his fingers firm on my jaw. "It was nice. He was kind."

The look she gave me felt like a strike to the knees. "*Kind.*"

My throat clamped. "I . . . I meant that he — I simply meant that I didn't fear him."

A woman beside me gasped and pointed toward the throne

room's tall oaken doors. She had not been the first to do so. Plenty of young ladies had swooned, leaning into their friends or escorts, at the sight of the Siren wing hanging above them, stark against the pale wall. The large feathers were stretched wide; bolts through the bone held it to its wooden plaque. The dim, golden candlelight didn't pull out the riot of colors on the wing's black plumage — the slash of iridescent blue and green near its base, the purple near its fringed edge — but I could paint it from memory. My gaze dipped to the inscription in the marble below it.

THE MONSTER IS ALWAYS SLAIN.

That motto was the black-tipped root of King Nemea's cruelty and the reason all the other rulers of the archipelago loathed him. It was why all these people had sailed for days across treacherous seas to visit a poor, near-barren rock of an island. For decades, King Nemea had obliterated all goodwill that might have once been his with the heinous practice of hunting divine Sirens.

I moved us away from the group of young women, whose eyes had found me and drank me in with condescension. Nemea had done well at making me a spectacle. We tucked in near the dais, where King Nemea stood speaking with the queen of the united kingdoms of Della and Gos. He was tall and barrel-chested. Wild black hair streaked with gray contrasted his fairer skin. That narrow, usually dour face of his looked so strange with a smile upon it. He gestured proudly and patted his chest, and the deep red coat he wore, boasting ruby buttons down its front, looked too fine against his rough countenance.

"He's positively glowing," Agatha drawled, a hateful frown on her face as she stared at him.

"I can't understand how you can look at him with such open

dislike." I pulled again at my bodice, gave a small moan of discomfort. "Aren't you afraid he'll notice?"

"I'm incapable of looking at him any other way. My face won't allow it." She attempted a crooked smile that did nothing to make her look less dismal. "I'll find you shortly," she said. "Going to get some more of Nemea's terrible wine."

I clung to the edge of the dais, illuminated in the wavering light of half a dozen candelabras. The brightly colored guests looked so carefree, flushed from drink and dance and laughter. Not one of them seemed to notice how King Nemea's highest-ranking soldiers skulked through their midst like death itself, clad in their night-black armor. I searched every one of them wondering where their captain — my fiancé — might be. In the candlelight, the large ring he'd given me seemed to trap the flame in its angles.

The spinel stone was the deep gray of the sea in a storm. Spinels were not found on the Leucosian archipelago. They were only mined on the northern continent of Obelia, and no captain from any kingdom could afford such a stone. I could only assume that Nemea had given it to him.

I twisted the ring with my thumb. It was a rare and expensive shackle. And I was stuck, yes, but more importantly, I was safe. On King Nemea's mountain, my mind did not often stray to its darker recesses, where thoughts of shredded flesh and dark water and rivulets of blood did their best to lure me. Here, I could live dulled and peaceful. I would do all I could to keep it that way.

King Nemea stepped onto the dais. The head table set upon it was laden with customary gifts from all the neighboring kingdoms. The swath of red silk draped across it was embroidered with twisting black eels. A gift from Della and Gos, I guessed, as they were famous for their silkworms. Blood-colored flowers sat in sprawling arrangements, likely gifted from Varya. Nemea fisted a new silver goblet, studded with rubies. "Don't linger in the dark, Imogen," he said, without casting me a glance. "Come up here."

Careful of my skirt, I took the stairs and came to his side. He took my hands and raised my arms. With impassive gray eyes he took in the intricacies of my gown. The pins in my hair, the heavy rubies pulling at the soft flesh of my ears. "The gown looks like a perfect fit," he said in a snide voice.

"It is, Your Majesty." I gave a weak smile.

He reached up with an inelegant hand and tugged at a dark curl that rested on my shoulder. "What's this?"

"The curl, Your Majesty?"

"You were to have it all pinned up." His already cool gaze turned frigid. "As I had instructed."

He'd given me no such instruction. I bent into a low curtsy. "Of course. I can go —"

He gave a quick shake, the gesture impressively withering and dismissive at once. "It'll do." He looked out over the glittering throne room, filled with guests. "It's something, isn't it?"

"Yes."

"And you..." He set a gentle hand to my cheek, and I went deathly still. He had never struck me before, but I'd seen the flex of his hand, as if it yearned to. I knew how his soft voice could boom, how easily he could order me locked away for a week. "Are you happy?"

I paused at the strange question. "I am. How could I not be?"

"Precisely. The gown, the feast — it's all more than you deserve."

"Yes, Your Majesty."

His gaze locked onto someone across the room, and it was as if a bolt struck him. He took me by the wrist and hauled me off the dais. "I don't imagine you think often of a king's duty, do you?"

"Not often, Your Majesty." My feet could hardly move fast

enough to keep up with him as he wove us through the crowd. "But I have thought of it."

"And what do you think?" The music rose. A swell of strings and a drum like a heartbeat filled my ears. Bodies pressed toward the center of the room, where the next dance was to begin. "Of *duty*. Do you think it is achieved by carving out pieces of yourself or by growing, collecting, so that you are equipped to do what is needed when it is time?"

"Your Majesty, I don't know what you mean. Both, perhaps?"

We came to a sudden halt before a wall of gold-armored soldiers. Six of them. All were broad and unmoving, with flowering vines carved into their breastplates, their vambraces. "Theodore Ariti," Nemea barked.

"Hello, Nemea," came a disgruntled voice from behind the soldiers. I recognized it, smoky and deep. The guards parted and there stood the man from the lookout. He was even more striking now, clothed in a beautiful deep green coat and wearing a perfect scowl. Tucked into his dark waving hair sat a golden crown of woven laurel. That scowl slipped toward me, and his eyes widened.

I averted my gaze quickly, feeling the heat rise in my cheeks, and sank into a low curtsy before the king of Varya.

2

My legs shook as I rose.

I knew King Theodore to be twenty-seven — a year older than I was — and ever since he had taken the throne seven years ago, Nemea had not ceased in his obsessive complaining. The "boy-king," as he still called him, was too haughty, too good, too loved, too honorable to be a ruler that Nemea could ever respect.

"I've brought the bride to meet you." Nemea's voice came sharp and cold. "This is Lady Imogen Nel, my ward. She and I were just speaking of kingly duty. She'd love to hear your thoughts on the matter while you take her for a turn around the dance floor."

King Theodore's scowl lingered on me for a heartbeat before he gave Nemea a beleaguered look. "Very well, Nemea. It's kingly duty that she's eager to discuss? If the dance is long enough, we can muse over just how thoroughly you lack it."

I gaped at his lack of fear. He did not bother to tend to Nemea's fragility the way the court did — the way *I* did. Before Nemea could even form a retort, King Theodore extended his hand and, mortified, I set mine within it. His calluses scratched, but his touch was warm, gentle. My mind rattled as I remembered our interaction on the lookout. I'd been emotional. I'd been disparaging and impolite. As King Theodore led me away, Nemea's meaningful gaze sank into me like a blade. What he wanted me to do was clear. Charm. Mollify.

"I beg your forgiveness, Your Majesty," I said, my voice small. "I didn't know who you were. I would never have been so familiar —"

"Where is your fiancé, Lady Imogen?" he asked, ignoring my apology completely.

"I —" I swallowed, trying to strengthen my voice. "I'm not sure. Perhaps the captain is hiding away with cold feet, preparing to beg His Majesty to be released from our engagement."

"Is the captain an idiot as well as a murderer?"

His words struck me, and I did not know if I should feel flattered or shamed. Silent and tense, we found our spot on the dance floor. His gaze pressed down on me, but I kept my eyes on the wall above him, on the disembodied Siren wing that hung upon it.

A lilting, plucky tune filled the air. The thought of dancing an unending reel with him forced a stilted smile to my face. I spoke above the music, trying anew for exuberance. "I'm honored by your presence, Your Majesty. I know you traveled a long way." He set a hand to my waist, and the quick steps began.

"I couldn't miss an opportunity to gape at Seraf's horrors, now could I?" he said, watching me keenly. I bit into my tongue. "I know your handmaid, Agatha." He nodded to her across the room, where she stood glowering at the sea of people, holding a goblet in her fist. "I was surprised to see her here of all places."

His disdain for *here* was clear in the harsh way the word slipped through his teeth. "I didn't realize you were acquainted." It was hard to imagine Agatha having a life before she had come into mine. "And how do you know her?"

"She was my governess — for a time."

"She was mine as well." She must have been in Varya immediately before she'd come to Seraf. "And would she scold you for dipping below the bottom line with your quill, like she did me?"

"No," he answered, with perfect austerity. "I never dipped below the line."

"Oh." I found myself missing the kindness, the warmth, that I'd seen in him earlier. "I see."

The steps of the dance were quick and twisting. I slid under King Theodore's arm, hopped and spun, and could barely breathe for the way my dress clamped as tightly as a fist around my ribs. I stepped back in front of him and set my hand in his, but his fingers wouldn't curl over my palm to hold it. He stopped us midstep.

"Is there a problem, Your Majesty?" I asked, wincing at the stitch in my side.

"Yes." He looked so severe, staring down at me with tight eyes. "You cannot breathe."

"Please keep dancing." I looked around, chest heaving, worried about causing a scene and riling Nemea's temper. "I'm perfectly fine."

"You're panting like a dog."

I could not parse whether the man was annoyed or concerned. "Please," I begged, "I have no desire to disrupt the dancers. I'm well. Thank you."

He stared at me for a heartbeat, gaze narrowing, and then he started our steps again, but at a half pace. He wove us through the other pairs, keeping us both in step with the music and out of step with the rest of the room. We were as close as my skirt would allow.

"What are you doing?" I whispered.

"I'm letting you catch your breath."

"I said I was fine." Panic edged my words. Out of the corner of my eye, Nemea watched us, angry color rising in his cheeks.

"Nemea made you wear this ridiculous dress?" His voice was deep and soft, sending a wave of prickling nerves over my skin.

I glanced down at my bodice. "It was a gift," I said tersely. "He wanted tonight to be perfect and had it made specially for the occasion."

"Remarkable."

"What is?"

"Nemea is even cruel with his gifts."

The music began to drone, one bar after the next. The laughter of the dancers grated at my ears, and King Theodore, annoyingly, kept our slow pace, leading me with ease through the reeling dancers all around us. I plastered an even, pleasant look on my face, eyes fixed over his shoulder.

He pulled back, just slightly, and cocked his head. "You look familiar." There was a question strung through the words.

"Do I? Perhaps our talk earlier has you confused."

He shook his head. "No. It's something else." He kept staring, just as he had on the parapet, meticulous and appraising.

"I assure you, you haven't seen me before today. I was born here. I've never left Seraf. When I was orphaned, King Nemea benevolently took me in as his ward."

He gave a bitter laugh. "And why would he do that?"

I kept my lips pinched, not eager to offer up the true answer: that my family had been wealthy, and it was my inheritance that kept King Nemea's kingdom afloat. "You'll have to ask him yourself."

"I'd rather not speak to the man, so I'll guess." I'd caught my breath, but King Theodore kept us at a maddening crawl across the dance floor. "You are a sprig of mint in a fetid mouth. You are the balm that soothes the lash of his cruelty. Why else would he dress you up in half the archipelago's available crystal if it was not to make it look like both his coffers and his heart were depthless? In

Nemea's mind, he cannot be seen as truly despicable if he's looked after someone so lovely and charming as you."

I didn't hide my wince. He'd given me no compliment; rather, his words curled with scathing distaste. I managed a wide, sweet smile despite the way my stomach sank. "And you, Your Majesty, are clearly too shrewd to fall for his elaborate scheme." I boldly met his gaze. "You seem far from charmed by me."

When our eyes locked, he stopped dead and stared in astonishment. His jaw slackened. He let go of my hand, released my waist. "I do know you."

"What?" I made a quick scan of the room. "Please, you're making a scene."

He shook his head, a small movement, but those keen eyes of his studied the lines of my face further — the arch of my brow and the swoop of my nose, and lower, to the bow of my lips and the sharp dip of my chin.

"What are you doing?" I raised my arms, waiting for him to take my hand again. King Nemea had come to stand at the edge of the floor, his head tipped back in suspicion. "Please, Your Majesty, you're drawing attention."

King Theodore took a step away from me. A young woman spun into his back, but even that did not break the way he stared. Finally, he strode toward his guards, leaving me standing in the middle of the dance floor as the music dwindled to an end.

Fingers dug into my arm, jerked me sideways. "What did you say to him?" King Nemea said gruffly into my ear.

"Nothing at all, Your Majesty." My heart was a lump in my throat. "He said he knew me. I have no idea what he meant by it."

"Come." Nemea took my hand and pulled me toward the dais. His grip was too tight, his body stiff, his long strides plodding. He stepped onto the dais, and I barely cleared the riser after him. My hand crushed in his grip as he took his ruby-studded goblet and drank. "What more did he say?"

"He complimented my dress." I fought to give him a warm look. I imbued my voice with as much gratitude as I could, but I did not dare take my hand from his. "He praised the feast. And I agreed. I can't thank you enough, Your Majesty, for giving the captain and me such a celebration."

His hold on my hand grew even tighter. The ring Captain Ianto had given me dug into my flesh. "You didn't truly think all of this was for you, did you?"

I shook my head, trying to keep the pain from creasing my face. "No, of course not, Your Majesty. I only meant to express my gratitude. As you've said, I've been given far more than I deserve."

He grunted at that, and my knuckles crunched with the force of his grip. But his voice — his voice was soft as a feather's touch. "You were meant to defang him, Imogen. To placate him. The last thing I need is a war with that arrogant twit."

Wet, sticky warmth filled the tight space between my fingers. "You're hurting me," I finally whispered.

But Nemea paid me no mind. His attention was now on Captain Evander Ianto, who stood before the dais looking formidable and hopelessly disarrayed. He held his black helmet to his hip. His sand-colored hair was windblown and sweat beaded over his tanned skin.

"There you are," Nemea snapped. He finally released me, and I curled my fingers into a fist to hide the blood he'd drawn.

"Forgive me, Your Majesty." Evander bowed. Exertion colored his cheeks. There were clumps of wet sand stuck to his boots. "I got delayed in Port Helris. The ships kept coming and my men needed help."

Nemea gave him an approving nod. His captain was nothing if

not a good soldier. "Take her." He dismissed me with a quick wave of his hand.

My curtsy was deep, reverent. While bowed, I mastered the pain that might have rippled my face before stepping to the edge of the dais. Instead of helping me down, Evander tilted his head back and took me in. He did not look at me like Nemea did, to assess whether I was sufficient. Nor did he look at me in the unsettling way the king of Varya had — haunted, dissecting, and scowling. No, he looked at me with solemn, surprising adoration.

I basked in it. Stared back. I'd always found the captain handsome, with his amber eyes, and the creases ringing them like sun rays. I liked the smatter of light freckles that sat on the bridge of his nose, the exceedingly pleasing cut of his features. The corner of his mouth tipped up. "You look... beautiful." He let his gaze slink down my body and dropped his voice to a whisper. "And very uncomfortable in that dress."

"I'm sorry to disappoint you, but I cannot dance a reel in it."

He smiled. "Then we'll waltz." He extended a hand to help me down, and when I stood before him, almost chest to chest, I froze. The scent of the sea clung to him. Salt spray coated his armor, his skin, and it wove itself straight into my nostrils. An intoxicating heat rolled through my body, like a wave ravenously lapping the shore.

"I'm not in my fancy clothes," he said, apologetically. "Would you like me to change?"

My stomach swooped. "No."

I set my stinging hand in the crook of his arm, and then he began to amble us around the outskirts of the room, watching the revelry with a smirk on his face. I'd known of the captain for years, though we'd rarely spoken. It had been only a fortnight since I'd been told of our engagement, but my tight muscles unspooled at his proximity. The knot that Agatha's disapproval had left in my gut loosened, fluttered.

"Shall I guess how many pounds your dress weighs?" he asked.

I gave him a full smile.

He stopped us. "Again."

"Again, what?"

"Smile like that again."

Our gazes locked and an ache began in me. I wondered what his touch might feel like. I wondered if his skin tasted like salt. "You're incorrigible tonight."

He gave me a wicked look. "Every night." His warm fingers wrapped around my hand, and I flinched. "What's wrong?"

"Just a cut."

He took it and turned it this way and that, inspecting the weeping wound on my middle finger. His brow knit. "How did this happen?"

"It's nothing. His Majesty didn't realize..." Evander knelt and stuck his hands beneath the hem of my skirt, where he fumbled with the petticoats. I glanced around the room with wide eyes. "Gods, stand up —"

"Wait." He looked up at me with a crooked smile on his lips. A quick jerk, fabric ripped. He rose with a strip of white linen pinched between his fingers. "Give me your hand." Gently, he wound the fabric around the cut. "Can you keep a secret?" he said, his graveled voice filling only the small space between us.

Startled by his question, I looked up into his desperate gaze. I felt as if I were made of secrets. "Yes, I can."

"If he were not my king..." Evander tucked in the loose end of the linen, then kept my hand in his. "I'd run him through for hurting you."

The sound of treachery spilling from the captain's mouth like a profession of love made me still. It thrilled me. It terrified me. "That's very chivalrous of you."

Evander took a step closer and the briny scent of him engulfed me. It beat through me, making my chest fill with thrumming heat. The look he gave me was expectant, earnest.

A protector, even if it was only in spirit, was not something I'd hoped to find in the captain. I'd only let myself wish for a thread of kindness, for him to be preoccupied enough with his job to let me continue with my quiet life still intact. I rose up onto my toes and set a quick kiss to his cheek. "Your secret is safe with me."

3

With each cup, the bitterness of King Nemea's wine turned sweeter.

Evander set another goblet into my hand. "A dance?" He smiled over the rim of his own. "It's been years since I've tried, but I promise I won't embarrass you the way the king of Varya did."

I found King Theodore across the room with a self-righteous pinch on his face. "Fine," I said to Evander, absently.

"You sound thrilled," he teased.

"Just swear you'll catch me if I swoon."

He came closer, and the salt on him sent shocks shooting through me. "I swear on the beloved deity herself."

We pushed ourselves onto the crowded floor, and when the music swelled, Evander's hand fell drink-heavy on my hip. He gripped the folds of my skirt, the flesh beneath, and then he pressed us together as he guided me across the floor. He surrounded me, the heat of his body spilling through my own.

It was its own kind of intoxication. To be touched, to feel his pulse beneath my fingers when I grabbed his wrist for another dance. Then another.

More wine. More of that sea scent.

There were women — I'd seen them — who were lit from within, and when they became wives that light dampened. I did not know if it was their husbands that doused their flame, or if they themselves curled up around it, their very souls trying to protect it from extinguishing. Regardless, I had been prepared to watch myself dim. But Evander's touch lit sparks inside me, and somehow, he coaxed the light within to burn brighter, to burn steadily.

The night, the music, the dwindling candles, all began to blur as we crept toward morning. My head hummed with drink. The dance floor still brimmed with bodies, and the music still beat through the air. Evander tightened his hold on my ribs and pulled me closer. He set his mouth to mine, his top lip slipped between my own, and the biting taste of salt filled my mouth. I gasped.

It felt like blood, hot and pulsing, flooded my back, deep around my spine. My body tensed. He slowed our dance. "What's wrong? Are you tired?"

I could only nod.

With a soft tug, he led me toward the grand doors, and in my haze, I let him. His strong arm snaked around me, his warm breath fanning against my neck. I arched into him mindlessly, tilting my head back, when my gaze snagged on the wing — on the etching below it.

THE MONSTER IS ALWAYS SLAIN

The king of Varya's words scurried through my mind, a bug inside my skull.

Is the captain an idiot as well as a murderer?

"You all right, love?" Evander's voice was gentle at my ear.

"I don't feel well."

His mouth quirked. "Too much wine. You need bread. Come on."

At the banquet table, he pressed a hunk of bread into my hand,

and grabbed the other, leading me out of the throne room with quick steps. Navigating the dark stairs took more focus than I'd anticipated. The wine in my blood had grown potent. I fought to cling to Evander's strong hands.

"This gown —" He swatted at the wide skirt, trying to keep me upright. "Bleeding Gods."

"I do what His Majesty asks of me." My words slurred together. "I wear the dress that steals my air. I marry the captain —" I cut myself off, suddenly aware. I looked up into Evander's piercing eyes. "It's what we do, isn't it? Obey."

He seemed to marvel at me for a long moment before he said, "It is." He sounded plagued by it. "Every day."

Evander tugged me the rest of the way up the stairs. At the top of the landing, he pressed me into the wall with a rough kiss. I jolted at the bite of cold stone against my neck. He spoke over my lips. "It starts to wear on you, doesn't it? Always doing what you're told. Having no say."

That shocked me. I wanted to say *yes, yes, yes,* but I was distracted by how badly I craved a full breath. I was distracted by the salt on my tongue, and how desperately I wanted more. He kissed me again, pressing me harder into the stone wall.

"Soon, when we're married," he said, between nipping kisses, "you won't have to answer to him." He gestured to the oaken door behind him. "This is your room?"

I nodded and he lifted me, fumbled with my skirt to wrap my legs around him, and then we were inside. There was the metallic slide of the door bolt, the glow of the low burning fire.

The harsh, dancing shadows it cast about the room swayed my vision. They cut across Evander's face, and a wildness grew in his eyes. I'd been with men before: pleasant, quick, passionate. This was different. Not the man — Evander's fervor was just like the rest.

I was different.

I wanted him with a strange sort of need. Like my body might wither if I could not taste him, feel him, press my nails into his flesh. He kissed me, hard and possessive, but I didn't mind. I dragged my mouth down the line of his stubbled jaw, to where his pulse sped in small, warm waves.

Salt from his sweat; salt from the sea. A moan filled my throat.

Too slowly, he untied the laces of my bodice and slipped it down my shoulders. When he finally loosened my stays, and I breathed the air in all the way down to the base of my lungs, my vision sparked. Unpleasant pressure built and scorched low in my chest and spine, down my arms. I pressed a hand to my aching head.

"Come here." Evander's dark voice made me jump.

A dark fog still shrouded me, but I took another complete breath and followed him to the bed. The firelight cut across his broad, muscled back, then across the lines of his chest as he turned to lie down. My body and mind had become two separate entities. Within the cage of my chest came a plucking sensation, like a string knotted to my ribs had been struck. I tried to shake the feeling as I set myself atop Evander. Slowly, I guided him inside me and pressed my chest to his. He held me, moved with me.

But even surrounded and filled by Evander, that sinister feeling grew. It was as if something lurked within me and thought to come alive, twitching, writhing, taking shape. Pressing my eyes shut, I tried to focus past it. I bit back the urge to hum. His fingers dug into my hips, and I squeezed my eyes harder. The rumbling sound of Evander's pleasure hit my ears, his mouth covered mine, and all I tasted, all I wanted, was salt.

In a sudden flash of white, I crumbled.

This was not ecstasy. It was a tumbling, pleasureless loss of self. A fire in my chest radiated out toward my back. The skin above my shoulder blades burned and pulled before it tore open. Wings stretched free. A painful moan shredded my throat. More fire ran down my arms, dripping down each finger, until my nails extended into dark-tipped talons.

Evander froze beneath me. In suspended seconds, his face morphed from slack-jawed shock to disgust. Then his handsome features contorted again, the heat in his eyes cooling.

Hate.

In my confused drunkenness, I cocked my head. I couldn't understand it — why it was not awe he beheld me with. Then comprehension lashed me like a whip.

He forced me off him. Threw me to the floor, where my head whipped back against the stone. I should have felt fear, should have felt pain. Instead, his sudden loathing, his willingness to harm me, prodded at the thing lurking inside. I couldn't quite place where it lived, but like a bruised bone, I could feel it deep within. It gnashed and swelled, drawing forth thoughts of clawed hands and ribboned flesh and streaming blood.

Evander moved quickly, coming over me to wrap his hand around my throat. His skin was hot against mine. His weight pressed me down, crushing the base of my wings. Both of our pulses beat through his grip. His, fast. Mine, even-keeled. Unchanged.

In a single, easy motion I mirrored him. My long fingers wrapped around his neck. The black tips of my talons sank into his golden skin, bringing forth ruby-red beads of his blood. He hissed through his teeth and withdrew his hand from my neck.

I breathed in the hot metal scent. "You're scared." I'd never felt so powerful — so unlike myself. He shook his head, but I could see the whites of his eyes. I sank my fingers in deeper.

"Imogen, please." His words were only air, but they struck me like a fist. Hearing my name — remembering who I was — shriveled the dark thing inside me.

I released him. My chest heaved with panicked breaths.

He sat back on his heels, rounded eyes darting over the whole of me. My naked body, the black wings beneath me, the dark talons at the tips of my fingers. "Fucking Gods."

Like a scolded pup, I rolled away from him and crawled toward the hearth. I covered my breasts in shame as he collected his clothes and pulled them on. His movements were quick, controlled. The flex of his muscled body filled me with petrified awareness. Those were muscles born of hunting Sirens, of heaving flailing, fearful bodies as they fought their executions. Evander stopped at the door, fury and disappointment rumpling his face. His lips parted as if he might speak, but he only etched one last withering glare over me before he left.

And with that, the steady, bright light that had grown within me snuffed out.

I sat awake, eyes on the bolted door, a jewel-encrusted dagger gripped in my fist.

The firelight set its rubies glinting and lit the short, dull blade gold. As the sun finally crept through my window, I twisted it in my fingers, feeling suddenly foolish. King Nemea had gifted it to me on my seventeenth birthday. With its profuse jewels and blunted blade, it was more ornamental than deadly — like me, I thought.

Even so, clinging to it through the night had given me a sense of safety.

From the moment Evander had slammed my door, I'd wept. I'd prayed to the Great Gods and Goddesses as if they could hear me, mindlessly asking them for some fleeting peace that never came. I'd waited for the clomp of Evander's boots on the stairs, for him to crash through my bolt and drag me to the courtyard for execution. It had been years since a public execution of a Siren — Nemea's men killed them too quickly to bother hauling them up the mountain for a show.

But I was already here.

I'd be made into a spectacle: the king's ward having her wings gouged from her back. Her throat cut deep, a pulsing curtain of red. When they were done, my body would be displayed on a stake to rot for days after. Perhaps my wings would hang on Nemea's wall too, this trophy a perfect set.

A quick knock sounded at the door. I tightened my hold on my dagger. "Yes?"

"Open up, Im." The heavy oak muffled Agatha's voice.

"*Shit.*" With Agatha, I might as well be made of glass. She'd know something awful had happened the moment she laid eyes on me. "Just a minute."

She gave another impatient rap.

"I'm coming." Everything ached as I moved toward the door. The raw skin on my back pulled as I reached for the bolt. At the sight of my outstretched hand, I paused. Dark brown crescents of dried blood sat beneath each nail.

Evander's blood.

Images of last night sliced through my mind. The feel of him, the salt on his flesh, the monstrous power I'd felt at the sight of those glimmering drops of red. I couldn't parse which was worse — that I'd nearly killed him or that I'd let him live.

I'd always known what I was. When I was growing up, there had been a beckoning whisper in my mind and a pull on my body to descend and meet the sea. I'd never heeded it, fearing it would make a monster of me. For the legends of Sirens and blood were true. We were created to yearn for it. To call it — hot and rushing beneath a sailor's skin — to us. To pull them fully beneath the spume.

Forcing a fist, I finally slid the bolt and opened the door. My voice scraped. "Morning."

Agatha rushed straight for my dressing room, not sparing me a glance. I locked the door behind her. "The ritual starts soon," she said. "Let's get you dressed."

I'd been so consumed with worry over Evander that I'd forgotten all about King Nemea's blasphemous ritual. For nearly three decades now, he had refused to worship the Great Goddess Ligea — the queen of Sirens. He claimed Sirens were vicious and pitiless as the sea, that they took joy in destruction, and over time he'd stopped honoring the Great Gods altogether. He made blood offerings to his water deity, Eusia, instead.

I wasn't even convinced Eusia was real, as the histories I'd read were bereft of her name. Yet Nemea was devout, gathering his court for an offering before making weighty decisions, before fishing seasons, before name days. And before weddings too, so the betrothed could ask for her blessings. I'd been forced to give my blood since I was small. Denying Nemea and his deity an offering meant death.

"The tailor brought the wedding gown," I called to Agatha. "Nemea asked that I wear it for the ritual."

My body dragged as I forced my way to the basin to scrub my fingertips. The brush's stiff bristles were sharp against my nail beds, and a shiver fell down my sore backbone.

"Imogen, I thought we might talk," Agatha called from the dressing room. "Last night, I was able to speak with King Theodore —"

She came in, brow buckled with thought, a clean chemise and the wedding gown of black lace carefully slung across her arms. She froze when she finally looked at me. Those big eyes of hers flared with worry, with the fierce, sisterly look she always armored herself with when I was hurt. "Tell me what's happened."

Suddenly, I was a girl again. Thirteen, slipping into a salt bath that a new maid had drawn me, forgetting that she should have forgone the salt. A sharp pulsing had filled my chest at the feel of it. My body had begun to ache. Agatha had pulled me out the moment I'd called for her. She'd had that same look in her eye then as she did now. She'd wrapped me in a towel, hurriedly drying the brine from my skin. "I'm like you, Immy," she'd whispered. "A Siren away from the sea. Salt water only makes the longing worse. Keep away from it."

Agatha had kept me safe. I was not so alone with her as my confidant. And so, I'd shoved the ugly, rearing head that was my true self below the surface. And last night, blinded by my unabashed desire, I'd hauled her back up. I'd let her gulp the air.

"Imogen?" Agatha's gaze darted over my disheveled body. My dark waves were knotted with hairpins, my chemise was wrinkled and hanging askew. A light smear of blood marred my hip. "*Imogen.*"

My throat clamped. I threw my arms around her neck, crushing the dress she held between us.

"Oh Gods," Agatha wheezed. She returned my embrace, hands pressing over my spine — over the open wounds left from my wings. I gasped at the pain. When she pulled away, her hands were red with fresh blood. Sudden understanding widened her dark eyes. "*How?*" She spoke in a rush. "We have to leave right now. We need to get down the mountain —"

A languid knock sounded at my door. My head snapped toward

the sound, hackles rising. "*Imogen*." Evander's taunting voice called through the wood.

Who is that? Agatha mouthed.

I gestured frantically for her to shut herself away.

"Open up, Imogen." A loud *thump.* "Or I'll open it myself."

"Agatha," I whispered, "go into my dressing room. Lock the door. Do not come out, no matter what you hear."

She straightened her spine, defiant. "What — absolutely not!"

"*Shhh.* Do it. *Please.*" I hurried to the chair I'd spent the night in and retrieved my discarded dagger. "*Now,* Agatha. I could never forgive myself if you were hurt. Go. Do not come out."

Finally, she rushed toward my dressing room.

Once the lock clicked, I raced to the chamber door. The bolt scraped. The hinges wailed as I opened it.

Evander stood, tall and imposing, wearing the black coat and trousers he was meant to have worn last night. His hand rested on the leather-wrapped hilt of the sword at his hip. Bright amber eyes slithered down my body. They creased with an unafraid smile when he saw my dagger. "You're not ready yet."

I took a step back, heart hammering. "What do you want?"

Evander pushed past me without answering, unbuckling his sword belt as he went. He laid it reverently upon the bed and perched himself at the foot. The man looked like a bad omen, all clad in black, stark against the light hues and harsh morning sun that filled my chamber.

"Close the door, Imogen."

My breath caught at the soft, emotionless command. I threw the door shut, never taking my eyes from him.

"Lock it and come here."

"I asked you what you wanted."

"I'm not going to hurt you, Imogen. Lock it. And come here."

He bent to retrieve the gown and fresh chemise that Agatha had dropped. "Let me help you."

I was a mouse, and this was the cat's gentle play before it sank its teeth in. "I can dress myself."

The way he looked at me was so close to the way he had last night. His gaze was heated, but a shadow swam through it now. He'd seen the dark thing within me, and it had changed him. Changed us. "Come here."

I took a cautious step forward. Then another. When I was near enough, he leaned forward and took my hand. Hard fingers kneaded my hips as he placed me between his open legs. I tensed as his arm slipped around me, holding me still and close. "I still want you." He looked up into my eyes. "I'll admit I'm . . . shocked." He dropped his voice to a whisper. "But . . . Nemea doesn't need to know."

I set my hands to his wide shoulders and pushed. "This is a trick."

"No," he said, his hold on me unrelenting. "No trick." I tried to hide my wince as he set the gentlest kiss to the middle of my chest. "I came to apologize. For hurting you." He pulled back and swiped at the angry red puncture marks I'd left on his own neck.

"I don't understand." My blood screamed in my ears. "You can't possibly still want me."

He gave me a solemn nod.

"You kill my kind. You are *ordered* to do so. Why would you want to marry me now that you know what I am?"

"Besides the fact that I've come to . . . love you —"

I flinched. *Love* was not something I'd ever hoped for. It was not something I'd ever felt. I'd read great love stories; I'd spoken to maids with blood in their cheeks and stars in their eyes over a quiet stable hand or handsome soldier. And always, love struck me as something soft and incessant. It seemed lavish, sometimes foolish, dangerous even, but it was never threaded with terror, like what I felt now. Like Evander had felt last night when I'd drawn his blood.

He drew his thumb across my lower lip, dragging my attention back to him. "You grew up away from your kind," he said. "You're nothing like the rest of them. You're docile. And there are benefits for me. Do you know of the Siren's blood bond?"

I knew enough. A Siren was tied to the sea and the air. Their power and instinct to drown was made stronger by their proximity to it. The blood bond dulled this instinct. It kept the person the Siren was bonded to safe from the lure of other Sirens. The bonded pair would be compelled to protect one another at all costs. But up in the mountains, I was simply a woman. My instincts and power were all but dead.

"The bond is painful," I said. "And there's no need. What happened last night won't happen again." I'd keep away from wine. He'd scrub himself clean after being on the sea.

His hand rose to my jaw, fingers curling around it. He spoke slow and clear. "I do not want a wife that can kill me."

My stomach plummeted. "The blood bond is treasonous."

"I said Nemea didn't need to know." He released me and shook out the gown. Guiding me by the hips, he turned me, so my back faced him. He slipped my bloodstained chemise from my shoulders, letting it fall to a puddle around my feet. The cold air on my naked body raised bumps on my skin. He set his fingertips beside the open wounds at my shoulder blades. "Did you know . . ." His lips brushed my shoulder. ". . . that if you were down by the water this would have healed almost instantly?" His knuckle bumped over the bones of my spine. "I could take you down there with me, when we're blood-bound."

My mind flooded with thoughts of all the things Evander knew about my kind that I did not. I pictured his hands covered in their gore, his face sprayed with it. "King Nemea doesn't allow me to leave the fort." And I wasn't sure I wanted to.

His lips touched my ear. "You wouldn't belong to Nemea anymore, Imogen. You'd belong to me."

I bent and pulled up my chemise, stained as it was, over my shoulders. I strode to the settee, where my stays had landed the night before, and forced my arms through the straps. "Help me." A tremor shook my voice. "Nemea will never forgive us if we're late for the ritual."

Evander obliged, walking toward me slowly. "Who else knows?" he asked, as he clumsily started on my ties. Each tug was agony.

I stopped myself from looking toward my dressing room door. I'd slice off my own wing before sharing that Agatha had spent years and years with my secret tucked safely behind her lips. "No one."

"Good." Another torturous tug, and then my stays were squeezing, squeezing, puckering my ripped skin. "Like this?" he asked, pulling them even tighter.

"Yes." I shuddered from the pain and stepped into my black gown. Evander fastened the glittering buttons up its back. At the looking glass, I ran my fingers through the knots in my hair and pinched some color into my wan cheeks. My gold-brown eyes looked glassy, empty. "There's a problem."

His lips pursed. "What's that?" Possessiveness thinned his gaze as he traced the lines of my body.

"The blood bond can only be performed if my wings are out. I'd never shifted before last night." Last night had been an unfamiliar swirl of wine and salt and heated skin. "I don't know that I could do it again."

I watched him in the looking glass as he adjusted his coat and said with frigid indifference, "We'll do what we do for executions."

I spun, gaze locking with his. "For executions?"

"I'll bring up seawater and use the siphon to force it into your lungs. It makes you shift." He came to stand before me, so close that I had to tilt my head back to meet his eyes. He bent to place a kiss on my neck. Then another. His lips might as well have been a clamp around my throat.

Crushing.

Silencing.

4

No amount of velvet coverings or gleaming wood could hide the fact that King Nemea's ritual room was subterranean, carved into the mountain itself. Its dank smell and webbed corners wouldn't be done away with. Candles glowed in their iron holders, giving off a secret kind of light.

My arm was linked with Evander's, and he slowed us just as we reached the heart of the vast, low-ceilinged space. "I'm to escort King Nemea from his quarters," he said. "Do not leave this room."

He left and my tight shoulders eased.

We'd arrived early to a few courtiers greeting each other, their voices pinging off the stone as they regaled one another with stories of last night's feast. Their laughter boomed and closed in around me. I walked the room's perimeter slowly, feeling caged. In the far corners, the statues of the Great Gods and Goddesses that had once stood in the courtyard gathered dust. Their faces had been chiseled off when I had been a girl, but I knew them from the items they held.

Milton of Della cupped silkworms in his crumbling palm and a hare was tucked beneath his arm to signify his power over beasts. Panos of Varya stood tall and strong, with a flowering vine snaking up his leg, over his shoulder, and around his open marble hand. I noted the tall, graceful lines of his body. He reminded me of his grandson, King Theodore. Panos had possessed the power of life — with just a thought he could make dying plants spring up green, mend ripped flesh. Diantan of Hera — the Great Goddess of craft — cradled a hammer and joiners. The plumb line that had hung from her other hand had long since snapped off and was likely now the grit I felt beneath my shoes. A prolific builder, she could machine what she saw in her mind's eye. Jesop of Gos lay on his side, his bearded head a foot away from the rest of him. He possessed the power of memory, which, combined with a God's divine, near-immortal life span, provided Leucosia with its first books of history, genealogy, and folklore.

And in the most dismal corner of the room stood the Great Goddess Ligea. I gazed up at her. Her delicate marble wings lay in pieces around her base. Her head was missing altogether, but her body was strong, swathed in a length of fabric that fluttered behind her in an unending breeze. A cresting wave kissed her bare feet. The other Gods said that she possessed the power of death — but they were wrong.

She controlled the wind and sea.

With a melodic whisper, she could kill a tempest or stir one to life. She used her power to fill nets with fish, to aid ships in battles. And when she was wronged, she would lure the guilty to a brutal, drowning end.

I stared and stared at what was left of her.

"Lady Imogen," came a low voice beside me.

I whirled. King Theodore stood taut with anger, a ferocious look on his face. I curtsied. "Good morning, Your Majesty."

"What is this place?" he asked, fiery gaze bouncing from one defiled God to the next. His eyes stuck to the effigy of his ancestor. "I was instructed to arrive here but was not told why."

My mouth gaped. The Great Gods — the Gods of Leucosia, made from its land and water — did not require offerings. They were not worshipped within the stygian belly of the earth.

"It's King Nemea's ritual room, Your Majesty." Shame weakened my voice. "It is where his court offers their blood to his deity."

His gaze shot to mine. "*You* do this?" A horrific look of disgust marred his face. "You give your *blood* to — to what? To whom?"

The water deity that I was moments away from offering my blood to was no Great Goddess, nor was she their descendant. If King Nemea was to be believed, she had been born with no power at all. Just like him. She'd made her own power with twisted, illicit magic.

"I do, Your Majesty." I couldn't meet his eye. "The offering is made to Eusia. Refusal means death."

The withering look he gave me was clear — the threat of death did not absolve me.

A hard hand met the small of my back. "All right, darling?" Evander said, glaring at King Theodore, who stared back with his own obliterating sneer.

The room had filled further. Nemea now sat in a wooden throne on the far side of the room, wearing the same scarlet coat he'd worn at the feast.

"Just fine," I said, and followed where Evander led me. In the center of the room, a throw of black velvet had been laid upon the dusty floor. Two bowls made of carved bone sat atop it. Beside them lay a pair of short, wickedly sharp obsidian blades. A small pile of white bandages sat in the very middle. The ritual for the betrothed.

Absent-mindedly, my thumb bumped over the mound of scars etched into my left palm. I'd sliced my hand with that blade so many times, I'd lost count.

"*Imogen.*" Evander jostled me. "Did you hear me?"

I shook my head.

"What did the prick want?"

"He wanted to know about this room — and the ritual."

Evander made a gruff sound of annoyance and adjusted his coat. "Have you decided what you will ask of Eusia?"

"Oh." Evander had never performed the ritual before, as only King Nemea's court was required to do so. He seemed eager, gaze intent on the implements at his feet. "I have nothing to ask of her," I said. "I only ever speak the ritual prayer." A prayer that made my stomach twist, for Nemea's beloved water deity was offered the blood of his court so that she might grant him his greatest desire: to rid the sea of Sirens.

"And what will you ask of her?" I asked, somber and soft.

Evander answered without pausing to think. "For power."

Power.

I shook my head, confounded. "Don't you have enough already?"

"You mean my title and my sword?" He gave a mirthless huff and his gaze cut to King Nemea. "I live my life in service of someone else." He shook his head, met my eye. "I want something that's mine. Something I can't be stripped of."

Perhaps Evander and I were not so different. After last night, after feeling my veins fill with such potency, I yearned for power too. I yearned for the freedom and choice and protection it could offer. If I were near the water, I'd command the sea and shape the wind just as the Great Goddess Ligea had once done. I'd sing those who would hurt me to a black, depthless grave. If I were near the sea, I'd have sway over the man beside me.

No — I'd have outright control.

A hush fell over the room as King Nemea cleared his throat. "We wish for goodwill between our kingdoms." He spoke to the other rulers — the Queen of Della and Gos, the King of Hera, and to King

Theodore too — in a rough voice. "For years, the Isle of Seraf has sought acceptance and respect. We have a right to worship who we choose. And we have a right to ask for blessings from a deity who actually answers."

The challenge in his voice sent a chill through the air.

Nemea went on. "Today, the betrothed shall ask Eusia for a blessing. May she give them what they request. Captain Ianto, Lady Imogen. Kneel."

The courtiers had pressed back against the rough walls of the room, their faces smudged by the dark. My breaths were shallow, hands damp, as Evander and I faced one another and went to our knees before our respective bowls. Evander's back was to King Nemea, which left me with a clear view of him sitting on the edge of his throne, a mad gleam in his eye.

But it was King Theodore who drew my gaze.

He stood beside Nemea's seat, seething. Deep lines were carved between his brows, and his jaw looked close to snapping with how tightly he held it. Even in the weak candlelight, I could make out the green of his eyes, wild and furious, locked on me.

Power radiated from the man. It poured from him, wove through his well-formed muscles. On the heels of the disgrace he'd made me feel came a burst of anger. He had never known what it felt like to be bent by someone else's will. He'd never been required to give something of himself that he did not wish to give. I met his blazing glower with my own, suddenly enraged that he would make me feel like my desire to survive was unforgivable.

"Begin, " came Nemea's dark voice.

Evander lifted his blade, and I watched him, frozen. He swiped it quickly over his hand, splitting it open. His blood spilled like dark wine between his fingers and over his wide palm, tapping into the bowl below. He whispered his prayer, then snapped his gaze to mine. A lock of sandy hair fell over his furrowed forehead.

"*Imogen,*" he warned through clamped teeth.

There was not even time for me to lift my knife. His shocking grip found my wrist, and with a sharp twist, he forced my palm up. The black blade bit deep into my skin and with a flick, my hand burst open. My entire body jerked at the ripping pain.

In my periphery, King Theodore moved closer, but I didn't look up. I could only focus on the sting and the growing pool of red in my palm. It oozed toward my sleeve cuff, seeping into the black lace. Evander twisted it over the bowl. "Say the prayer, love."

I tried to speak through the bitter taste of self-loathing, through the fiery anger. All my life I'd thought being docile and obedient would give me a sort of strength, safety. But I'd made myself fragile instead. I'd turned myself into something easily snapped between the finger and thumb of a person like Evander. My voice wobbled when the words finally came. "I give to the sand. I give to the water." The last bit of the prayer stuck, just as it did during every offering. "Hear me, heed me. Cleanse the sea."

When my blood stopped flowing, Evander stroked my wrist, a gentle back-and-forth, then took a bandage from the pile and wrapped it around my palm. How effortless it was for him to cut me, then mend me. To mix his barbarous duty with his endearment. I slid my gaze away from him, as if compelled, straight to King Theodore.

He'd stepped so close that his polished boots toed the black velvet we knelt upon, spear-tip eyes on me and me alone. Anger flushed his cheeks, and when he spoke, like a deep roll of thunder, the pressure in the room seemed to shift. "How much blood have you taken from her, Nemea?"

Not a single courtier pulled in a breath as they waited for King Nemea to answer. Even Evander had frozen, his hand hovering over the hilt of his sword.

"I have taken blood from my entire court and gifted it to Eusia for over two decades, boy." A smile colored his voice.

King Theodore finally unlocked our gazes to glare at Nemea. "I asked about *hers*."

Why?

Something dangerous hung between the two men, something unspoken that I could not decipher, but I felt myself — my blood — sitting at the rotting heart of it.

Nemea laughed, the sound rattling and bleak. "Look at the cogs of your mind trying so hard to spin. I have taken her blood since her infancy." Nemea sat back in his seat. "Since the day she became mine."

There was no time for me to parse Nemea's words before King Theodore reared back his long leg and swung it into the offering bowls that sat between Evander and me. They flipped and spun, spraying the blood within across my face. It spattered over his own cream-colored coat. I fell back, swiping the sticky, hot liquid from my cheeks, my eyes, when the room surged into motion. Guards' swords rang as they were pulled from their scabbards. Women gasped; men shouted. I tried to untangle my legs from my gown, scrambled to stand, but all the while I could not look away from the fearlessness that King Theodore possessed amid all the swords and muscle and sound.

Nemea's guards encircled him, and Evander pushed me back, clearing me from the center of the room. King Theodore was quickly enfolded by his own guards too, but there came no clash of metal. Nemea bellowed over the huddle of grunting men, "You cannot undo what has been done, you fool. But I hope you die trying."

"Imogen, get to your chamber," Evander yelled from where he stood between the two kings. *"Now."*

The courtiers cawed and clutched one another at the sight of the two rulers coming to blows, and I shouldered through them, toward the steep, uneven stairwell. The stone wall was cold beneath my bandaged hand, but I used it as my guide, forcing myself up and out of the belly of the mountain and into the slicing light of Fort Linum's entry hall. The front doors sat wide open to the courtyard, just as they did every day when the weather was fair. I started toward my chamber and stopped.

The sky outside was shrouded in clouds that rippled like gray waves. The mountains below sat in a bluish-white haze. How vast, how endless it all seemed, and I did not want to be locked behind a door. Trapped and amenable. I wanted out. A pitiful thrill of excitement raced through me as I disobeyed my order and crossed the fort's threshold.

The courtyard was a wide, barren circle, ringed in towering white pillars. At the very center sat an oblong stone, soaked with layer after layer of old blood. I strode past the stain, black gown dragging behind me, toward the cliff's edge. Beyond the peaks, through the haze, I could just see the fluttering stretch of sea. I pulled in a long, slow breath and imagined I could smell it. Imagined I was filled with it once more, like I had been last night. I had been fearsome. I had made Evander's eyes stretch wide. I had made him beg. Made him bleed.

"Imogen."

King Nemea's voice was harsh and scraping as he strode through the fort's doors. Behind him, his guards were an implacable wall of armor and blades. Evander stood at the center of them. He'd removed his dress coat in the tussle and his shirt was now rumpled and undone at the neck. In one hand he cupped his ritual bowl, in the other his sword. The disappointment in his gaze staked me to the spot.

Nemea's cheeks were mottled red and beaded with sweat. Those colorless eyes of his locked with mine.

"Your Majesty." I gave a stiff curtsy. "Is everything all right?"

His grunt sounded like scuffing stones. "That *fucking* boy-king can rot on the seafloor." He lifted a ritual bowl, still coated with thick, wet blood, from his side. He grabbed my hand like an eel striking prey and ripped the bandage from it. "He fancies himself a benevolent king." He took his thumb and dug it into the angry flesh around my cut. His touch was heavy, painful, forcing my stanched wound back to bleeding. "But it is not benevolence that makes a ruler mighty, is it, Imogen?" His eyes had grown bright with malice. Spittle collected on his lip like sharp white teeth as he forced each word out. I gasped as he squeezed and pressed, grinding the bones in my hand against each other.

My mind slipped outside my body from the pain. It floated above me. Heard my whimpering and saw my tears. "Stop. *Please.*"

Finally, he stopped, but he kept my hand in his. "It does not matter how powerful the ruler's blood is. It does not matter that a ruler is good, or just, or fair. What matters is that they can keep hold of what is theirs, by whatever means necessary." He turned my hand and placed a kiss on the back of it. "It is easy to be *good* when you're blessed by the bloody fucking Gods. It's when you are lowly, when you are nothing — like I was — that you learn to make your own power. And with it, you take what you've been denied."

He stared at me for a long moment, holding the bowl of my blood, before he turned and made for the stairs that led down to the mountain road. His guards followed him, and I knew precisely where he would go.

To the sea. To offer my blood to his deity. To make his own power.

Evander slowed before descending. "I ordered you to go to your chamber."

"I needed air —"

His eyes flashed as he shoved his sword into its sheath. "I don't care. I'll not risk you getting hurt."

I skipped over the irony that was my aching hand, carved open by him. "There was no danger —"

He was before me in a breath, fingers biting into my jaw. "That's enough." He lowered his lips to mine, but it felt nothing like a kiss. It felt like a cracking whip, slashing through my flesh. "Get" — another kiss that felt like a leash, notching tightly around my throat — "to your chamber."

He walked away like he knew I would listen, never once looking back. A blood bond between us would compel his true protection, but his protection was locked doors, and smothered needs, and obedience of my body and mind. A bond would bolster him and wear me down to nothing — I would become the headwater and he the river that I fed until I ran dry.

I needed to leave. I needed to get down this mountain, off this island, or every vital part of me would perish.

Inside, the courtiers were abuzz. I stopped at the top of the entry stairs, my wounded hand cradled against my chest, and watched them over the banister. They rose up from the ritual room stairwell, pooling in the center of the hall. They recounted the kings' fight with glassy eyes and cheeks full of ruddy color, like they'd just gorged themselves on a fatty meal. It was easy for them to be entertained by these men — they weren't at risk of being crushed between them.

The blood on my cheeks had dried and felt tight. I needed to wash quickly, bandage my hand, and then find Agatha. I'd tell her everything. Admit she was right about my engagement from the start, beg her to help me find a way out.

There came gasps and murmurs. The clank of armored men. I looked out over the banister once more. The king of Varya had ascended from the ritual room. He stood in the stairwell door, my blood flecked over his pale coat, looking severe as a graven image. The whole hall fell reverently, dreadfully still.

Envy ripped through me.

He could silence a room by simply entering it, could command awe, fear, without making a sound. He did not buckle under Nemea's barbarity the way I did. How clear it was that he was something different, something greater than Nemea and Evander, who grasped and gnashed for dregs. No, the king of Varya's greatness welled up from within, fed from a source that was entirely his own.

Clarity struck me, bright as a bolt. It pulled my spine straight and tilted my chin high.

It was not Agatha whose help I needed to get out of Fort Linum.

It was the king of Varya's.

5

King Theodore took slow steps into the hall, and the crowd split like water around a stone to let him pass. His chamber was on the same level as my own, and if I knew Nemea at all, he'd put him in the worst accommodations the fort had to offer. A small, drafty chamber at the northeastern corner, with crumbling exterior stones that had been harassed by the winds since the day they'd been stacked.

Flanked by his guards, Theodore started up the stairs. His every movement was filled with muscled grace, and when he neared the top, our gazes crashed together. His eyes rounded, and I could only imagine how shocking I must have looked. Severe in my black wedding gown, dark hair windblown, blood smeared on my cheeks, smattering my chest like gruesome freckles. He still beheld me with disapproval nearing abhorrence, but his gaze dipped to my injured hand, which I held protectively against me, and his full lips flattened in what looked like concern.

He might help. He might say yes.

"May we speak?" I whispered, before he could stride away from me, down the northern wing.

He paused for what felt like a lifetime, but finally, reluctantly, he dipped his chin in the barest of nods, then continued toward his chamber. I didn't miss the tension strung through his body, the lingering anger that trailed him like smoke. He was everything Nemea had always said he was — haughty and honorable and righteously indignant — but I did not wish to break him of those qualities, like Nemea did.

I wished to use them.

The crowd in the entryway below me began to disperse. Some made their way out into the courtyard; some huddled together toward the throne room. I made my way down the hall on what felt like new legs. Four Varian guards flanked the farthest door. Their golden armor glinted in a pool of light that slipped through the narrow window beside them. As I reached the end of the hall, one of the guards swung the door wide for me to enter.

"Thank you." I took a tentative step inside.

A fire popped in the small hearth. The hinges whined as the door shut behind me. The chamber was only a bed, a wooden chair by the fire, and a single window that King Theodore peered out of with his back to me.

"There's a cloth and water by the door," he said, his voice a deep, warm resonance in his chest.

"I'm all right, Your Majesty, thank you."

"Wash quickly. I'll wait."

I bit back my protest and wrung out the cloth. It came away from my cheeks with fat smears of pink. There was something in the action of it, in being commanded to clean up the blood he'd spilled on me, that made me feel almost as insignificant as I did with Nemea. The feeling hardened my jaw.

I finished cleaning and cleared my throat.

"Speak," he said.

"Your Majesty, thank you for giving of your time —"

"No." He locked his hands behind his back. "Speak about why you are here."

I gulped down the ball of nerves that clogged my throat. "I — I came to ask for your help."

He blew out a long breath. "Agatha sent you, didn't she?"

"I beg your pardon?" I shook my head. "No. Agatha has no idea I'm here. Why would she send me?"

Finally, he turned. The firelight accentuated his strong nose, the sharp line of his jaw and cheekbone, and I could not help but stare. He was captivating, even more so with the way his fury still sparked in the air around him. "She came to me last night after the feast. She said it was imperative you leave the fort before your wedding."

"I didn't know," I said. "Did she tell you . . . did she explain why?"

The kingdom of Varya was a peaceful one. Sirens lived among the ancestral Varians there, but still, the thought of anyone knowing my secret while I stood upon Serafi soil filled me with abject terror.

"She did. But the revelation that you're a Siren was no shock. I told you I knew you."

That insouciant surety of his gnawed at me. I longed to ask him more, to ask him how, but his gaze turned incisive. I stilled while he dissected the shape of my eyes, my nose, my mouth. His gaze lingered on my lips for a breath. Then another. As he stared, he slipped into some faraway place.

"Your Majesty," I said softly, trying to bring him back. "What answer did you give Agatha?"

He blinked, then cleared his throat. "Despite my many concerns about your current arrangement, I told her no."

"No." An ugly emotion surged through me. "May I ask why?"

"For one, you didn't seem like you wished to leave."

"Forgive me, but how could you presume to know what I want?"

A deep furrow carved his brow. "Lady Imogen, I have eyes. And though I cannot fathom the pairing — a secret Siren and her hunter — you couldn't keep your hands from your fiancé last night. The captain spent half the evening with his lips on your neck."

I prayed it was too dark for him to see the rush of embarrassment that heated my cheeks. "The captain also spent half the morning telling me of his plans to force a blood bond between us." He froze at that. "You saw how easily he sliced my hand in that ritual room. How thoughtlessly he hurt me."

Anger seemed to reignite within him. The heat of it filled his eyes. "Agatha left me with the impression that your identity is unknown here — that you both take great pains to keep it that way. How does the captain know what you are?"

I pressed a hand to my chest where my heart thudded against my ribs. "He . . . did not know until last night."

"Before the feast or after?"

"After."

His patience snapped. "Tell me plainly how he knows."

I hesitated, and he gave me a withering look. It surprised me, how desperately I wanted his poor view of me to change.

He strode toward me and stood so close that I had to look up to meet his eye. "Answer me or leave."

"I shifted," I said suddenly. "In front of him."

Confusion narrowed his gaze. "How is that possible? A Siren's power is tied to the sea. You shouldn't be able to change this far away from it."

"I . . ." My eyes dropped to his chest. "There was . . . sea salt . . . on his skin."

He paused. "On his skin?"

"Yes. And I . . . well . . . I tasted it."

"You *tasted* —" He pinched the bridge of his nose. "Are you without both honor *and* self-control? Giving your blood freely, and now this —" He paced away from me, mumbling to himself in a pious fit. "What kind of coward stays in this place, scraping to Nemea's whims? You're an imbecile to marry a man whose job it is to kill you."

Fury filled me, alarming and hot, and I heard Nemea's scathing voice in my head. *It is easy to be* good *when you're blessed by the bloody fucking Gods.* "How dare you!" I balled my hands to fists so I wouldn't shove them against his chest. "I belong to Nemea. What should I have done? Should I have told him I prefer to not marry? Tell me how you would treat a subject who denied you, Your Majesty." But he didn't. He merely watched me in quiet, wide-eyed shock as I went on. "I have twisted and broken myself to survive here. You could never understand what that is like —"

"You should have tried to leave a long time ago."

"Yes," I snapped. "I should have. But I am trying *now*." I held his gaze. "Will you help me?"

We stood in tense, heavy silence, breaths speeding and mingling. Then he gave a frustrated grunt. "Give me your hand."

"I'm sorry?"

"Let me close that cut."

I looked down at my gouged palm. I'd been so angry I'd forgotten about it, but he hadn't. He had the Great God Panos's power over life, the power to grow and mend. Slowly, eyes locked with his, I extended my wounded hand. "This is not the help I'm requesting of you."

"I know." His fingers were impossibly warm for the temperature in the drafty chamber. With a strong but gentle touch, he inspected the cut. "It's deep."

"Yes."

"There's too much scar tissue here." The anger in his voice had dulled, and all that remained was tension. "I can't prevent it from becoming another scar. I'm sorry."

I'd never received such an earnest apology. I spoke carefully, trying to hide my surprise. "I am not imbecilic enough to think I'd be undamaged, Your Majesty. What's another scar atop many?"

He gave me a quick, curious look before a heat built in his hands. A heat like the sun, coming from inside him. I held my breath and watched the red flesh around the gash start to soothe. "It would start a war," he said, his focus on my wound. "If Nemea knows I helped you escape."

Slowly, my skin began to knit together. I pulled in a shallow gasp as I watched it — a network of pale, fleshy lace, its stitches growing closer and closer together as the heat he poured into me spread.

"Forgive me," I said, my voice breathy from his ministrations, "but you have not seemed all that intent on fostering peace between the two of you. Your every action, your every word, has been inflammatory. Why did you truly come here in the first place?"

His jaw tensed and he finished checking his work. The wound had become a thin white seam across the mound of old scars in my palm. His warm hands remained on mine. "As you guessed, I came to see the state of this place for myself. To see Seraf's horrors. To see just how cruel Nemea had become." The calluses on his fingers scratched as he finally, slowly, let me go. "I have a deep hatred for the man."

"Then take me from him."

His gaze shot to mine.

My words tumbled forth in one desperate breath. "Nothing would hurt him more than to lose what he considers his."

"That's my fear." He shook his head, and he gave me that strange, lingering look once more. "I have a kingdom to protect. A war would put it in jeopardy."

"You came to witness his cruelty firsthand and then do nothing about it? If there is any person in Leucosia who has the power to alter the awful things that happen here, it's you."

Theodore ran a hand through his dark hair. He seemed to grapple with something, shut his eyes for a long moment. When he looked at me again it was with something akin to anguish. Pity coated his unsettlingly soft words. "He's done such a thorough job of diminishing you."

That hollowed me out. I stood before him, feeling bare and ill and embarrassed, and fighting to keep it hidden.

He moved back to the small window. "I will send you help. I leave tomorrow — I have no desire to stay for your wedding. When I'm back home, I'll make a plan to get you off Seraf. But it will take me time. It can't look like I was involved."

"I don't have time." I curled my healed hand, my nails cutting into my palm. "The wedding is tomorrow night. By the time you send me help, Captain Ianto will have already bound us. How will I leave him then?"

He straightened his bloodstained coat, and it was as if he'd donned a suit of armor. He looked at me down the line of his nose. "There are draughts to sever such bonds." His features smoothed into kingly austerity. "The appropriate response to my generosity is 'Thank you, Your Majesty.'"

I reeled back. "If you expect me to thank you for giving me the opportunity to suffer, then you are no better than King Nemea, *Your Majesty.*" His flinch filled me with satisfaction.

I wrenched the door open, letting it crash into the wall. "Move," I yelled to one of the guards who blocked my path. Panic scurried up my throat, blocked my breath. Agatha's chamber was on the lower floor. I could keep myself together until I reached her, but as I made my way down the hall from King Theodore's chamber, I faltered.

Two of Nemea's guards, clad in their ominous black armor, stood before my chamber door. They wore helmets that only showed their lower faces. One guard, whose jaw was covered in red spots and pock scars, shoved the other with a gangly elbow when he saw me. "She's there."

The older guard offered me a quick half bow. "Into your chamber, my lady."

"You have no right ordering me around." I spoke with authority, even as my heart plummeted. "I'm the king's ward."

"You're the captain's lady now," the pock-faced boy-soldier mumbled. "And he'll make my life hell if you're not in that room when he's back."

"I'll not be a prisoner in my own home." I trudged onward, but he reached out a single wiry arm and scooped me up. I yelled as he hefted me toward my open door. I thrashed and clawed before I was unceremoniously dropped to my rug and shut in. "I'll have the king skin you for this." The door rattled in its frame as I beat against it.

"Forgive me, my lady." The guard sounded unrepentant through the heavy oak. "Captain's orders."

6

The entire afternoon passed with guards barring my door. No one entered. Not Agatha, nor Evander.

I scrubbed my face with frigid water. Washed my hair and slipped on a clean chemise and dressing gown. All the while I thought on how I might escape. Perhaps there were passages I'd failed to discover when I'd been a curious girl exploring the fort. Dark and winding tunnels I'd missed that might lead me to the base of the mountain. But unsurprisingly, I found no secret doors behind the tapestries in my room. There were no cobwebbed halls behind my hanging gowns.

As the sun began to set, I sprawled over my mattress, staring up at the ceiling while a horrific maw widened in my stomach. My hope slowly slipped inside it, swallowed up.

Three quick knocks came. I sat bolt upright. The pock-faced soldier swung my door open, and Agatha walked in. Her hair was loose and wild, black curls haloing her wan face. She held a single lit candle. "I'm allowed to stay until it burns out."

My throat shut at the sight of her, so I nodded and patted the mattress beside me. Her gown was creased, and her knit wrap was pulled tightly around her narrow shoulders. She walked silently, grabbed a book from my table, and set it at the foot of my bed. She placed the candle atop it, then drew all the bedcurtains shut. She climbed onto the bed and propped herself up beside me. We both waited until the door snicked closed to talk.

"King Theodore came to speak with me," Agatha whispered.

Angry tears sprang to my eyes. "Did he tell you I was an imbecile? That I was a coward and that all of this is my fault —"

"Shhh." Agatha moved closer, wove her fingers through mine. "No. He came to tell me of your conversation. And that he would work on a plan to get you out."

I shook my head. "He said it would take him time. Time I don't have."

"He'll get you out," Agatha said, with assuredness. "I trust him."

"Tell me why." I peered up at her from where I lay. The firelight flickered around our little cocoon. "You only knew him as a boy. He's certainly changed since you were his governess. He's a dashing, priggish king now." Agatha squeezed my hand and I fell silent, and then, quietly, I asked, "How did you come to leave him and end up here?"

Agatha hesitated. "When I knew the king — the prince, then — he was about seven. I was only sixteen, and I fell in love with a young soldier in the king's guard." She swallowed hard. "After some time, we decided to perform a blood bond. In secret. Just the two of us one night in front of the fire." Melancholy filled her voice as she recalled it, and I wondered if she saw the flame-lit memory in her mind. "But when King Athan, Theodore's father, found out — well, he ordered that our bond be severed."

I turned to see her better. "Severed? But you loved each other."

"If only love were enough to overthrow the will of a king." She huffed a breath. "Afterward, I left and came to Seraf. Word hadn't spread yet that Nemea had started hunting Sirens when I set sail."

"I see." I propped my head on my hand. "Do you still love him? Your soldier."

"That was nearly twenty years ago, Imogen."

"Do you?" She shook her head too quickly and wouldn't meet my eye, which pulled a smile from me. "Well, when my future husband has tied me to some bed, or some mast, and I am no longer allowed to keep a handmaid, I hope you leave this place and go find him."

"*Imogen.*" She scowled at me. "I know Theodore. He will help."

"Was he imperious as a boy too, or is that quality something he needed time to grow into?"

Agatha snorted. "He was a sweet boy." She gave me a side-long look. "I remember him constantly whining for sugar cubes, though."

I grimaced. "Disgusting."

"Imogen." Agatha's voice went low and somber. "The news I hear from Varya is filled with stories of what a generous ruler he is. He is duty-bound to his core."

I quirked a brow. Fort Linum was a distance from Port Helris and the connected town of Stowand. Whatever information Agatha received about Varya and its king came from far outside the fort. Correspondence from the rest of the archipelago came sporadically, unreliably. "Who told you that?"

Agatha's pert nose scrunched up and a blush stained her cheeks. "Why do you ask?"

"It's just a curious and very specific detail, '*duty-bound to his core,*'" I said. "How do you know it?"

She swatted the question away with her hand. "Friends send me letters."

"About the king of Varya?" The blush on her cheeks darkened. I sat all the way up. "It's your soldier, isn't it? He still writes you?"

Agatha shuddered. She took both my hands into hers. "He's here. He's Theodore's commander now."

"He's here? Have you seen him?"

Agatha nodded, a soft but warring look on her face. "I asked if he could possibly help too, but . . . Not right now. It's too dangerous. Please, *please* trust that King Theodore will do what he's promised in his own time."

"I'll be bound to Evander by then." My voice shook. The hope of escape was slipping through my fingers like water. "It'll be too late to leave. What if I'm with child by the time he enacts his 'plan'? What if I'm nothing but a corpse?"

"Stop." Agatha's big eyes filled with a silvered rim of tears. "You serve no purpose to the captain dead. And you will not be with child — I'll make sure of it. A few months, Imogen. We can make it through together for a few months, can't we?"

My eyes fluttered shut. "You think I'm much stronger than I am." I could only bend for so long before I snapped.

Agatha threw her arms around me and tucked us back into the pillows. I let myself weep then. The profound, mourning kind of weeping. I could only suck in hiccuping breaths by the time she spoke again.

"Someday," she whispered, as her fingers played through my damp hair, "you will have a full life. A home, if you want one. And you'll see more than these stones and mountains and sky. And I'll be with you when you first touch the sea. You'll feel sand between your toes, and salt water on your tongue, and you will feel more joy than you can fathom. I promise."

We sat like that, watching the candle flicker across the bedcurtains until it burned itself out. Agatha kissed my forehead before she left. The darkness was thick as pitch, so I closed my swollen eyes, and I sank into the mattress where I floated between wakefulness and sleep — in a liminal space where the sheets around me became seafoam, and the tears in my mouth the waves.

Hours passed slowly, dragging me into the middle of the quiet night. The mumbling and shuffling sounds of the guards in the hall had finally ceased. I wondered if they'd left, or perhaps they'd fallen off to sleep. I pulled back the bedcurtain, swung my feet to the floor, and crept on tiptoe to listen at the door.

There was only the blood whooshing through my ears, but I stood like that for a long while, listening for breathing, for any sound at all. Finally, I set my hand to the knob —

And froze.

There were boots on the stairs. Heavy footsteps, far below, but they were drawing closer. Then there were many boots, ascending in unison — like soldiers did. I drew away and threw myself back onto the bed just as my door squealed open.

"Love, wake up." Evander spoke softly. He held a candle above me. "Come with me."

His gray shirt was creased and untucked. His cheek was stubbled with blond hair and his brow was damp with sweat. The contours of his face looked strange in the light, casting undulating shadows over the curves of his skull beneath his skin. I opened my mouth to ask what he was doing when he held a single finger up to his lips, silencing me. He took my hand and tugged me to stand.

"Take this off," he whispered, as he pulled at the ties of my dressing gown.

"No." I crossed my arms tightly over my chest. "What do you want —" Light glinted off a slim, curved pipe tucked beneath his arm. "What is that?"

Before he answered, a tendril of briny air wound itself into my nose and I knew precisely what he carried — the siphon. The one they used to force a Siren to shift before executing her. The scuff and fall of his soldiers' footsteps filled the hall. Like ants at work, they filed into my chamber, each carrying two buckets of water.

Seawater.

The sea and I had never met — not truly — but I knew it. It was in my blood and bones. I was made from it and would return to it.

Evander's men went into my dressing room. The *splash, splash, splash* of their buckets emptying into my tub sent a prickle across my skin. They kept coming, a dozen of them at least, and I watched, stunned still.

Evander set down the candle and worked on the ties at my waist, taking the dressing gown from my shoulders so I wore only my thin chemise. He took the siphon into his hand. Determination stained his countenance — fists rounded and jaw set. He moved toward my dressing room door. "Come."

"I do not want to."

Evander stopped midstride, his eyes filled with menace. His men were just winding their way back out to the hall. "You're relieved," he said to them, quietly. "Go." They obeyed. The door closed noiselessly, and Evander slid the bolt.

He grimaced at me. "Don't look at me like that." The siphon dropped to the woolen rug with a dull ping. "Don't you, of all things, *dare* look at me like I disgust you."

Something snapped inside me, my anger dislodging from where I'd tried to stuff it. "It's *I* that disgusts you. I see it in the way you look at me, I feel it in the way you touch me." The salty air was slinking through the room now, curling between us. I pulled in a deep, shaking gulp of it, and something in my chest vibrated. A string, plucked. "You can't possibly love me. You are so willing to hurt me —"

"Our binding will fix that," he spewed.

"It won't. It will only compel you to protect me." My words were tight and quick. "It will not change me or your resentment. I will still be what I am, and you'll only know misery because in your heart... In your heart you wish to kill me."

His amber eyes pulled wide, brows sinking. Tense and silent, he bent to retrieve the siphon and came at me with stalking steps. He stopped when our chests touched. "If I'd wanted you dead, my love, you would be." A sickening shiver fell down my spine as he raised a hand into my hair and gripped it in his fist. "I've loved you for so long. Did you know? Long before I begged the king for your hand. Long before I touched you." He shook his head. "You gave me a shock, yes, but in her own strange way, Eusia has answered my prayer by giving me you. Your blood in my veins will make me untouchable. No Siren lure will be a threat. My men will look at me like I'm a god." He pressed his lips to my temple, spoke against my skin. "I could never resent you for that, Imogen."

The way my guts heaved made me feel like I was falling. Down and down, and my entire being knew that impact was imminent. Touching him felt vile, but I threw my arms around his neck, hoping it would stop my plummeting. "*Please.*" My mouth was at his ear. "Please don't."

A hot exhale against my cheek was his only reply. It wasn't an apology. Not remorse, nor regret. It was a breath of disappointment, for I could not see and understand what he could — that this was best for both of us. He bent, breaking my hold, and hooked an arm below my hips. I wasn't petite like Agatha. I was tall, with well-formed muscles. My waist nipped in between full curves, but

Evander could lift me as easily as one might a child. He folded me over his shoulder and held me tightly as he carried me over the threshold of my dressing room.

"*No.*" I beat my fists into his solid back. "Put me *down.*"

The air within was thick and briny. I sucked it in as Evander dropped me to my feet. The seawater in the tub beside me glimmered in the faint light of an oil lamp one of the soldiers had left behind. Had I been alone, I would have climbed in myself, eager for the water to make me feel fearsome instead of fragile.

"I deserve this, Imogen." His fingers bit into my arms as he spun me. He grabbed my chemise and ripped the back open, straight down to my waist, making space for my wings. Panic clogged my mind. It froze my limbs. His body was hot against my back as he spoke over my bare shoulder. "I'll be the captain the Sirens could not drown, and you will live well and safe up here where your instincts can't taint you."

It was instinct that slashed through me then. It sent my arm rearing back, it crooked my fingers into a claw and sent my body whirling. My nails scraped over his forehead in an arch, then hooked into the lower lid of his eye. Welted lines of ripped skin rose on his sun-kissed face. A drop of blood slipped from his lashes like a crimson tear.

He growled through clamped teeth, but he didn't strike me. Instead, his bulky arms clamped around mine, pinning them to my side. "It'll be over soon." Then my feet were off the ground. He tipped me backward, over the lip of the wooden tub. I gasped as he dumped me into the water. Not from the cold, or the way my spine struck the wooden base, but at how it set me alight.

My panic dissipated. It was as if a million tiny teeth cut through me, into my sinew and bone. Into my very marrow.

Taking the water where it belonged.

Everything around me faded, even as Evander set the curved pipe into the tub near my feet and put his lips around the exposed end. He sucked until the sea began to pour through it, then spat. His strong fingers dug into the back of my neck, folding me toward the siphon's end. Its metal was sharp against my lips. Liquid spilled over my chin.

His fingers dug into my face. "Open your mouth."

Despite everything, I wanted to taste it. To be flooded with it. I unhinged my clamped jaw. The pipe nicked my bottom teeth, the sound echoing through my skull. Salt water poured over my tongue, down my throat, filling my lungs. They grew heavy, my chest widening. I did not blink. I did not move. I only stared up at him.

Horror contorted Evander's face. "Imogen?" His eyes darted over me, watching as the water that would not fit inside me trickled back out of my mouth, down my chest.

Drowning should burn, and I waited for it, only to remember that I could not drown. All I could feel was that odd plucking sensation between my ribs. An angry heat sparking to life in the very center of me. It grew and grew and grew until whatever was tied through me did not merely vibrate like a string — it pulsed like a vein. Like an artery, and it poured sludgy, oil-like power, black and sick, right into my gut.

It rolled through my body like magma and when the heat hit my back, my wings ripped through my skin and unfurled. My nails stretched into black-tipped talons.

Through the hum of coursing power came a voice so soft, I thought I imagined it. The water's words were frail and distant, like a breeze whispering round the shell of my ear, fighting to be heard.

There you are, dearest. I've waited so long.

I jolted. My gaze shot to Evander's. He knelt beside the tub, watching me with relief in his tear-rimmed eyes. He removed the siphon from between my lips, and in his other hand he gripped the curved dagger that had hung at his hip. He would slice me open, just as deep as last time, and shackle me to him.

No, no, no.

That pulse in my gut turned white hot at the thought of it. Then Evander went suddenly still, eyes drooping and muscles loose. The dagger he held slipped from his hand. It clattered against the edge of the tub as it fell to the floor. I retched up the water from deep inside my chest, and as if commanded, Evander stood, lifted a leg, and stepped into the tub.

Blood screamed through my ears; the dark pulse in my belly thumped. My essence slipped outside my flesh and bone and watched as Evander sank down into the water. He was large for the narrow tub, but he managed to bring his body over the top of my own, and wrapped his arm around my winged back. Reverently, he placed a kiss below my eye.

In a shadowy corner of my mind, I thought it curious that he would come in with me. That he'd dropped his dagger. His whole body was rigid as a new corpse above me, but his breaths kept coming. They fluttered across my mouth, like warm waves, rolling in, then sucked back out.

A Siren's domain was the wind and sea, and even his breaths felt like my own.

So I took them.

Through the part in my lips, I drew out his air until there was none left in his chest. His face reddened as he dipped his head just below the waterline to rest it on my breasts. The desire to drown him gripped me. I wanted his chest filled just as mine had been, and when I wished it, he pulled in a sea-choked breath. His nose and mouth flooded. I knew the paths the water took, sensed it as it pooled inside him.

His heavy body twitched against mine.

As the beats of his heart slowed, so too did the pulsing current inside me. It ebbed, stopped. It left me feeling full, but not satiated. Now that I had tasted such control, such *power*, I understood why Evander had been so hungry for it. My mind returned to me fully once he was waterlogged and limp.

My dressing room was silent, the lantern light steady. I pushed against Evander's heavy shoulder. "No." Panic sliced at me. "Gods, no."

For a moment, I wished I could drown. I'd let his weight pin me under, and I'd drink deeply, and before the light in my eyes went black, I would see, as if they were real, all the things I'd always yearned for.

Evander's body grew somehow weightier, bending my ribs and pulling me from the daydream of my idyllic death.

The one that awaited me would be so much worse.

7

I pushed against Evander's dead weight with my teeth gritted. My mind filled with all the awful things King Nemea's guards would do to me in retaliation. I'd ended one threat and invited in a myriad of new ones. King Theodore's voice echoed in my head —

You're an imbecile to marry a man whose job it is to kill you.

The water in the tub came up to Evander's open, unseeing eyes. Burst veins were stitched through the whites, like blood trails in the snow. Nausea rolled through me. I pushed against his shoulder once more, twisting beneath him, trying to wedge myself out. The effort had me gasping, had me cursing, but I didn't stop until I'd scraped my body over the side of the tub, and onto the soft rug on my dressing room floor.

Seawater ran down my body in thick rivulets. My torn chemise clung to me, a pale second skin ready to be shed. My hair hung like black ropes over my shoulders. I stared at Evander's body, all twisted and overlarge in the narrow tub, and I suddenly didn't care what the good and noble and just king of Varya would think of me. My one nascent thought was that I wished to live, and he alone could see that done. He'd already denied me his assistance — but there was another way.

I moved with primal single-mindedness. The unfamiliar weight of my wings had me off-balance, and I walked a staggering line toward my chamber door. At this hour, almost all the torches in the hall would be out of oil, but all those nights spent sneaking through the fort as a girl were not for nothing. I knew by rote how many paces it took to reach the end of the hall.

Evander's men had obeyed and vacated their post outside my door, but from the north end of the corridor came the soft clatter of armor, the mumbles of King Theodore's guards. He'd brought six with him. Considering how much he and King Nemea seemed to loathe one another, it was safe to assume he'd sleep with at least half standing watch.

That didn't stop me from hurrying down the hall toward them, water spraying as I went.

I had no sense of how to wield the shadowy, terrifying power that had overtaken me — it was even possible that it wielded me. I couldn't recall what I had done but steal Evander's breath, and I sent up a panicked prayer, hoping my power would make Theodore's men just as malleable.

Through the window, the moon was bloated and bright in the sky. Its light dripped like quicksilver over the sill, illuminating the guards. There were three of them. The one nearest me grunted and reached for his sword at my approach. In the next moment his body went slack. I felt it this time — a silent, heated lure that flew from my throat like a fisherman's line. The second guard staggered dreamily to the far side of the hall, while the third opened the door and permitted me inside King Theodore's chamber.

The hinges were maddeningly loud, whimpering as the door swung shut. King Theodore didn't rouse. His fire had burned down to embers, and it sent deep shadows and rusty light over the bed where he slept.

He looked so large, sprawled indulgently over the mattress. One arm was bent above his head; the other rested on his chest. A long leg had escaped from beneath the covers to show me golden-brown skin and dark hair over a perfectly drawn calf, a strong knee, a muscled thigh. He wore a white sleep shirt and what appeared to be nothing else. I took a step nearer and could make out his shallow, even breathing. I studied the line of his jaw, the part in his full lips.

I would do it quickly — slice his palm and press it to my own cut hand. A blood bond was that simple to forge, but I could not bring myself to move. He looked so soft in his sleep, all the sharp angles and harsh glares that I'd come to expect from him replaced by his open body and pouting mouth and delicate breaths.

This was wrong. It was treacherous and cruel to even consider this, but I steeled myself. I only wished to live. Mere hours sat between me and the discovery of Evander's body. Between me and my certain, gruesome death. The water soaking my hair and chemise would dry quickly, and when it did, my wings would curl back under my skin.

Now. I had to do it now.

My body ached with tension, but I forced myself to the side of the bed. I set my knee into the mattress, then flinched when it creaked under my weight. Drips from the ends of my hair beat into the bedding. With a trapped breath, I made a shallow slice in my palm with a talon and reached for the hand that rested on Theodore's chest, but before I could even touch him, he jerked. He seized my wrist, his grip as tight as an overdrawn manacle. A low growl, and he yanked me forward with such force that I fell over him and landed with my stomach pressed to his. Cold metal bit into my neck. This close, I blocked the dim light from the hearth and lost the details of his face. He pressed the edge of the blade further into my skin.

"It's Imogen," I wheezed, my throat moving against the pressure of the dagger. "It's me. Please, don't."

"Imogen?" His voice was thick with sleep. He pulled the blade away. "What the fuck are you doing?"

We both moved clumsily in the dark, tangling with the sheets, scrambling to put some distance between us. He reached for the candle and striker on the bedside table, and the room filled with a burst of warm light. He gave me a terrible, wide-eyed scowl.

I froze.

Just like I had been with Evander, I was laid bare before King Theodore. He took in the whole of me. The shape of my wings, tucked tightly against my back, my fear-drenched face, and then his gaze slipped down to take in the lines and curves of my body beneath my wet chemise.

I waited for his revulsion, for him to throw me to the ground and wrap a hand around my throat, but he only looked at me with bewildered awe. The seconds seemed to stretch until finally, he pinched his eyes shut. He reached for a blanket and quietly extended it toward me. I pressed it to my chest.

Some grim awareness shot through him suddenly. He held his dagger up between us. "You're covered in seawater."

The implication in his deep voice was clear. He was in peril. Sirens on the sea were dangerous, drowning and eviscerating those who would harm them. I shook my head. "I'm not here to hurt you." His distrust was palpable, scathing. I reached slowly for the hand he held the dagger in and guided the tip toward my sternum. "You have my word."

The rigidity in his shoulders eased slightly, but he kept the dagger where I'd put it. His voice was dark as the night. "Tell me what's happened."

I curled my talons into the blanket. "I need to leave Fort Linum tonight." My voice trembled. "Right now."

"That's not an answer." He shook his head like he was in some warped dream and wished to wake. He glanced toward his door. "How did you get in here?"

I blinked. "I — don't know exactly." It wasn't a lie. The power that had overtaken me bent the world to my will, but I'd not asked it to do so. I'd needed safe passage into this room; I'd needed Evander to not hurt me further. And that oily, awful power had seen it done. "Your guard opened the door for me."

"I doubt that very much." The tip of the blade pressed against my stomach, not hard, but enough to still me. "Answer me."

"I've killed King Nemea's captain."

His mouth dropped open. "You killed . . . your fiancé . . . and then you came directly to *me?*"

I spoke in an overloud rush. "He took the siphon — like they do for executions — and he filled my chest with water. I shifted, and then he just climbed in with me, and I drowned —"

"Shhh. Quiet." His free hand covered my mouth. He pulled the dagger away from me and stabbed it into the mattress beside him. "You have to keep quiet."

I nodded, tears welling.

Like a stitch pulled too tightly through fabric, his muscles bunched, and his face creased. He dragged his hand slowly from my mouth until it rested on my chin. "What do you mean he climbed in with you?"

"Into the tub," I whispered, eyes locked with his. "He had his men fill my tub with seawater and then he forced me in and —"

"Did you sing?" His hand fell away from me. "To drown him?"

"Sing?" I shook my head. "No. He climbed in with me, and he lay on top of me and then I . . . I don't know how. I took the air from his chest."

The look that he gave me sent cold skittering through my blood. It was a look of astonishment, like he could not fathom a more monstrous act, and it made the mattress beneath me slip away. It made the walls around me fade, until I was alone and adrift and hurtling toward my death.

"You killed your fiancé," he said in a brutal whisper, "and then you came here moments later to beg me to leave in the middle of the night and take you with me?"

"No." I looked him squarely in the eye — I had nothing left to lose. "I came to bind myself to you."

The air around us thinned. His voice was deadly quiet. "You're out of your mind."

"Perhaps." I didn't bother to hide the desperation in my voice. "But I have nothing left to armor myself in except your protection and you refused to give it."

His gaze was filled with the embers' light, with incredulity. "I did not refuse. I said I needed time."

"I'll be tortured." My words caught on tears. "I'll be given to Evander's men for them to do what they please before they slash my throat."

The silence sat like pins in my skin. It eked out until he finally deigned to speak. I would have preferred spiteful words, a curse dripping with disdain, anything at all besides the complete lack of emotion that he gave me instead. "That's what happens to murderers in a place like this."

My chest ached with the weight of my hopelessness, but still, I wouldn't leave without at least trying to make him understand. "He deserved it," I spat. "Had I been married and bound to him it would have been me that died. He would have sucked the life from me, one small cruelty at a time."

I scooted toward the edge of the bed. I left the blanket behind, and shivered as I moved toward the door. Death loomed just beyond, and I wondered if I should wait for it in my room, or if I should go out in search of it. Perhaps it would be better to trek out toward the fort's guards, wings wide, and suffer a quick death from an arrow to the heart.

"Stop." Theodore blew out a long breath and rose. His white sleep shirt was askew and rumpled, stopping just above his knees. A flinty look filled his eyes, but his voice was softer than I'd ever heard it. "Come away from the door." His gaze darted quickly down my body before he picked up the blanket and tossed it at me. "Keep this on you, Gods damn it."

When I finally had the blanket secure around me, he came nearer. He stood close, enveloping me in a wave of warmth. "What's this?" He reached out and grazed a finger over a sore spot on my chin.

I winced at the pain. "From my darling fiancé's siphon, I'd guess."

"It's bleeding." He shook his head regretfully. "I've told you, helping you now will start a war."

"Yes, I know." Hot tears rolled freely down my cheeks. "I'm not an imbecile, contrary to what you believe. I understand the repercussions. I understand why you are sending me away to my death —"

He swiped a hand down his face. "Shut up, please."

"What?"

"Shut up." He moved to cradle my face in his hands so quickly that I gasped. "I'm fixing this." He tilted my head back, thrusting my bloody chin forward and, with an angry glower, using his bright power to close the cut.

He finished quickly, his heat there and gone, but neither of us moved for a drawn-out moment after.

His hands finally fell from my face. "Were you truly going to bind us?" he asked in a strangely even voice.

"Yes." I locked my gaze with his. "I am tired of being diminished." I stepped toward the door. "But you were right, I'm too cowardly to save myself — "

"Do it."

"I beg your —"

"Bind us," he said. "A war with Nemea is unavoidable. He cannot be allowed to commit one atrocity after another. It's not ideal to start it with the death of his captain and the stealing of his ward, but I believe . . . I believe it's preferable to the alternative."

My mouth hung open. "The alternative being my death."

"Yes. So, I agree to our binding."

"But why?"

"There's no divine or earthly way that I would get anywhere near a ship with you unless I was immune to your lure."

My face flushed. "That's fair."

"There are three conditions."

"Of course." I sucked in a shaky breath as wariness surged. "What are they?"

"You denounce Nemea, and you swear fealty to me as your new king. Then, when we arrive in Varya, you go directly to the Mage Seer and have our blood bond severed in a ritual there."

It wasn't lost on me that he could ask me to remove my own hand and feed it to his dog while smiling and I'd say yes. "I can do that." I waited cautiously for the final condition. Theodore was a shrewd king, with a gaze like razors, and a mind just as sharp. He would require something of me, something far greater than my bending a knee and trekking to sever our bond. "The third?"

He began to rummage through a trunk at the end of the bed. Out came dark trousers, a white shirt. He bent toward the hearth and set some logs atop the smoldering embers. "When you return from the Mage Seer," he said, "you will complete one task of my choosing."

A warning bell tolled through me. *One task of his choosing.* I watched with a wary gaze as he dug through the trunk again. He checked papers, other small items shoved between the clothes, and I realized he was deciding what to burn. We'd be leaving too quickly for him to bring along his effects. "What's the task?" I asked carefully.

He avoided my gaze. "I don't know yet." He threw a small stack of papers into the fire and then began to pull on his trousers. "Quickly, my lady, your hair is drying. Your wings will shrivel up next and we'll have lost our opportunity." He began to remove his sleep shirt, and I looked toward the door. "Do you agree to my conditions?"

By every marker of what was fair, I should have. I should have fallen to my knees and kissed his warm fingers for being willing to cut himself open and tie us together. And if he asked that I risk my life, my safety, the prospect of a home of my own, I should say *gladly.* The king looked at me with disbelief, as if he could not understand my pause, and I thought: *He has never known what it is to exist purely for the use of others.*

The thought of submitting to the open-ended whims of yet another king, of owing obedience, of not being wholly my own, choked me with despair.

"I am willing to put my life in danger," he fumed, "to jeopardize the well-being of my kingdom, so that you can leave this place safely—"

His words landed like a spark on dead grass. They lit my mind with a dreadful realization. No good and fair and just king—no king who was *duty-bound to his core*—would do something this foolish. A king as virtuous and powerful as Theodore would let me, an orphaned ward of a vicious and lowly king, die here because his reign demanded it. Of course, he might feel the barest prick of guilt to deny me, he might even be so soft as to lament the loss of a young woman who had so wished to live, but he would not do *this.*

"Your decision, Lady Imogen?"

In the firelight, he looked as hard and imposing as a statue. Shadows tucked themselves beneath his golden-brown cheekbone, into the hollow of his neck and the furrow of his brow. I could see the shape of his ancestor in him. The Great God Panos had been strong and indominable too. He needed nothing from me. And I had nothing to give. But I thought of him in Nemea's ritual room, spun through with fury over *my* blood. He'd told me with surety, *I do know you.*

Who do you think I am?

Suddenly, I wondered if this lopsided favor was perhaps perfectly balanced.

"I agree to your conditions, Your Majesty." I tilted my chin up. "But if you prove untrustworthy, so help me, once our bond is severed, I will —"

Theodore cocked his head. "Are you threatening me?"

"I have little reason to trust men who say they will do right by me in exchange for my obedience." I'd grown so cold, so weary, that the words came out in one pathetic, trembling breath.

He raised his brows, conceding my point. "Let's do this before you accidentally kill me."

I lowered myself into the warmth rolling out of the hearth. Theodore didn't join me. He strode to the door, glowered at me, and said, "Keep your blanket on." Then he brought the three guards in, one by one. Each took me in with alarm and Theodore gave them a searing look. "Where's Commander Mela?"

His commander. *Agatha's* commander. All the men held themselves still, their faces unreadable, until finally one of them looked ashamedly to the floor. "He told us to cover his post." There was a heavy pause. "He went to meet a woman."

I'd not thought the king's mood could have gotten worse, but he grew even more glum, and his voice fell even lower. "Find him."

"He'll be on the floor below," I cut in. "Fourth door on the right."

Theodore's attention snapped to me. "Agatha?"

I nodded.

He swiped a hand down his face, then in precise, hushed tones laid out the plan of escape. "Wake the off-duty guards, and before you return here, go to Lady Imogen's chamber. There's a dead man in a tub of seawater. Collect some of that water and bring it to me. And for the love of the fucking Gods, do not leave my door unguarded."

Theodore's men swept from the room, and he forced the door's lock into place with a frustration that was surely meant for me. There came the susurrus of linens and the clink of metal, but my attention was on the engagement ring that still sat on my finger. A heavy, sickening feeling settled over me. "I have one condition of my own."

Theodore came to sit before me with his dagger in one hand and a heap of green silk in the other. "You don't get conditions — I'm the one doing you a favor." He tossed the pile of cloth at my knees. "Put this on when your wings shift away."

I gave him a determined look. "Agatha comes too."

He spun the hilt of the dagger in his hand. Shook his head. "It's too dangerous. You don't need your nursemaid to accompany you and — unlike you — she's perfectly capable of getting out of here on her own."

Tears tightened my throat. He was right. I gave an anguished nod and held my hand up between us, revealing the shallow cut I'd made before he'd woken. The scars across my palm looked twisted and pale. Undeterred, Theodore took my cold hand in his warm one and swiped a finger over the cut and gnarled skin, so softly that I winced.

"I have a soft spot for Agatha too." He'd said it like an apology, voice tender and steeped with regret.

The dagger gleamed as he brought it toward my palm. I went taut wondering how deeply he'd cut me, if he would heal me quickly after, or make me wait.

"Take it," he said, then pressed the hilt into my other hand. "I've heard a Siren bond is painful." There was no trepidation in his voice, but I wondered if he was afraid. "The way it settles in the body."

I nodded. I'd heard the same. "Don't go soft on me now, Your Majesty."

The corner of his mouth lifted ever so slightly, and when I placed the blade to my palm, his lips pinched. I sliced, a quick and shallow cut, and then I set the edge of the blade against Theodore's palm and made a twin wound. At once, we drew in a breath and pressed our bloody palms together. My heart thundered, beating through my entire body, but I focused on the sticky warmth between our hands.

Theodore gasped. His strong fingers clamped around my palm. The look that marred his face sat somewhere between pain and pleasure. Muscles shook, a sheen of sweat erupted over his cheeks, over the column of his neck. As his head fell back, he stifled a deep moan.

With bated breath, I waited. And waited. Theodore's body went loose, his pain cresting and falling, and then he looked at me with expectant panic. "What do you feel?"

I shook my head. "Nothing."

And then it came.

His blood felt like starshine. Bright and boiling, it climbed up the veins in my arm, into the pulse in my neck. It blistered me from within as it spread and spread through my body. I could hear myself moan, could feel my back curve with the hurt, but when it fell to knit itself through my stomach, the room went black. My jaw opened in a curdling scream.

Theodore's hand flew over my lips, and when that wasn't enough, he cradled my head and pressed my mouth to his chest. "Quiet," he pleaded into my ear. "Imogen, stop."

But I couldn't. I was being ripped apart from within. That thread inside me pulled so tightly that I thought it would snap and slash my heart and I would die right there in his arms. I clawed at his shoulders, at his back, and too slowly, the pain began to gutter. The bond sat in my belly, emitting a fluttering heat, and I was whimpering against his hard body, trying for steady breaths.

Theodore looked down at me, stunned. He raised a hand to my cheek and pulled away the hair that had stuck itself to my slick skin. "Are you okay? We need to go now. Tell me you're all right."

I nodded.

"No." His voice was hoarse, breathy. He gave me a little shake. "Say it. Let me hear you."

His worry over me was clear, a deep, consuming current, and I knew the bond had taken. That was what it did — compelled protection. I looked into his eyes and tried to hide how strange I felt. My insides quaked. I thought I might be sick.

"I'm all right."

He gave me a sharp nod and tried to school the stricken look on his face. Through the bonding, my wings had slipped back beneath my skin, leaving my shoulder blades raw and oozing. Theodore helped me keep my balance, gaze averted, while I removed the blanket and my wet chemise. He did not see the wounds my wings had left behind and I said nothing of how they hurt before I swung the robe over my shoulders and cinched it at the waist.

A soft knock at the door made me jump. Theodore permitted his guards in and this time it was his full retinue of six. One of them carried a vase that had been in my room — the scent of seawater met my nose. And trailing them all, with wild, knotted curls, flushed cheeks, and kiss-swollen lips, was Agatha.

Theodore looked at her and his mortification was complete. "Hello, Agatha." He glared at the tall, smug-looking soldier standing beside her. "Lachlan, I'll gut you."

"Yes, I know," said Lachlan. "Agatha informed me that she's coming with us."

Theodore shot me a scowl. "Blessed by the bloody Gods tonight, aren't you?" He pointed to the vase of seawater. "Give her that."

I cradled it to my chest and straightened under the king's dour gaze. It was dark and stern and the sheer intensity of it turned the cool air in the chamber stifling.

"You got past my men, my lady," he said, "now get us past Nemea's."

8

King Theodore's soldiers moved like specters, silent and
quick. Even their armor hardly rattled through Fort Linum's
too-quiet darkness.

We wound down the stairs that led to the empty entry hall in a
neat, long line. Outside, the winds cut through the valley, catching
on the corners of the fort. They moaned like a woman dying. I tried
to not take it as an ill portent.

Theodore descended ahead of me, Agatha behind, and I cradled
the vase of seawater to my chest like a mother would a babe. It was
this meager seawater that would allow me to use my power to get
us past King Nemea's men.

Agatha whispered over my shoulder. "You were in the king's
chamber. You're wearing his robe. You're wet with seawater."
The damp silk of said robe stuck to the open wounds on my
back. My long, wet hair covered the bloodstains. "Tell me what's
happened?"

I craned to look at her over my shoulder. "I promise, I will tell
you everything when we're safe on the ship. Please, please, just do
not panic when I do."

Her eyes flashed. "Panic! Why would I panic?"

"Gods, Agatha."

She bit her lips between her teeth, stopping up her worry and questions, and gave me a weak nod.

An ugly feeling seized me at the thought of confessing to Agatha. A braid of shame and pride twined through me like a second spine at what I'd done to Evander. As I descended the stairs and passed Nemea's throne room, I thought of the inscription upon its wall. *The monster is always slain.* I thought of Evander's blank, blue-lipped face, and a pang of uncertainty struck me. Perhaps I was just as monstrous as he had been. Perhaps my own slaying was yet to come.

King Theodore's commander — Lachlan — gathered us all close when we reached the towering main doors. "There are never guards stationed in the courtyard. We've always seen them gathered at the stables and barracks at the base of the mountain stairs," he said quietly. Then his stern eyes locked with mine. "We'll need you to get us past those guards. We need horses from the stables to get down the mountain road and to the king's ship in Port Helris."

My mouth went dry. A tremor had begun in my muscles, either from the cold or shock, I couldn't say. I fought against it and gave Lachlan a tight nod.

The lead guard pulled the massive door just wide enough for us to squeeze through sideways, and one by one, we wound our way through Fort Linum's entrance like a silent serpent. The wind had cleared the sky so only the bright, swollen moon and a speckling of stars filled it. It lit the pale stones an eerie, watery blue. Agatha and I huddled against the fort's rough wall. A gust whipped my hair up and into my eyes while the six guards spread through the courtyard, swords drawn, checking the smears of shadow cast by the pillars.

Theodore faced me and stepped nearer, his body cloaking me in sudden warmth. "Swear fealty to me now," he said, low and close.

"Before you leave Nemea's domain and while there's a witness. This way he won't be able to claim you were stolen."

I scowled and held the vase tighter. "You can't possibly think it will matter to him. And how will he know? He'll respond the same regardless."

"It matters to me," he said. "I won't have the disloyalty of stealing another king's subject in the night as a nick on my crown."

My scowl only deepened.

He stepped even closer, gaze bearing down on me, and my breath caught. "Considering what I have done for you tonight, the least you can do is bend the knee."

I held his glare for three beats of my hammering heart. It turned my stomach — kingdoms and the inane rules that shaped them. I did not want the gravel cutting into my knees. I did not want to step from one ruler's fetter into the next. The responsibility of honoring, and kowtowing to, and obeying another man who would not do the same for me in turn. And yet it was the way of things.

I turned to Agatha and shoved the vase at her. "Hold this."

With the courtyard cleared, the guards came back and made a wall around us. Lachlan leaned in, sounding nettled. "Quickly, quickly, if you don't mind."

I shot him an icy look. Then begrudgingly, shakily, I lowered myself to my knees. The gravel was as sharp as I'd expected. "What do you want me to say?" Theodore looked so severe staring down at me, his nose and brow highlighted in the moon's opalescence.

It was Lachlan who answered. "Make it up."

A gust ripped through us, raking my damp hair into the air. I clawed it from my cheeks and met Theodore's gaze with as searing a look as I could muster. "I denounce the ruler of the Isle of Seraf." Another gust boomed. Cold and howling, it pulled tears from my eyes. It muffled my soft words, sent a chill over my body. "I . . . I swear my . . . loyalty—"

Theodore lowered himself to his knees before me, his eye to mine, and my every thought dissipated. He was close enough for me to whisper and still be heard. My brow buckled with confusion at the gesture.

He gave a sharp nod. "Quickly."

I fumbled through my memory for the long and dismal oath I'd made to King Nemea when I'd been younger. "I, Imogen Nel, pledge my loyalty to you, King Theodore Ariti of Varya. I . . . will *try* . . . to honor you in word and deed, will and action. Before Eusia—" I shook my head. Cleared my throat. "Before the Great Gods, wherever they may be, I swear it."

The side of his mouth gave a wry downward curve. "You'll *try?*"

I nodded. "I swear it."

He gave me a hard look and helped me to stand. The shaking in my limbs was too much now to hide and Theodore steadied me with both hands at my waist. Agatha watched us with astonishment as she handed me back my vase.

"What?" I asked.

She shook her head, eyes blinking rapidly.

The group split up. Theodore and I, accompanied by four guards, hurried toward the stairs that led down to the stables and entry gate. Agatha remained with Lachlan and the sixth guard. We came to the edge of the first step and my vision rippled at the abrupt, shadowy drop.

"This is the way you entered the fort?"

"Yes." Theodore set warm fingers to my elbow when he saw how I swayed. "They're uneven. Some are very short. Others are much higher than they should be."

"There has to be another way." Panic skittered over my skin, through my chest. "Nemea couldn't have made all the guests climb these."

"My lady—"

"I'll spill it. I can't see three steps down in this dark and I'll misstep and spill it and we'll all die for it."

"That's a possibility." There was not a flicker of emotion in his voice, but his gentle touch on my elbow firmed. "But if you do not move forward, death—yours, mine, Agatha's—is a certainty."

Behind us, the wind screamed around the edge of Fort Linum in a pained warning. This was not where I wanted to die, in the place that had made me small and frightened. I straightened my spine under Theodore's scrutiny. The man who thought he knew me—who'd called me a coward. I adjusted my hold on the vase and took the first step down.

My progress was too slow. I felt with my bare foot for the edge of the step, making my way down with Theodore's hypervigilant aid, and feeling certain that I would never be warm again. My teeth clicked loudly in my skull. My whole body shivered. The silk robe I wore whipped against my bare legs. I stopped on a particularly narrow stone tread and tried to calm my trembling.

Theodore looked up at me from the step below. The terror—the worry—in his eyes made my stomach dip. "Ah, fucking Gods," he grumbled. "Come here." He reached up like he was going to wrap me in his arms.

I stepped back. "What are you doing?"

"Your Majesty," the guard behind me whispered. "We need to keep moving."

"A minute." Theodore scowled. "The lady is about to freeze to death. She needs to warm up."

"You're not suggesting that you warm me." His blood pumped

through my veins but the thought of being touched, of letting him press his body to mine, felt far too intimate.

He scrubbed a hand over his face. "The other people here are clothed in metal, so yes, it would be me."

The guards ahead of us came back. "We're only halfway down, Your Majesty. What would you have us do?"

Theodore's gaze lingered on me for a moment. "Go ahead. See what's waiting for us at the bottom. If you think we would be over-whelmed, return. If not, tuck yourself away among the rocks. We'll be down shortly." Theodore looked to the two guards behind me. "Wait for us ten steps down."

When we were alone, Theodore let out an enraged huff.

"I'm fine," I said, though my body quaked. It was foolish — I knew it was — to not accept his help.

"Clearly." His hands were propped on narrow hips. "But this incessant blood bond will not let me ignore the fact that you're shaking. You're cold. You're scared —"

"Don't you dare call me a coward again —"

He held up a hand. "I said you were *scared*." In the moonlight, I could just see the sincerity that softened his eyes. "I'm scared too."

My fingers flexed against the vase I held, but I said nothing. I couldn't decide if knowing that he, the descendant of a Great God and king, was also scared made me feel better or worse.

"Tell me what you need." Again, his voice was so perfectly empty of feeling, deep and resolute in his chest. But that look in his eye made me believe that he meant it.

"I need to stop shaking," I said. He nodded and our gazes held. Then he offered me a hand. It was so warm, with calluses over his palms and the pads of his strong fingers. Guided by his steady hold, I stepped down onto the wide slab he stood upon. He took us toward the rock face. It was slightly concave, and he stepped into its curve, placing himself at my back. Neither of us spoke as he swiped at my damp hair to pile it over my shoulder. Nor did we speak when he tugged me slowly backward, into the sphere of his warmth. My body tensed when my back touched his hard chest. The sore skin there ached, but quickly, the heat of his body seemed to soothe it. He looped an arm around the front of my shoulders, and it was as if a band of sunshine bloomed over my collarbone. Slowly, carefully, he wrapped his other arm over my stomach, below the vase I held.

"Don't spill it," I whispered, as if he were not already handling me with the utmost care.

I didn't think he was breathing as he gently pressed me further against his body. My twitching muscles were so exaggerated next to his steadiness. I could make out the lines and divots of his chest, his stomach. The hard press of his thighs against the back of my own. Self-consciousness leaked through me. If I could picture the intimate details of his outline, he most certainly could picture mine.

He spoke softly, lips beside my ear. "Your back. Why didn't you tell me you were bleeding?"

"There were more important things to worry over," I said, staring out into the darkness. "It hardly hurt compared to the binding."

"I can't heal the wounds with the silk stuck to it." We stood like that, listening to the wind, and my body began to mirror Theodore's stillness. He leaned against the rock, and I leaned against him, and for the briefest moment, I closed my eyes and imagined I lay on my stomach in the sun. That its rays sank through my skin and muscle, to my very center. It felt like the blood bond in my gut glowed.

"Are you ready?"

Theodore's low voice jolted me. My head had fallen back against his shoulder, chin tipped up toward the stars. I jerked upright.

"Yes." I moved too quickly, trying to pull my body away from his. His arm snagged on the bottom of the vase. Water sluiced over the edge, soaking the front of me. "Shit."

The water felt strange.

In the tub, it had sparkled over my skin and burrowed toward that dark, steady pulse in my middle. Now the water made that same place feel strained. It was as if something inside me were close to fracturing, as if the source of my power had become incongruent.

Theodore set his hands to my shoulders. "What is it?"

I shook my head, not wanting to speak what I'd felt, and started down the stairs once more. It was easier now, with Theodore's warmth lingering over me, but it sat uneasily. Every kindness, every favor, was a debt to be repaid, and I already owed so much.

Quickly, nimbly, I moved down the stones, relying on myself alone. His boots scuffed over gravel behind me as he tried to keep up. We came upon the first Varian guard crouched around a bend. I lowered myself beside him. Theodore knelt close on my other side.

The entry yard had come into view. A wide, stacked stone gate ringed an open paddock, and beyond it stood the well-kept stable house. Torches burned on either side of the stable doors, with two more at the paddock gate. They fought to stay lit in the gusts, which made their flames strobe through the clearing. Four guards were clustered at the gate. They spoke and laughed, but the wind carried their sounds away.

"Are there only four?" I whispered over the guard's shoulder.

"Four here. Another six or so at the entry to the mountain road." He pointed off into the blackness between two towering crags of stone. There were more torches at their base, illuminating a small huddle of guards, but the light was faint, and Nemea's men were dressed in armor that was the same color as the night.

I pulled in a breath and held it. Worry gnawed at me. Worry over how my tremors were returning, over getting us all down this mountain. Over Theodore and his safety.

"We need to go now," said the guard, impatiently. "Lure the nearest men. Then I'll retrieve the rest of the party."

He made it sound so simple, but it felt suddenly impossible. I had no sense of my power. It was a lump of clay, and I was an untried artist. Whatever form it had taken tonight had not been because of my skill and understanding of it. I looked down at the vase of seawater. What if it wasn't enough? What if I, in my shivering, fear-locked state, could not keep any of us from a brutal, bloody end, all because I was too craven to face a death that I'd earned?

"Imogen." My given name on Theodore's lips quieted my thoughts. The distant firelight flickered over his stricken features. "I'll be right behind you."

I could only nod. Slowly, I took the vase and began to pour the water over my chest, my shoulders. It soaked into the dark green silk and into my skin. Instantly, that string in my chest reverberated, but the strange, fractured feeling returned too. I closed my eyes and fought to focus past it. My heart galloped, breath quickened. Then the first ooze of oily power poured between my ribs. The bloody skin around my spine seemed to stretch with the pressure of my wings, but I smothered their emergence with a desperate thought and focused my intention. I wished to lure, and the darkness in my gut surged into my throat.

I stood and took a single step down.

Theodore's fingers grasped mine. "Be careful."

Our gazes stuck. "Yes, Your Majesty." I had to force myself from his side, past his crouching men, down the last of the crooked stairs. The pebbles in the clearing poked into the soles of my feet. The chill, though I felt it, didn't make me tremble now. With each step I took, however, I felt more and more amiss. I clamped my jaw against the stretching, twisting sensation in my stomach and stopped before Nemea's guards at the edge of the torch's orb of light.

The first guard to see me jumped. It was the pock-faced boy who'd forced me into my room earlier. I cocked my head, taking him in. He looked even younger with his black helmet removed, all round cheeks and unkempt hair. Though he reached for it, he never touched the hilt of his sword.

Silent lures had shot from my throat.

His face began to change — brown eyes bulging, cheeks turning a deep, ugly red. The wind in the clearing died completely. The torches burned steadier. The other guards slipped under my lures before they could make a sound. And one after another, the four of them choked and convulsed until they collapsed into an unmoving heap.

My eyes grew wet with tears. A swirl of nausea made its way up from my stomach. I'd not thought to kill them.

A shout echoed from the entry at the mountain road. The rest of the guards there had seen me. They assembled and panic fell through me at the sight of their swords and daggers and crossbows. I wished for darkness so no arrow could find me, and a gust extinguished the torches. I started toward them, intention on my lure once more, when an angry pain burst through my stomach. I hissed, pressing my hand over the spot, but I kept moving toward the advancing guards.

They were close enough now that my power should have stopped them, but they didn't freeze. Though I'd sent out my lure, their bodies didn't go slack. I squinted through the moonlit night, focusing past the way my blood raced, to see that they'd only slowed. They moved as if through water. The straining pain in my middle grew and grew. I clamped my teeth, trying desperately to keep the guards at bay.

"*Imogen.*" Theodore's agonized voice lanced the darkness. It stopped me dead in my tracks.

But Nemea's guards kept advancing, plodding yet barbarous. Teeth bared, swords raised. I stumbled backward, trying to keep space between us, but the pain was spreading through me like ink through water. I landed hard on my backside. Gravel crunched behind me as Theodore's men ran to my aid. A scream scraped through my gritted teeth when I realized one of Nemea's guards was already upon me. I clawed at the gravel, trying to scramble away on my knees, but the building agony in my gut made me slow.

My stomach clenched like I was going to vomit, when a searing pain lit my thigh. Nemea's guard loomed over me, his sword cutting slowly through the outside of my leg. I could feel the cold blade deep inside my muscle, flaying it wide.

One of Theodore's men slid to a stop above me, spraying stones with his boots. He moved so quickly, his sword arching over him and down into the guard's extended arm. A sickening wet crack rent the air. A guttural, pleading wail. The guard's arm came clean off at the elbow. It fell over my stomach, dark blood spurting onto my wet silk robe, the sword that had cut me still held in its clenched fist.

The rest of Theodore's men arrived, slashing easily into the slow-moving guards. Groans rang out, the foul rip and thud of swords slicing through flesh. Bodies folded to the ground, and then Theodore was beside me, pulling me up to stand.

The pain in my stomach fled completely.

His hands were in my hair, cupping my cold face, gripping my shoulders as he took stock of me. "You're okay. You're okay," he kept repeating to himself. Grooves sat between his inky brows. His face was sweat-strewn and terrified. Hard fingers swiped at the tears on my cheeks, and then he stooped and ripped aside the robe to look at my leg. "*Shit.*"

He hefted me up into his arms. As he ran us toward the stables, he set his lips to my ear. "I can fix it," he promised. "You won't even have a scar."

"I don't care about a Godsdamned scar," I hissed at his lie. He set me atop a horse and climbed up behind me. "Just get me off this mountain."

PART II
THE SURFACE

9

I did not often dream.

When I did, the images were fragile, broken, blurred. As if I viewed them from high above, through a veil of clouds.

But now I dreamed in lurid detail.

A faceless woman floated upon the surface of the sea, her body bobbing over the churning waves. She was naked, without hair. Where her eyes should be were seared, empty sockets. Something swam below her. Far below, where the sunlight could not reach. Like a great monster with a shriveled stomach, it frantically searched the depths with a clawed, unquenchable need. Its eyes were milky and veinous. Its skin slick and mottled with decay.

But its heartbeat was strong. It pulsed through the water and through the air. A steady *thump, thump, thump* of desperation. Of *want.*

Finally, the lurking thing strained up and up with delight, for it could sense the woman's warmth leaking from her and desired to feast upon it.

Right before it reached her — right before I woke — I realized:

I was the woman. I was the water. I was the monster.

My eyes shot open to bleary, amber light. I did not move. I couldn't. My body still seemed to bob atop waves, but now it hurt with such vibrant pain that I couldn't even moan.

I rolled my head over a cool pillow. Sleep still clung like spiderwebs, but I could just make out the large room. A few ornate lanterns swayed from the ceiling, casting their light through the dark space. Everything was gilded. The walls, the intricate vines carved into the bedposts, the settee. I squinted at the figure on the far side of the room. The broad yet trim shape. The dark hair and darker gaze.

I blinked, and the king of Varya came into focus. A black lock of hair hung over his creased brow. He rifled through a box of small glass vials and as I watched him, the memories came. The strange pain in my middle that had brought me to my knees in the gravel yard of Nemea's mountain. The slow, excruciating slice of a sword through my leg. Theodore clinging to me as we rode down the mountain atop a stolen horse. The jostling had tugged me in and out of consciousness, but I remembered the warmth of his power pouring through my bleeding thigh, the soft roll of his voice at my ear telling me to stay upright, to keep my hold on the pommel.

The bed lurched, swayed, and I realized . . . we were on the ship. I was on the sea. I could feel it in my body, through my pain, through the pitch and wood.

"We made it," I rasped. Then, in the next breath, "I'm gonna be sick."

Agatha was at my side in a rush, holding an empty washbasin below my chin. I heaved into it, coughing, then shuddered at how it flared my pain. Theodore moved himself and the box of medicines closer. The nauseating twist in my stomach eased.

"It's the blood bond that's making you ill," Agatha said warily, as she ran a hand through my knotted hair. "It takes some time to settle."

I held my throbbing head. "How much time?"

"Two days." Lachlan and Agatha answered at the same time. Lachlan sat at the far end of the table Theodore stood beside, sharpening a dagger with a whetstone. I could see him properly now. He was wiry but imposing, with wide shoulders, light brown skin, and brown-gold hair, cropped close. There was an upward curve to the corners of his mouth and a mischievous light in his eyes.

Irritation pinched Agatha's features. "Had you told me that you had performed a sacred blood bond with the king of Varya *before* walking into a horde of armed guards, I could have told you that you'd be sick. I could have told you that you'd need to keep close to one another until the bond settles. But instead, you told me nothing and nearly got yourself killed."

"Agatha," I groaned. "A lesson learned. The next time I frantically bind myself to a king and flee my home, I'll make sure to run all the details past you first. That's assuming that next time this happens, you're not in the middle of a liaison."

Lachlan snorted, and Agatha shot him a look that should have set him aflame. "Don't worry," she bit out, more to Lachlan than me, "it won't happen again." She swept away from the edge of the bed with the washbasin, her cheeks flushed bright. Guilt lanced through me, and I noted the strain between them. I wondered what had transpired in the short amount of time they'd been reunited.

I tried to sit up, to find a quiet way to ask Agatha what was wrong, but only managed to wince in discomfort.

"Don't move." Theodore's order was low and chagrined. "You'll make your leg bleed. It's not properly healed yet."

I met his icy gaze across the room and stilled. There had been a kindness to him, an attentiveness, while we'd made our way down the mountain. He'd kept a hand at my back and warmed me. He'd looked at me with something like compassion when I'd been scared. Now it was all gone. He possessed all the heat and civility of a marble statue.

A heavy rolling sound, like thunder, filled the cabin. "What is that?"

"Cannons," Lachlan said, attention on his dagger. "They're readying them in the very likely event that Nemea sends his ships after us. You know, since his captain was murdered, and his ward was stolen away in the night."

His harsh hazel gaze and the derogation in his tone made it more than clear: Lachlan did not think highly of me.

"If I didn't know better," he went on, metal ringing with each swipe of his blade, "I'd think you were trying to take advantage of Theo. He's always been susceptible to a damsel in distress."

Agatha flopped down onto the settee, where she cradled her forehead in her hand. "Shut up, Lach."

Theodore gave him an annihilating scowl, but Lachlan only raised his brows placatingly. The whetstone gave another scrape.

"Take advantage of him?" It was almost comical, to picture someone so implacable and intimidating as the king of Varya being victimized.

Lachlan looked at me like I was simple. "To make yourself queen."

"Queen?" I blinked. "What do you . . . I don't understand."

Theodore's deep voice was quiet, filled with a soft sort of tension. "Marriages are not performed as blood bonds on Seraf, Lach. She didn't know."

"Marriages!" My gaze bounced between all three of them. "We're married?"

Theodore rubbed at his eye.

"That's fine," said Lachlan, clearly annoyed. "But *you* did. And you agreed. So now, in the eyes of the Great Gods, you've taken a fugitive wife, right before you're supposed to meet your fiancée."

"Your *what?*" My glare shot to Theodore. A surge of inexplicable possessiveness raced through me like venom. Color sat high on his cheeks. His full mouth was a hard, flat line. I could hardly understand my emotions — the irrational, spitting jealousy, the impulse to defend him to Lachlan. "I gave His Majesty my word that I'd have our blood bond severed. I trek to the Mage Seer the moment I land on Varian soil."

The air seemed to thin. Slowly, Agatha raised her head from her hand. Lachlan set his dagger to the table with a deafening *clack*.

"You're going to the Mage Seer?" Agatha shuddered. "For a severance?"

A chill raced through me at the devastation that suddenly weighed on her. "Yes."

Agatha's voice went weak, impudent. "Your Majesty —"

Lachlan held up a hand. "Now, hold on." He gave Theodore a disbelieving look, a strained and angry tilt to his lips. "You're not actually sending her to the Mage Seer, are you? You wouldn't. The severance will happen in the safety of the palace."

Theodore's broad chest rose and fell with increasing breaths, but his features were even as ever. "The severance will happen in the Mage Seer's hut."

"No." Agatha rose from the settee so quickly I flinched. She stood like a bedraggled soldier, fierce and strong. Her black curls were a wild, sea-misted halo. Dirt and large tears marred her dress. "Absolutely not."

Theodore's gaze narrowed. "You're out of line, Agatha."

"I beg your forgiveness, then, because I do not plan on ceasing," she snapped. "*Please,* Your Majesty, you cannot send her there."

"Agatha." Lachlan's entire countenance softened as he made his way to her side. He reached out a tentative hand, but she stepped away.

"No," she said, resolutely. She looked pleadingly toward Lachlan. "He cannot. *Tell him.* He cannot do this." Her voice wobbled with tears.

I'd never witnessed Agatha in such a state. I wanted to go to her, take her hand, but as I tried to sit taller, I realized I was naked. With a violent tug, I pulled the sheets to my chin. My mind filled with questions, with dreadful, nightmarish thoughts of this Mage Seer and her severance ritual. They fell through me like stones, collecting painfully in my gut. "Tell me what's wrong," I said. "Is the Mage Seer dangerous?"

Agatha gaped at me. "Is she dangerous?" She rounded on Theodore. "Shame on you." Theodore went so still, so terrifyingly quiet, but Agatha went on. "When your father ordered that Lachlan and I sever our blood bond, he sent us to the Mage Seer with nothing but a pack of food and two horses. I nearly died in that rotting hut of hers."

The memory seemed to grind her down. Her shoulders drooped. Her voice faltered. "The severing draught . . . It turns the blood black and forces it through the nose and eyes and mouth. The pain of the binding is nothing compared to the severance. Lachlan could only sit and watch as I lost blood over days on a filthy pallet, without a healer, while the Mage Seer did nothing but slither around in her putrid smoke."

An ugly silence stretched between us all. Finally, Theodore spoke, his tone barbed and labored. "I am not my father." He paused. Pulled in a deep breath. "I know how terrible the Mage Seer is. That is why Lady Imogen will be accompanied by a retinue of guards and a palace healer."

"I beg you to send a rider instead." Tears slipped down Agatha's cheeks. "Let them bring the severing draught back to the palace. Let her endure the ritual under your care. You're the most powerful healer in all of Leucosia."

Tension strung through Theodore. He dropped his attention back to the vials on the table in front of him. "I can't do that."

Agatha gaped, her tears falling now in earnest. "You *can't*?"

I felt like I was sinking. Like the new shackle I'd stepped into when I knelt before the king of Varya was tightening, cutting in, pulling me down.

Lachlan's eyes were bright with fury. "Theo, I think —"

"You can both leave." It was an order, slicing through the room like a whistling sword. "Now."

Agatha reeled like she'd been struck across the face. She whirled and stormed from the room. Lachlan lingered to give Theodore a final damning look. "I'd thought you, of all people, would have chosen better than this. On all fronts." He strode with heavy steps toward the open cabin door, then slammed it shut behind him.

Theodore stood in the quiet, pinching the bridge of his nose. The moments strained, until finally, he swiped two vials from the table and came to the side of the bed. He pulled the stopper from one with his teeth and spat it to the floor. "Drink this."

I wished I were standing and clothed, instead of laid out over the man's bed, but I filled my voice with all the rebuke I could manage. "That was heartless of you."

"It was necessary." He held the little vial closer. "Drink."

Anger burst through me. Keeping the sheets in place, I clumsily pushed myself up to sit. A sharp pain hit my thigh and hot liquid gushed over my skin. "I will not drink," I said, ignoring it. "You tricked me. Why didn't you tell me that severing our bond could kill me?"

He raked a hand through his waving hair. "I did not trick you. You do not understand the complexity —" He tried for some control and failed. "Gods damn it, you have forced me to make impossible decisions, to do things I never thought I would, and yet you make me the villain."

"I forced you to do nothing! You agreed."

"Do you truly think I had any other choice when you broke into my room, all wet and winged —" He cut himself off with a scowl. When he finally looked back down at me, he winced. "You're bleeding through the sheet. I'll ask once more that you drink this and let me close that wound on your leg properly. We can scream at one another after."

The bright stain in the bedding spread quickly, but my anger did too. I glared at the little vial in his hand and spoke through my teeth. "What is it?"

"Nepenthe," he said, evenly. It riled me further that he sounded so composed. "It'll get rid of the pain."

Nepenthe did more than rid a body of pain. It blunted the faculties too. And the most I'd ever taken at once had been a handful of drops in my tea. I expected a vial's worth would send me into a dream-riddled sleep that I'd not wake from for half a day. I shivered at the thought and shook my head. "No nepenthe. Just do it."

Theodore looked at me like I was mad, but he knelt at the edge of the bed and waited as I struggled to slip my leg free of the covers. The small movement made me whimper. My thigh was a flap of bloody flesh. Only a thin layer of skin, that I assumed Theodore had coaxed into existence, had kept it from bleeding. When I'd moved it had torn.

"Hold this." He pressed the nepenthe into my hand. "You're going to change your mind." Then he set a tentative, but warm, grip on my knee. He swallowed hard and stared at my thigh, which was exposed all the way up to the curve of my hip. He didn't move.

I threw a fist into the mattress. "What in the bloody Gods are you waiting for?"

His mouth opened and closed. "Can I touch you?"

"You're already touching me."

"I need to touch you here." The wound was large, curving around my leg toward the underside of my buttock.

"Oh, for Gods' sake. *Yes.* Touch me."

For a tense moment our gazes locked. Anger and concern and annoyance churned between us until finally he palmed the flesh at my hip with such a firm hand that I gasped. He'd not hurt me, but his touch was fervent, frustrated, and somehow tender too. A heavy exhale slipped past my lips as he slid his hand down my rounded hip to the edge of the wound. His touch left a trail of gooseflesh in its wake. Then he met my eye. "Last chance."

"Do it."

He didn't hesitate. He tugged the flap of skin closed in one skilled motion as his hands filled with fiery heat. I screamed, then drained the little bottle of nepenthe in one swill.

"That's what I thought," Theodore mumbled, and his touch grew hotter and hotter.

I squeezed my eyes shut as the nepenthe carved through me. It trimmed away my pain until all I could feel was Theodore's power and the pressure of his fingers. It cut the flimsy ties that kept my anger in place too. "You'll come with me," I said, in an odd voice. It was not a question, or an order, or a plea, but some nepenthe-laced thing in between. "To the Mage Seer."

His fingers paused on my skin. "I've already said that I can't."

"Because of your dearest betrothed," I snapped.

His keen eyes found mine and I worried I'd let my asinine desire to guard him like some sort of treasure I'd never be able to claim slip into my voice.

"Yes," he said, carefully. "When we arrive on Varya, I am to meet immediately with the Empress of Obelia and her daughter, whom I am to marry." His grip on my leg tightened and a new flood of heat radiated through the healing skin. "That is why I cannot go with you."

I pushed up onto an elbow and scowled. "And why can't you send a rider?"

He kept his gaze on my wound. "Because it's not just the severance you need while you're there. You need a prophecy too."

I stared at him. My mind swam with worry over his words, his commands, over everything he withheld. I was overcome with fury and fear, but still, I could not help but notice that King Theodore was appallingly, tragically handsome. *Fucking nepenthe.* I squeezed my eyes closed. "A prophecy." The words slurred. "Is that your third condition?"

"Not exactly."

"Then I don't need to do it."

"You do." He rose in a huff and went to a clean washbasin beside the bed. He washed his hands, wrung out a rag, then brought it to my healed leg to clean away the thick smears of blood. "Because I am your king, and you swore fealty to me. And because the third condition, which you have already agreed to, hinges upon the prophecy."

My hand shot out and grabbed his hard forearm. I yanked him toward me, leaning in close enough to feel his breath fanning over my cheek. "I know you did not bind yourself to me out of the goodness of your kingly heart. You did it because I have something you need. Something, I expect, that you cannot get from anyone else." My words were sloppily strung together, but not without bite. "I will not live another life like my last, honoring the whims of a king who wishes to use me. I bent the knee to you, yes, but it will cost me nothing to denounce you and leave your kingdom with my blood still running through your veins. I will happily let our bond plague you with unending worry over my well-being until you are old and gray if you treat me like I am some palace maid to be ordered about. If you want a severance, if you want me to receive a prophecy so that I can fulfill your final condition, then I have some terms of my own you must agree to."

Theodore did not blink as he stared at me. I wasn't certain he breathed. His handsome face was unreadable, until his mouth parted in the barest look of offense. I wondered if anyone had ever spoken to him as I just had. I waited for him to rail at me for doing so. But his bewildered eyes merely slipped from mine and landed on my lips. One breath. Two breaths. Three. Then he jerked his arm from my hold.

"Later." His voice was rough, clenched. "When you're not flying from the nepenthe, we'll..." He rolled his jaw. "...negotiate." He strode to a built-in bureau and pulled a white nightshirt from within. He tossed it over my now clean and healed leg. Only a fine, silvery line of new skin remained.

Brooding, he went from lantern to lantern, turning them low. "A rule: If you somehow wake before I do, you are not permitted to leave this cabin without me at your side." He strode to the door and clicked the lock over with a key. Then he tucked it deep inside his trouser pocket. My heart thundered, the fog over my mind grew denser, and I watched the shadow of his strong body curl onto the settee. "Good night, Lady Imogen."

I fumbled the nightshirt over my dizzy head before falling back into the pillows. Sleep held me in its palm, but I could not help picturing it as the clawed, slick-skinned hand of the monster from my dream. I thought I could feel it writhe through the water below me, thought I could hear its roaring heart in my ears. Despite how I tried, my eyes wouldn't stay open. A terrified whimper filled my head as I finally slipped into midnight darkness.

10

The dress draped over the foot of the bed was made of the finest cobalt silk I'd ever seen. The distinct smell of armoire clung to it, and the hard creases in the skirt told me it had been shoved into a forgotten corner for some time, but there was no mistaking how expensive it was. I ran my fingers over the whirling stitches on the bodice, when my gaze snagged on my engagement ring.

The large, rare stone glittered and shone. Perhaps it would fetch me enough money to start a new life. New clothes and a small home. The king's discarded dresses and goodwill would very soon run out.

I tightened the dress's laces over my stomach and tied them into a bow at the swooping neckline. It was a perfect fit, and somehow I did not question that Theodore had known it would be. "You bastard," I mumbled, not knowing if I intended the curse for Theodore and his flawless gown or Nemea and his torturous one.

Frustrated, I shook out the wrinkled skirt and swallowed back a flood of saliva. It was sickness that had pulled me from a nightmare-suffused sleep. And from the way the light coming through the massive wall of windows had begun to melt into a luxurious evening gold, it had been a long sleep too.

The minutes passed and I only managed to nibble at a bit of apple as I paced the room. Then to the basin to heave up what little I'd eaten, and then toward the cabin door in hopes that Theodore would return and give me some relief. The golden light began to deepen, and I stood at the window watching the lambent sea ripple and slice. The spume haunted the peaks of the waves, there and gone, and there once more. I awed, and wondered if I should love it, or if I should fear it. If I should see something of myself in its changeability, in its ceaseless, churning want. In how I could never truly know what lurked in its depths.

My mind was yanked from its thoughts with my next round of dry heaves.

"Priggish ass," I groaned, wiping my mouth. "At least you're sick too, wherever you are."

I trudged back toward the door and tried the handle. Locked. I pulled back the green velvet curtain that hung neatly over the door's glass and stilled.

There, in a leadlight window, was a depiction of a Siren hovering over a rocky shore and a vine-covered ship. There was nothing ominous in her portrayal. Rather, she looked like she had been... adored. Her black wings were wide. Rays of yellow glass shone down on her from above. In comparison, the ship below her looked small, overshadowed.

I stared, curiosity swirling, for a long moment before I pounded on the door. "Let me out."

A shape rippled through the stained glass. The lock clicked. The door swung open, and there stood Lachlan. He seemed even taller now than before. A dark stubble had grown over his jaw. I stared up into his scrutinizing eyes, yellow-green shot through with brown, and said, "Ugh."

Lachlan arched a brow. "Not happy to see you either, but let's make the best of it, shall we?"

"Where's the king?"

"Working."

I looked over my shoulder at the paper-cluttered desk on the wall opposite the wide bed. Then at the long polished table that held two trays of food — the breakfast and lunch I'd slept through. "Why isn't he working in here?"

He lifted a shoulder. "Theo likes his privacy."

"Please," I begged, "I need this sickness to stop. Please, go get him."

Lachlan gave me a flat, unbending sort of assessment, and I knew he wouldn't.

"I hope he's vomiting all over his paperwork," I seethed. "All right. Agatha, then. Where is she?"

Lachlan's entire countenance changed. His shoulders fell and a long exhale pushed through his lips. "She's locked herself in her cabin."

I narrowed my eyes. "What did you do to her?"

"You sure it wasn't you?" He counted my sins on his fingers. "What with your murdering, and your almost getting yourself killed, and your king-stealing?"

We glared at each other for a beat.

"Fine." I crossed my arms staunchly over my chest. "I'll concede that I've very likely helped send her into a fit, but only if you tell me what the hell is going on with the two of you."

"There's nothing going on."

"Liar," I said, just as my stomach muscles clenched. I ran toward the basin and retched and retched until my ribs ached so badly, I moaned. As I wiped my mouth with a cloth, I heard the door close and lock.

Lachlan strode toward the settee and collapsed onto its cushions, propping up his feet. "I'm not lying. There is nothing going on between us, however much I would like there to be."

IN THE VEINS OF THE DROWNING

"But last night the two of you had obviously been kissing at the very least."

"That we had." He massaged his brow like it hurt. "She also yelled at me for writing so often, even though she always wrote back. Apparently, I have not let her 'move on' and we are 'no longer compatible,' but we felt pretty damn compatible last night, so I don't know what I'm supposed to fucking do with that."

"I think we're tied," I said, before I dry-heaved once more into my fist.

He snorted, then gave me a pitying look. "You're almost a full day into your bond now. One more day to go."

"I don't consider myself a petty woman." I made for the shelf where the box of little glass vials sat and searched for some tonic that might give me relief. "But I hope that the king is curled up in a ball right now, spectacularly miserable."

"Liar," Lachlan quipped. "I know for a fact that you're both riddled with worry for each other and that the only reason he hasn't run back in here is because the contracts he's poring over are eating away at him with sharper teeth than yours."

The glass clinked as I lifted one after the other to read the labels. "Contracts! Not war plans, or something else confidential? Why in the bloody Gods wouldn't he look through them in here, then?"

"They're marriage contracts."

A slash of envy lit my body green. My hand tightened around a vial. "Why would I care about his marriage contracts?"

Lachlan smirked. "Don't you?"

Silence stretched for a long moment before I relented. "Yes. I care," I admitted in an agitated rush. "Though I can't understand why."

"It's the blood bond." He lifted his wistful gaze to the ceiling. "It makes you believe *you* are the person best suited to care for him.

To see that he isn't harmed. The thought of him marrying another person should drive you mad."

"Why on earth would anyone *want* a blood bond?" My stomach cramped again with sick, and I pressed a hand to my sternum, praying it would settle. "I can't think of a more insufferable arrangement. It's like I'm being thwacked with a stick over and over and over . . . until I throw up."

Lachlan rose and strode to a little cabinet hidden in the gilded wall. He took out a crystal decanter and filled a glass with a healthy pour of honey-colored spirits. "Well, it's very nice when you love the person. Or can at least stand to be in the same room as them." His eyes twinkled — not with nostalgia, but with mischief. It was both charming and infuriating and I could see how Agatha might be at war with herself over someone like him. He held his glass up as if in a toast. "But alas, that's not the case for you two."

"And that pleases you, does it?"

"No." He made his way back to his spot on the settee. "I'm mildly amused. Theodore is so good. These last few years, he's followed every single rule every minute of every day. It's a little entertaining to see him flounder." He looked at me pointedly. "Despite the repercussions."

"I see." I gave up on the tonics, most of which were mixed with dream-inducing nepenthe, and made for the drink cabinet.

Lachlan eyed me over his shoulder. "You sure that's wise?"

"It might take the edge off the worry." I poured my own glass.

"Or make you more nauseated."

"Not possible." I took a deep drink and met Lachlan's gaze. "You said the king has been following rules 'these last few years.' What was he doing before that?"

"Oh no." He laughed, the sound warm and easy, and despite

myself, I smiled. I liked him. I liked him for Agatha. "I'm not telling you a single private detail about him."

I rounded the settee and sat on the low table before him. "I'll put in a good word for you with Agatha."

He went still, his hazel gaze narrowing in interest.

"Please." My desperation was too potent for me to rein in. "I cannot find a single crack in his facade. I don't trust that he'll do right by me if I can't find something, one small detail, that will knock him off his frustratingly perfect balance."

Lachlan leaned back and considered me over the rim of his glass. He tapped his fingers against the crystal. "All right."

"All right? You agree?"

"I do. You don't seem to understand just how off-balance you've already knocked him, but I want a good word with Agatha."

I straightened my shoulders and looked him square in the eye. "You really think I forced him, don't you? You think I stole him."

He lifted a shoulder in a shrug. "He mentioned that you climbed into his bed, in the dark, half-naked. At the very least you were *very* persuasive." I glared at him, and he gave me a defeated smirk. "Okay — I believe wholeheartedly that he agreed to your binding. Listen to me, though, I don't want to hurt him. I love him like a brother, so don't you dare." His gaze darted as he thought of what information to volunteer, until finally it landed on the wrinkled blue dress I wore. His eyes lit up. "Got it." He put his elbows on his knees. I leaned in too. "When Theo was a very new king, about six years ago, he would take this ship and turn it into a somewhat sordid pleasure cruise. Went on for a couple years. He'd fill it with beautiful women and his best wine and men from his court and sail it around from sundown to sunrise." He pointed to my dress. "That's where your dress came from. Left behind. No idea what the poor woman wore off the ship."

I looked down at the musty blue silk and back up to Lachlan. "*Somewhat sordid.* That's it? Not debauched. Or sickeningly immoral. Wasn't he nineteen or twenty? That's incredibly normal behavior for a young king. What on earth am I supposed to do with that information?"

Lachlan's mouth pulled into a wide smile. "It haunts him. He's disgraced by it. He thinks it was a massive, embarrassing waste of the crown's resources, and he's spent the years since trying to rectify the light that he thinks it cast him in with his chancellor. You'd think he'd killed an innocent man with his bare hands the way he carries on about it."

I took a sip of my drink. "Duty-bound to his core."

He dipped his chin. "That's right. Now, you tell Agatha that I've done nothing but think of her since I last saw her, and had she let me, I would have come to Seraf and whisked her away without a second thought."

"She told you not to?"

He nodded. "I suspect her refusal to leave had something to do with you."

"Oh." I felt the accusation, the touch of resentment. I cocked my head. "But is that true? That you've done nothing but think of her for nearly twenty years?"

He downed the rest of his drink, then pursed his lips. I was surprised when the pretense fled his voice. "I've taken lots of lovers over the years. Women and men, all of them witty and beautiful. All better than I could ever deserve. But one letter from Agatha makes me feel more alive, more full of hope and calm and elation, than touching any of them ever did."

His genuine smile tugged my mouth into a crooked one. "I'll tell her that."

He shook his head. "Please don't. Tell her the other thing I said."

"I'll tell her a variation — I'll skip the part about all the lovers."

He hesitated, scratched the dark stubble on his chin, and finally nodded. He paused. "You haven't thrown up in a while."

My gaze slid down to the glass I held, and I raised my eyebrows, hopeful I'd found some cure, when the door to the cabin flew open and Theodore strode in.

My spine straightened. Theodore was pallid, with deep grooves of lingering discomfort between his brows. He stood just inside the door, a thick leather folder of papers at his side. He met my eyes, and then his gaze dipped to the dress I wore.

"It fits," he said, his tone oddly flat.

"Yes. Do you like it?" I flounced the skirt over my lap and added in an overbright voice, "I'm fortunate that you kept it on your ship all these years."

Theodore's gaze sharpened and darted between Lachlan and me. A sudden flush of red colored his pale cheeks. "I beg your pardon?"

Lachlan's eyes bulged at Theodore's biting tone. "Good luck," he whispered before he rushed to stand and made for the still-open door. "If you'd both like some relief, may I suggest a hug?" He tried for seriousness, but there was no missing the delight that filled his voice. "A blood bond is happiest with some level of closeness, especially as it settles." He swung the door shut before I could throw my glass at him.

I set it down on the table instead, feeling a twinge of guilt for embarrassing Theodore. Perhaps I could charm my way into his good graces. I stood and swayed a little from the drink and lack of food, but I met Theodore's gaze with my chin high. Even if I'd drunk nothing at all, the whole room would have seemed to tilt. The king of Varya did that without even trying. He drew the air toward him, made the solid floor practically bow beneath my feet.

I felt a sort of pain to look at him, his beauty and rigid authority. It made me want to flee.

Since I couldn't, I smiled fully and inclined my chin toward the folder he held. "What's that? Do you need my signature on some official paper once you finally reveal our third agreement?"

He gave a grunt. "That's not a terrible idea, but no." He looked down at the folder and a lock of dark hair fell over his brow. "These are the contracts the Empress of Obelia sent over with her stipulations for my marrying her daughter."

"Oh." I stepped around the settee to stand closer, a soft smile still on my lips. The bunched bond in my stomach loosened and I let out a soft breath of relief. He looked at me with disarming intensity. "Are you . . . eager?" I asked. "To meet your bride?" I regretted the question instantly.

He considered for a moment. "If I'm honest," he said, carefully, quietly, "no. But eagerness isn't necessary. It's an advantageous match for my kingdom and fulfills what is required of me."

My brow buckled. "What if she's awful?"

He shrugged like he'd never considered it.

I half envied the ease with which he could deny himself so much and half pitied him for it. "Have you at least seen her portrait?"

"Yes."

I waited in vain, smile long gone, for him to say more. "Well . . . if you find yourself inspired to shirk your responsibilities . . ." I tried for levity, despite the frantic claws scraping through the inside of my chest. ". . . Perhaps I can offer you some guidance on how to rid yourself of an unwanted fiancée."

He shook his head and strode away from me to set the contracts upon his desk, but as he did so, he smiled. A real, full smile. It dimpled one cheek and crinkled his green eyes at the edges. His teeth were white and straight, and I found myself staring after him like an addle-minded girl.

"Is it so hard for you to imagine?" he asked, as he set the folder within a polished wooden box and locked it with a silver key. "To fulfill one's duty and be satisfied by it? I don't need a charming or beautiful wife. I don't need her to be a friend. None of that will benefit my kingdom."

"And you are your kingdom? There's nothing you need that it doesn't?"

He perched on the edge of his desk and crossed his arms. He beheld me with one of those frustratingly unreadable looks of his. "Like what, my lady?"

"Like . . ." *Like passion or humor or friendship*, but I couldn't bring myself to speak it. My mind went slippery with his attention locked on me. I shook my head and curled my hands into my wrinkled skirt. "You never answered me," I said, softly. "Do you like my dress?"

He regarded me, lips curling mirthlessly, then looked me up and down, very, very slowly.

I held my breath as his green eyes roamed.

"You look lovely." His voice was filled with graveled admiration, but it somehow did not sound like a compliment.

I bit into my cheek, annoyed by that tilting feeling he cast over me. "I cannot tell whether you mean what you say."

"I always mean what I say, my lady. It's my implication that you cannot grasp." He uncrossed his strong arms and gripped the edge of the desk he perched upon. "You *are* lovely. You're charming, and if our circumstances were different, I'd likely enjoy a meal with you, bask in your wit, but as it is your beauty and charm are like gnats that I must swat away from my eyes to keep my vision clear.

Your qualities are wasted on me. They do not matter, because your purpose and power exceed them."

The silence between us contorted, a mirror to my insides. I kept perfectly still, refusing to give him the satisfaction of seeing me shrink, of making me into some pest when it was his own self-importance that riled. "My purpose and power," I said in a glacial voice. "And what might that be?"

For once an emotion flickered over his face, but to my frustration, I could not place it. He let me see him tense. He made a moment of pulling in a full breath and slowly releasing it. "Your purpose — the reason I agreed to bind myself to you — is to ensure that you will help me track down and kill King Nemea's water deity, Eusia. And it's your power that makes me believe you can. That silent lure you possess is Gods' power. It's beyond what a normal Siren can wield."

I stilled. Blood raged through my ears. "Gods' power..." I breathed through the light feeling that began to fill my head. "No. You're... no —"

His acerbic tone fled, and he sounded suddenly like he was speaking to some spooked creature that was a moment away from a rampage. "I believe you're the daughter of the Great Goddess Ligea."

My thoughts came clipped and quickly. Theodore telling me *he knew me*. The Great Goddess Ligea's statue in Nemea's ritual room, her face chiseled to dust. I supported myself against the back of the settee.

I'd already given my word to Theodore, and it was my bleeding duty to honor it. I'd likely die trying. "Not possible," I squeaked. The sickness from our bond had settled, but I still felt ill.

"You have her face."

I shook my head. "That's why... that's why you look at me like that . . . isn't it?" I needed air. I needed to move. On weak knees, I bolted for the unlocked door and ran out onto the ship's deck. It teemed with sailors.

My feet slapped over the damp planks as I wove through the crew. The sky was a fiery red now and the salt wind whipped at my hot cheeks. Sea mist fell over me like the gentlest rain, sparking over my skin, clinging to the silk of my borrowed gown. I ran straight from the stern of the ship to the bow.

Behind me, Theodore's voice boomed. "Everyone belowdecks. Now."

I only heard the clomp of boots as the crew obeyed. The ship captain echoed the king, hurrying the sailors away. But I didn't watch them go; I bent over the ship's rail, not taking my burning eyes off the water. Though it frightened me to no end, though I dreaded what sort of monster it might make of me, I preferred its horrific mystery to what Theodore seemed so certain of.

He came up behind me with slow steps. "Lady Imogen . . ."

I whirled. "You ass. You sneaky, egotistical — this is just another ploy to keep me under your thumb, to use me."

The wind ran through his dark hair like fingers; it tugged at his black shirt. "No. That's why I need you to get the prophecy from the Mage Seer," he said, soft, impassive. "She will tell you the truth."

"What do you care whether I believe it or not?" My hands were fists, clinging to my now-damp dress. "I have this power — that I cannot control in the slightest, mind you. Why not just force me to use it regardless of whether a prophecy proves you right?"

He gave me a sullen look. "I do not wish to force you —"

"Oh, how *good* of you. Thank you, Your Majesty." I gave an angry laugh. "You want me to *want* to go on a mortal hunt for a powerful deity, because it's my divine duty." My anger was wholly untethered, whipping through me. "And what could possibly be more rewarding than fulfilling it? Who wouldn't want to die a hero in service of one's king? I have no desire to be like you —" I jabbed a finger against his chest. "To scrape myself empty for others and call it noble."

He'd gone rigid, eyes locked with mine. There was only the sound of the wind snapping through the sails. The sea crashing against the hull. That plucking sensation came again in my chest, deep in the middle, and I wished I could cut it out. Theodore and I stood still before one another, an abyss between us. I saw no way of bridging it.

I didn't bother trying to stifle the tears that rolled down my face. Theodore looked...stunned. Helpless. He blinked too much; his full mouth opened and closed as his mind clearly reeled.

"What the hell is wrong with you?" I demanded, through my weeping.

He shook his head. "I...I don't know what to do with you."

I swiped the windblown hair from where it stuck to my wet cheeks. "You do. You're sending me to my death —"

"Stop. No." He covered his face in his hands for a moment. "Right now. With you...emotional...in front of me."

I cast my gaze out over the horizon, toward the red, sinking sun. I tried to school my features, steady my breaths. The ship pitched and swayed, and even I knew that the crew would need to return to their posts soon to keep us on course. One last deep breath of salt air. "Another day and this bond will settle. Then we can both enjoy some space from one another," I said, gaze stuck on the last dash of sunlight. Without glancing back at him, I started for the confines of the stateroom. His warm hand wrapped around my wrist. I glared down at it, then up into his eyes.

They bored into me with a fathomless expression. "An embrace," he said.

"A *what?*"

He tugged on my arm, forcing me a step closer. "Lachlan said an embrace — closeness — might help ease things."

Had he not had the direst look on his face and a patch of red creeping over the top of his collar, I would have thought the suggestion was in jest. I might have laughed at the ridiculousness of it had my chest not felt like it were caving in.

I gave my head a confused shake. "You hate me."

His brow pinched. "I don't —"

"You called me a gnat."

"Imogen." His grip tightened on my wrist, and I stopped breathing. "I would like to find a way to make you feel better right now." His voice was all warmth, curling around me. "This is what I can offer."

I thought of our escape, when he'd held me to calm my shaking body and how the bond in my belly had glowed. I remembered the outline of him, the feel of his heart beating against my spine. The memories alone filled me with frisson.

There were many misguided things I desired, and I suspected it would always be so. Just as sure as I was made of flesh and blood and bone and sea, I was also made of want. Excising it, draining it like a bad humor, would never do, but this one time, with this one man, I could stop myself from being the fool.

"I don't want an embrace," I whispered. When he released me, my wrist was cold.

Head high, and with Theodore trailing in my wake, I made my way across the deck. There was an emptiness, a hopelessness, that rankled, but I tried to let this truth soothe me: Nothing good had ever come from me taking what I wanted.

11

A full day and a half later, I clung to the rail of the ship as it glided across a crowded bay, toward Panos Port. I was ready to be off the water and touch solid land. To sleep soundly, dreamlessly, without being jostled by the sea's merciless surface. I'd fallen into a malaise after my row with Theodore, and that Gods-damned plucking in my chest wouldn't cease.

Agatha stood close at my side, face pinched in a troubled scowl. Theodore lingered not far behind me. I could nearly sense what direction he paced in, bow to stern, and back again.

Our blood bond still had not settled.

"I think something's wrong," Agatha said, leaning toward me so he wouldn't hear. "The two of you shouldn't be ill any longer."

I frowned at the thought and stared into the water below. It was so clear, I could see straight to the bottom. Clusters of fish darted this way and that, looking like silvered arrowheads. Bright sprays of coral dotted the white sand of the seafloor.

"You don't know that." I tried to keep myself from sounding as worried as I felt. "It's not even been three full days."

She only offered me a sharp look, jaw tightly set. "And as I've said, it should only take *two*."

"You performed your binding a long time ago. Maybe you're misremembering."

"It was two." She was adamant. Then she paused to think. "Though our binding was different from yours. We didn't spend time apart during those two days. We..." She looked at me sidelong, then away quickly. "Were *together* often."

"Together?" I caught her meaning a beat later and grimaced. "Oh sweet Gods. Let's assume it's our lack of *togetherness* that's the problem, then."

"You could..." Agatha glanced at Theodore over her shoulder, then back at me. Her brows rose suggestively, disappearing into her thick curls.

"No. We couldn't." I scoffed. "He's more interested in sending me off to be tortured in a severing ritual than bedding me."

"Still — you can't be this sick indefinitely." She brought her voice even lower. "I don't think he'd say no."

"Think about what you're suggesting!" A briny gust rolled over the water and wound through my loose hair. "And he most certainly *would* say no. He thinks I'm nothing but a superfluous imposition."

Agatha shrugged. "I'd wager you'd be no imposition at all in this."

The suggestion was laughable. Theodore and I had hardly spoken since he'd told me what my task was to be. Since he'd told me that he thought I was the descendant of a Great Goddess. That was laughable too. I knew my story. I was an orphaned child of noble birth. Nemea took me in because of my family's money. Nothing more. But despite my lifelong surety, Theodore's belief had left me bereft. Agitated, I brushed my thumb over the heap of scars that sat in the middle of my palm.

"Do you think he's right?" I asked Agatha. We both leaned on the rail, and I pressed my shoulder to hers. "Do you think my power is like that of the Great Goddess Ligea's?"

Agatha stared out over the water. At the little white stone buildings clustered tightly around the docks. More fanned out to dot the sprawling green hills of Varya. She shook her head. "She was the last Great Goddess to survive, but I never saw her. I knew all the stories of her power, though. Sailors would say the sea called to them, but it was *her* pull they felt on their bones. It was her call that rushed silently through their ears. And she could ruin them all without lifting a hand. They would pray to her and ask that she fill their nets. They'd ask for calm seas. And she would oblige, where she saw fit."

My throat grew thick. "I can do none of those things."

"Not now. Not yet . . . perhaps." She looked at me with the shine of hope in her eyes. "Every God's power is different, but it's always the greatest among the descendants who can wield it with ease. I have to sing to lure, but you do not." She looked to Theodore. "And the king — he doesn't need to touch to heal flesh or to make plants flourish."

My attention snapped toward her. "I'm sorry — what?"

"What?" Agatha reared back at my reaction.

"Every time the king has healed me, he's touched me."

"Oh. Well." Agatha's lips curled into a knowing smile. "I can't imagine why."

I forced my eyes shut. The wind whipped again, blowing more salt mist into my nose. It should have calmed me, but it only fanned that unsettling hum in my chest. I glared at Theodore over my shoulder. He stood about ten paces away — as far as he could without either of us growing ill — looking resplendent. His golden laurel crown sat upon his head, twining through his black locks. His brown coat was cut precisely to the lines of his broad chest, his narrow waist. The emerald cape pinned to his muscled shoulders billowed in the wind. *Damn him.* I had to look away.

A wispy fog had rolled over Varya's port city of Voros, veiling the newly risen sun. A portion of the city was walled, with little stone lookouts sitting upon its corners. Flowering vines covered the wall like a verdant cage. My gaze followed it all the way out to the peninsula that Genevreer Palace sat upon. It was brilliant despite the fog, with its creamy white stones and tiled roof the color of ash. Even from the ship, I could see how Varya's famed flowering vines crept up its walls like dark veins webbing a fair body.

The city bustled and the land bloomed, all of it rich because of Theodore's power. I'd never felt so small. "Agatha, I can't do this. I can't control my power in the least. I have nothing to my name, no way to protect myself. I'll be alone —"

She curled her hand around mine. "I told you I'd be with you. I promised you." She squeezed my hand tighter. "You won't be alone."

We stood like that, hand in hand, as the ship kept its course for the docks. I watched the turquoise water ripple and froth, when suddenly, some energy rocked through my body. What had been a hum in my chest became wild tugs and jabs. They crescendoed and I set a worried hand to my stomach. It was as if that string inside me had become many and they were being plucked by a hand coming from somewhere far below.

I looked past the gentle waves to the seafloor. It had changed. It was no longer pristine white sand, strewn with colorful coral. Now it looked to be covered in dark, twisting rocks. I leaned farther over the rail, squinting, when I realized — they were bodies.

Many, many bodies. Their unmoving limbs were knotted and overlaid like the strands of a weaving. I gasped as a spindly arm appeared just beneath the ship's hull. A ghostly white shoulder, shadowed with decay, came into view next.

Then the whole corpse. A woman. Dark hair fluttered around her head like black fire. She was dead, I was certain of it, hanging lifeless not ten feet below the surface.

Then she moved.

She swam with the grace of a living thing. Like she was used to the water, meant to be in it. She strained toward the rolling surface, right below me, and her black eyes locked with mine.

Her face was blank, the edge of her jaw studded with a pattern of barnacles as intricate as white lace. She *was* dead. It was the sea that seemed to hold her together. She floated on her back over the waves. Leathery kelp had knit itself through the rotting edges of the holes in her torso. A stringy tentacle grew from her chest, right above her heart, and it curled down her shoulder to hold her arm in place at the joint. Bits of flesh were missing from her face, from her limbs — but her dark eyes saw me.

Rotting lips mouthed a single, silent word.

Home.

I screamed when two strong hands clamped onto me and jerked me back and off the ship's rail. I'd nearly climbed over. Theodore set my feet on the deck and held me so tightly around the waist I could hardly pull in a breath. His gaze locked with mine, all fiery and full of terror. "Bloody Gods — Agatha was yelling at you. Didn't you hear her?"

Agatha was pale beside me, a hand clutching her throat.

I shook my head. "No. There was a . . ." The jabs in my chest had returned to their quiet, even hum. I felt so cold, so strained with fear, that I threw my arms around Theodore's neck and held tight. I hated myself for seeking comfort in him, but he was so steady, so warm. The moment seemed to draw out, long as a string of honey, before he curled his arms around me in return. With a quiet exhale, he let his body soften against mine. It felt like a candle flared inside me — the bond — glowing bright. I raised my lips toward his ear. "I saw a woman. In the water."

"A nekgya." He pulled back to look in my eyes. "They hunt the waters closest to the islands."

Despite his proximity, a chill slipped through me. "What do they hunt?"

Those eyes. A mix of pity and wariness filled them before he drew me back into his embrace. He spoke softly, his voice heavy with contrition. "Sirens."

The carriage clacked over the blue cobblestoned streets, winding us through dense trees, their leaves a lush spring green. The boughs held large red blooms with centers like orbs of gold. I could hardly recall disembarking from the ship or walking over the docks to the shining carriage that had awaited us, but I remembered Theodore. He'd led me the entire way with a hand at my back, close and attentive. I sat beside him now, and across from us, in awkward silence, sat Lachlan and Agatha.

"They hunt Sirens," I said in a shocked voice, staring out the window. "Agatha, did you know? Why didn't you tell me?"

Her gaze rounded, but Lachlan spoke before she could. "You're aware that Agatha lived away from the sea for nearly twenty years too, right? You're not the only one who's been locked away from the rest of the world."

Agatha went rigid. "I do not need you to speak for me, Commander Mela."

Lachlan rubbed his jaw. "Don't call me that, please."

"It's your title."

"It's impersonal."

"Precisely." Agatha's gaze shot to me. "And you — I tried to teach you everything I knew. Have you forgotten how you shut me down every time I tried to tell you anything at all about our kind?"

I blanched. It had been difficult to learn the details of a life that I'd never thought I'd experience. Every bit she'd shared with me had felt like something to mourn, one small death after another. Ignorance had hurt less.

"And when I left Varya," she went on, defensively, "the nekgya were very few. I'd heard of only one or two attacks. I'd never seen one. I had no idea the waters had become so infested."

Theodore shifted beside me. "And the attacks have only grown more gruesome. They have started to go after Varians now too."

A shudder stole over me. "Have you not been able to do anything about them?"

"I'm trying." His tone, his look, made me want to curse him and fall quiet at once. "There are other, more pressing matters right now that we need to discuss. Like this negotiation with the empress. She's already here. I saw her ship in the harbor."

Lachlan gave Theodore a regretful look. "Well, your bond still hasn't settled. You'll have to take Imogen with you to the meeting with the empress."

Theodore scraped a hand down his face. "You know the size of her fleet, of her troops. The contracts she's sent are extensive and need discussing. If I waltz into that council meeting with a . . . woman like Imogen beside me —"

"*A woman like Imogen.*" I smoothed my undone tumble of hair. "There's no need to insult me while I'm sitting right next to you."

Theodore's mouth pinched. "Bloody Gods — I'm *not.* I'm saying that the empress will think I'm slighting her and her daughter if I bring such an uncommonly beautiful woman with me into the negotiations."

My cheeks warmed. "Oh."

Lachlan and Agatha stared at us for a moment, wide-eyed. Finally, Lachlan spoke in an oddly careful voice. "I'm your right hand. Have her come in on my arm and say she's your cousin, eager to meet her new family member."

I shot Lachlan an unpleasant look. Meeting the princess of Obelia, Theodore's fiancée, did not make me feel eager in the least. It made the bond in my stomach coil and strain with jealousy.

Lachlan shot me an unpleasant look right back. "You'll have to be nice."

Theodore huffed and looked toward the carriage ceiling. "Fucking Gods."

"I have to agree with His Majesty's sentiment," I said. "Bringing his pesky current wife to meet his future one is an awful idea."

"Vomiting on the Empress of Obelia is a worse one," said Lachlan.

Agatha nodded. "Lachlan's right."

"Thank you."

"Hush." Agatha pursed her lips, her eyes darting between me and the king. The look on her face was the one she always wore before she started an argument, gaze narrowed and lips quirked. I braced myself as she took a deep breath. "Your Majesty," she said, sweetly. "We also need to discuss you ordering Imogen to the Mage Seer."

Theodore closed his eyes. "Not today, Agatha."

"Please, let me speak, Your Majesty." But she didn't wait for his permission. "I am willing to accompany her on her trek. It's wretched of you to insist on sending her, but even with soldiers and a healer and me at her side, she will still be in danger."

At her words, Lachlan seemed to fill with hollow anger.

"What's your point?" Theodore's every muscle had clenched.

Agatha crossed her arms haughtily. "In the event that your bond does *not* settle — which at this point seems highly likely given it's been nearly three days — I'd like to know if you are prepared to accompany her yourself?"

Theodore's face went slack. "It'll settle."

"What makes you think it will?" Agatha challenged. "It should be two days. The stories say it's always two days. I expect there's something off, I can't imagine what, but regardless, how will you handle being on opposite sides of the island? Both of you will go mad with sickness and worry."

Just as the palace materialized through the mist and the wheels crunched over the gravel of the wide main drive, I saw something in the king of Varya that struck me with unease: panic.

It was such a small thing. So small, I doubted Agatha even noticed — but Lachlan did. His mouth thinned into a hard line as he watched Theodore's chest rise and fall with slightly increased breaths. I felt another layer of tension fall over him. His lovely eyes widened for the briefest moment, and it made my heart slam into my ribs.

Lachlan leaned forward and casually patted his knee. "We'll discuss this at another time." His smile was effortless, but there was a new trouble in him too. He looked out the carriage window. "We're here, so let's focus on the first terrible task on the list, shall we?" He clapped his hands. "Let's go meet your fiancée."

12

We exited the carriage to a horde of eager-looking servants and soldiers, all arranged into neat lines. Theodore strode up the wide steps first, mumbling quiet greetings to the official-looking assembly nearest the door. I kept close to Agatha, eyes down, and felt entirely out of place in the face of such opulence. My hair was undone and wild. I wore no chemise, or stays, or shoes. I was grateful that the hem of my gown was long enough to cover my bare feet.

We slowed just inside the soaring entry hall, where Theodore was accosted by a willowy woman carrying a stack of envelopes on a silver tray. I looked around, taking in the shining details.

The gilded, frescoed ceiling. The curving black marble staircases. One wound up to the eastern wing, the other to the western. Pale statues of Great Gods, their beautiful, stern faces fully intact, lined the railings. Their unseeing eyes were fierce, their hair upswept, their strong bodies carved into flowing swaths of fabric. I searched for Ligea but could not find her. They held candles, illuminating the risers, looking down on us with the same look of authority and self-importance that Theodore so often wore.

No one would doubt he was a God.

Lachlan turned to me. "Don't let them intimidate you. They were a lustful, violent, pigheaded lot. You'll fit right in."

Agatha *tsk*ed before their gazes caught on one another and lingered. Lachlan beheld her with fondness, with heartbreak. He set an absent-minded hand to his chest like it ached. "My rooms are the same, Agatha."

Agatha only gave him a sharp, cold nod, then looped her arm through mine.

Head bent, Lachlan started up the western stairs, taking them two at a time, then disappeared into the shadow of the hall.

"What the hell are you doing?" I chided. "You still love him. And he still loves you."

She rolled her eyes. "Lachlan loves everyone. And everyone loves him. He's charming and roguish and too witty."

"Opposites attract." I looked up the staircase he'd ascended. "I think he's hurt that you're willing to leave him again."

"I tried to explain it to him." She shook her head. "I told him I'd go with you when the king sends you off in search of Eusia too."

I stiffened. That was something else entirely. There was no way of knowing where the hunt for Eusia would take me, but it would most certainly be dangerous. "You can't come with me, Agatha," I said, firmly. "I'm hardly qualified for the task, and you have even less power than I do. I won't see you get hurt. I'd only blame myself for it." Her mouth fell open, her chest filling with a protest. "Please. You've looked after me for so long. You've given up so much for me. You should make up for it now."

"I'm not sure how." She looked overcome. I was not the only one who had been ripped from her old life, I was not the only one starting new. Selfishly, I was grateful to not be alone in the terror of it.

"Your Majesty!" A jovial voice echoed through the hall. A stout man with a bright smile approached the king. His face was as round as his stomach, his skin a dark, smooth brown. His crinkled eyes were a faceted amber. "It's good to have you back." He stopped before Theodore and gave him a grand bow. "Was the Isle of Seraf just as we suspected?"

Theodore's dark brows lowered. "There were a few surprises."

"Ahh, well. The empress and the princess have been here for nearly two days. They've been content to rest and wander the gardens, but I think it would be wise to plan the negotiations directly."

Theodore nodded. "Thank you, Eftan. Is all well with them?"

The man's wide smile dropped ever so slightly. He let his booming voice soften. "The empress is a woman of...high standards. I suggest the meeting be held in the Garden Room. I'll have the servants set the table." His eyes brightened, and he leaned in conspiratorially. "The princess, however, is lovely. Lucky for you."

Theodore gave an unaffected grunt.

"And who are these young women?" Eftan set a hand to his belly, shifting his weight from foot to foot.

"This is..." Theodore strained for words. "Lady Imogen Nel. She..." He gave up searching for an explanation for my existence and gestured to Agatha, absently. "And this is Commander Mela's former wife, Agatha. She was my governess once. Perhaps you remember her."

Eftan's face creased with distant recognition. "Why, yes. Agatha. I believe I do remember you." His cheeks rounded further with a full and friendly smile. "I'll find you both comfortable rooms. Come with me."

"Chancellor, it's good to see you again." Agatha's cheeks flushed pink, and she said, "Are there any rooms available near Commander Mela's?"

"I believe so, yes." He gestured to a nearby maid and then Agatha was making her way up the western stairs. She gave me an unsure smile before she disappeared.

"Eftan," Theodore said, "may I have a word?" He stepped closer to the little man and leaned in to whisper. As Theodore spoke, Eftan stood very straight, very still, then he shot me a quick, condescending look.

I choked back a groan.

Eftan gave Theodore a reverential bow. "I understand, Your Majesty." The man faced me without meeting my eye, bowed, and offered a clipped "Good day." Then he turned on his heel and strode from the hall, boots snapping quickly over the marble.

"What did you tell him?"

Theodore's eyes narrowed and an uneasy warmth fell through my stomach. "I told him to have the warships and land soldiers prepared for an attack from Seraf." His voice had sunk so deep into his chest I could nearly feel it rumble through me. "And I told him you would be sleeping in my room for the time being."

"Oh." I swallowed hard. "Did you tell him why?"

"I'll let him draw his own conclusions. They're likely better than the truth." He yanked the crown from his head and started up the eastern stairs.

I fisted my skirt and all but ran up after him. "He'll think I'm your mistress, and just as your fiancée has arrived —"

"Like I said — better than the truth. The poor man would collapse if I told him you are my blood-bound wife."

We reached a long hall, where he led us past large windows that framed flowering gardens, vine-covered outbuildings, and the wide, glinting sea beyond the cliff. The carpet was thick and soft, but I was desperate for a pair of shoes. For stays and underclothes that fit. For a hot bath.

Theodore flung the door at the end of the hall wide open. "After you, my lady." He stood with his back against the jamb, watching me with his chin tipped back, features hard. As I approached the threshold he stood upon, I stopped. The small space between us was charged. "You loathe me, don't you?"

He held my gaze, features unreadable as ever, but the rise and fall of his chest increased. As did mine. Then he cocked his head toward his chamber. "Get in."

It was as grand a space as I could have expected. The ceiling soared, coffered and painted with the island's flowering vines. The entire space was dressed — unsurprisingly — in shades of green and gold. At the center sat a bed even grander than the one on the ship. Wide, with stairs at its side. Heavy velvet drapes hung from its towering posts. Before an opulent mantel sat a large settee, but it was too far from the bed. We'd have to drag it closer so we could both sleep without growing sick.

I jumped when the door slammed. Theodore brooded his way across the room, unbuttoning his coat and tossing it over the back of a chair. "Keep close," he said, as he stepped into the washing room. I moved nearer and heard the burble and splash of water.

Crossing my arms tightly over my chest, I studied Theodore's room closer. There was a perilously tall stack of books on the table by his bed, one splayed open at the top, upside down to save his spot. A delicate crystal glass and a bottle of wine sat beside them. A desk as messy as the one on his ship sat before the floor-to-ceiling windows. Large, lilac-colored blooms sat in a vase amid the clutter. I itched to move closer and look at the papers there. I found myself wondering over the shape of his writing, if it was angular and prickly, like he was toward me. Or if perhaps he let the curling warmth he hid so well creep into its lines.

A knock sounded.

"Yes, what?" Theodore called. He emerged from the washing

room shirtless, golden brown skin flecked with drops of water. He toweled his hair, his face, and I stared dumbly at his strong, beautiful body. His chest was hard and muscled, with a smattering of dark hair. Divots looked like they'd been carved over his stomach, into the edges of his hips.

"Dressmaker, Your Majesty," came a weathered voice from the other side of the door.

"Come in." Theodore draped the towel over his wide shoulders. When the door opened and a hunched woman, black hair streaked with white, entered, Theodore smiled. "Hello, Antheia. It's been a while, hasn't it?"

The old woman giggled, chiming and unaware as a young girl would be. Slowly, she pushed a cart of hanging gowns into the room. She stopped and bobbed into a wobbly curtsy.

"None of that," Theodore said. That devastating smile of his dimpled his left cheek. "Let me." He took the cart from her and rolled it into the middle of the room. "I'm sorry to rush you, but the lady needs to be dressed quickly. Something subtle if you don't mind."

The old woman, Antheia, glanced at me and shuffled toward the cart. "Subtle!" Her dark, deeply wrinkled eyes twinkled. "Pity. I'll see what I can do."

Theodore looked at me, and his smile slipped away. "Go on," he said to me, the words empty and quick. He strode toward me to return to the washroom.

"I think you were wrong." I spoke quietly as he passed. He stopped, close enough for me to smell the vetiver soap on his skin, with a question in his green eyes. "You called me a gnat, but you were wrong. I'm a mosquito, I think. A nuisance you cannot be rid of, and I take and take and take —" I pulled the engagement ring from my finger and held it up between us. "Here. As payment. I do not want charity and I do not wish to be further in your debt."

His gaze bore down on me, amplifying that hollow feeling in my chest. "A mosquito." Then the corner of his mouth lifted.

It took effort, but I raised my chin. "Are you laughing at me?"

He shook his head, and before he could speak, I pressed the ring closer.

He sobered. "I don't need your ring."

"That's not the point." I nearly stopped myself from speaking further, but for some bleeding reason I wanted him to understand. "My care has always been dependent upon what I could provide in exchange for it. It was that way with Nemea, with Evander. With you. Agatha is the only one who has ever cared for me in earnest, and even she looked after me in exchange for compensation."

His look became fathomless, grave. "That's the end of it, then."

I shook my head, confused. "The end of what?"

He wrapped his hand over the ring, warm fingers touching mine. He pushed it away in refusal. "The end of transactions. We came to a deal, yes, but that is done. I offer my care now because I choose to."

His words made me feel placid and troubled at once. "But why?"

He didn't answer. It was a long moment before he broke our stare and glanced at the old dressmaker. "Antheia is waiting for you."

Not an hour later, Theodore and I were descending the grand stairs into the entry hall. He glowed in a light suit, his crown nestled back into his dark hair, but his mood had grown even more sullen.

I shot him a sharp look. "What are you upset about now?"

"I'd asked Antheia for something subtle."

The gown she'd put me in was anything but. The satin silk reminded me of a cherry blossom painting I'd loved in one of the books in Nemea's study. It was the palest, most delicate pink, the color deepening at the hem. The sleeves were sheer and flowing and cuffed at the wrists. The bodice was cut low, fitted, until it gave way to a skirt that moved like rippling water with my steps.

"This is what fit." We reached the last step and turned to move deeper into the palace's first floor. "Would a single compliment pain you that much? We are stuck together, and this fucking bond won't settle, and I'm alone. Away from home —"

"That place was no home. Home is where you're safe."

"It's also a place where you're wanted." I flustered, shook my head. "I am not saying . . . I don't need *this* place to feel like home. It won't. But sometimes you make me feel so small you could crush me under your heel. The least you could do is tell me I look nice in this Godsdamned dress."

His brow crumpled, a look like remorse filling his eyes. "I'm sorry," he blurted. "You are . . . You're one ambush after the next and I have yet to get my bearings."

I stared up at him. "One ambush after the next?"

There had been the barest softness to his features, to his full lips, that quickly fled. "Yes."

I gave an angry laugh. "Gods, even your apologies are deprecating." I stormed away from him, into the shadow of the towering staircase.

"Imogen." The stamp of his boots echoed behind me. "You want a compliment? You're stunning. You're —"

"*Shit.*" I stopped short in the darkened alcove of the stairs. There, like a phantom in the light of the candles at her feet, stood a statue of the Great Goddess Ligea.

Panic shook through me as I stepped closer.

Her hair swept up in a permanent gust. Her stone body had been carved into a blowing bit of cloth that covered one breast and encircled her hips. Her wings were spread wide at her back. She held out an arm, palm up, her fingers commandingly crooked, like she beckoned — or cursed — her watcher.

My gaze stuck to the swooping line of her slightly rounded nose. The fullness of her mouth, the pointed dip of her chin. I studied how her eyes, small and focused, pierced the nothingness before her. Her body too — the lean, muscled build of her legs and arms, the nip of her waist between her full breasts and hips.

My very countenance, shaped in stone.

I could feel Theodore standing behind me, unmoving, breathless. I blinked back a sudden swell of hot tears.

"Fuck you." I said it to Ligea. And to Theodore. And to Nemea too. I reached up to touch her frigid fingers as my tears won out. I'd always longed for power — for the right to a life I chose and a way to keep myself safe. But *this* . . . I could hardly breathe from the sudden weight of it.

Theodore let out a slow breath behind me. I swiped quickly at my wet cheeks, not wanting him to see me, but I was beyond restraint. Something inside me had ripped clean open, and everything I'd thought to be true — who I was, where I'd come from, the fragile, stupid hope of a life of my own — was melting into something I could no longer hold.

When Theodore's hand met my back, when his warmth wove around me, and the bond in my stomach flared, my tears only redoubled.

"Don't cry." The words were a soft plea. His arm encircled my shoulders, and he pulled me against him. "Not now."

"I . . ." I sniffled. "She . . . looks like me."

"I know." He pulled a handkerchief from his pocket. With a finger under my chin, he lifted my face and wiped my cheeks dry. "Breathe." His voice was so maddeningly soothing, so incomprehensibly even,

I wanted to scream. "Later, you can wail and break my things if it'll make you feel better. But don't go into the meeting like this."

I kept my eyes closed, pulling air deep into my chest. "I need to get to the Mage Seer." If I was the descendant of a Great Goddess, if her power ran through my veins and there was a mantle to be taken up, then I needed answers. I needed a prophecy.

Theodore kept dabbing at my still-falling tears. "One thing at a time, all right?"

Boots clicked to the side of us. Lachlan cleared his throat. "What'd you do to her?"

"She saw the statue," Theodore answered, eyes still intent on me.

Lachlan wore a neat black coat with medals pinned at his chest. He looked up at the Great Goddess Ligea, then back at me. "Oh shit." He came to my side and with a hand on my shoulder led me away from Theodore. "While I can imagine your shock, I'll advise you to not stand so close to the king when you're out in the open." He shot Theodore a scorching look, but Theodore only stared at me.

Some strange emotion had permeated him. He looked empty and terrified and furious all at once, and though I knew I should, I couldn't for the life of me look away from him.

"*Theo.*" Lachlan's voice was a jagged warning. He took my arm in his. Absently, he patted my hand and tried for levity, but his tone, the look he bounced between the two of us, was grave. "Look alive, Godlings. I hear the empress has fangs."

13

The Garden Room was not as quaint as it had been made to sound.

It was a massive, two-story ballroom, with an entire wall of glass that overlooked a perfectly manicured cutting garden. The other three walls were painted, floor to ceiling, in panels that mirrored the riotous hues of the flowers. Four massive crystal chandeliers hung from the ceiling, dimly lit, and as sparkling as the sea beyond the cliff's edge. A long table ran down its middle like a backbone, grounding the otherwise empty room. It was piled with fruit — far too much for us to eat — and enough decanters of amethyst-colored wine to slosh a small retinue of the king's men.

As planned, I entered on Lachlan's arm. Theodore walked ahead of us, toward the table, and poured himself a full glass of wine. He downed it in one desperate gulp, but still managed to look perfectly composed. Lachlan walked me as far away from Theodore as he could and filled two glasses.

"Your face," he said.

I set my fingers to my cheek. "What's wrong with it?"

"You're red as a slapped ass. Breathe. Try to look more collected, less like your entire life was just upended." He shoved a glass at me.

I took a long drink of wine, enjoying the way it shimmered over my tongue and swirled happily in my stomach. It was the best I'd ever tasted.

"A quick word of advice." He gave me a dire, knowing look over the rim of his glass. "Whatever is between you two . . . there's no harm in getting it out of your systems, but there's *much* harm in getting caught. I beg you, be discreet."

I glowered at him. "Has Agatha been speaking to you?"

"Not about this."

"Gods." I took another swig of wine. "There is nothing between us."

"Imogen." He adopted a sage tone. "There is nothing as insidious as denial."

Before I could retort, Eftan shuffled into the room cradling a neat stack of black leather folders. He wore the same round-cheeked smile he had when I'd first seen him. When his gaze landed on me it slid clean off his face.

"Oh." His mouth opened and closed. He blinked. "I didn't expect . . . you. Here."

Lachlan gestured to me with his free hand. "Chancellor, have you met the king's distant cousin? This is Lady Imogen Nel."

Eftan's brow quirked. "His *cousin?* Oh. I — well." He set the stack of folders onto the table with a loud *thwack*. Bewildered, he chewed on the air, then pulled a kerchief from his coat pocket and dabbed his upper lip. "Hello. Again."

I inclined my head politely, then glanced at Theodore. He stood at the head of the table, fist around his refilled glass of wine. He'd watched the entire exchange with a terrifyingly empty look on his face, then grumbled, "Ahh fuck."

The doors were swung wide by two liveried servants. I set my glass down on the table as three women walked in, all of them as glistening and pale as a midwinter's frost. I could place the Empress of Obelia on her presence alone. Tall and widely built, she moved through the room with refined authority, like it was a mere signature away from being hers. Her gown was velvet in a deep midnight blue. Her skin was so fair it revealed the paths of the green veins at her temples. Snow-colored hair, long and straight, fell over her shoulders, and atop it sat a heavy crown of diamonds. At her neck sat a collar to match the crown, set with hulking jewels. And her lips, thin and so red it looked like she'd eaten a fistful of mulberries.

I fell into a deep curtsy as she and Theodore greeted one another.

"Theodore Ariti." The empress had a reedy, melodic voice that lilted with her accent. Her greeting was friendly enough, but she did not smile. "You have the look of your father. More handsome, though." She gave a gruff chuckle. "I'm sure he hated that."

Theodore's lips lifted into a half smile, and though I had not known him long, I knew him well enough to see that the mention of his father set him ill at ease. "Hello, Nivala. I certainly was a thorn in his side," he said, charming and graceful as ever. "Please forgive my late arrival. I'm grateful you came all this way."

Her white brows rose. "It's an advantageous match. It's necessary we see it done properly."

Theodore gave an agreeing bob of his head and looked to the willowy young woman who stood behind the empress. "Princess Halla." He put an enchanting tilt on her name that set the bond in my stomach into a jealous spasm. He took her hand in his and drew her nearer. "You're even lovelier than your portrait."

And she was lovely. She was my antithesis. Where my skin was a golden brown and my hair a dark, waving chestnut, hers were pale. Her near-white locks seemed to shimmer and were crowned with a thin diamond-and-pearl diadem. She was tall, like me, but angular, sharp as a shard of ice. She wore trailing white like brides in Obelia did. I couldn't picture her fragile, airy countenance swallowed up by the harsh, customary black that Leucosian brides wore.

Or perhaps I didn't want to.

She smiled at Theodore, and it was like spring cleaving winter's hold. Her cheeks bloomed pink, her blue eyes were the clear sky, and her small, pouty mouth looked like a Godsdamned unfurling rose. Theodore brought her hand to his lips. The kiss took all of a second, but the way his full mouth pressed against her skin replayed slowly, distressingly in my mind. I felt Lachlan's boot press into the toe of my slipper and realized I was scowling. I attempted a smile, but it only flickered over my face before I picked up my glass for a hearty gulp.

"Very good." The empress strode to the far head of the table and sat herself down, mind clearly set on the business at hand. "Shall we begin?"

The third woman, dressed in less finery, laid out contracts and discussed with Eftan in hushed tones about what point would first be discussed. Lachlan pushed in my seat and sat beside me, promptly refilling my glass. It wasn't until they were about to begin negotiations that the empress seemed to realize there were others in the room. "And who are these people?"

"You know my chancellor," Theodore said, gesturing to Eftan. "This is my right hand and naval commander, Lachlan Mela. And my cousin, Lady Imogen Nel."

The empress's cool eyes landed on me. "Nel?"

I'd thought Theodore to be unreadable, but compared to the empress he beat with ready, effusive emotion. She was as feeling as a corpse, and I could gather nothing at all from her tone or her look.

I gave a warm, reverential smile, despite the way her gaze sliced. "Yes, Your Imperial Majesty."

Without another word, she snapped her attention to her servant and took the first contract. "Ahh, yes." Her eyes moved quickly over the page. "There is our differing religion to be discussed."

"The stipulations you laid out are acceptable," Theodore said. "I can commission an outbuilding for the princess to worship her saint within. I'll even have a garden built around it."

I fought to keep my eyes on the huge mound of grapes in front of me, trying to forget the way he'd stared at me in the entry hall.

"Good," said the empress, absently. "And with that are our differing marriage ceremonies. Blood offerings are necessary for an Obelian marriage to be recognized."

I tensed at the thought, my thumb going to my scarred hand on instinct.

Theodore shifted in his chair, like he could feel my discomfort. "I am cautious of blood offerings. However, with more detail, I am open to participating in an Obelian ceremony," Theodore said, carefully, "but she will be the queen of Varya — a Leucosian queen — and therefore it's necessary that Princess Halla participate in a traditional binding ceremony. For the marriage to be considered valid in my kingdom and for her to be crowned."

"Tell me of this binding ceremony," the empress said. "What power will Halla receive upon its completion?"

Surprise spiraled through me as I remembered my long-past lessons. Because Theodore and I were both born into the line of the Great Gods, our blood bond would let us share our power.

I pressed my glass to my lips and took a long drink. Over the rim, and for a fleeting moment, Theodore's gaze snagged on mine. "A marriage bond is a simple cut, usually on the couple's palms," he explained, "and the two wounds are pressed together. There would be no pain for you, Princess, aside from the slice of the knife. The blood mixes to make a symbolic bond. In the princess's case, since Obelians are not of the same lineage and do not possess Gods' blood, she will inherit none of my power. She will be as she always has been."

The empress shook her head, looking almost disappointed. "Then why do it at all?"

Theodore sat taller, an edge now running through his commanding voice. "It's a divine tradition, taken from the Sirens and adopted by the whole archipelago."

The empress clicked her tongue in distaste. "I've heard of Leucosian kingdoms forgoing it. I don't see why you —"

"Only one kingdom has shunned our Gods and traditions," Theodore retorted, "and we are not allies."

The empress's gaze sharpened. "I see."

"Princess Halla —" The ennoble softness coloring Theodore's deep voice sent a pang through me. I was mortified by the realization: I wanted him to speak to me like that. "Would you be willing to perform a Leucosian binding?"

Halla smiled wide. "Yes. Very much, yes." She had the same lilting accent her mother did, but on her soft voice, it sounded saccharine, like a string of flossed sugar.

With a pale hand, the empress reached out and patted her daughter's. She spoke quietly, but I caught the words. "Do not be vulgar in your eagerness, Halla."

The princess gave no reaction at all.

Theodore cleared his throat. "I'd like to note that I see nothing in these contracts regarding your plans for Halla ascending to your throne when the time comes. Perhaps those details should be —"

"I made no mistake," the empress snapped. A sneer crept over her face for a moment before she smoothed it. "Halla is not my heir."

Theodore cocked his head. Even Lachlan shifted uncomfortably at my side.

"Forgive my assumption," Theodore said. "If your only daughter is not the heir to your throne, then may I ask who is?"

It was Halla who answered in a meek but clear voice. "Our first-born child will be."

Theodore's throat bobbed as he swallowed. His sharp stare cut between the empress and Princess Halla. "Very well."

The bond in my stomach gave an ugly, protesting lurch.

Empress Nivala blew out a short breath and the air in the room seemed to clear. "With all that settled, we have the timeline to discuss. The trip here was ghastly. We will skip the customary two months' engagement and let the wedding take place in a fortnight. I have no desire for Halla to sail home and back again."

Theodore stilled, save for his index finger that tapped the surface of the table.

The empress smiled and I thought the gesture akin to a dagger being slowly unsheathed. "Is there a problem?"

"I expected the customary two months' engagement time," Theodore said, remarkably calm, but my own stomach had fallen. "I cannot guarantee that a feast and ceremony will be arranged in only a fortnight. Guests will not be able to travel."

"She has a dress. You have wine." The empress shrugged. "You have a bed for consummating. You're eager for this marriage, are you not?"

He was a marvel, his perfect austerity. The regal, unflinching command he had over himself. He offered up one quick nod. "Of course."

Gods. The bond — my asinine jealousy — ignited something primal in me. The urge to drag Theodore away with me, to shred the contracts, to make it known he was *mine,* raced through my body like hot, pulsing blood.

"However," Theodore said, with no timidity, "there are traditions —"

"You mistake my gentle tone, Theodore," the empress said in a new, rougher voice. "I was not making a suggestion."

Theodore froze. Lachlan straightened, as if on high alert, and I remembered Theodore's mention of the might of her fleet and troops. The empress was an excellent ally and a nightmare of an enemy.

"Your Majesty." Eftan spoke with diplomatic grace, and gave Theodore a nod that said *you must.*

Theodore cleared his throat. "I'll be scarce before the wedding," he said, "but I agree to a fortnight."

Suddenly, I wasn't certain that bleeding through my eyes and nose and mouth in a severing ritual was less preferable to this. The bond made the thought of Theodore marrying the princess feel more gruesome than having my guts pulled out through my navel. I needed to get to the Mage Seer immediately.

I poured more wine into my cup and the meeting droned on and on with clauses about legitimate and illegitimate children, trade tariffs, and haggling over what Halla's queenly expenses would be. And all the while the bond screamed a relentless *no, no, no.* Finally, when I was certain the fizzing wine would do nothing to dull my misery, I reached across the table and swiped Eftan's quill from where it lay, which earned me his menacing, silent glare. I dipped the nib, scratched a note onto a piece of discarded paper, and slid it in front of Lachlan.

He scanned it, then whispered, "Don't you dare."

"I can't do this," I whispered back. "It won't kill us. He'll be fine."

"You can last a few more hours. You must."

"No, I *mustn't.* I agreed to three of the asshole's conditions. *This* was not one of them."

But going to the Mage Seer, learning of my mother, and having our bond severed was. I rose abruptly, and the entire table's attention snapped to me.

I curtsied. "I beg your forgiveness, but I am too ill to stay any longer."

"Oh," said Princess Halla, with a dainty hand at her throat. "I do hope you feel better."

"Thank —" I paused. I stared at her pale fingers, or rather, at the large, brilliant gray stone that hung around her neck, just above them. It was identical to the stone on my finger. "Your necklace," I said, turning my ring so the gem was hidden on the inside of my palm. "It's unusual. But lovely."

That spring smile of hers reared again. "Oh yes. A spinel. They are only mined in Obelia. Very rare."

"Very rare, indeed." I curtsied once more and glanced to Theodore. "Please, excuse me, Your Majesty."

"Imogen, you cannot leave." His gaze burned. "*Stay.*"

"I'm sorry, Your Majesty." I set a hand to my stomach, right over where our bond sat in screaming revolt. "It hurts too much. I have to go —"

"For a stroll through the garden." Lachlan shot up and grabbed my arm. "Fresh air will do you good."

I tried, unsuccessfully, to remove his hand from me. "I'm not strolling through the garden, Commander."

"Yes," Lachlan said, tugging me around my chair. "You are." He gave Theodore, who had gone still with blank-faced anger, a meaningful look. "In fact, I suggest we all take a stroll. Give your fiancée a tour of your favorite garden, Your Majesty. We've been at it for hours. A break would be wise."

The sun was high and blinding. It made the flowers, pink and red and yellow, glow like flames.

Lachlan held my arm firmly to his side as we strolled down the gravel path behind Theodore and the princess.

"You can loosen your grip, Commander." I watched as Halla glided through the garden with a hand extended, her elegant fingers brushing the flowers' soft petals as she passed. "I'm not going to run away."

"I've never met a less convincing liar."

"I was in a state. The thought of them . . ." I gestured frustratedly at their backs. "This Godsdamned bond needs to be severed."

Lachlan gave me a suspicious stare but said not a word.

Theodore and Halla slowed to take in a wide, gurgling fountain at the center of the garden, and we had no choice but to follow suit. The water danced and sluiced over the sculpted muscles and splayed wings of three stoic Sirens. Light glittered through its spray, through the drips that fell from the tips of their elbows and feathers.

Halla looked on it in wonder and, slowly, she made her way toward me. "Lady Nel, did you grow up here? What a childhood it must have been. This place is like something from a storybook."

Theodore and Lachlan stood by, tense and silent, waiting for my answer.

"Oh no, Your Highness." My mouth opened and shut as I searched for a suitable answer. "I . . . I grew up in the north."

The princess nodded. "I expect the north here is not as cold as the north that I am used to."

I knew little of Varya's north but was certain there were no ice-laden valleys there. "Much warmer," I said through a reluctant smile. The princess was perfectly lovely. She and Theodore seemed well matched. A pang shot through me, beneath my ribs.

"I do hope you're feeling better," she said, voice melodic and light. "It was a long while to be in a chair in that room."

"It was," I agreed. "Your marriage contracts are rather thorough. Have you always been so detailed in your planning, Your Highness?"

"Oh, that's all my mother." A faraway look filled Halla's blue eyes. She dipped her fingers into the fountain's rippling water, flicked the droplets from the tips. "She's a plotter through and through."

"She seems to have thought of everything." I sounded worn, creeping toward annoyance. I forced a wider smile and hoped it was a convincing mask.

"She certainly has." Halla lowered herself to sit on the edge. She spoke quieter, a strand of emotion running through her voice. "I'm sure you won't understand, but it's rather a shock. To leave one's home and come to a new one. Where nothing is familiar and there are no friends or sights or smells that you know. I'm grateful my mother — and His Majesty — have taken my comfort into such consideration."

She gave Theodore a grateful look and he inclined his head in a regal bow. The swell of hurt I felt then did not come from the bond. It was true envy.

"Lady Nel, what can you tell me of the king?" She leaned in as if conspiring, but she never met my eye. Her gaze remained on Theodore, lashes fluttering, smile bright. *Bloody fucking Gods.* She was flirting. "I suspect you know him better than most, having grown up together as cousins."

I swiped my brow, laughed uncomfortably. "His Majesty and I were hardly close."

"I can't believe that. He chose to bring you to meet me. He must care for you, don't you, Your Majesty?"

Theodore looked to his shining boots. "Of course."

"See." Halla stirred the air with her hand, coaxing me on. "Tell me all you know."

Lachlan scratched at his neck, his eyes round with a look that seemed to say *Good luck*.

Buying time to think, I lowered myself onto the fountain's edge and peered up at Theodore. "Only nice things?"

The question seemed to catch him off guard. He smiled, almost nervously. It was full and dimpled and white, and a jolt of admiration rocked through me. "If you wouldn't mind."

A deep breath, a slow exhale, and I met Halla's gaze. "He's very rich." She laughed like I'd made a joke. "And..." I thought and thought and what came was the memory of his guiding hand at my back, his fingers at my chin, his handkerchief brushing over my wet cheeks. "He's very observant. And caring, when he chooses to be."

My gaze moved to Theodore of its own accord. To the even, but suddenly warm, look that had begun to fill his eyes. His arms were clasped behind his back and the sun accentuated the striking lines of his face and I felt so compelled to speak that I could not stop myself.

"He's gentle," I blurted, eyes locked with his. "And when you feel like you've been whipped and thrown, if you let him, he will be an anchor."

I broke our gaze and the four of us fell silent, listening to birdsong, and trickling water, and I felt quickly overwarm. I offered Halla a shrug. "That's all I've got for you."

"That's quite a lot," she said, with a smile in her eyes. "Thank you."

From somewhere behind the tall blooms, Eftan shuffled over the gravel and stopped in our midst. "The empress has requested we resume work on the contracts. She awaits you inside, Your Majesty."

Theodore nodded, and all of them started back toward the

palace. I remained seated on the edge of the fountain, stomach sunk and twisting. Theodore stopped. "Lady Nel, shall we?"

"No, Your Majesty." I straightened under his scrutinizing stare. "I don't think I shall."

Those eyes widened almost imperceptibly. "Go on ahead," he said to Lachlan and Halla. They left us, Lachlan with tight shoulders and Halla looking wholly unbothered, beside the fountain.

Theodore stepped toward me and loomed. "You have to come."

"I can't." I set a fist over the pit in my guts. "This bond sets me into a panic when I have to sit there and listen to all that. And in this new life, in this new place, I will not be bent and mistreated. I need to get to the Mage Seer now. I need my prophecy —"

"*Mistreated?*"

"Yes."

"No." Theodore was resolute, his jaw set.

"What the hell do you mean, *no?*" I stood and met his glower. "This was your plan all along. To separate and send me off."

"That was before —"

"Before *what?*"

He froze. Shook his head. "Before we knew this bond wouldn't settle. Before we knew I was getting married in mere weeks." He paced, back and forth, and I stared on at a loss for words. Then he stopped in front of me. "Come with me for the remainder of this meeting and I'll go with you."

Surprise shot through me. "To the Mage Seer?"

He straightened his coat uncomfortably and nodded.

"Another transaction, then?"

He flinched like I'd cursed, but that's what it was. Another bargain. Another sacrifice so that I might receive a kindness.

"And besides, you can't go with me. The empress is here. And your very pretty fiancée and those ridiculous contracts —"

A deep, remorseful crease wrinkled his brow. "I said I'd be scarce before the wedding."

He had. I couldn't help but wonder why he'd said it — how he'd known. "Still," I argued, trying to keep my hair from blowing wild in the sea breeze, "they'll feel slighted —"

"I'll gift the princess some jewels. Set off some fireworks in the bay for her."

I scoffed. "Of course. What woman wouldn't be distracted by sparkly things —"

"Do you want me to go with you or not?"

"Yes," I snapped.

"Then I'm going." He was so still, staring at me just as he had when he'd quieted my tears before Ligea's statue.

"Fine." Even angry, I sounded too breathless, too caught off guard.

He dipped his chin. Swallowed hard. "Fine." He turned from me and started toward the palace, but before he did so, I noted the flustered stain of color on his sharp cheekbones. The way his breath sped. Little glimpses of feeling that he didn't — or couldn't — control. He stopped, looked back at me, and spoke in a scraping voice. "If you wish to remain in the garden, you may. I'll still go with you."

Words wouldn't come. Just a deep bloom of gratitude. I stepped onto the path that led toward the palace and gave an appreciative nod. "We should hurry back," I said. "Duty calls."

14

Not two hours later, I stood in an empty, sun-strewn stall in the stables, shoving a saddlebag full of spare trousers and shirts Theodore had lent me. He'd taken great pains to fold them into small, tidy squares and tie them tightly with twine.

The stable hands had been sent away, and across from me, sullen and edgy, Theodore tacked a horse himself. I watched him — the tight way he pulled at straps and tugged on the saddle. The sullen eyes, the stony set of his jaw.

His mood had begun to devolve the moment we'd returned to the Garden Room and the seemingly endless contracts. He'd calcified further with each point discussed, began to bite on his cheek, tap his fingers on the polished tabletop. I could only assume he regretted his decision to accompany me, and it was his gallingly relentless honor that had kept him from withdrawing.

"Will Agatha and Lachlan be here to see us off?" I asked from where I knelt in the clean straw.

"Yes." He remained intent on his task.

"Are you all right?"

"Yes."

"Oh good." I tied off the last saddlebag with a jerk. "You certainly seem it." I hefted the bags toward him, and he snatched one from my grip. "I hope you don't plan on being this broody the entire time. I'm already aware you're regretting your decision to accompany me. There's no need to make it so painfully clear."

Theodore rounded on me. His green eyes blazed and pinned me still. "You've got me figured out, haven't you?" He took one step closer, and I couldn't speak. Some emotion had him by the throat. He took another step toward me. Then he raised a strong hand to my stomach and pressed me back against the wall of the stall. I gave a sharp gasp, overcome by him. "Would you like to know what's actually bothering me, Imogen?"

I managed the barest nod.

"I don't regret my decision, but I should." His fingers curled into my ribs, as if he were trying to grab hold of me. Our bond glowed with delicious, glittering heat. It rolled and pooled heavily in my center. "I called you a gnat, and I detest myself for it. *I* am the bug. A moth. And you are the moon. Drawing me, *pulling* me. But I'll never be able to reach you without destroying myself. All I can do is pray for the day." He gave me a pleading look. "Do you understand? I am doing my very best to keep a grip on myself, to keep my distance, but everything you do seems in service of thwarting that goal."

My heart rioted. I would have felt less shock had he pulled back the skin of his chest and shown me the fearsome, pulsing parts beneath. But this, his touch, his nearness, his outright admission. "This is a jest."

He was so close, face tipped down toward mine. I could kiss him if I pushed up onto my toes.

His brow creased deeper. "Gods, I wish it were."

My frustration rose at his tone of displeasure. "You speak of desire like it's an illness. Like I have infected you with it." I shoved halfheartedly at his muscled chest, only to curl my fingers into his shirt a breath later. "How dare you blame me. As if I've laid a trap for you, or as if it's vile to want. I may be the object of your desire, but I am not its source."

He blinked, mulled over my rebuke, and then fought to straighten himself. His warm hand fell away from my stomach, and I instantly mourned its absence. I released his shirt, but we remained close. Our eyes locked.

There was something between us after all, beneath the discord, the friction. I couldn't tell if it was simply the bond stoking our attraction, but in that moment, I was desperate to *know* it. To chisel away at his stony veneer, uncover, explore. From the way he looked at me, I thought he might want the same thing.

He stepped away from me. "Forgive my lapse." He turned back toward the horse to attach the second saddlebag. "It won't happen again."

The wall at my back was all that held me up. He was so adept at locking himself away. Suddenly, he was unflustered, unmoved by what had just transpired between us.

There came the sound of rustling straw and then Agatha appeared in the aisle. She wore a new wheat-colored dress and carried a basket filled with wrapped packages of food and bottles of wine. "There you are." Her face fell when she saw me. She eyed Theodore, then looked back to me. "Feeling all right?"

I nodded quickly. "Mmm-hmm."

Her face hardened at my lie. "Your Majesty," she said, to Theodore. "Princess Halla is here. She'd like to say goodbye."

Theodore's shoulders straightened, but before he could leave the stall, Halla was at Agatha's side. Her white hair was twisted up tightly and studded with sapphire pins. The pale blue of her gauzy gown was a perfect match to her eyes.

She dipped into a low curtsy, smile sweet. "I wanted to bid you farewell, Your Majesty."

Theodore was silent, but he stepped forward, took her hand, and placed a quick kiss to it.

Halla's gaze narrowed with confusion when it landed on me, still standing with my back to the stall wall. "I didn't realize Lady Nel would be accompanying you to liaison with your war captains."

Theodore glanced at me, then back at Halla. "Her family lives near one of the bases."

"How convenient." Her smile grew strained. She rose onto her toes and placed a lingering kiss on Theodore's cheek. "I'm eager for your return."

Theodore only gave a curt nod in response.

After one last glance in my direction, Halla hurried from the stables with her head bent. Guilt swarmed, and then Lachlan was bustling in, carrying bedrolls, and additional packs of provisions. I didn't miss how his wary stare cut between Theodore and me.

"Help me with these, Imogen," Agatha said, gesturing to the food packs she held, then to the stall behind her where our second horse waited to be prepared.

She began filling a bag at the horse's rump. She looked over her shoulder before whispering, "Let him help you."

I tugged on the belt I wore. The trousers I'd borrowed from Theodore were too big and folded uncomfortably at the waist. The wool felt strange around my hips and thighs. "I don't know what you mean," I said, distractedly.

"Listen to me." She glared, eyes deep with emotion. "You both seem determined to keep your horns locked, but that will only make what lies ahead harder. Let him *help* you. Let him comfort you and care for you." She shoved down a rise of emotion. "The Mage Seer and her ritual are dangerous. If you try to go it alone, I fear you won't come back."

"Agatha—" I shook my head. "I'll do my best." Accepting his

care would be difficult now that I knew it filled him with such resentment.

My gaze slipped across the aisle to Theodore. He wore a clean but dirt-stained brown shirt, with patched trousers and scuffed boots, claiming it was best to look unassuming in the Varian wildlands. The lack of finery did nothing to diminish him. In fact, I preferred him like this. With his waving hair catching the light, and his threadbare clothes draping over his lean muscles.

In silence, Agatha watched me. "I'll warn you . . . it won't be a clean separation."

My attention snapped back to her. "What do you mean?"

She spoke in a whisper, brow rippled with empathy. "I see what's between you two. It's barbed and messy, but there's something there."

I bit at my lip, determined in my avoidance, and shoved the hem of my overly large shirt into my trousers.

Agatha's look of empathy morphed quickly to one of harried pity. She huffed a breath. "Maybe you've deceived yourself, but not me. Not Lachlan either."

"What does it matter?" I asked, tense and quiet. "He's a king. And I'm . . ." I gave an angry laugh. "What am I? An orphan, a murderer. He's going to be married to a princess who is beautiful and perfectly suited to him. And even if our circumstances were different . . ." An unbidden memory of Evander, bent and submerged in my tub, flashed through my mind. I rubbed my eye, wishing I could tear the memory out. "Theodore will bring me back from the Mage Seer alive, because it's his duty to do so. Then I'll say my goodbyes and be off on my final task."

Agatha reached for me. "Imogen —"

I strode away, out into the stable yard where Theodore and Lachlan led the first horse. Agatha wanted to mine my emotions like they were jewels, precious and worth inspecting, but I was happy leaving them buried deep. I'd be damned if I complicated things further. "Are we ready?"

"Almost." Lachlan strode past to retrieve the horses' reins.

Out in the bright yard, Theodore didn't even acknowledge me. He'd slipped deeper into some unyielding, stolid exoskeleton of despondency.

I shifted in discomfort. "Should we eat before we go?" I asked, trying to cut through the unease.

Theodore tested a saddle strap with a tug. "You can eat on the horse."

I was tempted to meet his rough mood in equal measure. I raised my chin, then stopped. Perhaps . . . perhaps if I became like water — if I curved around him, wore him down — we might both survive the coming week. "That's a good plan," I replied, softly.

Theodore's jaw feathered. He put his foot in the stirrup and mounted in one graceful movement.

Agatha was at my side. "Be safe."

I nodded. "See you in a week."

My mare was pretty and shining black. I stood beside her and tried to mimic Theodore's easy mount, but I got my boot into the stirrup and froze. "I . . . I've never ridden alone before."

Lachlan let out a defeated breath. "Fucking Gods, you tell us *now*?" He strode toward me and stood close. As he tugged me around the front of my horse he spoke low, so only I could hear. "Be patient with Theo. He's as scared as you are. Maybe more."

"Over what? He's not the one going through the severance."

His gaze grew dark, sobering. "He'll have to be the one to tell you. When he's ready." Then he stopped me beside Theodore's horse.

I gave Lachlan a panicked glare. "What are you doing?"

"I'm sorry." Lachlan patted Theodore's knee apologetically. "Theo will give you a lesson."

"No. No, thank you —" But Lachlan was already forcing my foot into the stirrup, hefting me up into the saddle in front of Theodore. Clumsily, I threw my leg over the pommel and settled into his lap. Both of us went rigid.

Agatha put a hand to her temple and watched us with a grimace. An uncomfortable grin spread over Lachlan's mouth. He patted the horse's rump twice and said, "There's extra wine in the saddlebags."

With my mare's reins in Theodore's hand, he led us out of the stable yard and onto the road that carved through the outermost gardens. Sea mist swirled in over the palace grounds. I sat straight-backed, every muscle tight.

Theodore spoke over my shoulder. "You're too tense."

"Seeing as how you are doing your best to maintain some distance from me —" I noted the press of his body against mine. His chest and stomach were solid and hot. My backside filled his entire lap. "— it feels unwise to relax into this position."

"Is it really that difficult for you to focus on our task rather than our bodies?"

"Excuse me?" I craned to scowl at him over my shoulder. "What are you implying?"

"Nothing," he said, quickly. "Just focus on the damned horse."

I faced forward again in a huff. "Asshole."

He spoke near my ear in a low, rumbling voice. "Sit straight. Let your hips find neutral. You need to balance and feel the horse."

I blew out an annoyed breath and tried. We jostled over the dirt-packed road that led from the palace grounds into the tree-spotted meadow just beyond it, and I slowly loosened my muscles.

He gave an approving grunt. "Better." The encouragement was breathy and low, and an unbidden thrill fell through me. I slammed my eyes closed in annoyance.

The road grew uneven, and he tapped my hip twice, a reminder to feel the horse's shifting. I obeyed with my tongue between my teeth. "That's good." When he picked up the horse's pace and I began to lose my balance, he clamped an arm around my waist. "Got you."

He kept us like that, bodies pressed tightly together in a bumping trot, with his strong arm around me. My heart hammered at our nearness, and I wondered after all the loathsome thoughts that must have been running through Theodore's mind. In time, I eased into the faster pace, keeping my posture and balance.

"Take the reins." Theodore pressed them into my hand, and I led us through a curving dirt road lined with small yellow flowers. They swayed and bounced in the wind, as if dancing to some gusting melody I could not hear. The corner of my mouth lifted as I watched them, entranced.

"They're so pretty," I said softly, letting the thought slip past my lips.

"They're weeds."

"Bloody Gods." A shot of anger rang though me. "They're still beautiful."

He was silent as we wound away from the flowers into a green swaying field. I wished I'd held my temper, though it was not my fault that the man was a maddening, close-minded snob. Finally, and to my surprise, he leaned in close. His cheek pressed to my hair. "You're right." He sounded apologetic. "They are."

I wanted to see his face, his eyes. I wanted to see how they changed when his voice sounded like that. I kept my gaze ahead, but that single moment drained all the remaining strain from my body. Despite myself, I rested against him fully, and we moved atop the horse as if we had fused.

Halfway through the field, Theodore pulled hard on the horse's reins. We stopped and I sucked in a silent breath when I realized why. I could feel him, long and hard, straining against my backside.

Neither of us moved for a beat. My entire body rushed with fire, but I did my very best to douse it. Neither of us spoke as I ungracefully dismounted. When my feet were finally on the ground, I glanced up at him. His face was flushed, his lips pinched, and a part of me wanted to leave him alone with his mortification, but I shook my head in mock disappointment instead, and said, "You should have just focused on the horse."

He dropped my horse's reins and spurred his own down the road.

I couldn't help but grin. "Aren't you going to wait for me?" The bond was starting to stretch with nauseating discomfort. "It was a jest!" I clambered into my saddle and by some miracle got my horse to follow.

It wasn't long before my body began to ache. My mind, too, grew troubled. It filled with a maelstrom of worries and questions and thoughts, one circling the next, dragging me down and down. Not even the arresting beauty of Varya could soothe me.

Theodore rode ahead of me, our horses close. "Have you been to the Mage Seer before?" I finally asked.

He scrubbed a hand through his windblown hair. "Only once." The words were clipped. Final. He didn't want to talk, but the festering silence between us was eating me alive.

"And? Is it as awful as Agatha says?"

He adjusted in his saddle. Let the quiet stretch and stretch until I was certain he wouldn't answer. Then, "Yes."

Cold, choking dread overcame me. My fingers gripped the reins so tightly they locked up. I asked no more questions. I only watched his tense shoulders and cursed beneath my breath, hating that Agatha was always, always right. The thought that Agatha might also be right about us, that whatever simmered between Theodore and me might leave me permanently marred, was too dismal a thought. I wanted to be free of him entirely. And days spent with him like this, terror-riddled and unspeaking, would drive me mad.

"Let's have it out, then, shall we?" I waited for his reaction. Finally, he glanced at me over his shoulder, a question in his hard gaze. "Let's get it all out of our systems. Everything that's got you in a piss-poor mood. Everything we hate about each other, every grievance, so that when our bond is severed, we'll be properly purged of each other."

Theodore let out a low whistle and rode for a few more paces. "That sounds like an awful idea."

We'd crossed into a vineyard and a warm sea breeze rolled through the wide grape leaves. I spoke loud enough for him to hear me over their rustling. "You scared?"

That did it. He pulled in a deep breath, then slowed his horse until we were ambling side by side. He eyed me sidelong. "I'll go first."

I rolled my shoulders, readying myself for the blow.

"Your lack of responsibility astounds me," he said. "I've struggled to understand how someone so entrancing — the daughter of such a stunning, powerful goddess — could have spent her life content-edly curled up in the mountains, like a lazy, overfed cat. Willing to marry that captain. No — you seemed *eager* to marry him." Each word grew heavier and heavier with scathing anger. "Clinging to him, pressing your lips all over him when he'd done nothing to deserve you. What's worse — I'm inexplicably envious of the dead bastard. He killed Sirens, and you would have him anyway, and it gnaws at me." He took in a gulp of air, but it did nothing to quell him. "I struggle to understand why you wouldn't want to hone your power, to use it to *help*. Why you wouldn't be desperate to claim the lost seat of your mother's queendom for yourself. You're cowardly. And selfish. You gave your blood and prayed for the end of your own kind. You're only concerned with the parts of the world that touch you. You lack mettle and foresight and yet..." He clamped his jaw to stop himself from saying more.

I tried to blow out my hurt and embarrassment, my shame, but my throat had grown too thick.

He dragged a hand over his brow. "I used to stare up at that statue of Ligea as a boy. Lit candles at her feet and asked for the kind of courage the stories and songs about her told. Then I saw you, her very image, and I — I wanted... It's been a disappointment to learn that you are a beautiful shell of her."

The horses clomped over the dirt road as I tried to steady myself. My tight chest only let through short, shallow breaths. It was a long moment before Theodore finally looked at me. I kept my eyes on the road ahead.

"My turn," I said, when I was finally able to speak. "You're a pompous ass. You're so self-righteous that it's made you callous and closed off. You lack empathy. For me. For anyone who wasn't given choice and power and gold from their cradle, like you were. Your ridiculous sense of duty does not make you better than me. It makes you see in simple shapes, in black and white, and so it's made you see only pieces of me. And I hate that even though you are sanctimonious, and stubborn, and have treated me unkindly,

I desperately want you to see me as I truly am. To see that just because my courage does not look like yours, or Ligea's, does not mean I lack it. You wish to control me, and you're hardly better than Nemea for it." My voice became wobbly, and I spoke in a rush. "I've heard you laugh once, and it was to scoff at me. I've only seen you smile genuinely at your dressmaker. For fuck's sake, you think that simply thinking me beautiful might besmirch your hallowed name. And Gods forbid the paeans that will no doubt be written about you might mention you being virile. No, the great God-king Theodore was unplagued by evil desire. He made beautiful women wear sacks —"

"All right." Theodore's voice was desolate.

"No, I'm not done. You could use a Godsdamned fuck. A good, long one. Hopefully your new wife will enjoy your chaste kisses and rigid embraces and the fireworks you shoot off for her in the bay, because that's the most warmth she'll get."

My anger was vivid and beating and I wanted him to know it, but I'd spewed a half truth. I'd felt his warmth before, many times. Even now, the memory of his strong hand against the plane of my stomach filled me with a heavy, fiery ache.

Sullen, Theodore moved back into the lead. We rode through vineyard after vineyard without speaking a word. The sun curved in its wide arc over the sky, and as it fell back toward the horizon, Theodore pulled us off to the side of the road.

Jaw tight, he dismounted and rummaged through the saddlebag. He pulled out a bottle of wine. Wrestled the cork free. "Did that make you feel better?" He took a long swig.

"No." I threw my leg over my horse and winced as I fell to my feet. I groaned and met his glare. "I feel worse. You were right, it was an awful idea."

He huffed an agreement. Took another deep drink. He came closer, too close, and I stiffened. "Here." He stared down at me with heated, narrowed eyes as he waited for me to take the wine.

I took a long drink, my gaze stuck to his as I did. It was the same wine I'd drunk at the table in the Garden Room. Sparkling and sweet. I took another drink. "It's good."

"Thank you."

"Did you make it?"

He nodded. "The grapes came from two vineyards back. I tend to them."

I smirked. "You garden?"

"I do." He gave me a smile, though hurt still swam in his gaze. "Maybe they'll add that to those paeans they'll write about me," he said in a glum tease. "King Theodore, the gardening prude."

I returned a smile. "Lachlan told me you weren't always." His dark brow quirked. "He told me about your nights on your ship filled with women."

Theodore gave a deep laugh. It was husky and dark and I stilled at the sound of it. "I thought he might have. Fucking Lachlan." His cheeks were full of color, and an errant smirk curled his lips. He checked the deepening sky, the small clouds starting to grow over it like scales. "About a mile up there's a caretaker's cottage. They're open for travelers and land workers." His gaze locked with mine. "We can sleep there tonight."

I nodded and a peal of anticipation rang through me. When I tried to lift my aching leg into the stirrup, it slipped, and I nearly stumbled. A pained groan filled my chest, but Theodore was at my back, hands encircling my waist. He tightened his grip like he was readying to lift me, but he leaned in instead. His hand traveled up so his knuckles just grazed the underside of my breast.

His lips were at my ear. "If I had known you then . . ."

Heart on a rampage, I looked up into his eyes. "Yes?"

I couldn't breathe. He furrowed his brow, pressed his mouth shut, like he'd thought better than to speak the words that sat on his tongue.

"Tell me."

Slowly, he spread his fingers wide and dug into my ribs, as if he wanted to touch as much of me as possible. "I would have worshipped you," he said, husky and slow. "Laid you out over my bed like a goddess on her altar and gotten on my knees before you. And when we were done, after a very long time . . ." He brought me tighter to his chest, and I all but melted into him. My nose brushed his chin. ". . . I'd thank you for tearing me to ribbons with those pretty talons of yours."

Abruptly, he pulled away. He lifted me up into the saddle so quickly that my head spun. A protesting, throaty moan slipped past my lips, forcing an embarrassed flush to my cheeks. He looked up at me with a cocky smile.

"You're an ass."

"Yes, I know," he said through a chuckle. He mounted and clicked his tongue and both horses started down the road. For the first time, his body had relaxed, strong shoulders sloping with an easiness I'd never seen him wear.

"You're looking very self-satisfied," I snipped.

"Easy to do when you get a woman to make that sound."

Theodore kept the horses at a slow walk, and thank the Gods, because every muscle in my body hurt. As did my ego. But the air between us was clearer, less charged.

"I wouldn't have torn you to ribbons," I finally said, coyly. "I'm not that wasteful."

"Oh no?" That chuckle again. "What would you have done?"

"What any Goddess worthy of devotion would." He looked over his shoulder expectantly, heat and amusement in his gaze. "I'd have demanded you worship me a second time. And a third."

A grin spread over his face as he turned away from me. He tipped his head back toward the sky like he'd been swept into a pleasant daydream. I thought I heard a low, satisfied hum fill his chest.

I spent the rest of the short ride lost in a daydream of my own.

15

We turned off the main road for the caretaker's cottage and found three horses tied to the watering trough. A small, worn-down cart with packs and provisions sat in the small clearing. The little thatch-roofed building beyond it had no door, no glass in the windows. The floor through the entryway was made of the same packed dirt as the road. A small stone well sat beside it.

Low voices and laughter rose from the cottage's opening.

Theodore pulled on his horse's reins and dismounted. His hand hovered over the dagger at his hip. "Stay here." His unease swept away all the dreamy heat I'd been basking in.

Before he could duck into the cottage, three young men came out. Two looked like brothers, small and reedy. They reminded me of Serafi arrowheads with their black hair and sharp noses. The third was tall and handsome, with gold-streaked locks, warm brown skin, and mirthful eyes in the palest shade of green. All of them smiled. "There's room inside," one of the brothers said to Theodore. "We'll sleep outside. Weather's nice."

Theodore scowled and gave them a curt nod, but before he could do anything else, the handsome one looked up at me where

I sat upon my horse. He crossed to my side with a widening smile. "Need a hand?"

"Lay a hand on my wife and you'll lose it." Theodore gripped the hilt of the dagger.

The man's eyes went round as platters; his arms rose in surrender. "I was just trying to help."

I shot Theodore a scolding look, but he ignored it. Stormy and inexorable, he stole to my side and reached up to guide me off the horse. With pinched faces and muttered words, the men retreated to a little clearing behind the cottage, where a pit for a fire sat.

"What the hell was that?" I scolded. "They're not going to share that fire with us now."

"Pretend you like me." He reached up for the waterskin at my horse's side and pulled it open so I could drink. "Act like we're happily married — a stretch, I know."

I took an angry gulp of water. "Why? What's wrong?"

Theodore's brow buckled. He set a hand to his stomach, over the bond. "I don't know them, and the thought of him touching you —" He shook his head and took a drink of the water. "It's that Godsdamned bond. Just do this for me, please? Keep beside me. If they think you are anything other than my wife, then you're not safe."

"You're jealous." I gaped at him as he rummaged through the saddlebag. "You thought my reaction during those contract negotiations was ridiculous, but this is exactly the same."

He shook his head. "That was different. That was the Empress of Obelia —"

"See the handsome one?" Theodore frowned at him over his shoulder. "When you're asleep tonight, he and I are going to sneak away into the grapevines to make love, and then over breakfast tomorrow, you can listen as we discuss the fate of our future children."

He glared at me.

"Doesn't feel good, does it?"

"No," he conceded in a grumble. "It doesn't."

We troughed the horses, and all the while Theodore stewed. With a small bowl and a rag pulled from a saddlebag in hand, he led me to the little well. He rounded its stone wall, so his back was to the men around the fire, then sat upon its ledge. He scooped some water into the little bowl, set the rag into it. He spread his legs wide. Then tugged me by the hand, so I stood between them.

I stared for a moment — at the dark fan of his lashes, the slant of his nose, the bow of his lips. "What are you doing?"

"Acting like you're my wife." His eyes were level with my chin. He raised his hands and slowly, devastatingly gently, swept aside the stray hairs that had escaped from my braid. His fingers tickled at my ears, my temples, as he caressed the curls back. I held my breath as he reached around for my braid. He gripped it, wrapped it once around his fist, and gave it the softest tug. It tipped my chin up, baring my neck to him.

He made a throaty, approving sound as he looked from my lips to my neck and down further. Water droplets sprayed as he wrung the rag out with his free hand. Slowly, he dragged it across my cheek. Down the column of my neck.

I bit back a moan. "You don't have to —"

He dipped the rag again and brought it back to my flushed skin. "You're covered in dust and sweat," he said quietly, "and a good husband would see you cleaned up before feeding you and putting you to bed, wouldn't he?"

"That's not what you're doing." The rag traveled down farther, to my collarbone, where the shirt I wore — his shirt — was pulled slightly open. My eyes fluttered shut. I didn't doubt he could see the color rising on my cheeks. That he could see my breaths coming quicker, growing shallow. "You're getting back at me for what I said earlier. You're teasing me."

He shook his head. "I promise, I'm not trying to." The words were a hot caress over my skin. "But I'll admit, I wish I didn't care what you thought of me."

"Two days," I said. He swiped a bead of water from my chin with his finger, tugging my bottom lip down with the motion. "The bond will be severed. Then you won't care at all."

Our gazes locked and when he smiled at me, wry and full, my heart folded over on itself. "Let's hope." None of the heat left his eyes as he leaned back and let my braid slip from his hold. He held the rag up between us.

We'd reached a line, and now we toed it. I thought of Lachlan's and Agatha's pleas to let myself be cared for, to care for him. Despite the tumult of the past week, Agatha thought something more had woven and bloomed between us, like one of Theodore's flowering vines. It was desire — attraction — but nothing more. Nothing sturdy could grow under such conditions, and on the odd chance that something had sprouted, bolstered by our blood bond, we were two days away from ripping it out at the root.

I emptied the bowl and filled it with clean water. Dipped and wrung out the rag. My saddle-weary legs ached as I perched on his knee. "So we've established that you were once — and still can be — lusty and potent." He laughed and I couldn't keep from smiling at the sound of it. "But *I* have always been afraid."

Some of the heat in his eyes banked. I scooted closer to his chest, set my hand to his chin, and tipped it up. As I swiped at the strong column of his neck, he brought up his hand and rested it on the round of my hip. "Of what?"

"Everything. When I was little, I was afraid of the dark."

"So is every child."

I dipped the rag again and opened the collar of his shirt, letting myself enjoy the cut of his hard chest. "Maybe my fear was like a normal child's. But the darkness in Fort Linum felt different. It felt sinister. It's so dark, so thick, that it used to feel like its own kind of monster. Corporeal. I would forget myself and spend too long in the study reading and then I'd have to trudge through it to get to my chamber. I'd be crying and shaking by the time I'd reached my bed one level down."

His thumb moved back and forth over my hip. "Why didn't you sleep in the study?"

I shook my head as I swiped the bridge of his nose, his cheek. "I wanted my room. The comfort of a place that belonged only to me."

"Brave of you." He looked at me like he had the first night we'd met, like he was taking stock of all the pieces and parts of me, but now, he seemed to look closer. To a lower layer. Foolishly, I hoped that this time, those pieces would fall into a shape he found more pleasing.

I rose from his knee and threw the dirty water from the bowl, wrung out the rag. "I'm hungry." I looked past Theodore to the three men huddled around a roaring fire. "You'll have to make nice so we can heat some food."

Theodore grimaced as he stood, then swiped his hands on his pants. "I'll make our bedroll first."

"Bed*rolls.* As in two."

He came toward me and took the bowl and rag from my hand. "Bed*roll.* As in one. As in there is no way in all the sweet hells that this blood bond would let you sleep away from me when we are in the middle of the wildlands with three strange men sleeping beside us."

The line we toed began to break and blur. I could just as easily sleep safely on my own bedroll, under my own blanket, beside him. And the men who shared our camp were as innocuous as ever, laughing and telling poor jokes. But I couldn't bring myself to argue either point.

I *was* selfish, just as Theodore had said. I batted away my shame and nodded. "One it is."

Back at the horses, I helped Theodore pull our supplies from their restraints. The road we'd taken in had widened, cutting between the long, flat beach and the edge of the vineyard. The waves crashed quite a way out, but I could nearly hear them as the end of the day settled into a hush.

Theodore whistled quietly as he handed me a bedroll and a blanket. The tune was familiar, perhaps a song I'd danced to before. It was quick and rhythmic, but he whistled it at half speed. In his old worn clothes, with his dark hair mussed from travel, he looked roguish and at ease. A smile curled my lips. "You're different outside the palace."

He gave me a cautious look. "Am I?"

"I think so."

"You haven't known me very long." He smirked. "What if I'm always like this and you and I just met under very trying circumstances?"

I laughed and took a second blanket from him. "I don't doubt meeting me made many things worse for you, but I wonder if it's your responsibilities that make you so . . . surly. All that pressure you put on yourself." I walked around the horse slowly, toward the cottage, and he followed. "You seem to like it out here. In the sun and dirt. I like you better out here too, I think."

By the way he stared at me, I couldn't tell if I'd hurt him or complimented him. He took the load I carried into his own arms.

"I'm sorry," I said, when he was still close. "I didn't mean — you're right, I haven't known you that long."

He shook his head at my apology. "I find you rather terrifying, Imogen."

"Terrifying?"

"It's true you haven't known me long, but somehow you know me rather well."

He was devastating, standing before me looking windblown and anguished. I wanted to touch him, to smooth the lines etched into his face.

He turned toward the cottage, and before I followed, I glanced out over the waves — then froze. On the tremulous line of the horizon sat four little ships. They were no more than shadowy smudges at this distance, but something in my center dipped. I held my breath and crossed the dirt road toward the beach.

The bond sent rattling worry through my stomach as our distance grew.

"Imogen?" Theodore called. But I kept moving, knowing he'd follow.

My boots sank into the sand, my tired muscles burning as I tried to move over it. I'd spent my whole life looking at the sea from afar. Through my window in Fort Linum, a ship on the water's surface was nothing but a dot from the end of an artist's brush, but if I stared long enough, they distinguished themselves. And it was always easiest to tell when it was Nemea's ships that floated into the harbor.

The red, eel-stitched flag, flapping in the wind as if it were undulating through the sea. The dark sails, the same color as King Nemea's bitter wine. Theodore reached my side; our bond calmed. He saw what I did, and it morphed his countenance back into that of a king. His chin lowered. His gaze grew hard. "There he is."

There was not a hint of surprise in his voice. He'd been prepared, he'd known Nemea's men would come. So had I, but I found myself staring, slack-jawed, with terror wriggling through me as if it were that Godsdamned eel.

Nemea had come to take back what was his.

16

I stumbled over the sand and hurried toward the cottage and horses. "We have to go."

Theodore was at my heels. He grabbed my wrist and yanked me to a halt. "Go where?"

I looked back out toward Nemea's haunting ships. "We need to ride through the night, unbind ourselves as quickly as possible. I need to leave Varya. I need to keep as far from Nemea's men as I can."

He cupped my cheek, forced my gaze to his. "You need sleep. And food. I'm not letting you go to the Mage Seer tired and hungry. That'll only make the severance worse for you."

"Please." Fear wormed through me so deeply that I struggled to see his reason. "Please, just a few more hours on the horses. Then I'll try to sleep. I promise."

His brow furrowed, and then finally he gave me a quick nod. "A few more hours." His hand left my cheek. "Then I'm force-feeding you and tying you to your bedroll with a blanket."

My chin quivered as I nodded my agreement.

Once I was back on my mare, my sore body raged against my decision to ride on. The road grew so narrow that the grapevines were close enough for me to reach out and touch. I dragged my fingers over the soft, wavering leaves. Despite my discomfort, I was grateful to be moving rather than sitting in one place. It helped ease the clamp that had set itself around my ribs at the sight of those ships.

We passed row after twisted row of vines, and just as the rest of the daylight slipped away, Theodore looked at me over his shoulder. "You're tired."

I hadn't the energy to refute him. "Is there a place to sleep nearby?"

He shook his head. "We'll have to tuck in between the vines." He turned us down one of the rows. At the end, a thatch of flowering trees formed a small barrier between the vineyard and where the beach began. The sky had changed to a deep, inky blue, and we dismounted and tied up the horses. The clearing was tight. I skirted around horses and posts to get my bedroll, when one of the vines tickled my cheek.

I paused. "Your Majesty?"

He huffed a laugh. "Call me Theo."

"Theo." I liked the shape of his name on my tongue. "I need to learn how to control my power. Nemea's too close. Ligea could have swum out into the water and sunk those ships. I should be able to as well."

He stopped unspooling a bedroll. "I'll teach you how to use my power. Hopefully it will help you figure out your own." He rummaged through the saddlebag for the dried meat and bread and handed it to me. "In the morning. Once you're rested and fed."

He was right. Exhaustion cut through my every muscle, but my mind still whirred. I bit off a hunk of bread and threw open my bedroll. I wrapped a blanket over my shoulders, then settled onto my back, food forgotten at my feet. "Do you recall the princess's necklace?" I whispered as I stared up at the sky. Theodore lay an arm's length away. "It's identical to my ring."

"It's likely a coincidence."

"Hmm." That was logical and yet it pestered me like an itch I could not scratch. The waves hushed in the distance, insects sang, and the breeze shook through the leaves above us. "Theo?" I whispered.

"Yes," he said, groggily.

"Why is there a stained-glass Siren on your ship?"

"That's what you're thinking about right now?"

I rolled onto my side to face him. "I'm usually a far more agreeable bedfellow. I'm anxious. My mind is racing."

"All right." He stood up, then dragged his bedroll toward the base of the nearest vine. "Come here."

I propped up on an elbow. "What are you doing?"

"We'll do the lesson now. I'll tell you about the Siren." He knelt. "And then in the morning you'll let me sleep in."

I made my way toward him. "You strike me as the kind that rises with the sun." I sat in front of the vine.

"Scoot up." He set a hand to my back. "You need to be able to touch its base." He nudged me forward and just that small contact sent a luxuriant heat slinking through my whole body. It quieted the chaos in my mind. "Good," he said, when I was close enough. "And I wake with the sun when I'm well rested. Which you, my dear, are preventing."

His hand skated down my arm, tightening at my wrist. "Put your fingers into the earth. Dig them in." I dug through the packed soil to where it was cool. "Stay like that."

The night was balmy, the air light and comfortable. I could make out his features in the moonlight, the sharp cheekbones and jaw. Those full lips. The messy locks that fell over his brow.

I stared at him unabashedly, and damn him, he relished the attention. A slow smile tipped his mouth. "The Siren on my ship. Is that what you wanted to talk about?"

It was, blessedly, too dark for him to see my blush. "Yes. The Siren."

"When my father, Athan, was young, he fell in love with a Siren. Before that, she'd sunk one of his ships. He'd been furious. He had a notable temper, my father, and he went after her to seek some sort of payment for the loss. I'm unsure of his logic there — approaching a Siren like that is dangerous — but his temper and crown made him idiotically bold. Unsurprisingly, when he confronted her, she was utterly unfazed by him. She didn't care that he was a prince, nor that he was furious with her. He made empty threats of punishment, which she listened to with a blank face."

Theodore leaned forward to check my hands. "Still in the dirt?"

I nodded.

"Good." He leaned back and looked at me with his head tilted to the side as he went on. "Naturally, because this Siren thought nothing of my father, he fell head over heels. Eventually, thank the Gods I don't know the details of how, they became lovers. And they were for years and years. He had a new ship commissioned and immortalized her in that stained-glass window. But my father was the son of a Great God and as his father's strength waned and his time to take the crown grew closer, he was expected to marry a noble wife. To have an heir. And he did. He married my mother, had children before me that didn't survive. But he also kept his lover as his mistress. He flaunted her, brought her with him to balls and dinners. Lavished her with gifts that he didn't give to my mother. My mother loathed her. And my father too, I expect, though she was wise enough to never let on. His Siren disappeared one day, likely a nekgya attack. I was born a year or so later."

A moaning breeze filled the quiet between us. I rolled the soil between my fingers. "That's heartbreaking. For your mother, of course, being treated so terribly. But for your father and this Siren too. They loved each other and they weren't allowed to be together the way they wanted to be."

"I don't see them as the victims of that story." Theodore looked away, deep in thought. "When the blood of the Great Gods runs through your veins, you don't get to have what you want."

"Who told you that? Certainly not your father."

"No. He believed the opposite." Theodore cleared his throat, sat quiet for a long moment. "He thought his divinity guaranteed him his every desire. And that made him callous and indulgent. It made him hurt others."

"I see." Theodore took my wrist again, almost absently. "And so, you have tried to shape yourself into his opposite."

His thumb swiped over my skin. "According to you, doing so has made me into his very image."

My lips parted. "You seem far better than your father." I searched his face in the silver light, hungry for any emotion he might offer up. Suddenly certain that knowing him better would make me feel fed. "But I can understand now why I put you so ill at ease."

"I wouldn't say you put me ill at ease, Imogen." He released me and leaned back onto his hands. "Quite the opposite. Unfortunately."

"Oh." My voice was dangerously breathy when I finally asked, "How much longer do I need to sit with my hands in the dirt?"

He gave me a piercing look. "A week."

I froze. A mischievous grin spread slowly across his face.

"You're despicable." I threw a clod of dirt at him. "How long were you going to make me sit here?"

His laugh rumbled around me. I threw more chunks of earth.

"All right." He held up surrendering hands. "All right. I'm sorry. Stand up." His laughter rang through the night as he helped me to stand. A warm arm wrapped around my waist, and the solid heat of his body pressed against my back. The calloused fingers of his other hand took my wrist, and he extended my arm out toward a curling vine — not too close.

He pressed his cheek to mine as he asked, "What does your power feel like?"

Gooseflesh cascaded down my body. The bond flared like a lit candle. I had to swallow hard before I could muster any thought at all. "It starts like a hum," I finally managed.

"Where?"

"Here." His other hand rested firmly over my solar plexus, and I placed my own over it. "But it builds and climbs up to my throat."

"Mine is the same," he said. "But instead of building to my throat, it moves toward my hands." He gave my wrist a squeeze. "Tell the vine to curl around your finger."

"I don't know how."

"You haven't tried."

My nerves jolted at the thought of being incapable. At the thought of him watching me fail. I pulled a breath deep into my chest.

"Breathe out," he said, soft as mist. He pressed his hand against my stomach, the gesture both commanding and supportive at once. "Focus. *Try.*"

Focusing would be a feat with his body pressed against mine. He was solid, unflinching, and I flexed my sore muscles so as to keep myself from pressing into him. I'd staved off the exhaustion of the last few days as best as I could, but now, surrounded by the night and Theodore's body, all I wanted to do was give in.

His hand on my stomach flared with his warm power, and the hum in my stomach started. I couldn't tell if he'd coaxed it forth, or if he'd simply helped me focus my distracted attention.

Once I felt it, I had to fight to keep my hold on it. My heart sped as I focused my gaze on the thread-thin vine. Teeth clamped, I beckoned it toward me with a clear and singular thought. It didn't move. Theodore held me tighter. Again, I sent a command, a *plea*. Again and again, and Theodore remained a steady, quiet support at my back as I tried. Finally, as my emotion began to swell, my arm tingled, my palm turned hot, and the little green coil stretched, agonizingly slowly toward my finger.

It tickled as it slithered around me like a tiny serpent.

I pulled in a stunned breath.

"Look at you," Theodore crooned.

I turned in his arms and gazed up with a smile. We were heat and racing hearts. My senses tangled into an impenetrable mass — every one of them filled with him. I let my head fall back against his shoulder. "I did it."

His hand left my wrist, moved to my hip, and he looked down at me with wonderment. It struck me that my fears, my unease, felt as far from me as they ever had.

He lowered his nose to touch the end of mine. "You did."

Slowly, I rose up onto my toes. I could just feel the heat of his lips near my own when a curdling scream shredded the night's quiet.

We jolted, jerked free of each other's hold. The wailing sob ceased, only to start again a breath later. Theodore gave me a final look, eyes wide with alarm, before he rushed toward the horses and untied them. Quickly, he helped me into my saddle, took to his own mount, and then raced off toward the line of sea grass and trees that barricaded us from the beach.

"Keep close," he commanded, before he disappeared through the thicket of tall stalks. He was moving toward the keen, toward the danger, and I couldn't get my horse to keep up.

"Imogen," Theodore called, just as my stomach twisted with sickness. Finally, my horse moved into a canter and through the grass. But it wasn't fast enough. Nausea wrenched my gut.

We were on a long, flat stretch of beach. In the distance, a cluster of little grass-roofed huts sat in a wide circle. Torches dotted the spaces between them, flickering in the wind.

Theodore sped down the wet sand, his horse at a gallop. He was closing in on a huddle of villagers that stood just out of reach of the waves. Their attention clung to something at their center, though I was too far away to make out what.

I drew nearer and shivered as their faces came clear. Every one of them wore the same look of horror. Amid them, a woman — a Siren — lay on her stomach, face toward the water, hand outstretched, screaming. Her low-backed dress was clinging wet, her brown hair plastered to her face. Dark blood gushed from the exposed, muscly root of her right wing. It hung on by only a few threads of sinew. The flesh was shredded, as if it had been gouged with a saw-toothed blade.

Theodore was already off his horse, rushing to the Siren's side, by the time I pulled on my mare's reins. I fell to the sand as I dismounted, my knees too weak to hold me up.

"Imogen." Theodore came back toward me, awash with concern.

"I'm fine. *Go.*"

He seemed unsure about leaving me before he finally raced to the Siren and knelt. "A nekgya?" he asked as he set his hands into the gore at her back. Inexorable purpose bent his face.

I made it to Theodore's side just as he took the dagger from his hip. "I have to remove the wing."

The Siren's outstretched hand shook. I knelt in front of her, grabbed it and held tight. "He'll take care of you."

Theodore was covered to his elbows in slick, red viscera. He held the dagger in a firm grip and set it to the base of her wing. I looked away, into the Siren's terror-wide eyes. She shook her head and said through quivering lips, "My daughter."

"Your daughter?" Her hand was damp and shaking. "Where?"

When her wet eyes strayed to the water behind me I understood. "She's in the water."

My gaze shot to Theodore just as he dug the blade's edge deep into her back. Dark, sweat-soaked locks of hair stuck to his forehead. He moved efficiently, even as the Siren's screams sliced across the beach.

Focus. Try.

I squeezed the Siren's hand before I let it go. "I'll get her."

The sea's surface was calm as I rose to face it. In the distance, the moonlight illuminated a sandbar that cut the lagoon off from the rest of the sea.

Find the hum in your stomach, I thought to myself as I walked toward the water's edge. I'd been able to command that little vine; I could command the sea as well.

After all, it was *mine.*

The water was to my ankles, seeping into my boots, when it shot straight to that chord in my middle. It hummed until it broke into a pulse, and then I was filled with that awful, sludgy power once more. It built up toward my throat, filling me, and then suddenly it was as if I could see the whole of the lagoon in my mind's eye. I focused further and could feel the roll of the small waves on its surface. I could sense three bodies hanging in its depths.

Only one had a heartbeat.

Teeth clamped, I moved deeper into the water, homing my attention on the faint vibrations of that single beating heart rippling through it, and then, as Theodore had instructed, I commanded the power rolling through me to bring me the girl.

"*Imogen.*" Theodore's voice boomed over the Siren's whimpers. I whipped my head toward him. He looked murderous, hands covered in blood and sweat and sand, face carved with violent fear. His hands rested firmly on the Siren's back as he worked to stop the bleeding. "Get out of the fucking water, or so help me, I will —"

"No." My voice was quiet, but clear. "I can help."

He shook his head, face bending with desperation. "Gods damn it," he said through his teeth. "*Quickly.*"

The surface of the water began to ripple and roll. It had obeyed. It sped the girl toward me, but as I waited, the pulse in my chest began to burn like ripped skin. Like something was pulling against it. Fighting me. I gasped at the pain.

Theodore yelled my name from the shore.

I widened my stance as the body cutting through the water came closer. When, suddenly, it stopped. That ripping pain flared. I tried to command it to me once more, but it wouldn't move. Something broke through the surface of the water, only feet away.

I couldn't breathe.

Yelps and gasps and prayers erupted from the villagers on the sand.

A nekgya stood before me, holding the limp, adolescent girl in her arms. The girl's body was slashed with oozing wounds. But her chest still rose and fell.

The thing holding her — the dead woman — had long, matted hair that had lumped into tentacle-like strands. They covered her chest and arms, curving through gray flesh like a thread through fabric. A small, violet urchin lived in one of her eye sockets, but the eye that remained watched me with familiar regard.

My voice quaked. "Give her to me."

"There you are, dearest. I've waited so long." The nekgya's flat words came from its black-lipped mouth, but there was a second, identical voice that echoed the same words within my skull. The power in my chest blistered.

"What did you say?" Those words. *I knew those words.*

She moved toward me with hiccuping steps until she was close enough to set the girl into my outstretched arms. Her eye locked with mine. "There you are, dearest," she repeated in a slow, awful voice. "I've waited so long."

My shock had me stumbling backward through the water, clinging to the girl. Those were the same words I'd heard in my head when Evander had forced me into that tub.

The laugh that rasped from the dead woman was sterile and crackled like water was lodged in her chest. "Do not fear. You and I are one," the nekgya said. "Bound with your given blood. Bound with the words. We cannot harm one another."

"Bound to you?" I thought of the scars on my hand. Of all the blood I'd been forced to give over the years. Of the words — Nemea's ritual prayer. A trickle of cold, complete horror ran down my body. "You're Eusia."

The nekgya didn't answer.

Another body splashed through the surface of the water beside it, and I fell back another step. Her hair was fairer, the color of wet sand. The skin over her shoulders and ribs looked gelatinous, nearly transparent. Her large black eyes locked with mine.

"The bodies are reanimated by my power," said the fairer nekgya in an identical voice to the first. In an identical voice to the one in my head. "And I am animated by yours, dear, generous girl. There you are. Just like your mother. I have waited so long."

17

With fumbling steps, I walked out of the waves and onto the wet sand. The girl in my arms moaned, her head lolling over my forearm, but I could only stare after the two nekgya. They had turned to walk back into the lagoon. On either side of their spines sat two grotesque knots of flesh.

Wing stumps.

Theodore was at my side. He scooped the girl from my arms, speaking to me in low, commanding tones, but I couldn't grasp his words.

I could only think of the prayer I'd spoken over and over again, the blood I'd given. Shame stuck through me like barbs in my pitiful flesh. My knees hit the sand, mind spinning.

Bound to Eusia. To all the nekgya. That was why they didn't hurt me. Because it was *my* power that ran through their decaying veins.

"Imogen, help." Theodore had laid the girl on the wet sand behind me. His hands rested on one of the wounds on her arm that spilled red onto the sand. My stomach turned at the gruesome sight, at the heartbreaking way her mother dragged herself across the beach to be at her side. More villagers had filled in around them, torches in hand.

Even in the harsh, unsteady light, I could see how the crowd watched me. Carefully. With suspicion. On unsteady legs, I rose and set myself beside Theodore. I avoided the scornful glares of the onlookers, but I deserved each and every one.

My fingers shook as I touched a gash on the girl's stomach and closed my eyes. With my heart racing, and my own power still pulsing through me, Theodore's was easier to find and hold. It vibrated down my arm. Heat cascaded to the tips of my fingers. When I moved my hand away from the wound, the villagers gasped.

I'd healed it, leaving behind only a small white scar.

The girl's mother looked up at me, aghast. A man behind Theodore asked, "What is she, Your Majesty?" The distrust in his voice was clear as the cloudless sky. "Is she a Mage? A spell woman?"

The teeth-bared, fear-drenched question told me precisely how fearfully a spell woman was regarded. There was only one Mage Seer permitted per kingdom, their magic and spell work heavily restricted. What could I tell them? I was Ligea's daughter. Blood-bound to both their king and the monsters that hunt them. There was no way to explain who I was, what I'd done, without earning these villagers' ire and sending a ripple of contempt through the surrounding villages.

Theodore was calm and collected beside me. "She's your queen."

My head snapped toward him. "What are you doing?"

He ignored me, tending to the last of the girl's wounds instead. "Your daughter will be just fine with rest and care," he said to the astonished mother. He took my arm, helped me to stand. "We need a hut for the night," he said to one of the older women in the crowd, "if you'd oblige us."

The request moved the entire party on the beach into action. The villagers voiced their thanks and their welcomes. Some rushed back toward the huts to prepare for us. Others held their torches high, lighting our path.

"Are you mad?" I whispered at his side. "What the hell are you thinking?"

His face was impassive as ever. Ever the king, he held himself straight as he went to the water to wash the blood from his hands and forearms. Then he was pulling me along, trying to keep some distance between us and the crowd as we made our way back toward the huts. "Not now."

"Yes, now." My guilt was too tremendous to shake. "I'm not their queen. *I* did this to them. I've given my blood —"

There was a jerk on my arm, a grunt of frustration, and then Theodore's lips were on mine. They were soft, warm, but the kiss was forceful, laced with command. He pulled back just far enough to glare at me.

A quiet, forlorn moan rolled through my chest. "What are —"

His hand hooked around the back of my neck, and he spoke against my lips. "I am keeping you safe."

"But —"

He kissed me again. This time it was gentle, lips moving against mine painfully slowly. When he pulled away, taking my bottom lip between his as he did, he spoke in a clipped, heated whisper. "Gods, you don't know when to shut up." Then, as quickly as he'd kissed me, he took my hand and hauled me toward the village with determined strides.

My only response was a breathy, involuntary protest.

A gray-haired woman led us to one of the larger huts. Theodore urged me inside before requesting that our horses be cared for. I blundered across the packed dirt floor, toward the quaint hearth. My eyes burned and I squeezed them shut.

"Bloody fucking Gods, Imogen." Theodore forced the door closed and dropped the strip of wood into the metal anchors to bar it. Then he went about shuttering and locking the three little windows. "When I tell you *not now,* you listen." He'd worked to rein in his volume, but not a bit of his anger. "The sea villages are superstitious and zealous. They honor the Great Gods wholeheartedly. They shun whatever power they cannot understand. If you were not under my explicit protection — if I hadn't made a show of my care for and trust in you — they would have gone after you."

The lingering heat of his lips went cold. That was why he'd kissed me. I swallowed past the mass in my throat. "I'd deserve it."

"Don't say that."

"It's because of my cowardice, my selfishness, that these people live in fear. It's because of *me* that they're killed and taken."

Theodore scrubbed his face at a washbasin. "Keep your voice down, Imogen."

I kicked off my wet boots, skin crawling at the touch of the seawater. "Don't be gentle with me now, Theo. Tell me what a coward I am. Tell me how I am a shell of what I should be. Aren't you disgusted by me and what I have done to your people? To *my* people? Don't you want me ripped from your blood as soon as possible? I am the reason the nekgya exist at all!"

He rounded on me. "Keep your Godsdamned voice down." His wide eyes reflected the hearth flame. The effect was wholly fitting of his quiet rage. He pulled in a breath to steady himself and his gaze fell to my lips. He took a step nearer. Another. He tilted his head like he might kiss me again. "I won't punish you. You are doing a fine job of it yourself."

"That doesn't sound like you." My voice was sharp, but I couldn't deny the pull he had on me. I wanted to be soothed, consumed by him, but I forced a step back. "It's false," I said. "Whatever we *think* we feel for one another — that burst of warmth we feel in our stomach when we touch — it's a trick of the bond. I am everything you said I was. Fearful, and irresponsible, and you should give me what I deserve. Don't let the bond make you neglect to show me the same penalty you would any subject who caused harm to your people."

His gaze was impossibly dark, brows low, jaw severely set. "You want me to blame you? To punish you?"

My chest tightened. "Yes," I whispered.

He swallowed hard. "I blame *Nemea*," he said, voice dangerous. "It's Nemea who has used you since you were a child. Nemea who knew what you were and carved fear into you. He bent you into the shape he desired. And even after all that mistreatment you did not break. In spite of him, you are alive. I'd wager you are braver and fiercer than any Great God or Goddess ever was." His own voice had risen, and it boomed through the little hut, but he caught himself and stilled. His gaze cut straight through me. A slow breath pushed through his lips. One step, another, and he closed the little space between us once more. He spoke softly now, with awe in his voice, in his gaze, as if he were uttering a prayer. "You are peerless."

Amid the heaviness of my guilt and shame and terror, for a moment, he made me feel weightless. "No, I'm not —"

"I won't argue with you, Imogen." Theodore reached up and, so slowly, wrapped an arm around my waist. "Not tonight." His other arm encircled my shoulders and then he pressed my body to his.

A shaky exhale fell through my lips. I clung to him, willing my heart to slow. "Can the Mage Seer sever both bonds? Ours and the one I share with Eusia?"

After a long beat, he nodded. "We'll ride all day tomorrow. I'll get you there as fast as I can." His hand drifted up and down my back, fingers playing through my ratty braid. I let myself soften against him, let my head rest fully on his strong shoulder. A breathy, longing sound rose in me, and I couldn't tell if the resplendent heat flooding through my center was our bond or my desire. I looked up, noted the nearness of his lips, how hard and hot and inviting he was.

Our breaths slowed and knit together between us, and then with a final, remorseful exhale, Theodore released me. He took a deliberate step back. Color had bloomed on his cheekbones; his mouth was soft and parted. He adjusted his shirt and gestured to the little bedstead in the corner. "You need to get some sleep, Imogen."

I looked to the bed, then back at Theodore. It was comfort I wanted. Oblivion, distraction. I wanted to lose myself in him, wanted to let him burn away the scourge of despair that grew within me. The feel of his body still lingered over my own. I opened my mouth, the request just forming on my tongue: *Come with me. I am weary and empty, and you can make it right.*

But I stopped myself.

He stared at me with unreadable intensity, and the thought of him seeing me as some desire-riddled creature, unable to control myself after a night as awful as this one. *You are peerless,* he'd said. I couldn't stomach him thinking less of me again.

My gaze dropped to the ground between us. "Good night."

There was a tense, drawn-out silence. He gave a curt nod, took a cushion from the bedstead, and settled himself before the little hearth, curled up on his side. "Night."

A pit tore through my stomach as I crawled into the pillows and blankets. It gnawed and grew, and I wished I had a vial of nepenthe. I wished I'd dragged Theodore into the bed with me by his collar. I stared up at the ceiling, listening to his breathing.

It was a long while before either of us fell asleep.

With our horses at a gallop, we devoured the rest of the journey in two full days.

Night had fallen hours before we finally reached the northern shore of Varya and the cluster of little rocky islands on its coastline. A stormy gust clawed through my hair. Cold drops of rain began to prick at my cheeks. Even knowing the pain that awaited me, I was eased to have finally arrived.

Aching, I dismounted and made my way over the black sand beach, toward the glowing, foamy shoreline. A narrow strip of water separated the little islands — the Sacred Holms — from the rest of Varya. On the largest and closest holm, dark against the storm clouds, stood a tiny shack.

"How do we cross?" I asked Theodore, who rummaged through saddlebags at the tree line behind me.

"She pulls back the water." He sounded oddly hollow.

"How long will that take her?" Now that I stood within sight of the hut, the anticipation was too much. "How will she know we're here in the dark?"

"We're not going in until sunrise."

"Why not?"

"Because I refuse." His words cut like a whistling axe. He'd gone still beside the tree that the horses were tied to, and though the details of his face were lost to the night, I could imagine his glower. Could picture the unease tugging on his every muscle through the cool air and rain.

"You refuse." I crossed over the black sand, wanting to look into his eyes. "You raced me here for two full days, only to have me sit on this beach, and wait for the sun to rise?"

"The Mage Seer is dangerous. We'll wait for the added safety of the sun."

It was a kingly command, but I knew him well enough now to

note the fear in his voice, to see that the rigidity of his body did not come from a full day in the saddle but from something worse.

"What can she do to me by night that she can't do to me by day?" I closed the rest of the space between us. "I suffer either way. It's you who doesn't want to enter her hut now. Tell me why."

The only sounds were the tapping rain, the crashing waves. They drowned out his heavy breaths. Drops fell into my eyes, trickled down my neck.

"I need to get us out of the rain," he finally said.

"You're changing the subject." I crossed my arms. "First, tell me what's wrong. You won't set foot on the sand. Why?"

He thinned his gaze. "Let me build us a shelter. Then we'll talk."

"Fine."

He moved with efficiency, pulling food and a bottle of wine from a saddlebag, kicking away twigs and fallen branches from the sandy soil. Disquiet pulled his shoulders toward his ears. It clamped his jaw.

Movement at my side made me jump back. A single blooming vine had unwound itself from the trunk of the tree and hovered in the air. New vine shoots grew out of it, like little wriggling worms. They thickened and wove into one another until a small domed shelter took shape. The leaves broadened, each growing larger than my spread hand. White flowers yawned into existence, emitting their own faint light in the stormy darkness.

"Charming." I bent low to crawl into the little nest just as a bolt of lightning cleaved the sky. Theodore followed when the thunder cracked around us, so loud that my hands flew up to cover my ears.

Warmth rolled off him, filling the little shelter with the scent of rain and green earth and sweat and dust. The space was small, and Theodore was . . . not. His shoulder pressed hard against mine, and through the thin, wet layers of our shirts, his skin burned like a brand.

I pressed my eyes shut for a few breaths.

Soon I would feel the absence of him, and the thought sent sorrow cutting through me. I dug my teeth into my bottom lip and tried to focus on reason.

The low echo of a cork leaving its bottle grabbed me from my thoughts. Theodore brought the wine to his lips and tilted his head back, and back. So far that the bottle knocked into the vine roof above us. He took long pulls, like he'd come upon a spring after days in a desert.

"I'm out of the rain." I took the bottle by its neck and tugged. He let me have it. "Now you can tell me what's wrong."

A nettled grumble filled his chest. "You won't let me keep this to myself, will you?"

The light drops of rain had become a deluge. It roared against the leaves. I took a sip of wine. "You always panic when the Mage Seer is mentioned. Lachlan told me you were scared before we left. And now you're guzzling wine from the bottle like you wished you were at the bottom of it. It's unsettling. And I don't need to be unsettled before this ritual. So, no. I will not let you keep it to yourself."

"My story won't settle you in the least."

"That won't get you out of telling me."

He blew out a long breath. His fingers brushed my own as he reached for the wine and took one more gulp. "I was last here seven years ago. At my father's behest. He hid it, but my father was born with very little power. And he was not very skilled in wielding what he did have. Only the Gods know why." He brought the bottle to his lips, took another deep drink. "It was a source of deep shame for him. And I can understand why now — he was the only son of a Great God. By all accounts he should have been his father's equal, or close to it. I, on the other hand, was given a great deal of power...like his father. It was always a sore point between us. He pushed me to master myself, my power. None of my hard work seemed to be enough. It took years for me to understand that he envied me, perhaps worse. When I was twenty, he decided he wanted to perform a ritual of transference. He wanted to give me what little power he had, add it to the power I already possessed, and have me ascend to the throne. He said he was unfit compared to me."

He sat so quiet, for so long, that I thought he'd decided against telling me more. I leaned against him in encouragement.

"I didn't want to be king," he finally said. "But he dragged me here anyway, to the Mage Seer. We performed the ritual." We sat in silence. "The ritual of transference...it takes the life of the giver."

My body flexed in surprise.

Hurt laced his voice. "I left that little hut in the middle of the night, having watched my father die a horrific death, with a crown I did not want, with power I did not want — and with a stolen bottle of the Mage Seer's poison in my pocket. The poison she uses for the prophecies and rituals she performs." He stared through the shelter's opening, to the dark shore before us. "I couldn't take his body back with me. I...I drank the bottle of poison empty, right there on that beach while my head was still clouded from the ritual smoke."

I didn't realize I'd gripped his leg until his fingers bumped over my knuckles. He turned my hand over and ran a finger over the web of white scars on my palm.

"Days later I woke up in a room I didn't recognize. An older couple — Hector and Antonia — nursed me back to health. They live not far from here. Eftan ruled in my stead and allowed me to convalesce for a handful of months out here." He held up the wine bottle. "I learned to make this wine. Learned to cook Varian wildland dishes. Gardened, and mucked horse stalls, and washed clothing. I mourned my father. My freedom. But I'd also never been so content. I still visit them often." His voice snagged. "They've become parents to me, in a way."

"And now you're back here because of me." My stomach sank low. "I'm so sorry."

"No." He shook his head emphatically, twisting to face me. "Don't go searching for more guilt to pile atop yourself." His eyes were intent on mine. "I chose this. I agreed to it. Neither one of us knew it would have come to this." His free hand rose to my jaw and the tips of his fingers dragged across its edge. "And even if I had known . . ."

The space between my racing heart and ribs squeezed. Even with his pretty words, I felt scheming and selfish and wicked. Utterly undeserving of the understanding and care that Theodore bestowed upon me. I reared back, away from his touch.

His look hardened. "What's wrong?"

"There's nothing wrong," I said quietly. "I'm tired."

"Imogen?"

Something in me snapped. "I'm going inside the Mage Seer's hut alone. I'll get the draught, and then we'll find a safe place to perform the severance after I've left her."

His handsome face, that had been open and tender, broke into a scowl. "Is this a joke?"

"No." I blinked frantically as a sting began at the back of my eyes.

The rain beat loudly. His brows lowered; his jaw ticced once, twice. "If you think I'm letting you walk into that hut alone —" He scraped a hand through his wet hair. "What's come over you? Is this some twisted form of pity?"

"No."

"Are you upset I touched you?"

"What? No."

He stilled. Only his broad chest rose and fell as his gaze dragged over my face. "No?"

"I'm . . ." I shook my head. "I'm embarrassed. You have given me so much care when I haven't done a thing to earn or deserve it, and I've hurt you in return." I clamped my mouth against my rambling. "But, no, I'm not upset you touched me."

"There are no more transactions between us, remember?" he said in a husky whisper. "You're deserving because I say you are." Slowly, he raised his hand to my face. His touch was feather light as it dragged from my cheekbone, to my neck. I leaned into the warmth, relished the sensation of his touch.

"Are you upset I kissed you? On that beach by the village."

I closed my eyes, remembering, then shook my head. "No."

Relief enveloped him. A low, hungry groan filled his chest, and in one swift movement, he scooped me into his lap. He wrapped my legs snugly around him. Heat cascaded through me as his fingers twined through my hair, curled into a fist, and tugged. "Good."

For a moment, we sat like that, his strong body held between my thighs, and stared. His eyes were torrid; his breath rolled over my sensitive lips. I was a heartbeat away from begging when he lowered his mouth to mine.

His kiss was decadent, slow, and the world around me fell away.

I was lost to the softness of his lips, the firmness of his body, the languid heat of his tongue. I made a desperate moan when his teeth scraped over my bottom lip. He showed no restraint, and still, I wanted more. I rolled my hips over his and went nearly mad from the sound he made. His strong hands roved to my back, and lower, then to the front of my shirt where he raced to undo the clasps.

"I need to see you." His lips met my shoulder, my neck. He nipped at my earlobe and made his way back down toward my nearly bare chest when an icy shock of water wrapped around my buttock, my thighs.

We both gasped. Our bodies jerked. "What the fuck —"

Out of the shelter opening, the dark gray sky glowed with the faintest morning light. The storm still raged, but through the rain, I could make out the Mage Seer's grass-roofed hut and the out-line of a small, hooded figure on the rocks. Her arm was extended toward the sea. The wave she'd sent to us began to flow back in a curve of white foam, like a beckoning finger.

Theodore gripped my shoulders with determined force, as if he meant to keep me.

The sun had come. It was time to sever my bonds.

18

We stood with our toes at the water's edge. Silent. Staring across the channel at the unmoving figure. Storm clouds clotted the sky beyond, like towering, stony peaks. They reminded me of Nemea's mountains.

Beside me, Theodore's breaths came tight, shallow. If I laid my hand over his heart, I was certain I'd feel it strike with the force of a forge hammer. I was wet and cold but the heat of him, the pressure of his fingers, the softness of his lips, still clung to my body. Haunting me. I prayed that the severing ritual would excise that too.

The figure on the rocks raised her arm. The motion was inhuman, both jerking and strangely fluid at once, as if she were moved by something other than her own muscle and sinew. With the flick of her wrist, the water in the channel slid away from our toes as if it was a cloth being pulled slowly across a tabletop.

"She's a Siren."

Theodore nodded beside me. "Her father was Varian."

"But she's not a Goddess, is she? How can she command the water without touching it?"

"That's her magic. Her spell work," he said, grimly. "If a Mage Seer has any Gods' power, they can amplify it with magic. But where it costs us nothing to use our power, the cost of magic is great."

The water had receded enough for us to cross, revealing the rocks and shells speckling the seafloor. Neither of us moved. I glanced up at him. At the beautiful, defined line of his profile. His eyes had glazed, his look remote. I wondered if he was thinking of the last time he'd been here. If he and his father had stood side by side like this before crossing, rough salt wind making their eyes water.

Worry swarmed me like beetles over a corpse. I'd rather eat the sand I stood upon than force him to do such a thing again. I took a reluctant step forward. Then another. Finally, Theodore's boot crunched over the wet sand behind me, only to stop a moment later.

I spun. "You all right?"

He nodded too quickly. His features were drawn, hands fisted at his sides. I stepped back and lifted one of his fists. He tried to pull it back, but I held tight. Gently, I worked his fingers open and ran my hand over his. He watched me with a look that was both wonderous and bereft. "We may have muddied things for ourselves up there," I said, "but it — you gave me comfort." I wove our fingers together. "I would like to do the same for you now."

Hard fingers squeezed around mine and he raised my hand to his lips. He placed a kiss on my knuckle. We started across the seafloor, hand in hand.

"You are picturing a woman like you," he said when we were halfway across. "She's not. She is ancient and time hardened. Emotion doesn't rule her, only her poisons do — only her magic." He tugged on my hand, made me look at him. "Do not make the mistake of thinking she will do right by you."

I gulped. "I won't."

When we reached the edge of the holm, the sea slowly trickled back in behind us, nipping at our heels. The rocks were slick and steep, and our wet boots slid over bright green algae, over pebbles and sand, until finally we stood in the little clearing before her door.

It was warped and hung crooked. The large gaps between its slats had been filled with dried plants and pitch, the metal sashes had long been corrupted by rust, but it was sturdy still. I reached for the rough latch, then stopped.

Anticipation and fear had turned my stomach sick, but I was mere days away from being free. Days away from being rid of all the virulent ties to my old life — of my bond to Eusia. Days away from starting a new life that was all my own. I'd be rid of the deception of a blood bond that made me want a man I could never have.

Slowly, I turned toward Theodore and reached up to touch his stubbled cheek. He leaned into my palm. The edges of his eyes were strained, his full lips collapsed into a firm line.

"I'm sorry," I whispered. Then I flung the door of the hut wide open, slipped behind it, and slammed it firmly shut. I felt for a bolt, slid it into place. I pressed my back against the damp wood.

Theodore punched the door. "Imogen."

It was black as night within.

"Imogen. *Gods damn it.*" He hit the door again. "Open it now."

A voice came from the nothingness. A young woman's, deep and melodic and lovely. Her croon was so encompassing it seemed to vibrate through my chest. "There you are, dearest. I have waited so long."

Terror fell through me like a jagged stone.

Theodore redoubled his pounding at the sound of her voice. The wood rattled against my back.

"Imogen, open the fucking door." His shoulder must have slammed into it next, deep voice cracking. "*Imogen.*"

"He'll break my door," said the maiden.

"Then let's be quick."

"Quick?" Her voice hummed like a song. "Oh, my girl, what you require is a slow business."

"How do you know what I require?"

"You do not know me, do you?" She tutted. "I can feel your power through the sea. Just like you can feel the water that has seeped through the soles of your boots. I can nearly taste the God's blood that flows beneath your supple, young skin in the air." A faint rustling sound sent a shiver through me. "Your blood has spread through the sea for decades. I can only assume you are here because you want it back."

"I am the daughter of the Great Goddess Ligea. I need to know what... happened. Where she went. And how." I tried to swallow, but my mouth had gone dry. "And I hold two blood bonds. I need them severed."

A loud bang came from the door at my back. Another and another.

"Two bonds! Two is one too many, did no one ever tell you?" Her amusement was caustic. "Has it made you sick?" Another scraping, rustling sound came from the darkness. The quiet clinking of glass against glass. "I need your blood first, sweeting. To give you the answers you seek. And to know just what kind of severing draught to give you."

Theodore's next assault on the door sounded with a splintering crack. "Open the door, Imogen. Do not give her your blood without me beside you."

She gave a gentle, melodic laugh. "You're certain he wants a severance?"

"Of course he does. That's why he came here with me." She gave a simpering hum at my answer. "The blood bond is confusing us both."

"*Confusing* is not what I'd call a Siren's blood bond. The bond is clear as clean water . . . to *protect*. That is all it commands."

I shook my head, trying not to lose my nerve. This was the only way I could protect him. By keeping him out of her hut, away from her smoke and its memories. More rustling, and then the maiden's lovely voice fell low. "Your blood."

"*Imogen*." Theodore's voice turned begging, broken.

"Making a draught will take hours at the very least. A severance will take days. I'm afraid my door won't hold that long."

My breath raced as I scowled into the black.

"Now, now," she said condescendingly, as though she could see me. The dark was impenetrable, my eyes never seeming to adjust. Somewhere in the middle of the space three orbs began to glow. It was not like the spill of golden candlelight but a dampened brightness, like when a lantern cuts through the webbing between a finger and thumb. They filled the room with a sickly aura, illuminating a figure at their center.

She sat upon a mound of vines. The lines of her body were straight and youthful, unlike the hunched figure I'd seen on the rocks. But as the light grew brighter, I could make out the vines that snaked around her torso, shoulders, and neck, forcing her straight. The jaundiced light snagged on the hanging skin of her bare arms. It gleamed over a taut bald head and cast grotesque shadows over the sacks of loose flesh that hung beneath her eyes. Blank, still eyes the color of goat's milk, and yet I knew without a doubt she could see me clear as day.

My fingers twitched to unbolt the door.

"Cruel," she chided. "I know time and magic have made me monstrous, but there is no need to look at me like that. Open the door, Imogen." Her lovely voice turned sultry — covetous, possessive. "I'd like to see my king."

My own possessiveness seized me. The blood bond scalded me from the inside out. Without taking my eyes from her, I reached behind me and searched for the latch. I slid the bolt, and the hut flooded with gray morning light.

"Hello, Theodore." She spoke to him like a lover, her voice laced with the memory of shared private moments. The tips of my fingers burned as my nails stretched into talons. "Look how you've grown. From a sweet-faced boy to a hardened man in so few years. And still just as beautiful."

Theodore didn't look at me. Didn't touch me. Instead, he placed his body between mine and the Mage Seer's. His voice was knife-edge sharp. "Hello, Rohana."

"Oh no. You can't still be angry. After all this time?" Rohana hummed, eerie and low. The notes curled through the air like perfumed incense, intoxicating, stifling. A Siren's song. Panicked at the sound, at what it could do to Theodore, I gripped his shirt. As if that small restraint could stop him from being pulled toward her.

He didn't budge. "Not this time," he said.

Fury beat through me. *What had she done to him?*

Her song broke into a tittering laugh. "Of course not. Not now that you have her protection. Are you certain you want to give that up?" Rohana's smile was beastly and snarling, her mouth studded with sharp, blue-tinged teeth.

There was a long pause before he finally spoke. "Yes. I do."

"Shame." The orbs of light hovered around her. They were made of nothing but faintly glowing air, swirling and thick. The rattling of her vines filled the room. They wove around themselves, raising her to stand. They coiled around her emaciated legs, around her gauzy, stained wrap, and rolled her toward a rough carved bowl protruding through the floor. It was made of the same rock as the island, as if the hut had been built around it. "Come, then. Give me your blood and your payment. And I will give you guidance."

I moved my hand from Theodore's shirt to the bulk of his arm and held fast. My body hesitated at the thought of bleeding myself into yet another ritual bowl. "What will you do with it?"

"You would be worried about that, wouldn't you?" Her laugh changed. It was rough now, like sand on glass. "I remember the first day I tasted your blood in the water. You must have been just a babe. You've been quite generous with it since."

My fingers dug deeper into Theodore's arm. "Answer my question."

"I will not feed off it the way Eusia does, dearest. We will forge no bond. I simply need a drop of it so I can see you clearer. So I know how to help."

My head went light from quick breaths. I looked up at Theodore, who already watched me. His eyes were grave, but he gave me a small encouraging nod. We moved together toward the rock bowl and Rohana. Something clattered around our feet as we walked. Theodore kept his stalwart gaze up, but I looked down.

Bones. Human bones. And animal. Strewn all over the floor. The orb light caught on their yellow-white shapes, their broken ends, where it looked like the marrow had been sucked out. A whimper shook through my throat. Theodore pressed his arm around mine, pinning it harder to his solid torso.

At the bowl, I finally looked up, directly into Rohana's eyes. Up close, her face was even more repulsive. The large bags of skin beneath her eyes were rippling and white-lined. They drew up to her eyelids, marring the delicate skin there too.

"It's from the smoke," she said abruptly. "From hundreds of years of prophecies. My eyes used to be the same gold as yours. Hair like yours too." Bitterness colored her words. "We always give something up for power, don't we?" A vine wove through the air and dropped a small jagged-edged knife into the empty bowl. "Blood."

I let go of Theodore's arm and placed the crude blade on the lip of the bowl. I pressed my talon tip into the end of my finger instead and squeezed until a single drop fell into the basin.

"And you, my king," Rohana said, cloyingly.

I took Theodore's hand and gave him the same puncture wound. He let a drop of blood fall. Two more vine tendrils snaked toward us. In the coiled end of each was a small vial of black liquid.

"Drink."

"What will it do?" I asked.

"It will make you float." Her voice was beautiful, lit by a sinister smile. "It will loosen your lips and free your mind. It will unstring your muscles so that I may truly know you. I do not give prophecies that cannot be received. You must open to me, dearest. You must let me in."

I could think of nothing more terrifying. My tendons were strung taut, and I shook as I forced myself to take the vial from its coil.

Theodore took his and clamped it in a fist. "If the smoke makes her ill, you do not touch her. You will not rip at her hair or pick at her skin. Your foul mouth will not touch her body. She owes you nothing for your prophecy."

"Payment is req—"

"Yes, I know." Theodore's voice filled the crooked hut. "But she is not yours to take from. She is mine."

Rohana grimaced, showing her stained teeth. "Not for long, Your Majesty."

Theodore was terrifying in his stillness. "Agree that you will not touch her. Or I'll cut your head from your shoulders myself."

Rohana held his stare for a moment before she gave a sharp nod of agreement. He lifted the vial to his lips and drank. I took his hand to stop mine from shaking and drank from my own. The liquid was thick and muddy and foul. It coated my tongue, my throat. I swallowed, coughed, gagged, trying to clear it, but it clung and only grew thicker. Theodore squeezed my hand as a prickling feeling filled my chest. A boom of thunder rocked through my head. I pressed at my temple, desperate for the feeling to ease.

Another coiled vine rose into the air and emptied the contents of a third vial of black sludge into the bowl where the drops of our blood had fallen. It hissed, bubbled, and then Theodore let go of my hand. In one slime-coated breath, he fell to a knee and groaned.

"Theo?" I took his face in my hands. His skin was cool and slick. "What's wrong?"

"Sick," he grumbled. Then he was tilting backward, toward the bones that littered the damp wood floor. I did my best to guide his dead weight down slowly, but he was too large. I slipped, sending us both to the floor with a rattling crash.

I moaned from the pain, but it was the blood bond in my gut that had me clambering, fighting my way back to Rohana. "What did you do to him?" I seethed at her through the tendrils of smoke that were lifting from the bowl.

"He's all right, my sweet," Rohana said, lowering her face to the smoke. "He expected it."

"Expected it?" I lunged for her, but her vines yanked her back. "*Undo it.*"

Whatever I'd drunk from that vial was beginning to affect me too. It made me feel like I was sinking. Like time and the world around me were suddenly submerged in thick water, rippling and slow. I blinked, trying to clear the way Rohana's visage began to blur.

"I slipped him some hedera. I cannot *undo it.*" Her empty eyes locked with mine. "Payment is required before we begin. Magic must be fed, Imogen, and I know my God-king very well." She gave a chuckle that only stoked my blistering anger. "He'll prefer paying me while unconscious."

The three glowing orbs winked out. There was abject darkness, filled only by the slithering, rattling sound of her vines. My senses were so overwhelmed that I couldn't place where in the little room she was. Then Theodore's body jerked at my feet.

I looked down to see the faintest bloom of yellow light. A pale arm, snaked in vines, hooked over Theodore's torso. Rohana was there, sliding her decrepit body up his. Her bony fingers dove into his thick hair, gripping like she would pull some of it out. Her lips scraped up his cheek, teeth settling against his ear.

Without a thought, I lunged and forced my talons into the thin, sagging skin around her feeble biceps. My other hand sliced through her robe, stuck into her ribs, and drew an ear-piercing shriek from her. Rohana was only bone. With ease, I hoisted her up and slammed her down onto the floor, placing my body between hers and Theodore's.

My voice ripped from my chest. "You touch him again and I'll tear your limbs from your fucking body."

"He must pay." Her voice had turned weak and begging. "The ritual has already begun, the smoke is already in my chest. I must replace what is taken."

I was nearly choking on the rotting mist that was filling the hut. And I needed my severing draughts. I needed a prophecy, but my anger was consuming. I dug my talons in deeper.

"Please," she moaned. "I need flesh."

Flesh. There was no way I could let her touch him.

Her thin lips pulled back in a snarl. "There is an order, a balance that I keep. Killing me will ruin it. If you will not let him pay, then you must so that I may continue to serve."

"I've grown tired of paying with my body so that monsters may keep living." My talons scraped against her rib bones as I forced them even deeper. Her scream bounced off the walls.

"Do not be like Eusia and kill your own. What kind of monster would *you* be if you took me from the people I am here to care for?"

I'd grown into a woman believing I was a monster. Living in shame and fear over what I was. But even with my talons tapping against Rohana's ancient bones, that feeling had momentarily fled. I was not like her. I would never be.

"What exactly do you require?" I ground out. "How much flesh?"

"Just a piece. With fat still attached," Rohana answered in a relieved wheeze. "And hair. Pulled out at the root."

The foul, sweet scent of the smoke sat heavy in my lungs. It smelled like dead things, broken down, nearly gone. My head beat with the pressure of that brew she'd given me, but I managed to pull my talons from her crepey flesh. "Don't move." I sounded like I'd downed an entire flagon of wine.

It took all my concentration, but I wrapped a clump of hair at my nape around my fingers and ripped it from my scalp. One of her vines stretched longingly for it.

Rohana's empty white eyes watched hungrily as I lifted my shirt. I dug a talon tip into the soft band of flesh beneath my navel, pulling out a small round of bloody meat. The vine took both my hair and skin and tucked them inside Rohana's gaunt cheek.

Her entire body relaxed, instantly satiated.

She was dragged back to the bowl, looking like a pale corpse in the lone orb light. The brown mist crested the lip, and the vines heaved her up, holding her so her face hung above it. A rank sucking sound cut through my ears as she gulped the thick, brown fumes deep.

I could hardly see her now with how thick the mist had become. My sight began to fracture with the more breaths of it I took. I adjusted myself so that Theodore lay protected between my legs just before the orb light went out once more. In the dark, I felt like I was floating.

The voice that came was not that of a maiden. It was the voice of a crone, reed-thin and wobbling.

There is a crown. Ripped, ripped, ripped from the head.
There is a bond. Cut, cut, cut from the blood.
The queen lies drained of her divinity.
The king sits wrecked and ravaged beneath her wing.

Rohana made an awful gasping sound that droned on for what felt like minutes.

What they have made will decimate the order of all things.

I shook my head. My voice was dreamy and slow. "I don't understand."

Rohana cackled through the darkness.

What they have made will bring chaos. Will bring ruin. Will
bring death.

Feeling disembodied and confused, I had the sensation of resting atop coarse, pleated waves. Rocking, swaying, dipping. I fought through the meaning of her words and a chill fell over me as understanding snapped into place.

I was the queen, drained of her power.

And Theodore . . . the king.

Wrecked and ravaged because of me.

And together . . . Panic slipped through my body as my thoughts and fears slowly crystalized.

Together we would bring chaos.

We would bring ruin.

We would bring death.

19

Time stuttered. Perhaps it stopped. My vision rippled and went black. When I came to, I lay upon the floor, the gleam of orb light above me. Beside me, Theodore was still unconscious. The tinkling of glass, the hiss of smoke, the sound of all those slithering vines, filled my ears.

Sluggishly, I lifted my arm and pressed my hand to Theodore's chest. Even, shallow breaths. I rose onto my elbow and watched Rohana working over her bowl, her bald head reflecting the sickly, yellow glow.

"Speak, Imogen," she said, sounding once more like a young woman. "I know you wish to."

"I want my severing draughts," I croaked.

"I am making it."

"I paid for two."

"You will get one."

I rushed to stand but her vines tightened around my calves and wrists, keeping me down. I focused, tried to find Theodore's power through my smoke-addled haze, but I was too sick, and she was so strong.

"I can sever the bond between you and your king, and that is all."

Her awful, cloudy eyes locked with mine. "And what a shame too. You are so much better together."

I reeled, head hammering. "What do you mean?" I yelled. "What about my bond with Eusia? The bond that you just told me drains me of my divinity." I thrashed against the vine's hold. "You told me that I will ruin Theodore, that we will bring death and chaos. How can we be better together?"

Rohana gave an eerie, skittering laugh and loosened the vines. "How young you are, how new and bright. You see things with clear, crisp eyes. But let your vision blur and break. Let yourself see deeper."

I pushed myself up with a hiss. "If that's your way of telling me to look for more meaning in your prophecy, then *fuck* you."

She was too still, her little body sagging against the cage of vines that held her up. She set a small glass bottle into the loop of a vine and sent it toward me. "It's time for you to leave. This will remove the God-king from your blood —"

I nearly screamed. "What of my bond with Eusia?"

"You made that bond with a despicable spell, and it is always the Mage who makes the spell that must break it."

Hopelessness pummeled me. My voice grew small. "What should I do? How?"

A vine curled around her chin, cocking her head for her. Her unblinking eyes were locked with mine. "Go home."

My brow creased. "Go home?"

The room erupted with the scraping of moving vines. Like a bed of verdant snakes, they began to creep around Theodore's supine body and ferried him over the bones and wood, toward the hut's crooked door.

Go home.

The blood bond pulsed like a racing heart, filling me with worry, and I rushed to his side. I touched him, needy for the assurance of his warmth. Gently, I traced the edge of his cheekbone. I ran a fingertip over the slanting line of his nose, down to the contour of his lips.

Home.

The word was a changeling, twisting its meaning from one breath to the next. My mind was still sluggish from the lingering taint of the ritual smoke, and that word — *home* — spun it and filled it.

Then I was transported. I stood in my old home. In King Nemea's icy-white throne room, cold penetrating to my bones. I looked to the wall. To the splayed black wing that hung upon it.

It was just like mine.

The king sits wrecked and ravaged beneath her wing. My heart began to squeeze. *What they have made will decimate the order of all things.*

"What they have made...What the queen and the king have made..." I whispered, clinging to Theodore's sturdy shoulder. My stomach dropped. "Is Nemea..."

Rohana began to giggle, and with sickening assuredness, I knew.

"He's my father."

"Good girl." She sounded approving of my revelation, but I was undone.

The features of Nemea's face, the notes of his voice, even the remembered touch of his hand, swarmed me. "I'm not..."

Then Rohana was in front of me. Her skeletal fingers clamped onto my jaw, and she jerked it toward her face. "You are what will bring chaos and ruin and death. You are the fount of desolation and change."

My throat tightened with tears. "And Theodore..." I was the daughter of the man he hated most. "Will I ruin Theodore too?"

She blinked slowly. "His power and duty are as incorruptible as ever. And yet he would give up his throne for you."

"No." I shook my head. "He's a good, loyal king —"

"Chaos. Ruin. Death," she whispered through a flash of bluish teeth. Her wrinkled mouth pulled back in a smile. "I'll tell you what I would do if I were still young and beautiful like you." Her white eyes shone. "I would keep him. I'd use his power and body to keep myself safe. Your journey to sever your bond with Eusia will be dangerous. You'd be a fool to go it alone." Her vines brought her even closer to me, but I was too stunned to recoil. "Damn the war I feel brewing in the water. You are a Goddess-queen. Take what you want while you can." Her voice dropped low. "For someday you will be like *me*."

I batted her hand from my face. Her laughter was coquettish, completely at odds with the monster before me, but her guidance struck me square in my chest with intoxicating force.

Keep him. I wanted to. Desperately.

Despite all the destruction Rohana saw following in my wake, despite there being no clear path toward remaining together, I yearned for it. My stomach turned with sick, my eyes burned with tears, but I refused to fall apart in this hellish place.

Unanimated vines still draped Theodore's body, and I tried to focus on his power within me. I set my fingers to them, fighting to command them to drag Theodore the rest of the way to the door. They were slow at work, sputtering under my weak control, but I managed to get him near enough that I could drag him the rest of the way myself, out into the daylight and sea air.

The waves churned against the rocks. I tried to let the sound soothe me, but each word of Rohana's prophecy was a needle-thin blade, slipped through my skin. There they sat now, aching, refusing to be ignored. I pulled Theodore farther into the clearing and slammed the door.

"Goodbye, Rohana. I hope you rot."

In the light of day Theodore looked so much worse. His golden-brown skin had been drained of its glow and was beaded with cold sweat. The rise and fall of his strong chest had lessened, now nearly too shallow to see.

"*Shit, shit, shit.*" I cupped his clammy face, dragged my hands down to his neck. His pulse had grown sluggish.

I squeezed my eyes shut and saw Nemea's face once more. I remembered bouncing on his knee as a girl. The terror his nasal voice would send ricocheting through my body. The gifts he'd lavished upon me after he'd been particularly cruel — gowns and jewels and books. His thumb digging into my flesh to take my blood. The unsettling, empty way he would lose himself to some remote place while looking at me. I wondered if it was my mother he thought of then. My mother — whose wing hung upon his wall.

I lurched to the side and vomited onto the rocks.

Coughing, I swiped at my mouth and crawled halfway over Theodore's inert body. "Theodore. Please." I hit his chest with a fist. "Theo. Get up."

He gave a hoarse groan.

"Theo." I grabbed his face again, begging. "You need to get up. We need to get back to the shore."

The water in the channel was high. The storm gusts turned its surface into a frenzy of toothy white peaks. I rose to my knees, tugged on his heavy hand. His head lolled to the side.

Panic rammed me so powerfully that I was certain something cracked. I was alone. Utterly alone save for a confluence of fear and fury, crashing through me like the sea. I stood and walked over the jagged rocks, down toward the edge of the water. I stared and stared at the waves. "Listen to me," I said through my teeth. "Listen."

The power in my stomach rose, and I focused, focused on twining it and the sea together until they could not be rent apart. Until they were indistinguishable.

Finally, when I pulled in a deep breath, the surface swelled. When I blew it out, it ebbed. I told it to steady, and the frothy peaks smoothed. A narrow path of water between Rohana's island and Varya's shore went flat. Calm. I could feel the waves at the tips of my fingers, and with the curl of my hand, the sea rose up the rocks, toward me.

Higher and higher the gentle flood climbed, until it rolled around Theodore's body. The dark fan of his lashes fluttered at the contact, but he didn't rouse.

"Theodore?" My voice cracked at the sight of him. "Shit. Wake up, please wake up." I urged the water to move quicker. It cradled him, carried him down over the rocks and into the now-glassy channel. With a hand clamped around the severing draught in my pocket, I followed. Cold water met my hips, my navel. When it reached my chest, I swam.

He looked like a dead man. Motionless, empty. I swam faster, commanding a current to aid me, and when my boots hit the other shore, I ran up the sand and urged the water to carry Theodore up the beach, toward the vine shelter and our tethered horses. He sprawled over the black sand, white shirt clinging to his skin. He made an aching sound, cracked his eyes.

I fell to my knees. "Theo." I forced a smile, swiped the wet hair from his brow. "I'm going to take care of you. Tell me how to get to Hector and Antonia's. Can you tell me?"

His eyes shut. I tapped his cheek too hard, and this time he opened them wide enough for me to see the faceted green of his irises.

"Road," he croaked, before he dropped away again. A bead of dark muck dribbled from one of his nostrils. Like oil. Like black blood. I frantically swiped it clean and bent to place kiss after kiss on his cold lips, his chin. He didn't flinch.

In my single-mindedness, I lost all sense. I cursed and focused to near exhaustion and somehow commanded the vines of the shelter that Theodore had built us to help me bundle him up and over his horse. I sat behind him, straining to keep him steady, and started us down the road with my horse's lead in my hand.

Rain started and stopped as we traveled through the mud, though I hardly felt it. For over an hour I kept silent, a hand firmly over Theodore's back, counting his breaths and feeling his heart.

If I stopped counting, stopped pushing, I feared what would become of me.

We took a bend in the road and a well-built wooden house, tucked behind a lush, fenced garden, revealed itself. It was painted a creamy white, with those ever-present blooming vines climbing up its walls.

The day was dying. I stroked Theodore's shoulder. "I wish you could tell me if this is the right place." Quickly, I dismounted at the garden gate. With some force, the rusted latch gave, and I led the horses into the clearing beyond. On the large, covered porch dozed an older man. The tight coils of his white hair were stark against his black skin. A small pipe dangled in his loose grip.

I glanced back at Theodore, slumped over the horse's back. The sight alone sent a shot of worry through me. I cleared my throat. "Excuse me."

The man sucked in a startled breath. Sat up on the edge of his chair. "Yes?"

"Are you Hector?"

The man's jade-colored eyes were kind, edged in a soft cross-hatch of wrinkles. They narrowed on me. "I am."

He took in my appearance. The soaked, dirty clothes. My knotted tumble of dark, wet hair. Those kind eyes turned hard when they landed on Theodore's unconscious body.

"Who do you have there?"

"Theodore, king of Varya," I answered, softly. "He's sick."

Hector's eyes bulged. He moved quicker than I expected him to, stepping off the porch and coming to Theodore's side with long strides. He set a knobby hand to Theodore's wet cheek. "Let's get you warm and dry, my boy."

Together, we lowered him from the horse, set one arm over each of our shoulders. We started slowly toward the cottage through the mud. "And who are you?" Hector asked in a strained voice.

"I'm Imogen." I ignored the weight of the severing draught in my pocket. I ignored the shame that made me want to admit all the things I truly was. "I'm Theodore's wife."

20

Hector's footing fumbled for a moment before he righted. "Wife?" He shook his head and yelled toward the open door. "Antonia!" He spoke to me. "Theo would have told us if he got married. He would have sent a letter."

"It was a quick binding. Surprised the both of us." We reached the porch and heaved Theodore's impressive weight up the small step. "He told me of you two. That I could find you up the road."

"You went to the Mage?" Hector craned around Theodore's broad chest, bewildered eyes darting over me.

"Yes," I said, carefully. "It was merely a prophecy we needed. The ritual brew made him ill."

The man nodded too quickly, clearly concerned. At the door, we sidestepped over the threshold. I dripped onto the ornate rug that nearly filled the entire floor of the main room. It was finely made, at odds with the simple lines and rough-hewn woods of the house, and I wondered if Theodore had gifted it to them. The entire home, in fact, was a mix of rustic wildland wares and pieces that looked like they belonged in a palace.

The warmth of the home surrounded me like an embrace. I gripped Theodore's solid middle more firmly. The scents of herbal tea, cut flowers, and a stew simmering over the fire all wove around me, and I blew out a long breath.

This. I wanted *this.* And I'd never have it.

"This way," Hector said, guiding us toward a door on the far side of the room. "Antonia?" he called out again. "Where is she?"

A tall woman, lean and strong for her later age, pulled open the chamber door. Her lovely olive skin was dappled with sun marks. Her white hair was piled high atop her head, braided and pinned. "Turning down the bed," she said in a thin voice. Her troubled eyes were only for Theodore, tripping down his sodden body, taking stock. "He doesn't look good."

Together, we got him into dry clothes and tucked into the bed. He'd mumbled and moaned as we jostled him and bent his joints. His skin was still too cold. I dragged my fingers through his hair, combing the knots from it as best I could. I wiped the black sand from his forehead and cheeks as Antonia brought tea and Hector boiled water for a bath.

"There are clothes in the wardrobe there," Antonia said, finally looking at me. She watched where my hand lingered at Theodore's temple. She noted my ring. "Nothing too fine, I'm afraid, but it looks like we were close in size. They should fit you nicely. Your Majesty."

I winced at the title. "Please call me Imogen."

She gave me a cool look. "I'll be in later with broth for him, and stew for you."

I had no energy to try to make her like me. I barely managed a pleasant "Thank you."

When she closed the chamber door, whatever force had been holding me upright disintegrated. My shoulders slumped. I pulled the severing draught from my pocket and set it next to the pain tinctures on the table beside the bed. Looking at Theodore made me ache, so I made my way toward the tub.

I peeled off my wet clothes, stepped into the steaming water, and cried.

You are so much better together, Rohana had said.

Of all the words she'd spoken to me, those were the ones that played through my mind in a steady, deafening beat. There was no telling the pulse of my heart from the pulse of the bond we shared. They both echoed a similar rhythm — *keep him, keep him, keep him.*

Take what you want while you can, she'd said, *for someday you will be like* me.

I shivered despite the hot water and pressed my hands over my face. I wanted to scream, wanted to rip everything to pieces.

"Any room in there for me?"

I jumped at Theodore's groggy voice. He had turned his head on the pillow and watched me through heavy lids.

The tangle in my chest began to unfurl. I gripped the tub's edge and set my chin upon my knuckles. Gave him a half smile. "I think sharing baths with men has lost a bit of its appeal since the last time I tried it."

His chuckle sounded painful, like the Mage Seer's smoke had congealed in his chest.

"How do you feel?"

"Everything hurts," he managed.

"Antonia left some nepenthe. I'll get it for you." I searched for a bath linen and found them on a stool — beyond my reach. Theodore watched me with a hint of bemusement in his tired gaze. "Close your eyes."

A mischievous smirk tried to lift one corner of his mouth. "You're joking," he mumbled. "That wet shift you barged into my chamber wearing was worse than seeing you bare. I think about it all the time."

"Do you? Then it sounds like you need no reminders. Eyes shut." He gave a weak groan and all I could do was laugh. "You're quite amorous for a man with such a limp and aching body."

He fixed me with a steely gaze, all humor leaving him in a rush. "Tasting that brew again reminds me of death, Imogen." He pushed back a burgeoning emotion. "You remind me that I am alive."

For a moment I was lost, swarmed by longing and hope, stilled by how he looked at me. I shook my head. "Damn you, Theo." The water whooshed as I stood in one quick motion and reached for the folded linen.

He made an aching sound deep in his chest at the sight of me, but I wrapped myself in a rush, trying to ignore the way his attention sent a torrent of heat through my middle.

"Imogen." His voice was suddenly severe. "You're bleeding." I looked down at the small red bloom of blood that had soaked through the towel. "Why are you bleeding?"

I stepped out of the tub with a glower. "I had to pay the Mage Seer. Thank you for telling me in advance that she charges in flesh."

"She was supposed to take payment from me," he said, his brow lowering in anger. "You stopped her?"

"Yes, of course I stopped her, you dolt. You expected me to let her slither up your body and feed off you while I watched? I nearly ripped her apart for trying."

"Fuck." He managed to raise his hand to his face and press at his temple. "Come here."

"It's nothing."

"Will you come here?" His fist hit the mattress with a dull thump. "*Please.*"

We stared at each other across the room, the air between us crackling.

Slowly, I crossed to the side of the bed and perched on the edge. I managed to keep my face serene, but within me sat a violent clash of feeling. I scooted closer, pressing the side of my body to his, selfish for the comfort of his touch. He draped a heavy arm over my lap and his fingers played with the corner of the towel I wore. "What happened?" he asked. "What did she say?"

I didn't want to speak any of it aloud. I wanted to lie, to barricade what I'd learned behind my teeth, and keep us locked away from the rest of the world for a little while longer. I looked to the filthy severing draught on the table beside us and shame upended my want. "She can't sever my bond with Eusia," I finally said. "I have to do that myself somehow. And I need to do it quickly. Every day that passes with her connected to my power sees more Sirens hunted and killed." I picked up the draught. "This is for us."

He said nothing. Only stared.

"When you're well enough . . ." I had to concentrate past the anxious twist of our protesting bond. ". . . I'll ask Hector and Antonia if we can do the severance here. The sooner it's done the better." The words rang hollow in my ears.

His jaw ticced, and he swallowed hard, but his face remained impassive as ever. "Tell me the prophecy."

I pulled in a deep breath. "There is a crown. Ripped, ripped, ripped from the head. There is a bond. Cut, cut, cut from the blood. The queen lies drained of her divinity. The king sits wrecked and ravaged beneath her wing." I paused. And left out the final line.

What they have made will decimate the order of all things.

His brow creased, but some tension within him seemed to unspool, like he'd resigned himself to a certain fate. "I'm the king, aren't I?"

My stomach fell. I shook my head and spoke with conviction that I did not feel. "No. Not you." I replaced the severing draught and took up the tiny vial of nepenthe. The cork gave a hollow pop. "For the pain." I pressed it to his lips, my fingers cradling his stubbled chin, and tipped it back. "She meant Nemea." I relished the way he looked at me — with hungry, admiring eyes — and readied myself for that look to change. To color with disgust the way Evander's had when he saw what I truly was. "He's..." I set my hand in the middle of his chest and focused on the thump of his heart. "He's my father."

His fingers gripped my thigh. His eyes rounded, but not with the look of disgust I'd anticipated. They were wide with concern. "Bloody Gods, Imogen. Are you... how are you?"

My mouth gaped. His reaction stunned me. "Fine."

"You're not." He searched me, then took my hand and tugged me forward until I lay over the top of him. My surprise made me pliable, and I melted into him as he wrapped me in his arms.

"What are you doing?" I whispered with my face tucked below his chin. "Aren't you... Aren't I repellent to you now —"

He gave an amused snort. "I'm sorry, Immy," he said into my hair. The use of my name, sweetened and short, had me lifting my head in surprise. His stare was reverent, warm, steadfast. "You are far, far from repellent."

I squeezed my eyes shut and rested back upon his chest. My relief was complete.

"Let's decide together," he said, softly, "that our fathers have no power over who we are and what we become."

I managed a slow, grateful nod. The pace of his heart soothed me. Reluctantly, he finally loosened his hold, and I settled onto the mattress beside him. My head on his shoulder, a leg draped over his.

His thumb stroked my bare knee. "Did Rohana say anything else?"

A rush of bitter tension moved through me. I hadn't the strength, nor the courage, to tell him the whole of it. To tell him that I would bring ruin. That he might abandon everything he held important because of me. His kingdom wouldn't survive a war with the continent of Obelia, and if I tried to keep him, as Rohana said I should, it would certainly mean war. Earning Theodore's resentment would grind me to dust.

I burrowed in closer to him, knowing I shouldn't, but unable to stop myself. "My mother's wing hangs on Nemea's wall. I wonder if it's his crown Rohana saw ripped from his head. The familial bond between us cut. I wonder if I —"

"Your mother's wing —" Theodore's grip on my knee tightened. "He hung Ligea's wing on his fucking wall?" He twisted to meet my eye. "You're thinking of going after Nemea, aren't you? Absolutely not."

"When our bond is severed, you'll care far less about where I go and what kind of danger I'm in."

His gaze sharpened. "Do you really believe that?" His voice was harsh, but his touch gentled as it coasted up my leg. He gripped my hip through the thin towel, spoke soft and close. "If you are hurt, then all Sirens continue to suffer. My people. And yours. You need to keep yourself as safe as you possibly can. Climbing back up that mountain to face Nemea in the name of revenge does not see your bond with Eusia broken. We need to do that first."

My breath shook at the way he touched me, at the intensity of his stare. There was desperation and longing in it, like he'd been sucked under a vicious tide for too long and was now taking his first gulp of precious air.

"What do you mean *we?*" I asked shakily as his hand slipped beneath my towel. His fingers traced delicately over my bare hip and every thought in my head turned to shimmering vapor. He played over the curve of my backside, the dip down into my waist. The color rose on his cheeks and his movements seemed to come easier. The nepenthe was working.

"You need to rest," I whispered.

"Not now." He coaxed me over the top of him and guided me with strong hands, so I straddled his stomach. I kept my towel tight around my body, breaths heavy, and met his eyes. They were smudged dark, drooping, but more ardent than ever. So gently, his fingers traced the line of my thighs, then slipped beneath the towel, where they grabbed onto my hips and held me tight.

This was foolish — I knew it was — but the outside world had turned battering, and touching him blunted my hurt, it stifled my fear.

"Tell me what you want." His voice was like embers. Heat filled his palm as it skated around my hip to the bleeding spot on my stomach. When he finished closing the wound there, his hand inched up, slowly, slowly, until it rested between my breasts. Over my ragged heart. "Your wildest dreams."

I could hardly breathe. "I don't know."

"You do." When his fingers moved to trace the underside of my breast, he let out a dark groan that set me alight. "Tell me."

My eyes fluttered shut, back arching as he slowly dragged his hand up to hold my breast. "I want a home, where it's quiet and lovely." My face warmed to speak something so trite. "Where I'm safe. I want to know others like me, so I feel less alone." My body loosened, towel slipping down around my waist, as his fingers teased the tip of my breast. Slowly, Theodore sat up and wrapped an arm around my waist, pressing our chests together.

I gasped at the sensation, at the heat and hardness. I held still as he brushed his lips over mine, just barely.

"Immy," he groaned into my mouth, forcing a decadent thrill through my body.

Then he kissed me. It was so fervid. So laced with want and promise, I thought he was trying to undo the impossibility of my desires with it. Each swipe of his tongue felt like a declaration, *I will give you all that and more.* I wove my fingers through his damp hair, letting the strands snare me. I'd never felt more wonderfully divine with my body wrapped around his, eagerly taking and taking and taking his lavishment. And it was more than I deserved, considering everything Rohana had revealed.

Chaos. Ruin. Death.

Theodore's soft lips pressed to my chin, my jaw, down to my neck, and for a moment the terror of the prophecy burned away. Frenzied, I pulled at his buttons, then peeled his shirt down his shoulders. He rolled us and pressed me back into the pillows, only to grunt in frustration when his body ached too much to let him come over the top of me as easily as he wished. "I'll curse the Gods for this until I die. I finally have you naked in a bed and I can barely move."

I laughed, pressed my lips to his. He was nothing if not determined. There was an urgency to the way he kissed me back, to the way he ravished every inch of me. His teeth scraped over my nipple, and then he pulled it into his mouth, banishing the pain with a swipe of his hot tongue. His large hand hooked around the back of my knee and splayed my leg wide as he kissed between my breasts.

"Where's the severing draught?" he mumbled against my stomach. He kissed lower, lower.

I blinked, trying to think clearly enough to answer. "It's there." Breathless, I pointed to the table, to the little bottles on top. "The black one."

A deep, breathy moan left him as he slid a finger inside me. My head fell back as he curled it perfectly, as he took it out and back in. He pressed a second finger inside me and said, "Throw it in the fire."

My head flew up off the pillow. "*What?*" I was gasping.

He looked up at me, flushed and bewildered, fingers still making my stomach coil with pleasure. "What?"

"Wait a minute. Stop." He did and I was struck with a pang of regret. "Why on earth would I throw it in the fire?"

He looked at me like I'd spoken a different language. "Because we're not unbinding."

"Why not?"

"Because if we do, you can't keep yourself safe. Finding Eusia and unbinding yourself from her is too dangerous without our combined power."

I fought to catch my breath and stared at him agape. "What happened to you? You would never have said that a few days ago. You would never have even thought it. You're getting married in less than two weeks. Our bond makes us sick. How will I go searching for Eusia if we can't be more than ten paces apart?"

His face bent with confusion. "Did you think I'd make you go alone?"

I sat all the way up, hiking the sheet over my naked body. Rohana's words suddenly rang loud in my head once more. *He would give up his throne for you.* "I don't need to explain your duty to you, do I?" I snapped. "What about the empress? Your fiancée?"

Muscles flexed as he pushed himself onto his knees. He rolled his jaw. "Seeing that my people are safe *is* honoring my duty. And I've signed none of the empress's contracts."

"But you've given your word. What damage will it cause if you go against it?" I pressed my hands against my eyes. "I can't believe I'm trying to convince you to marry her."

He looked overcome. "I'll figure it out."

"Your head is muddled from the Mage Seer's smoke, and we've been too close." Our cheeks and bodies were aflame, our hair tousled, the bedding all twisted and half on the floor. "I'm just an itch you need to scratch."

His swollen lips twitched. "An itch." Sarcasm coated his words. "It was you who said that I needed a Godsdamned fuck, wasn't it? Maybe after, I'll be able to think clearly again."

"Theodore, that's not what I —"

His chest flexed, and he winced as he moved to the opposite side of the bed. "None of this is ideal. None of this is how I planned it to be." He lay down, giving me his back. "Don't let your stubbornness kill you, Imogen."

"My stubbornness? That's not fair —"

Three quick knocks came at the door. I jerked the sheets all the way up to my chin and sank back into the pillows. "I have stew," Antonia called from the other side of the door, "and broth."

I squeezed my eyes shut as my stomach hollowed. Both of us sounded equally disgruntled when we called back in unison, "Come in."

21

By late evening, Theodore felt well enough to sit before the fire in the main room. His eyes were still shadowed underneath, his skin was still wan, but he reclined with his feet up. His head leaned against the chairback, a cup of cooling tea in his hand.

We hadn't spoken save for a few terse words since the moment we'd had in bed.

I sat on the floor before the hearth, staring into the flames, remembering. Theodore's touch lingered over my body, inside it. As if his kisses, his hands, were but an extension of his power, taking root despite our tumult. I adjusted my skirt and wished that I could go back, wished that I could have kept my mouth shut and let him take me with him into the oblivion we'd both wanted. The unfinished memory wouldn't be enough to suffocate the horror of the tasks ahead.

Find and kill Eusia. Sever our bond. And find some way to make Nemea pay for every lie and cruelty. I let my gaze slide toward Theodore. He watched me with heavy lidded eyes, chest rising and falling just quickly enough to make me think he was remembering too.

Hector pushed through the front door with a large bundle of

firewood in his arms. "Ahh, you're both up!" He set the wood next to the hearth, then took in Theodore's reclined form as he clapped the dirt from his hands. "You've looked better."

"I've looked worse." Theodore chuckled weakly.

Hector laughed alongside him, the sound ringing and bright. He gave me a broad smile that I couldn't help but return. "And you — you're looking far better than you did all soaked from the rain." He pointed to the dress I wore. I'd pulled on a simple linen gown of Antonia's from the wardrobe. It was studded with the smallest embroidered flowers in shades of lavender and periwinkle. "I recognize that gown. Looking as lovely as Antonia used to in it." His gaze moved toward where she stood in the kitchen, preparing a platter of fruit, bread, and boiled eggs.

He shuffled toward her and kissed her on the cheek before pouring himself a cup of tea. "Did you hear, Theo? About the attack on Ammos?"

Theodore tensed. "What?"

"I was talking to the baker's son traveling the road there." Hector looked to me. "Ammos is just an hour up the coast by foot, if you don't know. Three ships sacked it. Lit it aflame. Two were unmarked. Mercenary ships, he said, but one was Serafi."

I gasped around the fear that lodged in my throat. Theodore sat up, spilling his tepid tea onto the ottoman.

"When?" He stood so quickly, he swayed. I jumped up to steady him.

"Two nights past," Hector said, jade eyes wide. "I'm sorry. I thought maybe that was why you went to the Mage. Getting guidance."

He shook his head. "No. I had no idea." Theodore looked utterly adrift, his attention darting around the room helplessly. Finally, he strode toward the front door, closed it, and barred it with the wooden beam.

"What are you doing?" Antonia asked, a nervous hand at her chest.

"It's not safe." He moved to the window and began securing the shutters. "They're looking for her."

Hector and Antonia stared at me with twin looks of astonishment. "Who is?" asked Hector. "What do they want with the queen of Varya?"

I shook my head, my stomach all the way at my feet. "I'm not the queen of Varya." I swiped at my brow at their growing confusion. "I mean, I am, but not by choice. His choice. He didn't choose me to be queen, per se. I just — I don't know what I am."

Antonia crossed her arms and glared at me. "Are you married?"

"Yes," Theodore and I answered at the same time.

He secured the next window. "She's a Siren. We bound ourselves when I helped her escape from King Nemea's fort where he'd been abusing her. I've been skirting a war with him for years. Taking her set it into motion."

"Oh, Theo." Hector shook his head. "Why'd you do it? Why not plan for something like this?"

Theodore stopped, shoulders perking in offense. "I *did* try to plan." I felt a punch of shame for my lack of patience, for not accepting how he'd told me to *wait* when we'd been on Nemea's mountain. He looked to me then, but I saw no prickling of conscience in his gaze, no regret in it. Only a tormented certainty. "But I couldn't leave her —" He cleared his throat, suddenly self-conscious. "She's the daughter of the Great Goddess Ligea and King Nemea. She can kill the monster that hunts the Sirens." He looked to Hector and Antonia and said quietly, "In truth, it did not matter who she was . . . I couldn't bring myself to leave her behind."

Warmth rose to my chest, my cheeks. *He would give up his throne for you.* Rohana had been right. He'd already done it.

Hector and Antonia gawked at me. She bobbed into a quick curtsy, to which I only opened my mouth like a stranded fish.

Renewed determination filled Theodore. He piled a plate with fruit and bread and eggs. He gave Hector and Antonia each a kiss on the cheek. "It's likely those ships left and took all their men with them, but sleep with your sword at the ready regardless. With your door and windows barred. We'll leave at first light."

Antonia held up a finger. "You're still too sick —"

He shook his head and gave her a smile. "Your broth healed me completely."

She swatted at him, still concerned. "I'll pack food for your journey," she said, reluctantly. "And Hector will see that your horses are ready in the morning."

My heart thundered. My terror was weighty, keeping my feet stuck to the spot.

Theodore started toward our shared bedchamber, hands full of food. He stopped at the threshold and looked toward me. Everything sat in his gaze — the heat and hurt of the moment we'd shared. The fear and uncertainty of the days to come. His voice left him like a lure, like he'd used my own power against me, if such a thing were possible. "Come to bed with me?"

The request all but turned my bones to water with how weak it made me. I gave Hector and Antonia a quiet *Good night* and followed.

Only a few candles were lit within the chamber. The small fire in the hearth was down to coals. Theodore set the food on the small desk in the corner. I closed the door, slid the lock. When I turned to cross into the room, Theodore was before me.

His attention bore down. The news of Nemea's ships, the residual sickness from the Mage Seer, it all morphed into barbed words and piercing eyes. "Tell me again," he said, gruffly. "Tell me again that you want to take that severing draught. That you want to move ahead through war and uncertainty without each other. Without the ability to heal yourself, without me there to help keep you safe."

My lips parted. I wanted no such thing. I wanted to keep him. The thought of parting from him filled me with the worst sort of anguish. But I couldn't bring myself to ruin him further. To watch his kingdom fall simply so I could have what I wanted. I had to make my own safety. And if my life was forfeit because I tried to go it alone, at least I wouldn't take him with me.

In my silence, Theodore pressed toward me, making my back bump against the door. "If you truly think I just need to get you out of my system, that you are merely an itch that needs scratching, then let's. Let's spend the night seeing ourselves satisfied and then unbind so we can move on."

He raised his hand to my chin. He tipped it up and let his lips hover over mine. "Say it, Imogen."

I opened my mouth, trying to get the words to form on my tongue. I knew the whole of the prophecy. Keeping one another was an utter impossibility, and yet I couldn't bring myself to speak.

He waited, gaze locked with mine, and then he lowered his mouth until our breaths became one. "Tell me that *this*—what's between us — is just our bond."

I couldn't breathe, couldn't move. Finally, I shook my head. "There's too much against us," I whispered. "This — what's between us — will end, and it will end terribly."

"You can't know that."

I can. I do.

My eyes fell shut, chest crushing, and still, I couldn't bring myself to speak the words I should. "Let's get to the palace first," I finally said. "Then we can decide."

He let go of my jaw. Took a wide step back, so we each stood on one side of the rift that sat between us.

"We should eat," I said, flatly. "And sleep." He nodded, slipping behind a stern mask. "We need to get back as soon as we can."

The next morning, the sky was a deep gray, low and thick with yesterday's storm clouds. I fed my horse an apple as Theodore said his goodbyes. Last night, we'd eaten in silence propped up against the pillows. We'd fallen asleep almost instantly on our respective sides of the mattress. When we woke, we were so knotted together, it was as if we'd tried to climb into one another in the night.

We mounted and started down the muddy road, the air between us strained and misshapen. The horses' hooves squelched. The sky released a light misty rain over us in fits and starts.

"Rested enough to try to ride through the night?" I called up to him.

"Yes." His answer was cold and concise.

We made good time, and as we rode, my mind scrambled for a plan. When we finally did reach the palace, Lachlan and Agatha would make Theodore see sense. We would perform the severing ritual, free ourselves of our compromised blood bond, and then I could leave and sever the one I shared with Eusia. Only, I had no idea where to find her.

The day darkened, the sun a shocking spill of red over the horizon. The horses drank from a storm-swollen stream while Theodore and I perched on two rocks, eating the bread and cheese Antonia had packed us. "What do you know of magic?" I asked, picking at the crust. "Of the Mage Seers' spells."

Theodore shook his head, his dour gaze somewhere off in the distance. "Not much."

I gave an annoyed huff. "That means you know some."

He finally deigned to look at me, only to give a scowl.

"I'm tired of your snit," I spat at him. "You're mad at me. You think I'm being illogical and absurd to even suggest we unbind. I get it. Be big enough to help me come up with a fucking plan regardless." I ripped off a bite of bread and chewed. "If I can understand how magic works, then I can possibly narrow down a way to find and end Eusia. She uses magic the way Rohana does, I expect."

Angry color had risen high on Theodore's cheeks, but he kept a hold on himself. "I don't know where she would have learned it," he relented. "It's highly regulated. A Mage Seer is permitted one apprentice ten years before her tenure is done." He rose and went to his mare, guiding her from the stream and back to the road.

I followed, thoughts churning. "How long is a Mage Seer's tenure?"

"Four hundred years." He put his foot in a stirrup and mounted. "Rohana is two hundred and seventy-eight years into her tenure."

"So if I'd killed her, like I nearly had, Varya would have been left without a Mage Seer indefinitely."

"Correct."

I groaned as I pulled myself up into my saddle. "Where did Rohana learn magic?"

"None of them are old enough to have been taught by the First Mage, I don't think. I can't remember when she died. Spells are passed down, but Rohana and all the other kingdoms' Mage Seers create a lot of spells that are entirely their own too."

"They create their own spells?" I could only assume the spell that Eusia had used to bind us was her own.

Theodore gave a solemn nod. "The transference ritual my father performed — Rohana is the only one in Leucosia who can do it." He was thoughtful for a moment as we moved out of the stream clearing. "I don't know much about the First Mage, but I do remember that she was executed, gutted if my memory is correct, for the way she used magic. There's little in the histories about her. She was executed back in the First Years, when the Great Gods were new. That's all I know."

We wound down a sloping hill, back into the vineyards we'd traveled through on the way north. "Rohana said that our bond — mine and Eusia's — was forged by taking the Siren bond and mixing it with magic. She said I was the one who had performed the spell — that I would have to be the one to break it. But I have no idea how."

We rode side by side. "The ritual," he said. "The prayer Nemea would make you recite. What was it, again?"

"'I give to the sand. I give to the water. Hear me, heed me. Cleanse the sea.'" The words left an acerbic film over my tongue.

"The spell should have made you ill." He narrowed his gaze, contemplative. "Would you feel unwell after performing the ritual?"

"No." The night was settling over us, taking the last of the day's warmth with it. "I didn't feel much of anything up in those mountains. I expect if I perform a spell at sea level I will." I wrapped myself in the knit shawl that Antonia had gifted me. "Do you have books on magic back at the palace? Anything the Great God Jesop wrote."

"Yes. There are quite a few," Theodore said carefully. "But they're not allowed to be accessed."

"You mean by commoners?"

He dipped his chin and looked at me with a sheepish eye. "No, not even I am allowed to take them from the lower study."

A harsh wind cut through the vineyard, prickling my skin. I could feel his attention linger on me. "Who dares to tell you no?" I gave him a sardonic smirk. "I'd like a lesson from them on how it's done."

His chuckle was dark as the twilight shadows. "There's a very tightly wound hermitess down there that does not let me — or anyone — enter."

"Well, Your Majesty" — I straightened in my saddle — "your hermitess has not met the likes of me. I'm rather an expert at making people do what they don't want to, aren't I?"

He gave me a smoldering look, the barest edge of a smile on his lips. The warmth of his quiet laugh cut through the night's chill. "May the Great Gods go with you. The hermitess carries a very knobby stick that she would swing at me when I was little and tried to sneak in."

I laughed, but soon that awful, strained quiet that we had begun our journey in settled back around us. He picked up our pace, riding at a gallop through endless vineyards. It must have been midnight when my eyes were finally growing droopy. A thundering sound rocked the air, jolting me fully awake. Horse hooves.

Theodore pulled on his reins. "*Whoa.*"

I slowed my mare too. "Is that coming from up ahead or behind?"

Before he could answer, a horn sliced through the night.

"Soldiers." Theodore called out into the darkness. "Slow up ahead! This is your king. Slow your mounts!"

The retinue came into view and slowed into well-ordered rows. Bringing up the rear was a small carriage. "Your Majesty?" called a familiar voice. Lachlan rode toward the head of the group, fully outfitted in his gold armor. Even in the moonlight, I could make out the strain on his face, the worry strung through him. "I thought you'd still be with the Mage Seer. We were coming to find you."

"What's happened?" Theodore asked, bracing himself for the reply.

But Lachlan didn't answer. He looked to me with derision in his gaze instead. "You're looking surprisingly well for being in the middle of a severing ritual."

"I . . ." I bristled in my saddle. "We didn't —"

Theodore cut me off. "I asked you what happened, Commander."

"Ammos was sacked," Lachlan said, grimly. "So was Notos on the west shore. Nemea's doubled the size of his fleet with mercenary ships. More than we anticipated. He shouldn't have the money for it." Lachlan gave me another withering glare. "The empress isn't pleased. She's sent a missive for her own fleet to come and aid you. She's demanding you rally Sirens and force them to use their power to bolster the navy. Sink the fleet so that her daughter becoming queen need not be delayed. Tell me you performed the severance, and that Imogen is just uncommonly resilient."

Theodore was stoic as ever, sitting tall and unmoving. But I could sense that what Lachlan had just shared ripped at him.

"Your Majesty?" Lachlan's gaze darted between the two of us.

"We didn't do it," I said. "Not yet. We . . . There was — a complication."

"A complication?" Lachlan gave an angry laugh. "What was it? Like a 'you lost the draught' type of complication? A 'didn't quite feel like going through the trouble' type of complication?"

"*Enough*," Theodore snapped. "You won't speak to her that way." He dismounted and made for the carriage at the back of the line. Called out to the riders in a barking command, "Back to the palace." He glared at me, then Lachlan. "With me. We need to talk."

22

The carriage was small and tight, jostling Theodore and me into each other's sides as it raced down the North Road, back toward Genevreer Palace.

Across from us, livid on the narrow bench, sat Lachlan. His dark brows were lowered, menacing eyes on Theodore. "What happened to you, Theo?" The question was withering, accusatory.

Theodore stiffened. "What does that mean?"

"It means that you have been so tightly fucking wound for years. You've been perfect. Always in line — to the point that I started to wonder if there was something wrong with you." Lachlan raked his fingers through his short hair. "And now — since *her* — you can't make a sound choice to save your life. What complication could possibly have prevented you from unbinding the second you got that draught?"

Defensiveness, shockingly, rose up in me like hackles. I spoke before Theodore could. "King Nemea is my father," I said, crossing my arms tightly over my chest. "I share a blood bond with Eusia — with all the nekgya. If I want true safety for myself and Sirenkind, I need to find and kill Eusia. Theodore wanted to remain bound because doing so would offer me additional safety from the danger I'll face."

Lachlan's face creased with confusion. He looked between us. "That's not a Godsdamned complication. That's Imogen's responsibility. And it should have no bearing on your own, Theo."

Theodore bristled. "The Sirens are my citizens. They have been my people since Queen Ligea disappeared. Imogen's success in this falls under my responsibility as king."

Lachlan's gaze cut between the two of us once more and a slow realization slackened his face. "Oh shit. *Shit.*" He squeezed his eyes shut. "You're kidding me."

"What is it?" I glanced to Theodore, then back to Lachlan.

"Of all the beautiful women I've thrown at you over the years." Lachlan pinched the bridge of his nose. "Of all the very eligible, very safe, very unproblematic women you've had your hands on, *this* is the one you fall in love with!"

Theodore went so still beside me that time seemed to halt.

The silence that followed let me hear how my heart raged. It stretched out, so long that it was an answer in itself. A mingling of dread and elation filled me.

"Are you going to deny it?" Lachlan asked, shaking his head. "Shouldn't be surprised. This is what happens when you try to be impossibly good. You fall apart for the first naked woman who forces her way into your bed."

Theodore launched himself across the small distance between them. One hand gripped Lachlan's throat, and the other hauled back, ready to land a blow.

I screamed, pulling at Theodore's shoulder. The carriage was too small. It filled with groans and flailing arms. Theodore managed to reach around me, clipping Lachlan's nose with his fist. I wedged myself between the two men, pushing my back into Theodore's chest and my palms into Lachlan's breastplate.

"*Stop* it. What the hell is wrong with you?" I bellowed at Lachlan.

A clot of red dribbled from his nostril. Both men gasped for control on opposite benches, but I still knelt on the carriage floor between them, not trusting them in the least.

"I need him with his head on straight." Lachlan swiped at his nose with the back of his hand, then sneered at the smear of blood.

"I know," I snapped. "I know you do." I shoved harder against Lachlan's breastplate. His lips flattened into a severe line. "But that's not how you get it, you idiot. He should have hit you harder."

The carriage suddenly lurched, throwing me forward, then backward. As I fell back, my head rammed into Theodore's chin. He gave a pained hiss as he wrapped an arm around my waist to steady me. There was a loud clatter outside. Horses whickered; soldiers shouted to one another.

Both Lachlan and Theodore tensed. Lachlan went for his sword that lay on the bench beside him. Theodore pulled the spare from the wall above his seat.

"What is it?" I whispered.

The carriage had slowed and now it sat at a complete stop.

"Stay in the carriage," Lachlan said as he slipped his gilded helmet back on. He peeked around the window curtain, but all I could see from my vantage was darkness. He threw the door open and slipped out. Theodore closed it and turned the puny lock. He lowered the flame in the small lantern that swayed from the ceiling until we sat, breathing tightly, in the dark.

Our sides were pressed against each other's. "Should I go out there?" I whispered. "If there's a threat I could help. My lure is better than shooting an arrow into the dark."

"No." Theodore sounded immovable. "They're more skilled than you are, and you're safest in here."

I bit into my lip. "I used both your power and mine well enough when you were unconscious after the prophecy." He shook his head, but I scolded him before he could tell me no again. "I'll be in danger, Theodore. Over and over again, death and danger will cross my path, and you cannot be the one to beat them back every time."

I couldn't see his face in the darkness, but I could hear the long breath he pushed through his nose. The soldiers' voices were muffled through the carriage walls, the clinking of their armor dampened, but I could still make out their every sound.

One of them called into the vineyard. "Come out. Weapons down."

There came a ping and a whistle of air followed by a dull *thunk*. A groan rang out, followed by the heavy, metallic crunch of an armored body falling to the ground.

Then all hell broke loose.

Shouts rang through my ears. Clanging metal and whinnying. Theodore swore as I dove past him. I twisted the little lock and threw the carriage door open. My boots slipped over the mud. Theodore gripped my elbow to steady me. His soldiers looked like beacons, gold glowing in the moonlight, and in their midst moved a handful of wraith-dark figures. They were merely men, but they moved with treacherous grace, quick and nimble amid the metal-clad soldiers.

Theodore stood at my side, sword at the ready. I kept my back to the carriage, inching around it until I was close enough to one of the men clad in black.

I sent all my focus to the center of my body. To the place where my power sat, where my sick bond with Eusia stuck to me like a parasite. I latched onto it, felt the place heat and open like a ravenous, unhinging mouth. A frisson of power crept up my chest, into my throat, and in a blink an invisible lure flew forth, hooking right into the man's spine.

He froze. His back arched. He took an unsteady step backward, boot splashing through a puddle. As if he were puppeted by strings at the tip of my fingers, he turned with jerking movements to face me. A shock ran through me. It was one of the men Theodore and I had met at the caretaker's cottage. I recognized him — the handsome one. Blond, waving hair, and eyes so light I could see them in the moonlight.

"Im, get back." Theodore's grip was protective and strong on my arm. He tried to jerk me away, but I resisted him.

The man's jaw fell open as he tried in vain to suck in a breath. My panicked gaze tripped down his body, over his black, worn clothes, to the bandolier slung over his chest, then to the red band that was wrapped around his biceps.

A twisting eel, fangs bared, wove around the edge of the band. "You're a mercenary?" I asked. "King Nemea hired you?"

He was shaking, his face reddening with strain. I eased my lure, allowing him one quick breath.

"Answer me." I pulled a dagger from his bandolier and held it to his throat. Metal clanged around us, shouts rang out, and fists landed blows on flesh behind him. Theodore set his sword arching toward a mercenary to his right with a grunt. I tightened my lure on the man before me once more. His eyes bulged. He gave no answer.

But the band on his arm was answer enough.

My rage rose in a wave, and I slashed the dagger across his throat. Blood spewed from the cut in a curtain of red, spraying over the front of my shirt. Theodore winced at my side. I released my lure the moment the man fell to his knees.

Seeing that eel, knowing how close Nemea had come to me — I'd not known this sort of consuming terror. Spurred by it, the power in my middle became hotter, thicker, prompting a slew of lures to fly from me. They sank deep into the mercenary men scattered through the road, making them spasm and collapse to the mud.

Theodore's soldiers stepped back, watching in astonishment as the men they'd just been in combat with writhed on the ground, choking and grabbing at their throats. My vision had blurred with fury. I tightened my hold on the lures, eyes stinging, breath fast, when Theodore's fingers gripped hard into my arm once more.

"Imogen, stop." He shook me, urgent. "Damn it. *Stop.*" He ran through the handful of convulsing men. He lifted one of them into his arms, screamed my name again.

It wasn't until Theodore heaved the man further into his embrace that my vision seemed to clear. It was Lachlan.

Horror struck me in a searing bolt. I pulled in a hiccuping gasp and cut every lure I'd sent out. Sucking sounds scraped at my ears as the mercenaries all took in a frantic breath at once. Theodore's soldiers moved toward them so quickly that I stumbled back a step. The tips of their swords pierced through skin and rib, conjuring a gruesome chorus of death cries. Dark, thick blood spread over the mud, seeping through the puddles like the earth itself was bleeding out.

Slowly, Theodore helped a shaken Lachlan to stand. He looped his arm over his shoulder and together they moved over the bodies of the dead and dying. "On your horses," Theodore ordered in a weary voice. "Onward."

The soldiers' distrustful gazes clawed at me. Some of them scooped up the limp body of the soldier who'd been shot from his horse. A snapped arrow protruded from the side of his neck. They removed his breastplate and threw him over his horse's back, belly down.

"Lachlan. I'm sorry," I said as they passed me for the carriage.

Lachlan shook his head. "We're even." He tried for a crooked smirk. Theodore's gaze was downcast. "I should know better than to make you mad."

His voice was hoarse from how I'd strangled him. It made my

stomach roll with sick. Lachlan climbed into the carriage, but Theodore lingered for a breath. I waited for him to look at me, to see how I was rattled, to give me his ever-steady comfort and pull me up from the darkness I'd too easily slipped into.

Instead, he rolled a tight shoulder, then entered the carriage. In his absence, the world grew overloud. The ring of swords forced back into their scabbards, the horses' nickering, the soldiers' voices. The incessant echo of the waves in the distance; the unending rattle of the grape leaves. My mind played cruel tricks too, showing me Lachlan's face contorted, and Theodore's etched with brutal worry. The meaty smell of blood from my shirt sat heavy in my nose. It had grown sticky and cold. I stepped through the mud, head hung, toward the carriage door. I decided then that the moment after our severing ritual was complete would be the last I would see Theodore. For I was as undiscerning as a storm, as ruinous as a tidal wave crashing, and I could never live with myself if he was caught in my devastation.

Theodore's hand found my leg, gave it a shake. "We're here."

Two days had passed. The carriage wheels crunched over gravel. I peeked through the window and yawned. Genevreer Palace seemed like a skeleton lit aflame in the night. Its stone walls were pale as bone, its windows glowing bright against the black sky.

The carriage rolled to a stop and a short line of servants greeted us. Theodore exited the carriage first, but he did not reach back to help me down himself. A servant came swiftly on his heels, his glove soft against my hand as he helped me down the narrow steps.

"Thank you," I mumbled.

His brown eyes raked over the filthy shirt I still wore. It was creased and stiff with dried blood. In the melee, the saddlebag that had held my spare clothes had fallen from its restraints, left behind among the bodies and blood. The dress Antonia had gifted me had been in that bag. It brought a strange sadness over me to think of it lost — one more thing I'd ruined.

I looked down the front of my body. I wore Theodore's ill-fitting trousers, tied with a frayed rope. Mud caked my boots. My hair was stiff in places with mats. At least Theodore had taken a moment to bathe in the shallow stream beyond the city boundaries that afternoon. I watched him cross the gravel drive. Even with his threadbare shirt rolled to the elbows like a worker's, even exhausted, there was no mistaking precisely who and what he was. He stood at the base of the marble palace stoop, chin tipped back regally, shoulders square and strong.

I'd not realized just how much of his armor he'd let fall away while we'd traveled. Alone with me in the wildlands, he'd been someone else entirely. Now, all the soft, vulnerable pieces of him were suddenly hidden away.

I stopped at his side. "I'd like to bathe."

He gave me a quick nod. Something had shifted between us since I'd lost my control. Since I'd nearly killed Lachlan.

It made me certain of at least one thing: The king of Varya could not allow himself to love me. Here, in his world, we could never be. I was something fearsome, untrustworthy. And he ... he wore his crown so well.

The severing draught sat heavy in my pocket. "Tonight, we should —" I started, but Theodore's attention was elsewhere.

"We should what?" he asked, absently. A deep line creased his brow as he took in a long line of opulent carriages, tucked one after the other down the long drive like a string of gaudy beads.

"What's the matter?"

He shook his head. "I don't know why all these carriages are here." He turned and took the stairs two at a time. I moved quickly to keep up, racing behind him down the middle of the entry hall. Ghostly music echoed off the walls, the tune delicate, almost melancholic. Theodore followed the sound all the way to the ornate door situated at the palace's back wall. He heaved it open and halted right upon the threshold.

It was his throne room. It was a soaring space, drenched in crystal and gold, and brimmed with extravagantly attired guests. It was as if Theodore had lifted the gilded lid of a jewel box that held the brightest of stones. Varya's nobility had a wealth that Seraf's could only dream of.

Theodore took a rigid step into the room and the herald's voice boomed over the violins and murmurs and laughter. The music cut out as every guest bowed. I wanted to bolt behind the door, but Theodore plodded farther into the room, eyes scanning the scene in shock.

"The bridegroom has returned." The empress appeared from the center of the crowd, arms spread wide in benevolent greeting.

I lingered as far behind as I could without our bond cramping with sick. Boots scraped behind me and Lachlan was there, helmet in hand.

"Fuck me," he mumbled when he saw the way Theodore's anger had rounded his wide back and curled his hands to fists.

"What is this?" Theodore asked the empress through a locked jaw.

The empress tilted her head, a bland look on her pale face. It was a wonder her massive diamond crown didn't slide to the floor with the movement. "An engagement party, of course. The wedding is in just over a week."

Princess Halla emerged from amid the guests and swept into an absurdly grand curtsy before Theodore. Her white gown was tight and studded with sparkling beads. A sheer, flowing white hood billowed over her shoulders and hooked to her tiara. "Your Majesty, I'm happy for your return." She stood once more and gave him a blooming smile. "I'm sure you'd like to refresh yourself, but may I request a dance before you do?"

Theodore was still. Red crept up his throat, which bobbed as he swallowed back his temper. He gave Halla an almost polite nod. "One dance."

The princess's smile grew somehow brighter as she lifted her arms. Theodore held her hand and, keeping their distance, took her by the waist. The music swelled. The crowd cleared away. With the first steps of their dance the blood bond made my stomach feel like it was stretching. It gave a deep ache, a protesting surge of discontent. Saliva trickled over my tongue. I didn't budge. I merely clamped my jaw, chest squeezing, and endured the discomfort.

I could feel Lachlan's gaze on me. "You okay?"

"Don't act like you care."

"I care." He blew out a fast breath. "I was mad when I found you on the road. It's been stressful."

"The severing draught is in my pocket." I watched a stoic Theodore glide the princess through the steps of the dance. "Can you find Agatha for me? I'd like her to be with me when I take it."

Lachlan gave me a heavy, searching look. "Does Theo know?"

"No." I shook my head. "Don't tell him. Please."

He pursed his lips, looking ill at ease. "I'll find Agatha."

As soon as he left my side, a smooth, lilting voice trilled in my ear. "It looks like your travel was quite harrowing, Lady Nel." Empress Nivala sounded benign enough, but her lapis eyes were keen as she took in the state of me.

I stepped back and dipped into a curtsy. "Yes, Your Imperial Majesty. Quite."

Her gaze cut away from me, and she watched contentedly as her daughter and Theodore continued their dance. "They're lovely together, aren't they?"

They were. He was the sun, fervent, constant, and it was *she* that was the pale, glittering moon, brightened by his presence. What was I then, I wondered? The slinking darkness, perhaps, burned away by the light of them both.

When the empress's attention returned to me, the wrinkles at her eyes deepened with puzzlement. "Is there a reason that you linger? You're covered in days-old blood."

"No, Your Imperial Majesty." I curtsied again, my stomach twisting further. "Excuse me."

"Ahh, a moment." She'd gone oddly still, all her icy attention zeroed in on me, or rather, on the engagement ring I still wore on my finger. I stopped in my muddy tracks. "Your name, my lady — *Nel*." Her casual tone was so at odds with her piercing gaze. She extended a hand toward mine, the fingers long and bone pale, but her touch was warm, soft. She took my hand — the one with the ring — and began to stroke the back of it with the pad of her index finger. "I'd like to know its origins."

Cold skittered through me, but I offered her an agreeable nod and worked to clear my mind enough to answer. Nemea's family name was Miros. I couldn't even remember what Ligea's had been, though I'd learned it in my lessons. "I was born on Seraf," I answered with a shaking voice. I could only offer her the story I'd been told.

"Seraf. I see." Her eyes shone with cunning. That finger still traced a repetitive line over my hand. "It's an interesting name," she said through a small, unfriendly smile. "It's Obelian." Her finger stopped moving, but she did not let me go. "Did you know?"

My throat tightened, senses on alert. I shook my head.

She looked out at the collection of beautifully dressed nobility, at Theodore and Halla. Then her gaze sliced to mine. "I'll tell you of it," she said, as if sharing a secret that was to be kept between us. "Years ago, back when King Athan still ruled, when Seraf's king, Nemea, was still young, my husband died. Sweet man. Simple. He liked horses. The blandest consort an empress could ever hope for." She gave a cold chuckle. "All the Leucosian rulers came north for the remembrance. Queen Rillion. Queen Ligea too. Some of them had never visited the continent before — it's quite a distance. The Nels were a very rich, very old Obelian family that I had been close with since my youth. Our families intermarried for generations, but by then, their members were few. A matriarch remained, her sickly grown son, and his mousy wife. They had a quiet little girl with the most perfect white curls. That first night, they hosted an elegant dinner for the Leucosian royals in their manor home.

"Between courses, we toured their gardens. It was summer and the night was unusually balmy for the north. When we returned for the next course a half an hour later, the bodies of the Nels — all four of them — were piled in the middle of the dining room, beside the table." She tutted as if to say *such a shame*. "They'd been sliced open from their necks to their groins, so deeply that their insides spilled out onto the lovely rug." Again, that finger traced a slow line down the back of my hand. Down the middle. Mimicking the way the Nels had been sliced. "The matriarch's body had been stripped of its jewels. A spinel necklace and earrings to match. A ring too."

I jolted. "That's an awful story."

"It is."

"Why did you tell it to me?"

"Oh well." She brushed her thumb over my palm quickly — over my many scars. She smiled. Then she let me go. "You, born on Seraf, with that name. It brought forth the memory." She gave a thoughtful hum. "Nemea was very handsome then. He was very attentive to me in my shock and grief over my late husband. I wonder how he's fared."

My pulse sped. "How many years ago was this?"

Her blue eyes rolled upward in thought. "Halla was not born yet, so, twenty-five years ago now. My, time is a savage thing, isn't it?"

In that moment, it was not time that I thought to be savage. "Good evening, Your Imperial Majesty."

I dipped into a shaky curtsy, stole one last glance at Theodore, and blood bond be damned, fled the throne room.

23

I staggered up the candlelit stairs. The Great Gods lining the banisters stared down at me and I steeled myself against their empty, searing gazes. Against the relentless, stabbing pain in my stomach. I scowled up at the uncanny statue of Panos, but there was something to be learned from all the Gods — my mother included. Something in their stoniness, in their implacability. Theodore had those qualities, but I... I was prone to dissolve in the face of my want, of my fear. It took all of me to not run back to Theodore's side.

And alongside everything else, I was certain the Empress of Obelia knew precisely who I was.

At the top of the stairs my stomach clenched. I ran quickly toward the end of the hall and the door to Theodore's chamber. Perhaps I should have gone elsewhere, but the palace was winding, and I yearned for the comfort of a familiar place. I twisted the knob and raced toward the washroom. At the basin, I heaved and heaved until I sweated. The retching settled, but not the pain. I splashed cool water over my burning face and peeled my filthy shirt from my body. Before I stripped my trousers, I carefully took the severing draught from my pocket and set it on the table beside Theodore's bed.

It was as if a stone had been set on my chest where it gradually pressed down, cracking through my bone, pressing on my heart. I scrubbed with soap that smelled like Theodore. When I was clean, I wrapped myself in a towel and curled onto the tiled floor, waiting for the next roll of nausea.

The hinges of the chamber door squeaked. I rose quickly. Raced into the room. "Theo?"

Agatha stood in a lovely charcoal gown, her face edged with concern, and my eyes burned.

Gods damn it. I'd wanted it to be him. I wanted it to always be him.

"Lachlan told me everything." Agatha's look gentled.

"About how I almost killed him because I lost control?" I sucked in a shaky breath. "About Eusia, and Nemea?"

She gave me the barest nod. That look on her face slid too close toward pity. "At least you made it back in one piece."

"I don't think I did. I feel like I've been split wide open." My voice snagged. "I think . . . I might love him."

Agatha froze. Blinked. Nodded once. "Let's get you dressed."

Another painful twist of nausea moved through me. "Did you hear me?"

"I heard you." Agatha pulled open Theodore's wardrobe. A handful of dresses hung within that I recognized from the dressmaker's cart. Agatha picked one in wine-colored silk from the rack.

"I'm just going to throw up on it."

Agatha strode toward me, determined. "I don't know how this is going to go, Imogen. I don't even know what to think about it all. You might have to fight for him. You might have to let him go. But whatever will be required of you cannot be accomplished while you're naked."

A sad laugh bubbled up in my chest. I let her help me into a chemise and stays, pausing to dry-heave into the washbasin. She tugged on the laces at my back. "Tell me your plan."

Plan seemed a grand word for the jumble of tasks that crowded my mind. "I don't know...I have to find Eusia. We learned she's a spell woman, or she at least possesses some magic, like a Mage Seer does. Theo said there were books on magic in a study here. I need those books." I swallowed back a surge of nausea. "We need to unbind first. I'll take the draught now —"

"Imogen?" My head snapped toward the open door. Theodore stood there, sallow, with a hand clutched at his stomach. His wide eyes bounced between me and Agatha. "You were going to take the draught?"

Agatha let go of my laces while they were still half undone. "I'll go." She gave my hand a quick, parting squeeze. "Call for me when you need me." She skirted past Theodore to leave.

The pressure in the room changed. With slow steps, he came closer, and my sickness abated. His green eyes were pained, his voice gruff. "Answer me."

"I was. You haven't spoken to me in a day and a half. The empress..." I couldn't find the words to explain our interaction. "And you and Halla — you're so lovely together. It's your engagement party. And I have my own responsibilities to see to —"

"I cannot even see her for the way you encompass me." Emotion etched his face. "You fill my every sense. You stalk my waking mind. You make up the entirety of my dreams. I couldn't speak to you after what Lachlan said because it shocked me — that he was right. About what I feel —"

"Theo," I whispered, cutting him off.

He shook his head sharply. "It's not the blood bond. We both know it's not. There is something between us that that Godsdamned bottle of muck cannot sever." He closed the rest of the distance between us, cupped my face in his hands. He spoke over my lips. "What I feel for you is beyond reason — beyond duty and desire. You have tipped my whole world on its side, and you are the one clear thing in the chaos." His nose brushed the end of mine. "You. I want *you*."

I closed my eyes at the impossibility of his admission, at the danger in it. Rohana's words lanced my mind. It was no wonder he couldn't see reason. For my soul was the water, shifting, wild, rolling through destructively, but Theodore's had roots. They burrowed deep, held strong, and I had poured through their empty spaces — drowning him.

He kissed me then and every clear thought I had muddled. His lips were hot and soft, and they met mine with a desperation that cracked straight through my flimsy resolve.

I rose up onto my toes. I kissed him like he was air, like he was light, and I had spent my whole life gasping in the dark. He moaned into my mouth as his tongue swiped across mine. Hard fingers curled into the strands of my hair. He set his lips across my jaw, my neck.

"Don't think me selfish," I breathed. "Don't resent me for this when I should be finding and reading those books. When I should be taking that severing draught."

There was agony in his look. "If you are selfish" — he gave me a deep, luxurious kiss — "then I am a gluttonous, greed-riddled fiend for how badly I want you."

If I thought myself weak when it came to Theodore before, I'd been wrong. I met his kisses with shameful abandon. He pulled at my half-loose bodice, dragging his mouth over my bare shoulder, over my collarbone. He grunted in frustration when he couldn't get the bodice any farther down.

"Turn around." He spun me, kissed my neck from behind as he walked me toward the bed. He pressed me over its edge, curling his body over mine as he undid the rest of my laces and set his lips and teeth and tongue over the expanse of my back. He set indulgent kisses over the skin that hid my wings. As he peeled my gown and stays and chemise off, his lips dragged lower, lower, all the way to the base of my spine. His words were husky, curling steam across my skin. "Too many clothes."

Finally, they were a pool of fabric encircling my feet. Theodore made a low, smoky sound of approval as he took me in, bare and bent over the side of his mattress. With the softest touch, he swiped a few errant strands of my long hair away and placed the softest kiss upon my middle back. "Perfect," he whispered, sending a shiver through me. "You're beautiful."

He set kiss after gentle kiss down my back, until he knelt behind me. I let out a shaky breath as his lips brushed slowly over the curve of my backside, as his fingers grasped and kneaded my flesh. He nudged my thighs wider. The first swipe of his tongue coaxed a moan from low in my chest.

The world narrowed to him alone, to the heavy spiral of heat that he sent through my belly with each flick of his talented tongue. With a forceful grip, he moved my knee up over the edge of the bed, and deepened his attention. That heat spread through me in a cresting wave. "Theo," I called out, weak and high.

"Not yet," he ordered, speaking against the soft skin of my inner thigh. He slid a finger inside me, groaning as he did. Then another. My hands clawed at the blanket, my hips bucked, but he pinned me still with a strong arm. With those fingers moving in and out, with his hot tongue set perfectly over the most sensitive part of me, it was impossible for me to wait any longer.

My cry filled the chamber. My entire body was beaded with sweat and pulsing, shaking under the fluid, sweet way his tongue, his lips, still worked at me. He rolled me onto my back, pushing my legs wide. He dragged his mouth over the inside of my thighs, biting and kissing me there. When I reached for him, utterly spent, he reared back.

He rested his cheek on my knee, gave me a wicked smile. "Did you forget that I'm greed-riddled when it comes to you?" He set his lips over me again — sucking, licking. "I'm not done yet."

It wasn't long before the candlelight guttered from euphoria, before I was moaning and arching against him again. I was splayed over the bed, limbs weak as sapling branches, and Theodore loomed over me wearing the smuggest smile I'd ever seen. "Do you need a moment?"

"You're feeling very proud, aren't you?"

He bent over me, that smile still on his beautiful face, and set his lips over my breast. "Mmm-hmm."

I curved my back, urging him to take me deeper into his mouth. He obliged, flicking his marvelous tongue over me. "Take off your clothes," I breathed.

He sat back on his knees and started on his buttons. I reached for his trousers with clumsy fingers, eyes stuck on the way his flat stomach and strong chest bunched and flexed as he removed his shirt. He was exquisite, shaped as perfectly as the statues that littered his palace. He watched me with dark, heavy-lidded eyes as I took him in. The curves of his muscles, the dark hair on his chest, the thin trail that ran down toward where my fingers hovered. I undid the fastening, pushing his trousers and underclothes over his hips.

I reveled in seeing him bare, in seeing his eagerness and the large, straining shape of him. I wrapped my hand around him, and he let out an aching breath.

"Lie down," I said, my lips against his chest.

"You don't have to —"

"Shut up." I pushed him back into the pillows with my own

self-satisfied smile curling my mouth. I set my lips around him, and elation fell through me at the hiss of air he pulled into his chest. His hand clasped the back of my neck, fingers gripping my hair. His head rolled back against the pillow, his swollen lips open in a quiet moan.

I was greedy too. I wanted to possess him completely, wanted to be consumed by him, wanted to string the memory of him through my sinew, my marrow, and carry it with me for as long as I lived. Finally, he gave a dark, frustrated growl and hauled me up into his lap.

He looked up at me with a warm, sweet emotion I didn't bother to decipher. It would be hard enough to cut him from my blood, let alone from my heart. His lips were fervent, adoring, as they met mine, as they dragged to my neck, my ear. He guided my hips over his and watched with taut attention as he lowered me, so slowly, around him.

"Gods." I gasped at the rapturous strain of being filled with him.

"Imogen," he said against my neck. He adjusted himself, grasped my backside, and sank all the way inside me. "*Immy.*"

I didn't breathe when he first guided me up and back down around him. He whispered his approval, his awe. Ecstasy was carved into his features, his heated gaze clinging to my every movement. A slow, replete smile lit his face.

"What?" I asked on a moan. He shook his head, hooked an arm around my waist. I squealed as he rolled me back and set a new pace above me. "Tell me."

He stopped, breath heaving as his smile faded into an open, wondrous look. "I have never wanted anything..." He paused. "...the way I want you."

My heart burst. He kissed me before I could reply, and we became a huddle of heavy gasps and trembling muscles and rapturous moans. He swept through every part of me on a rising tide, dissolving all lines, all rationality. Together we sank irretrievably into the sweetest, darkest deep.

The middle of the night was quiet and still. I dozed with my head on Theodore's chest and a heavy leg thrown over his. My finger traced circles across his stomach. Over the weeks, I'd grown to know his mood by the rhythm of his breaths. They came soft and easy now. No tension pulled at his graceful muscles, no agitation splayed through his fingers, as it so often did.

He was at peace. And I envied it. My mind was an eddy of schemes, worries, and awful thoughts. It wove itself into knots trying to piece together some plan that would let me keep him, that would let me stay, but no matter how it twisted and spun it could not find one.

Theodore's breaths were growing shallow as he slipped off to sleep. As his hand fell from where it rested in the narrow of my waist, a knock sounded. I raised my head from his chest.

"Your Majesty?" came a man's voice from the other side of the door. "I got the books."

Theodore grunted, then called out groggily, "Leave them."

"Yes, Your Majesty." A thud sounded. "Night, Your Majesty."

"What books?" I asked Theodore in an overloud whisper. I rose from the bed and padded toward the door, listening closely to make sure no one remained on the other side.

"You have too much energy after all that," Theodore mumbled. "I feel like I've failed you."

"No, I am wrung dry. Utterly spent. Delightfully sore." I smiled at him over my shoulder. "I'm just too anxious to sleep. It's like there are bees in my skull." I pulled open the door. Close to a dozen small books, bound in old, cracked leather, were piled into a basket on the floor, a folded piece of paper laid on top. I dragged them over the threshold and scooped up the topmost book with the folded note that lay upon it.

Theodore watched me with dreamy, tired eyes, the barest smirk on his lips. "Beautiful."

I gave him a coy smile. "As are you." I unfolded the paper and crawled back into bed to read it.

Hermitess Vasili,

I have taken a wife. As a gift, I humbly request use of any and all of the Great God Jesop's books that pertain to magic, the Mage Seers, and the like. As you say, the books belong to the realm of Leucosia. Please know that they will be used to aid, protect, and keep it.

Your King,
Theodore Ariti

Praise be to the memory of the Great Gods that you have found a wife worthy enough to kneel before. You were growing too old.
Here. Return in two days. Just as they are.

I snorted at the curt reply. Theodore chuckled as he looked over the note.

"She lives in the palace," I said. "You should have said you're 'soon to take a wife.' She'll realize the wedding hasn't happened yet and come after you with her stick."

"The woman hasn't left the basement in forty years." He kissed my arm. "Besides, I meant you."

"Oh." My cheeks warmed. "What's this mean?" I asked, my voice soft with overwhelm. "'A wife worthy enough to kneel before'?"

"In Leucosia, a king or queen will kneel to their betrothed, and only their betrothed, as part of the binding ceremony." His eyes were closed. He shrugged. "My father never did it. The hermitess must have remembered that, and stickler that she is, she's likely trying to guilt me into honoring tradition."

I remembered Nemea's mountain the night I'd escaped. The howling wind, how terribly I shook, and Theodore dropping to his knees before me when I swore my oath of fealty to him. I set the book on the mattress, turned on my side, and swiped a lock of hair from his forehead. "You knelt for me." The words were timid, laden with a question.

That dimple of his appeared and disappeared with a quick curve of his mouth. "And I'll do it again later."

I pushed weakly at his shoulder. "When we escaped Nemea's."

He opened his sleepy eyes, looked into mine, then closed them once more. "I've been besotted from the moment I saw you on that overlook in that ridiculous dress. It was easy to kneel."

"You lie," I said, breathless.

He shook his head, eyes still closed. He whispered through a crooked smile. "Besotted." Theodore wrapped an arm around my waist, pulled me close. He gave me a long, slow kiss. Despite his heat, a chill crackled through me. He fell off to sleep, but I remained awake, my eyes on the bed's canopy. Rohana's decrepit voice ran through my head in a taunt.

You are a Goddess-queen.

Take what you want.

24

Sleep never came. I lay at the edge of the bed, propped on the pillow so I could read by the faint light of a single taper. With drooping eyes, I scanned over Jesop's exacting scrawl. It was page after monotonous page of lineages, and tales of the Great Gods from when they were new. Marriages, and deaths, and births, and I found myself cursing Jesop's power of long memory and wishing it had been a gift for fine prose instead.

The sun was sneaking up slowly, brightening the sky beyond the window in a wash of steely gray. I wanted time to stop. I wanted to pore through these books in a blink and find precisely what I needed, but with each useless page turned, my hope dwindled. Even if I learned where Eusia was, even if the exact spell I needed was written out in stark black and white, it would not give me what I truly desired.

I closed the book and looked at Theodore. He slept on his back — full lips parted, brow smooth. The entire world was stacked against us, but my body, my heart, did not seem to care. I had spent the whole of my life wondering what it might feel like to truly belong somewhere, and now I was starting to know.

I picked up the next book. A little blue leather tome with

browned paper and a crumbling spine. With renewed urgency, I flipped through the brittle pages, one after the next, until my eye caught on a section title:

THE FIRST MAGE.

The blanket slipped from my body as I sat up straighter. Knees pulled toward my chest, I gripped the book's case tightly and read on with wide eyes.

> Spell magic was born of malice and jealousy, but I cannot say that it does not have its uses. Its merits are many. It can heal, can divine, can locate the blood through the sea or land or air. In some cases, it can do what Gods' power cannot. There are recorded events of ships surfacing from the deep with the aid of spell magic. Of bodies rising up from their graves. But my warning must be stated clearly:
>
> For all that spell magic can give its user, it will take from them more than double.

The temperature in the room seemed to dip. The grotesque memory of the loose, marled skin hanging from beneath Rohana's milky-white eyes lit my mind. I thought of her bluish teeth and useless body. It was magic that had remade her from maiden into monster.

> When the First Mage began her spell work, it was rumored that she wished to overshadow her sister, the Great Goddess Ligea, who was given immeasurable Gods' power at her birth. The Mage was given very little. Her mind, however,

was shrewd. By spilling her own Siren blood, mixing con-
coctions, making sacrifices, and reciting well-worded
prayer, she was able to make a new kind of power. One that
her sister, the Great Goddess, did not master.

My heart clanged like an incessant noontide bell. The room
was brightening. Theodore roused, but only just enough to scoot
closer. He pressed his sleep-warm body against mine, gave a low
hum, then draped a heavy arm over my middle. I adjusted the book
around him and read on.

The first spell performed was one of goodwill. The Mage
provided a prophecy for a woman who was increasing
with child. She used a single drop of blood, a round of the
mother's fatty flesh, and a potion of seawater and smoking
herbs. The mother wished to know the child's future and
fate, as she had been suffering from portentous dreams.
The Mage predicted the babe would be a great seer. The
Mage called the babe Rohana and saw that she would
advise and protect the Leucosian archipelago for a great
many years.

But at that time, the Mage did not yet know that her new
magic was wholly unlike the power of the Great Gods. The
magic used for spell work has a limit, and a price. With
time, the Mage began to weaken, realizing too late that she
needed to find a way to replenish what her magic took. It
ate her body away, and what had once been robust and vital
grew small and feeble.

The Mage's magic had earned her certain acclaim. She
was known throughout the realm, just as the Great Gods

were. Some feared her, some were awed, and others cursed her, unwilling to trust a rare magic they could not understand. As her health declined, so did her ability to perform spells. When her notoriety dwindled too, a madness set in. She began to seek out past payment from those she had served, and while some chose to pay her out of fear, many did not. For the price was steep.

There is a strange account regarding the mother to whom the Mage had given a prophecy. Based on the account given by the young girl, Rohana, this is what I know:

The babe had grown into a child when the Mage came to her mother for past payment. By now, the Mage's body was so used up that she'd hired herself companions to carry her across the archipelago. They took her to the northern shore of Varya, where the mother and Rohana lived. She entered their small home without invitation. She left two days later with her muscles renewed of their vigor. Her body was once again whole, her clouded eyes bright, and her skin taut once more. Rohana's mother was not seen again.

From then, the Mage consecrated the Sacred Holms as the ritual site for Varya's magic. She tied herself to the soil and sea on a little island there and was able to sustain herself, beaconing seekers of her power to come to her, and conserving her meager energy. So has every island's Mage created a sacred ritual spot to sustain themselves and perform their craft.

"Bloody Gods." I raced to the next page, needing more, but it only gave me rules and laws pertaining to the Mage Seers and their magic. A long list of the divine lineages sat on the page beside.

Rohana's hut rose to the front of my mind. Bones had littered the floor, human and animal alike. I thought of Theodore's story of performing the ritual of transference. He had not been able to take his father's body with him from her awful, rotting hut. I understood why now — it had been payment.

"For the price was steep," I whispered to myself, caught in a dark rush of thought.

Theodore stretched out beside me, a honeyed sound rolling through him. I let him pull me closer, desperate for the contact. Cold terror had seized me.

I glanced at the book once more. The page where the lineages were recorded resembled a web of soft black lace. Jesop's writing was small and precise, the lines connecting the names penned in the thinnest threads of ink. I found the Great God Panos's name first. He was the first in a line of two younger brothers and a sister, all created from the past generation of Gods of the earth. Panos's line dropped down to Theodore's father, Athan. The book was too old for Theodore to have been recorded in it, but his older siblings were. Three of them, and every one had passed before their tenth year.

I saw Ligea next. There were no delicate lines dropping from her name, but there was one line that jutted to the right. A younger sibling.

My body jerked when I read the name.

Eusia.

Eusia. My mother's sister. The First Mage. The monstrous thing that fed on my power and hunted my kind had been the First Mage of the realm.

"Theo." I shook his shoulder. "Theodore, wake up."

His fingers curled into my side, and he gave a sleep-thick groan. "What's wrong?"

IN THE VEINS OF THE DROWNING

"I found something. Tell me of the First Mage's execution. Didn't you say she was killed?"

He blinked, rubbed at his eyes. "I think. If I remember my lessons correctly, she was disemboweled and thrown into the sea off the coast of Anthemoessa."

"Anthemoessa?" I shook my head. The Sirens' home island was far west and now it was uninhabitable due to blight. "She made Rohana's island on the Sacred Holms her ritual spot. How would she have gotten to Anthemoessa?"

He shook his head sluggishly. "I'm sorry, Immy. I don't know. Maybe Agatha would." He pressed a trail of slow kisses over my shoulder, down my arm, but even as his touch poured an indulgent heat through me, I couldn't give myself over to it.

"Eusia is the First Mage," I whispered. "She was — *is* — Ligea's sister."

Theodore froze. His hand rose to the side of my face and forced me to meet his eyes. "Imogen, that's impossible. She was killed."

I shook my head. Held up the book. "It's in here."

"How?" His gaze darted, thoughts seemingly frantic. "How are you supposed to kill something that is already dead?"

"Magic."

Theodore's brows lowered in question.

"Magic," I repeated. The thought of it sent a sick feeling racing through me. "I was going to have to use a spell to break our bond in the first place. I can use a spell to find her. One to unbind us, and one to end her completely."

Tension began to build in his body and his fingers gripped my hair frustratedly. "No. One spell is entirely different from *three,* Imogen. You know what magic does — you've seen Rohana."

"She's used magic for hundreds of years. Three spells won't —"

"*No.*"

"If Eusia remains tied to me, then the Sirens continue to die," I said. He pressed his forehead to mine. "If Eusia and I remain tied to one another, then you and I . . ." I swallowed back the rest of the thought.

Theodore gave me a searching look. "Then you and I what?" There was panic behind the heat in his eyes. I felt it too. The outside world was coming for us with a chisel and hammer, ready to knock us apart, to crack us to dusty pieces. In a breath, we locked in a frantic kiss, both of us desperate from fear. He tugged at my hair, baring my neck to him. "You and I what?"

"Nothing."

He used his other hand to reach between us and spread my legs. He caressed me until I was slick and gasping. "Tell me."

"It's impossible." The blood bond I shared with Eusia was not the only thing that would keep Theodore and me apart. But the contracts and the marriage and the prophecy all fled my mind as he settled his hips above mine, positioning himself.

He looked at me like I were as precious and faceted as a jewel. "You think we're impossible?" My fingers bit into his shoulders as he filled me in one frenetic, claiming thrust. I moaned and his lips met mine. He tried to beat back the terror of what we faced with that kiss. His lips were scorching, purifying, but a darkness lurked at the edges of my mind. It pressed against my flushed skin—a threat cold as death. "You're already mine, Imogen," he said against my cheek. "Mine."

The rising sun gently lit the lines of his muscled body. It filled his eyes. I tried to lose myself in him. Tried to let his words settle over me like it was our very own prophecy, like it was a blessing.

Through our heavy breaths came a clicking sound. We froze. The lock I'd turned over last night was being undone by its key. The door flew open just as Theodore pulled away and jerked the blanket up and over our naked bodies.

Lachlan strode in, eyes on us for a second before he looked straight down to the ground with a curse on his lips. Beyond the threshold, Agatha stood frozen out in the hall, hands at her cheeks in mortification.

"*Out,*" Theodore bellowed.

"I'm sorry. I am." Lachlan dropped to a knee, awkward gaze stuck on the ornate rug. His voice was flat, but I didn't miss the downturn of his mouth, the harshness of his words. "The empress is up and in a piss-poor mood that you never returned to the engagement party last night. She's insisting that you accommodate her and the princess's ceremony on the beach. They want the wedding and the war blessed today."

Theodore's gaze on Lachlan smoldered like embers. His fist turned white where he held the blanket around us. I set a mollifying hand to the middle of his chest and his heart raged beneath it.

"Lachlan." My voice quivered with embarrassment. "Leave. Please. We'll be right out."

He dipped his chin and rose in flinty silence. "Lady Imogen." He spoke my name with unsettling formality. "You spent the night doing exactly the opposite of what you told me you would."

Theodore's eyes flashed. "Get *out.*"

Agatha cursed at Lachlan from the threshold, but Lachlan ignored her and met Theodore's glare. "As your commander and right hand, it is my responsibility to advise you. After the Obelian ceremony, it's best that you and Imogen follow through with the severance."

"I'm the fucking king —"

"If you refuse, I will set the severance to a vote with the council."

"The council has no say in my personal affairs."

"No, but your blood bond is, for all intents and purposes, the catalyst of this war. And it has the potential to create more problems with the empress." He tipped his chin up in a challenge. "We have a say when your personal affairs compromise the kingdom."

Agatha's voice was unfathomable. "*Lachlan.*" His head snapped in her direction, an incredulous look straining his face. She shook her head, brown eyes wide and wounded. "You cannot force them. You cannot do to them what was done to us."

Lachlan's mouth fell open. "Agatha." His voice turned imploring. "Agatha, this is different." The way Agatha shut herself away, so thoroughly and efficiently, made Lachlan rear back. "Agatha —" He rushed after her, slamming the door behind him.

Everything was crumbling. Theodore and I lay twisted in the blankets, silent and stunned. His eyes fell shut as he pulled away from me and moved to the edge of the bed. His strong shoulders stooped. Guilt rose in me like bile. I understood so keenly now why Theodore had not been able to abide my lack of duty, my selfishness, and my cowardice. They were calamitous, and he had fallen headfirst into their depths.

The blood bond in my stomach rioted like I'd disobeyed it. I had caused him harm. My gaze slid to the severing draught on the side table, next to my ring. "Theo," I whispered. "There was another line to the prophecy that I didn't...I couldn't bring myself to tell you. The last line was '*What they have made will decimate the order of all things.*'" Theodore didn't move. "What Ligea and Nemea have made — me. I will ruin everything...I already have —"

"That's enough," he said softly. The shuddering silence stretched as Theodore rose from the edge of the bed. He retrieved clothes and dressed himself, face stern and body tense. Wrapped in a sheet, I pulled myself off the bed and made for the washroom with my head slung low. As I passed the side table, I reached for the severing draught.

"Stop." The word landed like a punch. I whipped my head toward Theodore and his burning gaze. "You are so determined to believe you are some dark harbinger, some monster. I cannot believe — I *refuse* to believe that knowing you, that binding myself to you —" He swallowed hard. "That...that caring for you could possibly be the cause of my ruination. But if you are to devastate me, then let it be completely. Lay waste to me and everything that's mine. A life without you in it is not one I wish to lead."

I held his impassioned gaze, my heart swelling and sinking at once. Words knotted on my tongue. "Think of what you are asking of me, Theodore," I finally managed, my voice raw. "The people who would suffer if we stayed bound. The cost of it for your kingdom. I can't fathom it."

"I don't have the solution yet. I don't know —" He shook his head and gave me a crushing look of desperation. "Do you think we are fated to be as we always have been? You, blighted by fear, and me, devoutly, miserably dutiful. We were both fading away." He crossed the space between us. "You have shone a light on me. You made me feel fury and terror and joy and longing. How do I curl myself back into the darkness after being so alive?"

My throat clamped around tears. Something cold and hard began to spread through my chest. Perhaps it was armor growing around my heart, or perhaps it was my heart itself, shriveling, calcifying, because I understood clearly what I had to do. And I knew just how awful it would be.

I took in his disheveled appearance, his waving hair that looked very much like my fingers had run through it all night. He did not resemble the untouchable king I'd first met. No, I had peeled back his defenses, and he had hardly put up a fight.

"We should hurry," I finally managed. "Be sure to wear your crown."

25

Lachlan and Agatha had not been in the hall when we emerged, and I thanked the bloody Gods. My wine-hued gown was wrinkled from lying in a heap on the floor all night. My hair was wild and loose down my back, and the severing draught in my pocket bumped against my thigh as I hurried along beside Theodore.

We reached the stairs that led down into the entry hall. "I should walk behind you." Theodore stopped hard, affronted. "I'm worried enough about the empress seeing me trail you, never mind me walking at your side. I have a feeling about her . . . I think she knows who I am."

His brow quirked. "Why would you think that?"

"I'll tell you everything when the ritual is over." I gestured toward the stairs. "After you."

With the Great Gods' statues looming overhead, and a deprecating look on his face, he started down the stairs. I kept ten paces behind. The sounds of the palace rose up around us. There were bustling servants and trooping soldiers and courtiers draped in jewels and finery. They moved about the hall in lovely bunches that reminded me of spring bouquets. Theodore reached the bottom of the stairs and lingered, looking up at me with scintillant eyes.

I shook my head at him. "This defeats the purpose."

"I don't want you behind me," he said, in a low and too-fond voice. "I want you at my side." Some kingly defiance straightened his spine. It told me he would not be bent by rules that displeased him. He would not be ordered to give me up by a council that he himself had appointed.

I blew out a resigned breath and his gaze fell longingly to my lips.

"You're very beautiful." His voice was a quiet rumble.

"You're very foolish." I glanced around us, remembering Lachlan's warning to be discreet, then tried to smooth the deep creases in my skirt. "I look like I've been scooped up from the wildlands."

He nodded his agreement. "Even so." He tucked my hand into the crook of his arm. "It's best to keep you like this, I think," he said, as he led us toward the door to the garden. His gaze smoldered as it skipped over my hair, my mouth, the scoop of my neckline. "If I am made a fool by you like this, I'd be incapacitated to see you dressed as you should be."

His attention forced a smile to my lips. "And how should I be dressed?"

"In a crown." He held the door open and looked down at me. "Made with stones the color of honey to match your eyes."

My heart quickened, even as I realized I did not want to be a queen. I did not want the neck-breaking weight of a crown — not as my father's heir, nor my mother's. I wanted to tuck far away from councils and wars and frivolity for something still and quiet and safe.

But perhaps, in another place and time, at Theodore's side, I could bear it.

A cool mist swirled over the garden, dampening the bright blooms. It turned the paver stones slick beneath my slippers. A short path led us to a run of wooden stairs that dropped straight to the socked-in beach. Lachlan and Agatha stood away from the waves, speaking closely with Eftan. The chancellor looked particularly dour this morning, his hands clasped behind his back in balled-up fists. When he saw me on Theodore's arm, his mood somehow darkened further, but Agatha's eyes lit up.

She rushed to my side and took my hand, tugging me closer to the water. A small group of robed Obelian women huddled off to the side, preparing for their ceremony. "I'm so sorry." Agatha held my hand tight. "I tore into Lachlan for barging in on you two like that. I'll never forgive him for suggesting the council vote on your severance." She stared out at the cresting waves, her look sober and dark. "You can't let Lachlan decide for you. You have to make your own choice."

I watched the water too. I could feel it breathe and pulse, a mirror of my own body's rhythms. I guessed it was a mirror to Eusia's too, wherever her split, decrepit carcass might be. "I understand Lachlan's frustrations," I said. "And the weight all this has put on him. Please, don't let it topple what you two are trying to rebuild."

She let go of my hand and scoffed. "It's already toppled." Her gaze was vacuous as she peered at him across the sand. "No. That gives the impression that it can be rebuilt yet again. It's a heap of ash that sits between us, I think." A gust tousled her curls, and she brushed them back with a sad smile on her lips. "We were a long time apart. We used to be complementary shapes, but now we don't quite fit."

An indescribable sorrow overtook me. "But you still love him?"

"Yes. I love him." She swiped quickly at her cheek, at the tear she'd let slip her guard. She looped her arm through mine and squeezed. "That's the worst of it."

"Then keep trying." I wasn't sure if it was sound advice or not, but I wanted her to have what I couldn't. "Perhaps you're trying to make things look the way they used to, but you are different people now. You need time to relearn, to explore what you have each become."

Agatha looked at me with teary, blinking eyes. "All right." She gave me a grateful half smile and I could see a prickling of hope in her look. "That's enough of that."

I peeked over my shoulder to see if the ceremony was to begin, but the Obelians still rifled through an array of small wooden boxes.

My breath hitched when I realized one of the women among them was Princess Halla. She and the two others, her ladies-in-waiting, wore identical robes in a light, fleshy pink. Halla's pale hair hung straight and unadorned, slipping around her shoulders in the breeze. Her angular cheeks were without any rouge, and her lips lacked their usual petal-pink coloring too. When she turned, I stifled a jolt. From her neck to her hem hung a deep red sash the precise color of blood.

The effect was so stark, so jarring, that I had to fight to smooth my features. I could only think of the empress's story of the night the Nels had been slain. Sliced open from nape to groin, bowels spilling to the rug, no doubt by one of King Nemea's men. All so that he might snatch some jewels. It had the mark of him — of his contemptible, craven scheming.

I leaned toward Agatha. "Where is the empress?"

She gave me a troubled look. "She told Lachlan she refused to speak to or be around the king until he apologized for slighting her daughter last night."

"Fucking Gods."

One of the ladies took a tapered crystal stake from a wooden box. It was smooth, flawlessly clear, and its point was terrifyingly sharp. Upon inspecting it, Princess Halla turned to face the small group of us that had gathered on the beach. When her eyes landed on me, they went wide. "Lady Imogen, what a surprise to see you here."

I dipped into a curtsy as her blue gaze darted over my rumpled dress, then up to my unsecured, waving hair. I wore no jewels save the spinel on my finger, no color on my face. I looked like I'd risen directly from a fitful sleep.

Halla sent her attention over the beach once more and said, quietly, sternly, "I'd like a word."

I squeezed Agatha's hand from nerves. "Of course, Your Highness."

The princess started down the beach in a stroll, her arms clasped before her, head bowed. The sand and the water and the sky were all a melding shade of cloudy gray. I couldn't walk much farther, and stopped just as the bond in my stomach began to twist with discomfort. "Your Highness, what would you like to speak of?"

She stopped and spun. "Do you know what the ritual I'm about to perform is for?"

"I was told it was for a blessing." I kept my voice even. My face still. "For your forthcoming wedding. And the war."

"Yes, that's correct," she said, in her lilting way. "I expect you can understand why I would want such a thing."

My brow creased. "Of course."

Halla stepped closer, her white hair pulled back from the breeze, her death-pale face pinched. "Then you will not interfere. I have been tasked with a job here, and I believe that your presence, and the . . . ample time you spend with the king, will prevent me from accomplishing it."

I held her stare, unable to determine if that job was simply to make an heir, or if it was something more sinister, but both prospects made my insides churn. "What is the job you are here to do?"

Her brows lowered. Her soft words came clipped. "That question is out of line —"

I spoke on undeterred. "I know you have lost favor with your mother, Halla. You have done something to make her pass you over as her heir. I expect you want desperately to find her favor again, but I do not trust her, and by proxy I do not trust you. I need to know if you intend to hurt Theodore or his kingdom to get back in her good graces."

I waited for fury, for her to rail over my defamation, but she only looked at me with welling tears. Her silence stretched.

"Answer me truthfully," I said over my thundering heart.

"I have no intention of hurting him." She blinked her tears away and looked out at the roiling gray waves. "I just need to give my mother a grandchild."

There was no comfort in knowing that I would leave both Theodore and Halla to do their duty in providing their people an heir. I should aspire to it as well. To carry on a line, a kingdom, but I could find no purpose in it. No fulfillment or joy. I could not fathom such a thing in a world where I had no safety, no home. I could not fathom carrying on Nemea's line. The prospect smarted like a beating switch.

"Very well." I gave her a sharp nod and made my way back over the wet sand, toward Agatha and Theodore, who both watched me with attuned stares. I avoided each of them with determination.

Princess Halla hung back for a moment, collecting herself. Finally, she made her way toward Theodore, and her diaphanous robe billowed behind her. She lowered herself before him with a flourish. "Your Majesty, I'm grateful for your presence," she said in her winding voice. "Blessing our union is very important to me."

Theodore clenched and unclenched his jaw and stared down at her with unreadable eyes. "It's my pleasure."

She took a step nearer, tilting her head back flirtatiously to look up at him. "The ceremony tends to make me feel ill," she said, her voice turning sweet. "I ask that you do me the honor of standing beside me, as my future husband and king, to catch me when the sickness strikes."

Theodore straightened. "Wouldn't simply kneeling better suit?"

"Not in the least, Your Majesty. I must stand with the sea to my ankles." She lowered her voice. "And I must confess, I fear it."

His lips flattened and he offered her the barest nod before she wove her fingers through his and led him toward the edge of the water. She took slow steps in, waves biting at her hem, weighing it down. Theodore stood behind her and she guided his hands up, so he held her waist. She looked over her shoulder at him, a curving smile on her lips. "Just so."

Writhing possessives overtook me. There was no need for it, but our blood bond lit in a painful, sparking protest. Agatha came to my side and tugged me back. I'd stepped closer to the sea without even realizing it, as if beckoned.

"Deep breath," she said, so only I could hear her. "If we've learned one thing, it's that your control is poorest when your emotions are high."

I sucked in the salt air, but it did little good.

Princess Halla turned in Theodore's hold and gave us gathered on the beach a beatific smile. Her voice rose above the roiling waves. "I know you do not pray to my saint, as I do not worship your Gods, but I ask that you all kneel during the ceremony out of respect."

We lowered ourselves to the sand. I spun through my memories of Agatha's lessons from when I had been a girl, searching for what I'd learned of the Obelian saints. All I could recall was that each family chose their own. The two other robed women walked into the water. They faced the princess and lowered themselves to their knees. The red sashes down their centers floated over the white foam, a thick stream of deep red.

Halla's voice wound through the damp air like a song, reaching high, then dropping low into her chest. It was filled with heart and adoration. "I come with gratitude, with praise, with unending reverence. I come to keep our counterpoise. To take and to give in equal measure."

One of the ladies in the waves raised the crystalline stake and Halla cradled it in both of her hands. "I ask for a happy marriage. I ask for a union that begets many children."

My stomach felt slimy, flipping with sick. I dropped my gaze to my lap, where my interlaced hands had gone white.

Halla's voice softened. "I ask that you strengthen the waters with your power. I ask that you aid King Theodore's fleet. Twist the currents in his favor, fill them with your minions, so that the enemy may be lowered to your devouring dark."

My gaze shot to Halla like a loosed arrow. Cold crackled through me as she twisted the stake and gripped it in one hand. Halla held her other hand out, palm up. "I give you my blood as payment for your blessings." Halla's eyes closed, and she whispered, so quietly I could hardly hear the words over the breeze, "I remember your body sliced open, and your blood spilled." She set the sinister tip of the stake to her index finger and sliced the end of it clean open. Red dripped into the waves. "I give to the sand. I give to the water. Hear me, heed me. Cleanse the sea."

Panic slammed me in the chest. "*No.*" I was on my feet to a chorus of gasps. I strode into the waves, water flying through the air in a wide spray.

Lachlan's sword rang in my ears as he pulled it from his sheath and raced after me. "What the fuck —"

"Stand down, Lachlan," Theodore shouted.

"Theo, you've lost your —"

"Stand *down.*"

I stood before Halla and ripped the stake from her fist. Our gazes stuck. The whites of her eyes were suddenly red, shot through with bright, snaking veins. Somehow, she looked even more like death now with white lips and sunken, gray cheeks. Her knees gave and Theodore braced to hold her up. "Who is your saint?" I demanded, holding the stake between us. "Tell me her name."

"You gave your word — you would not interfere." Her sweet, melodic tones were gone. Now she spoke with the crackling voice of a crone.

Theodore's eyes widened at the sound.

"Answer me." My hand fisted into the front of her robe, jerking her. She could not move at all now. The entirety of her body's weight slumped in Theodore's strong arms.

Halla let out a screeching yowl of frustration, of pain. "Do something, Your Majesty."

"Imogen." Theodore's voice was alarmingly even. I met his gaze over Halla's shoulder and there was something in it that stilled me. Disorientation. The steady, noble man did not know what to do. "Let her go, Im."

I couldn't bring myself to obey. My voice turned heavy and begging. "She worships Eusia."

"*Eusia.*" Halla's red eyes rounded at the name, and her jaw went slack. "You know Eusia?"

"I know her well." My chest heaved with quick breaths. "Why do you worship her? What magic did she perform for you?"

Halla gaped, affronted. "She performed a miracle. For our family."

"She performed a *spell*," I said through my teeth. "What was the payment required for it?"

Some realization crashed over her at my question. Her face went blank. Her mouth closed into a thin, refusing line. My talons slipped from the tips of my fingers and sliced through the front of her robe.

"*Imogen*," Theodore yelled, "let her go."

I shook my head, and with a jerk, I forced her easily from his hold. He wasn't expecting my force. Her body crumpled into the water, but I held her above the surface as I strode in deeper. It was cold and cutting when it reached my thighs. "What did your family pay for the spell?"

The water obeyed when I told it to envelop her like a coiling serpent, and she sucked in a rattling, terrified gasp. "Get me out of the water," she cried in terror. "*Please*."

"You should fear the water, Halla." I pulled her nearer, locked my eyes with hers. "It belongs to *me*."

I sent another current to wrap and writhe around her body. Her trembling cry cut through the morning mist.

"A body," she finally said. "The price for her miracle was a body."

"Whose?" My voice was strange to my own ears. I sounded as vast and powerful as the crashing sea. I blurred into it, losing myself.

Halla jerked in my grip like a fish snagged at the end of a line. Tears poured from her reddened eyes. "My father's. Eusia ensured that my mother would finally have a child. She became pregnant with me. And as payment, she gave her my father."

My face bent with disgust. I looked up to Theodore, who stood frozen behind her, and our gazes stuck for a long, awful moment. "Eusia is a monster," I said to Halla, "and you worship her all the same?"

Even at the stomach-knotting thought of what the empress had done, my mind still slunk back to Nemea. How the empress had said he'd been attentive while she'd mourned her husband. I thought of that disemboweled family, of my ring, plucked from one of their limp fingers. I thought of the red sash that ran down the front of Halla's robe. Of the story of Eusia's execution, her body sliced open and flung into the sea. I thought of the prayer Halla had spoken over the water and how Nemea had taught me the very same one when I was a little girl, bouncing blithely on his knee.

Below the plucking in my chest, below the oily darkness of my bond with Eusia, and the shining warmth of the one I shared with Theodore, was a knowing. A sudden, terrible clarity.

"Imogen." Theodore's voice was an anchor. It brought me back to my flesh and bone. I could feel the distinction between the water and my skin once more. My gaze fell upon him, standing before me like a signal fire, and my eyes burned at his radiance. "Bring her back to the sand, Immy."

I couldn't make myself move. For one step would beget the next, and now I knew where the heartbreaking path forward led.

Theodore walked farther into the waves, and I watched him with studying eyes. The slant of his nose, the hard cut of his jaw, the dark hair that edged his furrowed brow. I thought of his breaths in my ear and his lips on my skin and the shape of my name on his tongue when he'd whispered it in the darkest hour of the night.

"*Now,* Imogen. I am your king." He said it firmly, as if the statement were a solid grip on a trusty hilt. A weapon that had never failed him.

I towed Halla a step closer to the shore. "And what am I?" The question was strung through with more emotion than I cared to reveal. His brow smoothed at the question. "Your subject? Your mistress? Your queen? The heir of Seraf and queen of Sirens? I am none of those things and all of them at once. I belong nowhere and everywhere."

Hurt passed over his face like a storm cloud. "You know where you belong."

"I don't." My throat narrowed. "The only piece of me that has found a true home is my heart." A breath trembled through my lips. "But I am more than that, aren't I? You want this to be tidy and painless. You want things to stay as they are, but I fear everything must be undone before either of us can hope to have what we want."

There was a war within him; I could see it in his eyes. Halla shook in my grip, and I hauled her up, so her face was mere inches from mine. "I will see an end to your *saint*." Unceremoniously, I released her. She fell with a shriek below the surface, and I sent a wave to carry her back to the sand.

Theodore helped collect her from the tangle of sodden silk that she lay in. The effects of the spell she'd performed had slowly worn off. Her color had returned. The red had left her eyes. Her legs shook, and she let herself lean into Theodore's chest. "She said she was your queen," she whimpered, looking up at him, distressed and needy.

Theodore looked to me, then back to Halla. I'd been foolish to speak so plainly, to reveal that I was a threat to her claim on him and her title, but I could only hope that Theodore would neutralize it. He took a full breath. "She is."

I stared at him, dumbstruck.

There was a note of promise in his voice, as if telling Halla the entirety of what sat between us might let him keep me. "Imogen is the Siren heiress. We share a blood bond, and as a result, she can use my power. Our bond will keep her safe as she travels to find . . . to find Eusia."

Halla stood leaning against him for a long moment, stunned. Slowly, she raised a trembling hand to Theodore's cheek. When she spoke, her voice was once again sweet and smooth. "My mother will crush us all for this."

Theodore's face went stony.

"You gave your word, did you not? That *I* would be your queen." Her thumb traced the line of his cheekbone. "And isn't the word of a king as binding as a scratch of ink from his pen?" Her words turned cutting, menacing. "See your bond broken, Your Majesty. Our wedding is in one week."

Her threat stung me, sent my need to protect him surging. I clamped my jaw against the impulse and reached into my pocket for the severing draught. I stopped when I felt something through the water. The plucking in my chest sped faster. Cold fingers brushed my ankle. Broken talons scratched up my calf.

"Not *fucking* now." I sent a command shooting through the waves. The nekgyas rose up at my behest, breaking the surface with empty eyes. Halla screamed and scurried out of the water completely. Lachlan, Eftan, and Agatha all reared back too. Three Siren corpses stood before me. Their blue-gray flesh was knit through with seaweed and rot.

They spoke in unison through their black mouths, as Eusia's voice echoed through my skull. *"Home. Home. Home."*

Eusia had sent them to mock me. To tell me once more what she'd been trying to tell me from the start. To tell me what I'd tried so hard to ignore.

"I know." I hoisted my clinging skirt and turned toward the shore. The water curled up my shins as I strode out of the sea. The nekgya still chanted their taunt, even as my wet slippers met dry sand. Everyone gaped, Theodore included, as I kept moving up the beach. When I reached Lachlan, I stopped. "I'll need a ship to escort me to Seraf when I wake."

"When you wake?"

"Yes." I reached into my pocket and pulled out the severing draught so only he could see it.

He gave me a grave nod. "I'll see it done."

Head hung, I moved past Eftan and Agatha, clutching my dripping skirt in my hands. Eftan made a sound of protest as Theodore crossed the sand after me. "Your Majesty, leave her."

Theodore had left Halla drenched and shaking behind him. "We need to speak." He reached for me, and though it cracked me in two to do it, I stepped back from his touch. "Will you come with me, Immy? Please."

"Go to your fiancée."

"Eftan will look after her."

"She's *yours* to look after," I said. "See to your duty, Theo. And I will see to mine."

Theodore flinched like I'd struck him across the cheek. "Imogen... I refuse to lose you —"

"You were meant to lose me from the start." My voice was shredded and weak. "I gave you my word in Nemea's fort. Please, let me keep it." I clutched the draught in my fist and turned away from him, hurrying toward the stairs to put distance between us.

This isn't the end, I lied to myself as I wrestled the cork from the vial. We'd have more time. We'd tease one another again, and fight, and I'd feel again the deep timbre of his voice reverberating through me when we lay chest to chest. I told myself he was still mine, even as I set the bottle to my lips and tilted my head back.

"Imogen?" There was anguish in Theodore's voice. "No."

I picked up my speed. The sludgy draught slid over my tongue and stuck in my throat. At the stairs that led up to the garden I fought to swallow it down. It tasted like rot, black and thick as tar. The pain came a beat later. A hot dagger that sliced slowly through the middle of me. My knees buckled on the first step. My vision blurred. My head rocked like a club had struck it.

There were strong hands on me. Sounds that were muffled by a high ringing in my ears. I could only focus on the rushing ache in my chest. The liquid that was filling my lungs.

I tried to breathe in and a gurgling sound came from my throat. "I can't . . . I can't breathe."

"Imogen."

I knew that voice. It pierced through the pain, through the heartache.

My chest burned and swelled. *You cannot drown,* I told myself, trying to ease my panic, but I *was* drowning. Someone carried me and I gasped and gasped. There was a blur of color in my periphery — flowers. Bubbling in my throat. Metal on my tongue. Liquid, hot and thick, rolled over my lip and down my chin. It filled my nose. I blinked and I could feel it, sticky in the corners of my eyes.

My body jostled, cradled within those strong arms. I coughed and felt the liquid spray and fall over my cheeks. As my vision left me and my lungs scorched with the anguish of drowning, I felt the sun.

Theodore.

His power.

Hot and unwavering, it poured through me like molten gold. It tried desperately, determinedly to beat back the darkness.

But the darkness won.

PART III

THE DEEP

26

There was nothing in the darkest, deepest part of the sea but pressure. The kind that morphs a living thing into a grotesque, slanted version of itself.

And that was where my body lay. Under all that water. Moldering. Changing.

An unbankable heat hollowed out my stomach. It was not a heat like Theodore's, gentle and warm as daylight. It was hellfire. It boiled my blood, scalded my veins. My sight was gone, my hearing muffled, and I was being emptied. Theodore was leaving me, one drop of glistening Gods' blood at a time.

I'd never known the sea without his power stitched through me. I'd never known the sea with only my bond to Eusia lingering in my gut.

Theodore's absence would bring me more than heartache. For awful things filled empty spaces. And it was in the darkest, deepest part of the sea that monsters were made.

27

I sucked in a breath like I'd broken the surface of the water. My body was overwarm, covered in a clammy coating of sweat. I stared up at a ceiling I didn't recognize. It was unadorned — no gilded trimming or painted vines. It didn't smell of vetiver soap and summer, like Theodore's room did, but of dull mint and lavender flower and the sharp note of nepenthe.

For a moment, I wondered if I was still in the palace at all, and it felt like my chest collapsed in on itself. The narrow bed creaked as I sat up and let my legs fall over the edge. My entire body was sore as a swollen, beating bruise. The thin gray sleeping gown I wore was rough against my tender skin.

I scanned the little room, my mind stuck in a thick fog. There was a glass of water and small bottles of medicine on the shelf beside the bed. A washbasin sat below the window where glittering beams of afternoon sunlight sliced through the glass and pooled on the floor.

My eyes stung. The damned shafts of light reminded me of Theodore. I was empty, scraped clean of the warm spot where our bond had resided, but he still lingered. He was everywhere. On my skin, in my body. I could still hear the echo of his voice in my ear.

It was bitter determination that forced me to stand. That forced me to bite back my tears and set my mind to my task. I could not sit alone in a nightdress, weeping at sunlight, or I would fall apart entirely. I had to get to Seraf. Nemea held the answers I searched for.

I made for the washbasin and paused at a new weight that hung around my neck. I reached up and tugged a long gold chain from where it rested beneath my clothes. It was finely made, with a little diamond set into the clasp, and at its end hung my engagement ring. The stormy gray spinel. My teeth clamped. I let it fall against my sternum, then set to scrubbing my skin with the frigid water.

There were folded clothes on a bench at the foot of the bed. My gaze stuck to the dark trousers and tunic. They were folded into neat, small rectangles and wrapped tightly in twine, just the way Theodore had folded our clothes while we'd traveled through the wildlands. A pair of lovely black boots sat beside them. When I noted the second pile of clothes, I stilled.

It was a gown. Black as night, but the rich fabric held the faintest sheen of iridescence. Like Siren wings. I let my fingers play over the deep V of the neckline. Tidy little stitches of midnight thread depicted a scrolling vine. It curled up to the shoulders, the splay of leaves and star-shaped blooms beautifully rendered. My fingers froze. Tucked into the vines, so the eye could not tell where one ended and the next began, were feathers.

I pulled a breath through my tight throat. He'd had a binding gown made for me. Black to resemble the endless blood bond, when the boundaries of two faded to nothing and they became one. I tried to douse the flare of hope that lit in me. I picked up the gown to shake out the skirt, and something small fell from its folds. It landed on the wood floor with a *ping*. My joints rioted as I bent to retrieve it.

Another ring. Clawed into the gold filigree setting was a large, honey-colored jewel. The very color of my eyes. I forced them shut. "Gods damn you, Theo."

The door swung open on silent hinges and a young, bright-eyed woman with smooth, brown skin strode in. "Oh! You're up." She gave me a small smile, but her gaze skipped over every part of me, taking dutiful account. She wore her black hair pulled tightly back and under a gauzy white cap. Her dress was a deep, Varian green, its lines simple beneath her stark white apron. "Are you feeling well? You look like you've seen a ghost."

Theodore's ring pressed into my palm as I curled my fingers around it. "No ghosts," I breathed. But I did feel as if I were being haunted.

"Well, thank Panos for that." She closed the door behind her. "Let's get you dressed, Your Majesty."

My gaze shot to hers. "Excuse me?"

The woman's eyes went wide. She dipped into a fast curtsy. "Forgive me. I'd been instructed by the king to address you as Your Majesty."

"By the king. But *why?*" My heart pounded heavily in my ears. I lost hold of reason and wondered for a breath if Theodore had found some way around Halla and her mother.

She gave her head a panicked shake. "I assumed because you are a queen, Your Majesty. Ligea's heiress, I was told."

"Oh." I blinked, feeling foolish. "Of course." I looked to the bed, brow furrowed. "How long was I . . ."

"Three days." Eyes cast down in uncomfortable reverence, the woman shook out the new chemise and stays and underclothes that had lain beneath the gown.

"I'll wear the tunic."

She looked up at me, puzzled. "But it's wrapped so neatly for your travel. His Majesty was very careful in how he folded them. I believe he was eager for you to wear this gown. It's lovely, isn't it?"

My thoughts blurred. "Was he here?" Distracted, I let her pull the sleeping gown from my shoulders and slip the chemise over my head.

"He carried you here himself yesterday morning." She wrapped the stays around my rib cage and began lacing them. "He saw to your care the first day and a half himself. Once you stopped bleeding . . . that's when he turned you over to us healers."

"I see." Sorrow ran through me, violent as a surge. He'd left me. I'd told him to do as much, to see to his duty, and yet I couldn't stamp out the pain of it. I donned the underclothes and stepped into the gown. She lifted it up over my hips, then strung the bodice around me with gentle tugs.

"It's not my place, Your Majesty," she started, carefully, "but if it helps you to know, he did not leave you willingly." She tightened the bodice and tucked in the ties. "Chancellor Eftan dragged him out." I nodded, unable to discern if that news was a twisting knife or a soothing balm. "Your companion, the one with the curls, was worried sick over you as well. Even the Empress of Obelia came to your bedside last night — quite vexed over your state. And this was left for you." She pulled a sealed envelope from her pocket and my heart lurched.

The wax cracked as I opened it. I crinkled it in my tight grip when I realized it wasn't from Theodore.

Imogen,

*A ship has been readied for you, as you requested.
Please do not sink it. The Hercule is quick and small*

*and has been fitted with a hearty crew. Each sailor is
Siren-bound and will be immune to your lure, but I
wouldn't be surprised if you found some way around
that divine protection. You do so love denying us men
our breath. A carriage will carry you to the docks
when you wake. Find Chancellor Eftan so he can send
for it.*

I wish you a successful endeavor.
Cmdr. Lachlan Mela

The letter felt like a rough push out the door. I folded it closed. I set the ring I held on the bench and quietly slipped my boots on. Before I made to leave, I gathered the twine-wrapped clothes that Theodore had left me. "Thank you."

"Don't forget this!" The young healer plucked the ring. It caught and glinted in the shaft of sunlight as she handed it to me.

I stared at the warm, shining stone, and anger burst through me like a flint strike. I'd certainly not been fool enough to think that our severance would have been a clean, painless excision, but neither did I think Theodore would have been this naïve.

He should have let me go completely. No ring, no binding gown. They were promises that he could never keep.

The healer watched me staring at the ring, and her brows rose expectantly. "Do you feel well? Is there anything else you need? Some nepenthe for any lingering pain, perhaps."

I slipped the ring quickly onto my finger. "No." I strode out into the hall. I'd change once I made it to my ship.

The entry hall was being decorated for a wedding. Deep blue Obelian flags hung beside Varian ones. They lined the black marble banisters and hung above lintels. It looked like a fucking garden had been planted at the base of each of the curving stairs. Vines wove through their balusters and curled around the ankles of the Great Gods' statues. Servants darted beneath them with baskets of tapers and bundles of flowers in their arms.

Just as those vines seemed to wind through the palace with abandon, so too did a black, plaguing anger begin to creep through me.

I nearly strode past the palace's front doors myself, perfectly capable of arranging my own carriage, when my gaze caught on Eftan. He and a woman in a servant's uniform stood at the base of the far stairs, looking over papers and taking stock of the state of the entry hall.

When he saw me, his round face puckered. He strode toward me with short, quick steps, his widened gaze skipping over my visage, over the gown I wore, and finally, it stopped at Theodore's ring on my finger. His thin lips curled back. "The king is a fool."

I sucked in a tedious breath. "Hello, Chancellor."

"You beguiled him. You tainted him." He took me by the arm and, short man though he was, began to haul me toward the palace doors. "You have pushed this kingdom toward utter ruin, and he dresses you up like a play bride for it. Leave. Leave now, before he sees you."

I ripped my arm from his hold and nearly threw him off his balance. "He marries the princess in four days," he spat, "and you cannot return. Not as his mistress, not as his —" He gave a violent gasp, face going from red to a deepening purple.

I cocked my head at how easily the lure had slipped from me, at how quickly my power obeyed my barest desire. It was different now, without Theodore's bond strung through my middle. "Dear

Eftan," I crooned, as the man pawed at his throat. "I've come to you for a carriage. So that I may leave and never return. Will you help me?"

He gave a frantic nod.

A slow smile curved my lips. "How good of you."

I turned on my heel for the doors and released the lure, listening eagerly for the echo of his desperate inhale as it bounced off the marble.

The afternoon was warm and clear. Damp, flower-scented air pushed through the cracks of the carriage door. I'd grown so used to the scent and how it mingled with the sea that I hardly noticed it anymore, but I pulled in a heavy breath now as the carriage jostled me over the blue cobblestone road that led toward Panos Port.

My mind churned like the surface of the sea, with black and lashing thoughts. They kept leading me back to Nemea, to his empty gray eyes and unyielding cruelty. To his cold, dry mountain, far, far from the sea. I'd never thought I'd return. I'd done all I could to avoid it. But of all the people in the archipelago who might know where Eusia was, it was him.

Before the carriage lurched to a stop, I slipped the ring Theodore had given me onto the chain around my neck and huffed a breath thinking about the future I could fund with my collection of engagement jewels. My hair had been washed while I'd been asleep. It smelled of sweet flowers and orange, and I plaited it down my back in a long braid. When I was done my hands had stopped shaking.

As I adjusted on the bench, something sharp poked my thigh. I searched the seat beside me, ran a hand over my dress. I froze at the square of folded paper that I felt in its pocket. A letter. Sealed in green wax, pressed with Theodore's sigil — a hand wrapped in vines.

My shaking returned as I tore through it. I pressed the paper over my lap to keep it still enough to read.

Immy,

I begin uncertain what to write you. I am overcome by the empty space you have left behind. Please know, I had no intention of leaving you. I was ordered to do so by my council. They said I have forgotten my duty, that I have brought war upon us with my lack of control. Eftan refused to let me give you the binding gown and ring until I threatened to have him permanently removed from the palace.

All this to say, I am adrift.

I am bereft, but I think my purpose is growing clearer than it ever has been. My duty, my desire — they have become one entity. They are both unquestionably tied to you. The absence of you has shown me that, if you will let me, I will happily carve myself open again and pour you back inside me. I cannot see how yet. I don't know the way. But if you will have me again at the end of all this — even if you won't — I am yours.

For now, I must do terrible, punishing things to keep my people and you safe. Come back to me and absolve me of them.

Yours unendingly,
Theo

I smoothed a hand over the creased paper, my heart weighty and pained in my chest. "Gods, Theo." He would completely forgo his duty to his kingdom if I ever returned to him. He would let me utterly ruin him. And yet, if I were honest, that was precisely what I wanted. Eyes burning, I refolded the paper and tucked it beneath my stays, above my breast.

Terrible, punishing things.

The driver pulled us to a stop beside another palace carriage, this one large and drenched in carved golden vines. I choked on a breath. My carriage door swung open, and the footman reached in a hand.

I shook my head. "Is that the king's carriage you parked us beside?" If he saw me with his ring, in his gown, his scant resolve — and mine — would disintegrate.

"Uhh." He walked away from me, then returned. "Aye, Your Majesty. It is."

"What the hell is he doing at the bloody docks?"

The man pushed his lips forward, taking me in with round brown eyes. "I can't say. Should I find out?"

"No, no, no. I'll just walk fast. Do you see him?" The man looked left, then right. Then he shook his head. I gripped the little bundle of traveling clothes Theodore had left me and bounded out of the carriage without taking the footman's hand. "Thank you."

The docks were crammed and sprawling. Rows and rows of damp wooden planks and a forest of masts surrounded me on all sides. I was swallowed up by sailors and merchants hauling goods up and down gangplanks, their whistles and shouts piercing my ears. Squinting through the sunlight, I read the nameboards on the bows, and when I reached the end of the first run of decking I stopped. The water in the harbor was so blue and clear, so gentle and rolling, that I nearly forgot what swam through it.

A ship in the distance caught my eye. I raised a hand to block the glare. Those were Obelian flags flapping at the top of each of the ship's four masts. A cluster of ice-blue runes on a sapphire background that had always reminded me of snowflakes.

That was the empress's ship.

The wedding was currently being prepared for — the entire palace in a spin to see that everything was done and ready. I couldn't comprehend why the empress would leave just days before her beloved daughter wed, what with her demands and detailed contracts ensuring Halla's devoted care. All that talk of heirs and allowances and gardens to worship her monstrous saint in, and she was leaving before seeing Halla in her bridal gown.

The ship slunk past the breakwaters and realization struck me. The empress would never have left unless she'd gotten what she'd truly come here for.

Her contracts.

Her trade routes secured, treaties guaranteed. My stomach fell. Theodore must have signed them. For why else would a woman like the empress come all this way south? She could have shipped Halla off to be married on her own, like all rulers did with their children. She did not make the treacherous journey for the love of her child, even if she had sacrificed her husband to have her. Everything the empress did, every choice she made, every order and request, secured her own power.

A chill slithered over my skin despite the warm afternoon. I gritted my teeth at the building pressure in my chest when resounding whoops and cheers drew me in. Behind me, the crowd shifted and fanned out as the metallic clacking of armor sounded. I rose up on my toes and saw a flash of gold.

It was Theodore's retinue. He must have seen the empress off. Princess Halla's halo of white hair came first, luminescent as a pearl stolen from the seafloor. The glimpse was quick, as his soldiers soon barred my line of sight. Mindless and foolhardy, I pushed my way to the front of the throng. It was as if my body were being drawn by a magnet, my gaze hungry for a parting view of him.

A boot landed on my toe; an elbow jabbed my sternum. I tucked myself behind a tall, broad dockworker and when I saw Theodore, I lost all sense of pain and place. I evanesced into nothing but yearning. He looked like a myth, as stern and beautiful as the God he'd come from. His soot-colored coat and trousers accentuated the stunning lines of his body. The wind had pulled at a few dark locks, and they waved over his brow. I was close enough to see the green of his eyes, the curving line of his full lips. His mood was gloomy, his head bent down to the decking as he passed.

That weight on my chest crushed down harder. I wanted to scream *Look at me,* but I drove my teeth together. I stared at his back for one more tight breath before I forced myself away from the crowd of onlookers.

"Imogen?"

I froze, then whirled to see Lachlan, suited in his golden, vine-etched armor. He'd broken away from the procession and taken me in with startled hazel eyes. He closed the space between us in a few long-legged steps.

"I'm leaving. I'm just looking for the —"

He threw his arms around me. His rerebraces and vambraces pinched my arms. His breastplate scuffed my chin.

I grunted. "What the hell are you doing?"

He pulled away and held me by the shoulders. "Glad you're not dead."

My brows quirked. "Was I nearly?"

His mouth popped open as some memory seemed to surface in his mind. "Theodore certainly thought so," he said, somber. "Agatha too. They mourned that first day as if you'd gone."

I shrugged out of his hold, hating the way my eyes stung. "But not you, right, Commander? Death would have been a much cheaper way to be rid of me, after all."

His mouth twisted sardonically. "You think I wanted you dead?"

"The lover of your king is your enemy, and all that." My brows rose. "I almost killed you too, don't forget."

"I hadn't." He shook his head. "I don't want you dead. I don't want Theo miserable, which he currently is. I just need this kingdom whole and safe." He stared out over the bustling docks. He bore a new burden too. It was in the grim line of his brow, the somber set of his mouth. "How do we see all that done?" I gave my head a resigned shake, which he met with a condescending look. "Come now, you're the embodiment of a Great Goddess. Ichor in your veins. Stubborn and greedy for what's yours. You'll find a way." He pointed to a ship behind me. "That one." His half smile left his eyes flat, cheerless. "Goodbye, Imogen."

Despite his words, it was a hopeless farewell. I could only nod in reply as he started on his way. "Lachlan," I called out, surprising myself. He returned with a question on his face. "I . . . could use your advice. You spent all those years away from Agatha . . . How? How did you keep yourself together?"

He scratched at his chin with a gauntleted hand. "You don't want my advice."

"I'm low on options, Commander."

He huffed an uneasy laugh. "All right. If you must know — I drank and I whored. Then after a few years, I took proper lovers. I was never without one. I felt worst when I was alone. It wasn't until many years later that I took a friend as a lover. And he . . . he was good for me. He showed me care and helped me climb out of the low places that I'd made my home."

"And you were happy in that time? With him? Without Agatha?"

Lachlan shook his head. "I'm sorry, Imogen. I was content. I was satisfied and enamored. But I was never happy like I was with her." He gave me an apologetic shrug. "But you're not me. Plenty of us fools move on to find better love. Perhaps there's hope for you yet."

I blew out a long breath. "I feel worse."

"I tend to have that effect."

I laughed, then glanced behind me. *Hercule* was carved into the nearest ship's nameboard, the scrolling letters painted red. I moved toward its gangplank. "Tell Agatha I love her."

"As soon as I can find her."

I stopped. "What?"

He was unbothered, but an alarming prickle sped down my body. "Haven't seen her since last night. She's likely just taking some time to herself after everything that's happened. You know how she is."

The oddity of it struck me. Agatha would never have left my side. She would have refused to let me wake in that strange room alone — but I was being absurd. She was no longer my keeper, and I did not want her to be. Besides, Agatha was sharp claws and full of mettle, with a spine like steel. I had no reason at all to feel such foreboding. I gave Lachlan a pointed look. "Find her. The second you get back to the palace go search for her. Tell her I'll come back safe."

His brow knit like I was being ludicrous. "All right," he said, flippantly. He sobered at my stern glare. Nodded. "All right. I will."

"Good. Thank you." I started for the *Hercule* feeling like my heart was close to rupturing. "Take care of them both," I said over my shoulder. He flattened his lips, nodded his head, and disappeared into the crowd.

The gangplank bowed under my weight, and I held my skirt in my hands, studying the way the light shifted over the fabric.

Purples and blues and greens swirling over its black surface. I made straight for the cabin the captain appointed me, locked the door, and tie by tie, I yanked the gown from my body, peeling away the vines and feathers like they were an old skin. A lump sat in my throat as I folded it carefully and set it safely at the end of the cot.

The twine burned my fingers as I tore it from the folded trousers and tunic. They'd been made to fit me. My fingers bumped over the little gold buttons down the back of the tunic. It was designed to be opened to make space for my wings.

I forced the tunic on, when clanging rang through the side of the ship. A tolling bell. A low, eerie horn reverberated through the air, pulling my muscles taut with its warning. I ran from my cabin, out onto the deck, where the crew was frantic. They hurried to retie ropes that they'd already undone. They looped the mooring line back around the cleat. Even the docks below were clearing, people running toward the cobbled streets of the island, away from the harbor.

The ship's crew was starting down the gangplank. "What's going on?" I asked a sailor, pulling her arm to halt her. Her cheeks were sun-weathered, freckled, and lined.

"Enemy ships," she said, inclining her head out toward the horizon.

I had to squint, but I went deathly still when I saw them.

Those familiar smudges.

Those red sails.

Serafi warships.

28

Half a dozen Serafi ships sat on the line of the sea. The fleet moved toward the harbor quickly, their ominous sails full of a northeasterly wind. Beyond the breakwaters, Varian warships weighed their anchors and cast off. They moved at a clip, out to the open water. There were other warships docked too, hundreds of sailors on their decks, hurrying to get their vessels pushed away from their slips.

I felt an unfathomable responsibility for them all.

It was because of Theodore and me — joining our blood on the floor of that drafty chamber at the top of King Nemea's crumbling fort — that they were now in harm's way.

The rope above me bit into my palm as I gripped it and pulled myself up to stand atop the ship's rail. I took in the whole of the docks. Another Varian warship was two slips away from the *Hercule*. Sailors readied the ship to sail, climbing over the rigging as easily as spiders did the strands of their webs.

"Your Majesty." The *Hercule*'s captain looked up at me from the deck. His dark red hair was cropped short. The sun had darkened his skin with a thick covering of freckles. He narrowed his light brown eyes as he reached a hand up, a silent order that I come down. "Protocol states that the docks empty until the navy clears the threat."

I pointed behind him, toward the warship. "I'm going with them."

He spun to look at the ship. "Going where?"

"Toward the Serafi fleet. I'm going to sink them."

He smiled, a patronizing twist to his brow. "The king and commander were very clear in their orders. You are under my protection till your task is done. You've set foot on my ship, you're my responsibility now."

The thought of being "his to protect" set a burrowing fury through the vacant space in my gut — where Theodore's bond had sat. I had no time to reason with him. I refused to beg his permission. With half a thought, I threw out a silent lure. The captain only gave a shake of his head, then looked up at me with foggy eyes. "What the hell was that?"

My brow knit. The lure hadn't hooked in. I remembered Lachlan's letter — the entire crew was Siren-bound and therefore immune to my lure. I jumped down from the rail and blew out a frustrated breath. "I hope you're prepared to grovel before your king, then, Captain, because I have no plans to remain under your watch." I skirted around him, but before I reached the gangway, he grabbed the band of my trousers and hauled me back like I was a misbehaving cur on a lead.

I spun, breaking free of his hold, and threw my fist into the edge of his jaw. It was a poor punch, and a driving pain shot through my hand, but he went stumbling backward, groaning and holding his chin, nonetheless.

Heart as loud as the tolling alarm bell, I hurried down the gangplank. When the captain raced down behind me, I threw my arms wide to keep my balance. The man was my height, thinly built, but

I was hardly faster than he was. I took a turn on the docks, leaping over the corner where water sloshed up to wet the wood. His boots drummed on the planks, the sound growing louder as he drew steadily nearer. The port had mostly cleared now. Those who remained were naval sailors and soldiers, tending mooring lines before their ships pushed out to battle.

I sent out four lures and praised the bloody Gods when I felt them slice into the sailors before me, taking hold deep in their chests. It had been effortless. My command had hardly formed in my mind before the men obeyed it. Once I raced past them, they made a blockade to bar the captain, tangling him in their arms like an animal in a snare. I ran faster toward the warship, my power suddenly bursting through my chest more intensely than ever, a mass of hot, gurgling sludge.

Two uniformed sailors were loosening the warship's mooring lines and readying to hurry back up the gangplank. "Wait," I yelled to them, stalling their progress.

A guttural scream from behind me hitched my strides. I whirled, peering through the windblown strands of my hair, as one of the sailors I'd lured pulled a dagger from their belt. Another wrestled the captain of the *Hercule* to the docks and set a heavy boot to his shoulder, pinning him as another held his legs.

Panic shot through me like lightning. "*Stop.*" I'd said the command clearly, I'd thought it with intention, but my lures would not dislodge. That pour of hot sludge continued through me and I gritted my teeth, trying to rein it in. It was *my* power, after all, but the bond I shared with Eusia had changed since the severing ritual. It had strengthened.

My bond with Theodore must have kept her hold on me at bay.

The sailor pinning the captain reared his dagger back, just as the ship's gangplank ahead of me was being lifted from the dock. "*Shit.*"

I was mere feet away from boarding. "Put it back," I yelled. "Let me on!"

But the sailors only looked at me with befuddlement and continued hauling the gangplank up.

My attention was too splintered, my terror a buzz in my ears. My entire body was power-riddled, consumed. Possessed. Reluctantly, I sent out new lures, this time to the sailors on the ship, commanding them to return the gangplank to its position. Their faces slackened. Their eyes glazed. As they returned the gangplank, I ran back down the docks, toward where the *Hercule*'s captain fought and shouted.

Two sailors held him down at each shoulder. One sat upon his legs. And the fourth sailor drove his dagger down. I screamed, sending new lures, tugging on the ones that were still hooked through their ribs, but nothing I did knocked them from their task. The dagger sank into the captain's belly with a sickening, wet thud. His scream shredded the air as I reached the sailor who held the dagger. I extended my talons and sank them into his arm, but the man who sat upon the captain's knees lunged. He locked an arm around my neck. With all his weight, he brought me down hard onto the docks. I shredded at his arm too, sending his blood pouring down the front of my tunic, but he made no sound, he gave no quarter.

I could only watch as the dagger sawed through the captain's belly, straight down in a vertical line. From sternum to groin. His entrails bubbled from the gash and spilled to the dock. Blood ran thick and dark through the cracks, it seeped into the waterlogged wood, and still he screamed and screamed and screamed. In a few horror-struck breaths, the captain quieted.

That was when they spoke the prayer. "I give to the sand. I give to the water. Hear me, heed me. Cleanse the sea." The sailors stood.

They used their booted feet to roll the captain's limp body off the edge of the dock and into the empty slip.

A trembling breath fell through my lips as all the burning power in me began to cool.

Finally, the sailor who held me let me go, and he too walked to the edge of the dock. Blood streamed from his ruined arm, but they all stood blank-faced, watching as shadows passed through the water below them. I rose up to my knees, gaze riveted on the dark streaks cutting through the sea.

The nekgya had come for the body. For the offering. The water frothed and turned pink and then, as if instructed to do so, all four sailors mumbled Eusia's prayer once more. I held my breath as they stepped off the dock, into the deep, bloodstained water.

I marched up the gangplank, shaking and cold. My tunic was wet with the blood of the sailor who'd held me back, and it clung to my stomach. The bond I shared with Eusia was like a hand slipped inside me. I'd become a puppet, and she the master.

My gaze locked on the sailors at the top of the gangplank. The sailors that my lures were still strung through. Their eyes were glazed, their bodies loose. The thought struck me: *They are marionettes at the end of your strings. You are no better than her.*

When my boots hit the deck, I released their lures in a rush and waited with bated breath. I waited for praying lips and fisted daggers, but they both shook their heads like they'd awoken from a feverish dream.

One set a hand to his brow like it ached, but both went about their business as they had before. They heaved the gangplank onto the upper deck, and soon the ship cast off into the harbor. It bobbed beneath me, and once its sail caught the wind, it lurched.

"Who are you?" The woman's voice behind me was rasping and harsh.

I whirled and knew precisely who I faced. There was no doubt, what with her perfectly pressed uniform, her steely eyes, and the abundance of medals pinned to her chest. The warship's captain. She was reedy and time-hardened, twice as old as all the other soldiers and sailors around us. Her eyes cut down to the bloodstain on the front of my tunic and narrowed further.

My mouth dropped open, my mind blank. I was still dazed from the gutting I'd just witnessed. "I ... I'm —" I couldn't even think of what to call myself. "Captain, I —"

Her fair brow lowered dangerously. "A stowaway, then."

"No." I still shook but tried to stand straighter. I tried to imbue my body with the easy command that Theodore always wore like weightless armor. "I'm Imogen Vathia." All this time I'd been unable to remember Ligea's inherited name, and now it fell from my mouth as easily as an exhale. She'd been *Vathia* for the spirit of the deep water that had helped create her. "Daughter and heiress of the Great Goddess Ligea. I'm here to help you sink those ships."

The captain's eyes widened as she studied me. "I knew Ligea. She aided my ship once before, when I was a new captain, many decades past." She pursed her lips. "You have the look of her." She scanned her crew as they milled over the deck. "We have rules about Sirens on our ships, Your Majesty," she finally said.

"And they are?"

A deep thunderous boom rent the air, pulling our attention. The Serafi and Varian ships were close enough to exchange cannon fire, and the first shot appeared to have hit a mast on one of the Varian ships, snapping it in the middle like a branch in a windstorm.

The captain took a deep, uneasy breath. She glanced down once more at the dark stain of blood. "If a Siren is on board, wax is required for all sailors, so they aren't affected by their song. But seeing as you are the Goddess's daughter, I expect wax will do little to keep them safe from your silent lure?"

My mouth went dry at the mere thought of my power. At how tangled and dangerous it had become. "No," I managed. "It won't."

"I'll need your word, then," the captain said, holding my gaze.

"My word?" The wind sliced, pushing salt mist up my nose, setting my power strumming through my middle.

"If I let you remain on this ship, Your Majesty, then we are all at risk. I am entrusting the safety of every crew member and soldier into your hands. The Goddess could be a terror, but she was precise in the execution of her power. Are you like your mother?"

My entire body stung from the onslaught of shame and worry, from the responsibility she was asking me to bear. Dark, sticky blood stained my vision. The *Hercule*'s captain's death screams echoed in my ears. I knew nothing at all of my mother, and my power was anything but precise. I was certain, too, that Eusia would relish an offering as grand as an entire warship of Varian bodies. But despite all that, I opened my mouth and said, "I am."

The captain gave me an approving nod. "Then welcome aboard."

The cannon fire grew louder. The ship rolled and dipped over the striated sea. I raced toward the bow for a better view. The Serafi and Varian ships had formed two rows, sides of the ships facing one another. Blooms of white smoke exploded between them. The whistles and cracks of cannonballs bunched my muscles. I could not stop one with my power, and the ships floated so close to one another that I had no idea how I might sink the Serafis without pulling the Varians to the seafloor too.

The wind was rough and dragged hair loose from my braid. I firmed my stance, despite how I felt like I was tipping. The captain's voice rang out behind me. "Trim that sail. Cannons at the ready." The ship was pulling up alongside the sixth Serafi vessel.

She gave me an authoritative nod. "Whenever you're ready, Your Majesty."

I stared out at the Serafi ship, taking in the black leather armor I knew so well. My fear felt like fingers curling around my throat, stifling my breaths. Across the narrow strip of water, I spotted the Serafi captain, foreboding in his dark helmet. For a moment, I thought of Evander.

I pictured his face, stretched with disgust as he beheld me. I pictured Nemea's throne room and my mother's wing on the wall. I pictured the words below it carved proudly into the marble.

THE MONSTER IS ALWAYS SLAIN.

Black, burning power ruptured through my chest at the memories. I wanted the Serafi crew to freeze, and a wave of lures shot from me, spanning the space between our ship and theirs. My throat burned and I grew cold, like I'd been sliced at the neck and left to bleed dry, but at once, every sailor, every crew member, fell still.

The Varian captain's voice boomed. "Fire!"

My ears ached from the cracking of gunpowder, but I stood unmoving. I watched as the Serafi ship suffered our assault. Cannonballs split through its side, wood splintered, and clouds of dust climbed high into the salt air. But it was the way the Serafi crew and soldiers slowly began to move that had me most transfixed. One unnatural step at a time, they began to walk toward the ship's bulwark and climb over its rail to jump, one by one, into the sea below. I'd not ordered them to do it. I'd only intended to make them freeze. As their ship crumbled, as the sails ripped and the masts snapped, I watched the way their mouths moved in perfect unison.

With all of them speaking as one, I could just make out the words.

I give to the sand. I give to the water. Hear me, heed me. Cleanse the sea.

"No." Eusia was ravenous. Since her creation she had starved for power, for recognition in the shadow of her sister. For years and years, she'd sought a way to fuel her insatiable magic. And now, she'd found a way to keep herself fed.

Me.

My mind sat in a grief-stricken fog by the time we came alongside the next Serafi vessel. It was badly damaged already; massive holes had been blown through its upper hull, but it took on no water.

The captain patted my shoulder proudly, nostalgia and pride deepening lines around her eyes. "Once more, shall we?" she said, inclining her chin toward the Serafis.

I nodded absently. "Of course." I gripped the ship's rail, resigned to the awful reality of it all. There was no way to keep Varya and its people safe without giving Eusia the bodies she so yearned for. I focused once more on that sickening, oily power in my middle when I realized what ship sat before me.

It was Seraf's flagship. I recognized the squared-off stern, the four tall masts. The fanged eel painted on its largest sail. It had been Evander's ship, and decades ago, when Nemea had been a seafaring king, it had been his. He had pushed it to the farthest edges of the world, to every island, and the northern continent too. There were stories of the haunting collection of Siren bones that decayed in its hull, of the Sirens who had been tied to its masts, left to blister in the sun for days on end.

The fabled ship belonged at the bottom of the sea. The cannon smoke was thick and white, stinging my eyes. I pulled myself above it to cling to the ropes and scanned the flagship. My heart crushed as I let the lures build within me, as I set my intention on the vast crew, but I clamped down on them all when I saw a flash of gold through the lingering smoke.

I froze as I made out the shape of that old, crenellated crown. It was Nemea. *Here.* He had not been on a ship in nearly thirty years. He'd refused, keeping himself safe from all its threats by remaining cloistered in his mountain fort.

His unfeeling gaze seemed to sense me through the smoke. A dark apparition, he stood in the middle of the deck, wearing worn, ill-fitting black armor. Those stabbing gray eyes locked with mine.

My mind couldn't process the sight of him. On a ship. In Varian waters. I was supposed to go to him. Rohana had told me as much. Eusia had taunted me with it, pointing me *home, home, home.*

Power swirled through me, surging like a storm, but I held it in. I pulled at the buttons over my spine and ripped them open, one by one. The captain's order to fire sliced the air. Cannonballs flew from both ships. One of the Serafi volleys cracked through the bulwark to the side of me and I shielded myself from the splintering wood, but I felt the sharp pieces pierce my flesh. My cheek, my neck, my arm, burned from the stuck shrapnel.

I fought to keep my mind clear, then set my intention on the water and ordered a deep current to slice between our ship and Nemea's. In two beats, the Serafi ship careened, forcing their cannon aim to skew.

"What the hell are you doing?" the captain yelled to me as I pulled the back of my tunic even wider. "Freeze them! Lure them into the water!"

My wings broke through my skin. I stretched them wide and tried to keep my balance with the new weight tugging me back.

Our ship was badly beaten, splitting further with each blow. But the Serafi flagship had not been able to overcome my current. It listed, its sails going slack.

"I'm boarding that ship," I called back to the captain.

Her face was red, spittle at her lips. "Get them in the water first, Gods damn it."

I shook my head. I couldn't risk accidentally luring Nemea over the side of that ship.

She drew her sword. A cannonball flew over the deck, and she ducked, darting around sailors at work. "You gave your fucking word," she yelled, sword tip pointing at my throat.

"Tread carefully." My body had grown taut — my power tremulous. "I have a poor history with captains."

The lines on her face deepened with my threat. She bared her teeth, her nose wrinkling with disgust. "Get off my ship."

The strike of her enmity felt familiar, and I bore it well. I held my chin high and got my footing. Nemea's ship was close enough for me to glide across. When I called it, a gust blew under me, and I stepped off the ship with my wings spread wide. My stomach flipped at the sensation of moving over the air. Ungracefully, I landed on the Serafi ship's shroud and held tight. The square-hatched ropes burned my palms, my knees, my shins.

My presence unsettled Nemea's crew. My dark wings set them on edge, like hounds scenting their quarry. They nocked arrows and prepared ropes as they dodged the cannonballs that still flew at them. With a clamped jaw and all my focus, I sent out only three lures. I shook to maintain them, to not let Eusia take them from me. They pierced the chests of the men standing nearest Nemea. The men's shoulders slumped as they surrounded him. As they hauled him toward the nearest mast, that burn began once more in my throat.

Nemea didn't fight them; he didn't rail and scream. I kept moving, trying to keep myself from arrows' paths, trying to keep my hold on my power, and watched through the ropes. I waited for his face to redden and his eyes to bulge as they always did when his ire was up, but he only leaned back, head tipped against the mast as they tied him to it. He looked me directly in the eye. His graying hair whipped, and he held my stare even as they took his sword from his scabbard. They bound his hands and pulled the wax from his ears. And as my body began to drain of its warmth, they took the dented gold crown from his head.

The sword and crown clattered to the deck as the three men turned toward the port side of the ship. I'd sent no command. I'd not even felt when the lures had putrefied, but Eusia now tugged on the strings. The three men mouthed the prayer as they stepped over the deck with jerking movements and threw themselves into the sea.

Arrows whizzed past me, and I climbed up, fighting to keep my balance, when Nemea called up to me.

"You're tarrying, girl." The slice of his voice through the din made my body lock up. I felt like a child, small and powerless and in want of discipline. "I thought I taught you better. We die when we tarry, Imogen. Do what you mean to do before we both meet our ends."

He was right, and it anguished me to admit it. It anguished me to do what came next. I closed my eyes and let my power fly. I could not count how many lures, but my power — or Eusia — knew what was required. They hooked in and the sailors on the deck all let out a breath at once. I whimpered at the searing pain in my throat and the chills that broke out over my skin. Bodies went limp, weapons clamored to the ground. And then they all began to climb over the edges of the ship. Like a wave of tar, they slowly crested the rails and spilled into the briny water.

I looked to Nemea. I'd set all the focus I'd possessed on keeping him safe from my lure. The wind rolled over the deck, carrying with it the incessant splash of bodies and the mumbled prayers of the crew up to me on the shroud. Our gazes locked.

When Nemea heard his crew speak the familiar words of Eusia's spell — the one he'd taught me so long ago — a slow smile curled his mouth.

29

I jumped to the deck. Pain shot up my shins when I landed. My attention narrowed on the poor knots the sailors had tied around Nemea. The ropes were slung loose across his barrel chest. It would take little effort for him to remove them. Yet he didn't struggle. He sat at ease, gaze on me.

His stillness — his peace — sent a spear of anxiety shooting through me.

His sword lay on the deck a few paces away, gleaming gold in the early evening light. It gave a metallic scrape as I retrieved it. Cannon fire still quaked through the warm air, but the volley from the ship I'd been on had ceased. They were sailing away, up the line to support the others, leaving me and Nemea on his flagship — alone.

With a forceful current and a steady wind, I guided the ship away from the tight cluster of firing vessels. I let us drift out farther from Varya's shore, yawing and pitching with the chaos of the sea. The sun limned Nemea's silvering hair and shadowed his narrow face. I stared, forcing my adrenaline-sodden body to still, and looked for something of myself in him.

I'd inherited so much from my mother. Her features, the shape of her body too, were nearly identical to mine. But I feared I'd inherited my father's heart.

All the deaths I'd caused did not pierce me like they should. I still stood on my own feet, I still pulled breaths into my lungs without collapsing under the weight of self-detestation. I wished to feel the sting of these terrible, punishing things, to feel absolution, as Theodore had said, but I was numb.

I must have gotten that from Nemea.

The sails flapped overhead, unmanned and now loose in the breeze. I'd never looked at Nemea with such clear eyes before. I could picture what he would have looked like with the years peeled away, back when the empress had known him. The dark hair and light olive skin, the narrow slant of his gray eyes. How they pierced like pointed steel. I walked nearer to him, toward where his crown lay on the deck. My heart knocked into my ribs as he watched me. I bent to pick it up, weighing the heavy, sun-warmed gold in my palm.

"Hello, Imogen," he finally said, over the snapping sails. "Have I surprised you?"

That voice. Low, nasal. It sent a host of rotting emotions spreading through me. "You have."

"You left," he said simply, head leaning back against the mast. "I had no choice but to retrieve you." His gaze slid to my wings. "I'll admit, you've surprised me too."

My fist tightened around his crown, its edges denting my palm. "Don't pretend you didn't know what I was," I spat. "And I am not yours to retrieve."

He gave a chuckle. It was unamused, rough, empty. "But you are. In so many ways, you are."

"What is your strongest claim to me, Nemea?" I asked, adjusting my fist around the sword's hilt. "That you are my king? My warden? That you fed my blood to a monster since I was a baby?"

Slowly, I rested his crown upon my own head.

He scowled. Then the expression on his face slackened as he realized I knew precisely what his strongest claim to me was.

"Take that off." The words were clipped, frigid.

"It's where it soon belongs, isn't it?" I hated the feel of it, the way it pressed down and cut in. "Am I not your heir?" The vitriolic look on his face moved through me like a slow poison. "I disgust you, don't I?"

"Disgust." Nemea was so still. "The Sirens disgust me, yes." He shook his head. "But you never have. She never did either."

She. My mother.

He must have seen the questions springing through my mind, the longing that shadowed my face, because he said, "Would you like me to tell you of her?"

Nerves tingled beneath my skin. He pulled fear from me as easily as he had blood from my palm. He adjusted himself against the mast like his body ached, and the shoddily tied rope across his middle slipped lower. I saw the glint of something silver at his hip. A dagger. I set my teeth and moved my other hand to the sword's grip. But Nemea only sat there, uneasily still, waiting for my answer.

As much as I was tempted, the story of Nemea and my mother was not one I needed. I needed to know of Eusia. Of the empress, and the princess, and the tangled web that I was stuck in the middle of. But I drew in a shaky breath and nodded.

He made a thoughtful sound and focused on something in the middle distance, seemingly slipping into the past. "You remember the stories of the years that I was missing at sea?" His voice was strange. It went soft and lank, rolling between us like an eerie morning haze. "I was with Ligea for most of them. The stories boast that I set out to conquer, but I was never fool enough to think that I, the lone mortal king of Leucosia, would ever amount to much in a realm where Gods exist. If I wanted power, I had to make it." His haunted gaze locked quickly with mine. "Isn't that right, Imogen? Isn't that what I always told you?"

I didn't answer him.

He pursed his lips at my silence before he continued. "I took a small fleet to seek out the Mage Seers. They had succeeded in making their own power, after all, so why couldn't I? I'd thought magic could give me what I lacked. I was foolish in my youth, though. I had no knowledge of its cost. When I saw the Mage Seers, what the magic did to them . . ." He shook his head, lip curling. "That was not a price I was willing to pay.

"I remember the Mage who told me to go north. She could hardly speak. She lay in a ball on the floor of her tower like a dried-up insect. She was the one who told me there was a way to gain power without paying for it. She told me how I could serve Eusia."

Fury ignited in me. The sword's grip ached against the knot of scars on my palm. Proof of the *cost.* I lifted the blade and strode forward so the tip hovered before him. "*I* paid, Nemea."

Whatever hold he'd had on himself snapped. His cheeks burned red. His gray eyes stretched with rage. "Let me *speak.*" The words hissed through his clamped teeth. "I paid. I paid, dearly. The fucking Mage lied."

The tip of the sword fell to the deck with a dull *clunk.* I staggered a few steps back, startled by the depth of his emotion. He looked anguished. Tormented.

He spoke then like he was giving a confession. Quickly, eager to be rid of the words he'd held in for too long. "Eusia was one of Obelia's saints. Centuries before, she'd washed up onto one of their beaches. She was old—old as the Gods. She'd been gutted, her insides missing when they found her. But she wasn't dead. She could speak and move, and they worshipped her for it. For an offering, Eusia would grant her faithful a miracle. So I went.

The empress, Nivala, was . . . she was a force. She was as hungry for power as I was. She welcomed me, a young Leucosian king, with open arms, eager to learn what sort of power I possessed. I never told her I was mortal. She lavished me with food and wine, took me to her bed, and I stayed in Obelia for months, preparing for my first sacrifice and blessing from Eusia.

"I remember the day that she finally got it out of me — that I was powerless, just like her — she laughed in my face. But she took me to their temple anyway and I made my offering to the little sunken pool inside it. I poured my blood into its water and said the prayer. I asked Eusia . . . I asked her to end the Sirens that had decimated my fleet. They'd cost me men, and money. My pride. They brought nothing but ruin, and I was determined to see them pay for it."

A chill took me. The far-off cannon fire, the ship's creaks, faded under the grip that Nemea's story held me in.

"When Eusia's head broke the surface of that pool, I screamed. She was so small. The size of a child. No hair. Flesh had grown over her eyes and down her cheeks, but she could see me — I knew she could see me. Her voice sounded strangled, but she had been eager to speak of her sister with me. Of Ligea. She spoke of how Ligea had been given everything and remained golden and hale and unmatched after so many centuries. And she had become a monster trying to best her. Our wants aligned. So I told her I'd help her."

"Eusia is in Obelia?" I asked quickly.

Nemea shook his head. "She asked me to take her home. So she could perform the spell needed to end Ligea."

"What did you say?" My entire body had filled with a terrible, crackling cold. A dread so deep that it ached. "She asked you to take her *home*?"

His eyes lit like I'd revealed a weakness. "You're looking for her."

"I am blood-bound to her," I yelled. "Of course I'm Godsdamned looking for her."

His thin lips tipped. "You're very like her. Like Ligea," he mused, through his annoyance. "It was absurd of me to think Captain Ianto would have been enough to keep you holed up in my fort indefinitely." He shook his head. "You and her both — so damned stubborn, so arrogant, that you'll see yourselves killed rather than fall in line."

That struck me. Theodore had said something nearly identical. That Nemea might truly know me, my flaws and my strengths, turned my stomach. "Finish your story," I said, voice thick.

He glared, made me wait. "I moved Eusia from Obelia. It was an undertaking. Making sure she had all that she needed for the journey. Before she left, the empress requested a final miracle. A large one. She made a final sacrifice —"

"Her husband," I said, breathless. The realization cleaved me in two. "And the Nels. You didn't kill them just for jewels. You killed them to feed Eusia while she was journeying on your ship, didn't you?"

Nemea jerked. His eyes flared with confusion. "How do you know that?"

"I've been busy." I lifted the sword once more.

Nemea cracked his jaw, a dangerous energy building through him. "Eusia wanted me to have a child with Ligea." He said it so simply, as if he were remarking on the mundane. "There was a reason your mother never had children. She feared her sister, feared what she might do to them. Eusia wanted generations to feed on. Bodies kept her alive, but mortals did not give her Gods' power. If she could capture her sister, and her sister's children, she would be able to swallow their power *and* use her own magic. She would be endless."

"And so you did." I didn't hide how despicable I thought it was. "How? Why would Ligea ever let you —"

"She bound herself to me." He'd never spoken with such softness. Not even in my memories of him from when I was a girl, when he would greet me with a fleeting smile and a sweet in his palm, did I remember his voice sounding quite like that. "She was no fool, your mother, but binding herself to me was the most misguided thing she'd ever done — the beginning of her end."

I took a step back. I needed space between us, I needed to remember his callousness and cruelty, for the look that swam in his eyes now set me too off-kilter. He was heartsick.

A gust cut across the deck and my balance swayed as the ship pitched over a set of high waves. The temperature was dropping as the sun fell behind a wall of dark, bulbous clouds. In the distance, a deep boom rolled over the water.

I searched the sea. The boom had been thunder — the cannon fire had ceased. The two Serafi ships that remained had retreated. Half of the Varian fleet had returned to port, and we had drifted far away.

"Looks like you lost," I said.

"I had no intention of winning this battle, Imogen." His eyes were depthless. Glittering with a terrifying sort of hunger. "Like I said, I came for you." He slipped a hand through the ropes around him and tugged. They fell as readily as dead leaves. My arms shook with the weight of the sword, but I held it firmly between us and stepped backward across the deck. Nemea hardly noticed. He rose, unfurling his long limbs slowly, and then he adjusted his ill-fitting armor, the gesture easy and unafraid. He looked out toward the storm clouds at the horizon and asked, "What will you do?" He mocked me with the question. "I think only Ligea could have manned a crewless ship through a night storm. And you are so like her, yes...but you are also so much less."

The air knocked from my chest. I watched him, quietly, waiting for him to take the dagger from his hip. He never did. He lowered himself onto a nearby crate instead.

"Did you love her?" The question slipped from me before I could stop it.

He huffed, rolling his shoulders before he answered. "I liked possessing her. That damn bond we shared was tricky, though. I wanted to hate her. I reminded myself that she was the root of my suffering, of my kingdom's struggles, but the thoughts wouldn't stick. That bond convinced me I loved her."

I winced like his words had hit a bruise. "That's not what the bond does."

He froze. He'd been at ease, but now his body began to lock up with awareness. With a tilt of his head, he said, "You speak as if you know."

"The bond compels you to protect."

Disbelief, and the barest thread of amusement, curled his lips. "Dear Gods. That's how you got that boy-king to help you, isn't it? You stole him." He scoffed. "Just like your mother."

"I didn't steal him. He agreed."

"Oh, what benevolence! What sacrifice! And has he proclaimed his love? Has he sworn himself to you always?" He hit his knee with a fist. "He'll be even more insufferable now, Panos's grandson bound to Ligea's daughter. As if the bastard wasn't powerful enough already, he went and gathered up some more."

The insinuation rocked something in me that had once felt unshakable. Theodore had first bound himself to me because of my power, because of who he'd thought I was. I suddenly couldn't bat the thought away: Had Gods' blood not flowed through my veins, would Theodore have left me in Nemea's fort to wither and die?

Nemea stood quickly, his body coursing with familiar anger, and plucked the dagger from his belt. He rolled it in his fist and paced. "That bond..." He looked haunted and then locked our gazes. "Your mother learned of what I'd done. Of how I'd helped move Eusia. I was sailing back to Seraf through a narrow sea stack and there sat Ligea." He pointed with his dagger, like he could see her before him. "Ligea, winged and speckled in salt water upon the rocks, looking like a glorious, brutal bird of prey. She dropped onto my deck and froze the entire crew without making a sound. I'd never seen anything like it. Power seeped from her, but she stared at me like *I* was a threat. She'd come to me like *I* was the one who possessed a vicious lure. She said, 'I know you wish to harm me and my people. I shall see to it that you can't.' She sliced me open and bound us."

My arms had begun to shake. The wind cut, covering my eyes in mist and stray hairs. I could sense our time running down and I still didn't know where Eusia was. "How did you kill Ligea?

"I didn't."

"Don't lie to me. Her wing hangs in your throne room, Nemea. How did the blood bond permit you to cut it from her?"

He took a menacing step toward me. "I *never* hurt her. I never wanted to. I lived with regret over my service to Eusia for years because of my feelings for Ligea and did all I could to keep her safe. I kept her from the sea so Eusia couldn't sense her. When she... when we... Ligea was determined to give birth to you in the sea. Despite how I begged her, how I demanded she stay on land." The color drained from his face. "She slipped out in the night. We were on Seraf, at the old keep on the western shore. The mountain fort wasn't finished yet. I realized too late she was missing from our bed. I should have tied her to the post like I'd threatened to, but I couldn't bring myself to scratch her wrists with the Godsdamned ropes." He scrubbed violently at his eyes. "When I got to the beach, the sun was just rising. The spume was still colored with her blood. You were screaming, lying up on the dry sand — like she'd tossed you to safety. And her wing floated on the breaking waves. Bits of her flesh still hung from its root. Eusia took her, but she didn't kill her."

"How do you know that?" I whispered.

"Our bond didn't break when she left me. I still felt it. For years and years." He looked up at me and I could just make out the sneer and dark amusement on his face in the fading light. His laugh came angry and low. "This might be the first time you've ever looked at me like I have a heart." He shook his head. "Don't be fooled."

"Why didn't you gut me and throw me into the sea?" I fought for balance against the rolling ship. "Why didn't you make Eusia all-powerful? Get rid of us Sirens once and for all."

"Eusia doesn't want you dead," he said in a snarl. "She kept Ligea alive as long as she could. And she'd do the same to you. She'd use you up slowly."

I stared at him in slack-jawed disbelief. "Are you telling me that you kept me as a mercy? That you made me give my blood in that ritual so that I wouldn't suffer like my mother did?"

Alarming anger filled him, bringing color back to his cheeks. "I did it for *Ligea*. Not you. I've kept my word to Eusia. I've fed her. But I swore that while our bond still lingered, I wouldn't let Ligea's daughter suffer her same fate."

"Your bond," I said. "Is it gone?"

He paused and seemed stunned by the question. As if he'd never before considered it. Eyes darting, he searched himself inwardly. Set a hand to his stomach. His voice went low and, unbelievably, a lovelorn look filled his eyes. "I can't feel it."

The change in him was instant. Intent built through his body, bringing him nearer to me.

"Where is Eusia?" I demanded, firming my stance.

"With all that you've learned while you've been away, you still can't figure it out?" His shoulders rose. His weaponless hand curled into a tight fist. "I kept you up in that fort, away from the sea, as a mercy because you have always been so weak. You were so small when you were born, so sick. The sea would have swallowed you whole had I ever let you near it. Eusia would have plucked you from the sand with no effort at all. Even now, you stand there with a sword, letting me speak and asking me questions you should know the answer to." He gave me a disgraced shake of his head. "Harden up. *Fight.*"

"If I am fearful and weak, it's because of you," I yelled. "You have made me this way."

"And what will you do about it?" He held his dagger up between us. "Will you come back home with me where you're safe, and we can pay Eusia for her blessings where she cannot reach you, or will you make me gut you now, and let her monsters carry you to her? I know the spell that will keep you alive until you reach her. The very one she used to save herself from death."

The water had grown choppier, the troughs of the waves deeper, and it made the ship sway steeply. I met his gaze through the gloaming. My voice filled with steel. "Neither."

30

The sword's weight combined with the rocking of the ship had me fighting to stay upright.

With all my strength, I hefted it and set the blade slicing down toward Nemea in a wide arc. He dodged. His hand flashed in my periphery, and then a bright striking pain lit my cheekbone. My head snapped to the side and the crown I wore went flying to the deck, where it landed with a wobbling roll. Sparks flew across my vision. I waited for the next strike, for the dagger to my gut, but it never came.

My face smarted, my eyes watered, but I found my footing. On the far side of the deck, Nemea paced. His shoulders were hunched, and he kept swiping his hand through his mussed hair, as if distraught.

"Is that your measly conscience, Nemea?" I yelled over the howl of the wind. "Did it hurt you to strike me?"

He shot me a glare. "No."

I moved toward the rigging and grabbed hold. The storm threw the ship over the surface of the water like a loose flower petal. "I look like her. How can you not picture her face when you strike mine?"

The rain started. It fell sideways, plastering his hair to his brow.

"Use your power and let this be done," he said, over the crash of the waves.

"You want me to kill you?"

"You cannot understand my misery." His voice cracked. "I lived all those years with an intact blood bond, never being free of the worry or the compulsion to keep her safe, and there was nothing I could do."

"Nothing you could do?" Something inside me cracked. I hauled the sword up and started toward him. "How dare you try to justify your cruelty." I charged, bringing the sword down just above his shoulder. He dodged again, swiping at me with his dagger. "All the ways you've terrorized me. You made me into what you wanted me to be — into what served you. You made me small and timid. You made me everything my mother was not so that you could use me."

His eyes flashed. The dark was pressing in, making it harder to see the details of his movements. Nemea lunged. I made to move out of his reach, but the ship pitched and sent me stumbling directly toward him. He was more prepared than I was. He grabbed my hair in his fist and yanked me sideways. A scream tore up my throat at the pain.

Nemea seethed, his breaths coming hard through his teeth. "All I have done is keep you safe and require your obedience in return. Is that not how a God treats his worshippers? Is that not the agreement a king has with his subjects? How a father treats his child?"

He released my hair with a shove. I fell flat to the deck and the air rushed from my chest. Teeth bared, he took the dagger from his hip once more and fought the ship's swaying to trudge toward me.

My power was swirling, an eddy in midnight water, eager to break free of its confines, but I couldn't pull in a full breath, couldn't focus on sending out a lure through my pain. Slowly, I rose to my knees and set all my intention on Nemea's withered heart. He was right before me, dagger gripped in his fist, when I let my lure fly.

Silver light glinted off the blade in his hand as he reared back. I waited for him to freeze under my control, waited for the dagger to clatter to the deck . . . but my lure never sank in.

He lunged, eyes locked with mine. I sucked in a ripping breath as the dagger tip cut into me. Fire blistered through my middle, through muscles and organs. Right through the spot where my bond with Eusia sat.

A cry bubbled up in my throat.

Nemea froze. His eyes blew wide. The rain rolled down his stunned face like tears. "No," he whispered, releasing the hilt of the blade like it scorched him. He shook his head, mouth gaping. "You tried . . . didn't you? You tried your lure?"

I gave a weak nod. My hands went to my stomach, to either side of the half-pressed-in dagger. "It didn't take."

He nearly lost his balance as a wave crashed over the deck. It washed me off my feet. Threw me on my side. My gut exploded in agony as the dagger shifted and drove deeper into me. No scream came forth, no rush of pained breath. My body locked up instead, stiff from the consuming press of metal into my soft flesh.

Nemea's fingers dug into my arm. He hauled me up with such force that my shoulder popped loudly from its socket. I screamed then. I flailed, dragged my talons over his cheek and summoned forth dark blood.

He hissed, but his fingers dug deeper into my arm. "*Stop.*" He hauled me to the stairs that led to the quarterdeck and forced me down. My spine struck the risers. I only saw his shaded outline, a flash of teeth as he yelled, "She's still alive. If your lure didn't work, that means Ligea's still alive. Our bond remains."

He was frantic. The stormy twilight lit his horrified face. "The spell." He set his hand on the hilt of the dagger in my middle like he meant to remove it.

I whimpered and spoke through gritted teeth. "Do not touch me."

"The spell will keep you alive."

"So I can keep feeding Eusia for you?"

He shook his head, face crumpling as the pelting rain beaded down it. "Ligea. She was gone. I swear, I thought — as long as she lives, I swore I'd keep you safe."

It was incomprehensible, how the blood bond he shared with my mother had formed this twisted moral compass of his. He was despicable, deceitful, but I'd never seen him like this. Heartsore and broken. Willing to offer me life when I'd spent so long certain that he wanted me dead — after he himself had struck the killing blow.

Regardless of how I could not understand him, I was clear in one thing: I wanted to live.

Lightning ripped through the sky, illuminating Nemea's intent. He didn't wait for my consent. His shaking hand gripped the dagger, and he ripped it straight out of my gut.

A cry gouged my throat.

Lowered on one knee, Nemea kept himself steady as the ship rocked. As water washed back and forth across the deck. He dragged the dagger over his fingertip, then scooped up some seawater as it rushed by. He let the bloody mixture trickle over the gash in my stomach. The salt burned my open flesh. "Will I be sick?" I asked, through a cracking voice.

"I don't know." He'd gone pale, tense.

My gushing blood looked black in the quickly fading light. I was growing cold. My body began to shake.

"Keep still." He pressed his hand against the weeping gash. I squirmed from the feel of his fingers on my skin, all cold and gentle and wet. He closed his eyes and an unnatural calm came over him. He was a foil to the chaos of the rocking ship, the slashing rain, the gusting wind.

He spoke with reverence, with purpose. "In the wake of the ruined, when the spirit rends, mend and loop and seal. In the veins of the drowning, when blood fills the throat, clear and wash and heal."

I felt nothing. Warmth still gushed from beneath his fingers. Then, at the very moment that Nemea sucked in a scraping breath and pulled his hand from me, my body arched with an awful, stabbing pain. It was like the dagger had been driven in once more. I looked down. The flow of blood slowed to a dribble, but it did not stop. The skin did not close. The wound was the width of my palm, a red-stained maw.

Nemea fell to the deck, wailing, as the spell sought recompense. His fingers flew to his eyes like they seared. Water crashed over him, sending his large body sliding until it hit the base of the mast. Water gurgled in his throat, and I couldn't tell if it was the seawater or the spell that choked him.

I didn't move from where I sat. Instead, I watched him flail and slide as the wind and water saw fit. With another sway of the ship, he managed to wrap his arms around the mast and curl himself around it. I waited for his watery breaths to even the way Halla's had after she'd performed her spell. I waited for him to stop scratching at his eyes, but he writhed instead, fighting to stay put as the storm tried to dislodge him.

My gaze slipped back down to the dribbling wound in my stomach, and a flood of sickness filled me. I had been so close to suffering a death like Eusia's. And then something struck me — Theodore's account of her execution.

She was gutted and thrown off the coast of Anthemoessa.

The Sirens' island. The seat of Ligea's queendom. Where she and her sister had been created.

Home.

"It's Anthemoessa, isn't it?" Nemea's breaths were coming easier now. "Answer me," I yelled. "How did you get there? The waters are supposed to be impassable."

It had been blighted by a spell and abandoned. A spell I could only assume Eusia herself had cast. Its land had grown black and toxic, as did the waters around it. There was no passing its outer reef, no touching foot on its inner shores without the blight seeping through the soles of your boots. As a result, Ligea had lost her seat. She'd been a queen only in title after that. The Sirens had spread out through the rest of Leucosia's islands, welcomed by all — at first.

I crawled toward him and yanked at his shoulder, forcing him to look at me. His eyes bled, shredded and nightmarish. "How did you get on Anthemoessa?"

He shook his head like he wouldn't answer me. It was growing nearly too dark to see, but as the ship rocked, I could hear the slide of metal on the deck behind me. The sword. I followed the sound, scraping my body toward it. My pain was deep and beating but I managed to take the wet leather hilt in my hand.

The storm cracked the sky. I rose, dragging the sword tip over the wet planks as I stumbled back to him. Nemea didn't move. Only the faintest of groans filled his chest. I stood above him and positioned the blade so it hovered over the soft hollow of his throat. "How did you get on Anthemoessa, Nemea?"

He stared up at me, unmoving, and had the gall to laugh. Like I was no threat to him at all. Like he believed he'd done such a thorough job of defanging me that the worst I could do now was gum him.

I jabbed him quickly with the sword, enough to just break the skin. He snarled like a feral animal. "Eusia allowed it."

"You and your whole crew? She let your whole ship past the outer reef?"

He shook his head. I couldn't tell how well he could see me through the blood in his eyes and the impending night. "She let my ship pass the outer reef. She only let me and Nivala on the main island."

Oh Gods. Foreboding choked me. My hands cramped around the sword's grip. "The empress?"

He nodded. "She still feeds her." His teeth gritted, he tried to move, but I held the sword above him steady.

My voice shook. "The empress still feeds her bodies?"

"She feeds her *Sirens*."

Dread hollowed me out as pieces of the past day fell into place. The empress was not simply a devotee of Eusia, she was all but a priestess, working vigilantly to keep her alive. She knew who I was — she never would have told me the story of the Nels otherwise. She'd come to my room in the healer's quarters that night, distraught by the state I was in, as the healer had said. She'd meant to take me, but I'd been too ill to leave. Lachlan hadn't been able to find Agatha.

Agatha.

She'd gone missing the night before the empress had left.

Agatha.

"*No*," I breathed. She had taken Agatha. She had taken her — but she'd wanted me. "*No, no, no.*"

The wind and rain slashed at me, roaring as loud as the blood in my ears. I could just hear Nemea's strained chuckle rise up from his sprawled, soaked body.

"You've lost, haven't you?" he asked in a shaking voice. "Did you just realize?"

I pushed the sword tip down and held it firm against his neck. The next pitch of the ship, the next crashing wave, would send it straight through him. He sobered. Raised his hands in surrender.

But I didn't wait for the next roll of the ship. The raging storm and lurching vessel would not be the executor of his fate.

I would.

I shoved the sword down. I felt it crunch through the tough pieces in his neck. I felt when it hit the bones of his spine, when it hit the wood beneath him.

I was grateful for the shroud of night.

I released the sword. Stumbled backward. Fell to my knees and vomited.

31

The seabirds roused me.

Aching, I rolled my head to the side, then rushed to cradle it in my hands. I cracked open my eyes. Dim light . . . morning. Above me, the dregs of last night's storm clouds hung low, gray-hued and wrung out.

My eyes began to focus, and I traced the lines of the drooping sails, the ropes swaying in the humid breeze. Panic tightened around me as my mind cleared fully of sleep.

Agatha. I needed to get to Agatha.

I'd huddled beneath the risers that led to the quarterdeck in the night, and I gripped them now as I pushed myself up to sit. My panic only grew as I took stock of myself. The air was warm, but I shivered. My skin looked gray, covered in gooseflesh and cold sweat. The thumping pain in my stomach was consuming, profound. I blew out three slow breaths in a weak attempt to ease my racing heart, then peeled back my wet tunic.

"Shit." The hole in my stomach oozed a steady, thin trickle of blood. The skin around it had grown tender and red, and I let out a wobbling cry when my cruel mind pushed forward a memory of Theodore. His bright, healing warmth, the press of his calloused fingers, the way his presence and power beat back the darkness that nipped perpetually at my heels.

"Nemea did it wrong."

I gasped, head snapping toward the creaking voice that had come from across the deck. My body pricked with awareness when I realized the voice had come from within my own head too.

Eusia.

One of her nekgya sat on the deck, right where Nemea's body had been. Her dark, silken hair stuck to her shoulders. She was wan and smattered in black, ragged wounds. Decay crept over her mouth and fingers, over her chest and arms. The sea held her together with bits of kelp and a patchwork of delicate, pale barnacles.

She cradled Nemea's crown in her crooked fingers. His sword lay on the deck before her. Beside it sat a mound of wet sand and a slimy ribbon of kelp.

"Where is he?" I croaked.

Her eyes were rimmed in deep purple skin, her irises the color of the water off Varya's shore. "Do you truly care?" Eusia's voice asked through the nekgya's rot-smattered mouth.

I hated the man. I was relieved he was gone. And yet his death snapped a tether that had tied me to this world. Bits of my life — memories of me, of my mother — that only he held had died with him. That realization filled me with lonely grief.

"Tell me where he is."

"The sea, of course." She set the crown on the deck with uncanny, jerking movements. "Come. We must close that wound. You're running out of time."

"Why?" I said, in a groan. "Why help me?"

"If you die, in a short time, so shall my power."

The impulse overtook me — to let myself fade, right there on the deck of Nemea's bobbing ship. To let my death be the severance that finally brought an end to Eusia. But my selfishness was a stubborn, inextinguishable fire. My desire to live burned bright. I thought of Agatha and the danger she was in. Of Theodore, days away from marrying an enemy bride.

I rose to my knees, shaking from the pain, and crawled across the deck toward her. The ocean was calm, rolling the ship gently. I knelt across from her, with the sword and sand and kelp between us, and looked into her dead eyes. My voice trembled. "I'm inclined to die if it means your end." She remained silent, unblinking. "Tell me how to get to you and I will agree to your spell."

There was only quiet. Only her hollow stare, until finally she said, "It is not perfect."

I shook my head. "What's not?"

"Our bond," she said, simply. "How I have used up Ligea is preferable. If I had you beside me, like I do Ligea, I'd be stronger. This bond we share—I can access your power, you sustain me. But despite how I'd like to, I cannot harm you." The nekgya's dead eyes met mine and ice shards sliced through me. "Do you feel that too?" Her voice was a scratching whisper. "The desire to end me? To win. But if I let you come to me, if you stood above what is left of my body, ready to sever our bond, you could not do it."

"Is that why the empress tried to take me?" I asked. "To bring me to you. She is your aide. She *can* harm me. She can help you perform the spell to break our bond and help you make a new one that is just like the one you share with my mother."

The nekgya's pallid head tilted unsettlingly to the side, the movement almost human. "Yes. Her veneration and fear have served me well."

Warm blood dribbled down my lower stomach. My head seemed to float and the tremors that had begun to rack my body were too strong to stanch. As hopelessness settled over me, I thought to curl up on my side beneath it. We had reached an impasse. There was no way for me to succeed.

"You're dwindling," Eusia said, her voice empty as ever, but I could practically feel her panic. A thrum, a worried sort of whirr that stirred my blood.

I clamped my chattering jaw. Pulled in a painful breath. And a spark lit my mind.

I was fearsome too. I was worthy of veneration, and if none would devote themselves to me as the empress had done Eusia — then I would make them.

And I knew precisely who I would take as my aide. Who I would make assist me in breaking my bond to Eusia and ending her.

"Permit me onto Anthemoessa and I will perform this spell. I will keep you alive," I said in a rush, my heart thumping quickly. She didn't answer me. "Quickly, Eusia." My voice scraped. "I have a bride to steal."

The nekgya stared at me for a long moment and I knew Eusia was considering my terms. I would come to her on Anthemoessa and one of us would win. Her nod was sharp and quick. She blinked, then moved like a spider, inching toward me on all fours, and Theodore's warnings against spell work pealed through me. He'd outright refused to let me even consider performing more than one spell — the one to end Eusia. But there was no hope without it.

"Will I be the same?" I leaned my body against the mast. "After the spell?"

"What magic takes, it never returns."

My vision began to smudge the sails and rigging above me. My pain began to numb. "What do I need to do?" I sounded like a terrified child.

Her empty eyes did not meet mine as she knelt beside me. She cupped the sand in her decaying fingers. "The sand meets the blood. The fat fills the mouth. The kelp knits the flesh."

I looked at her own rotting body, at the smattering of kelp and barnacles, at the patches of gelatinous skin. My stomach turned at the thought of making myself into her likeness, but I clamped my teeth and pulled my damp tunic over my head. "I put my blood in the sand?"

She nodded. I shook as I cut the familiar line over my palm with a talon. I let my blood run into the sand she held, and she crawled closer to me, reaching for my wound. I shuddered as she pressed the bloody sand into it, sucking in a harsh breath from the sting. She shoved the kelp at me. I bit a piece of it off, set it over the spot, then looked at her for approval.

"Fat," she said.

My stomach fell. "I . . . I don't —"

"Magic cannot make something from nothing."

The price was steep.

Once again, I twisted my talon into the soft skin below my navel. I took the smallest piece from myself and remembered Rohana. How she had tucked the piece of my flesh into the hollow of her cheek. Gagging, I set it on my tongue and fought to swallow.

"The words." The nekgya waited like she expected me to repeat them from memory.

My senses swam. "I don't remember . . ."

"Repeat. Hold them in your head." I could only focus on the nekgya's black lips as they moved with the words. "In the wake of the ruined, when the spirit rends, mend and loop and seal. In the veins of the drowning, when blood fills the throat, clear and wash and heal."

I repeated after her, each word torture to speak, and waited. When nothing happened, I met her empty gaze.

"You will feel pain," she said, voice even. "You will only find relief in your king."

"In my king?" My face bent as I tried to parse her meaning. "A healer will do, won't they?"

"There is no power like that of the Gods, dear girl. Only the king will do."

I froze. Eusia's meaning had morphed. I could nearly feel her yearning through my body, through our bond. A warning shot through me. "You want him. You want his blood like you want mine, don't you? This . . . this spell was a trick. To get me to return to him."

A slow pain started in the middle of me. I winced, and the nekgya smiled. "No trick, Imogen. The spell will keep you alive. And you, all on your own, will find your way back to him." The nekgya was so still, so horribly lifeless. "And if you don't . . . well, one way or another, I'll have his blood too."

I opened my mouth to speak, to scream, when the spell consumed me. My eyes seared like hot oil had been dripped into them. My scalp, my skin, my lungs, all felt like they were being pierced by thousands of burning needles. My mind left my body from the sensation. It slipped into another plane where there was only insatiable hunger and endless want. It took me to a place where I yearned for Gods' blood like it was precious, flowing gold. Yearned like it was the only thing that would sate me.

Beneath the spell's influence, terror took me. Magic was headier than I'd anticipated. It was like nectar — ambrosia. And despite the horrific pain, I wanted more and more and more. I wanted power in all its forms. Safety and control and influence. I wanted revenge.

I wanted Theodore and the potent, shimmering blood that ran through his veins.

I would do awful things to ensure that it was mine…to ensure that I was fed.

There was no grasping the passage of time, but when I returned to my body, it was with a shriek. The nekgya was gone. I was alone. Only Nemea's crown and sword remained at my side. My body felt like it had absorbed the entirety of the sea. I looked down quickly. The seaweed had stitched itself into my skin, sealing the wound and stopping the blood. I pressed my hands to my burning eyes. I ran my fingers over my scalp and a clump of dark hair came away stuck to the tips.

My cries seemed to come from outside myself, mixing with the slap of the waves against the hull, with the hammer of my heart in my ears. Using the mast behind me as support, I rose, and the effort nearly made my vision go black. The bleeding had stopped, the spell had worked, and just as Eusia had said, I was filled with a crippling pain.

For a long moment, I simply stood there. I fought to remember what my own want had felt like before I'd been tainted with Eusia's. *Kill Eusia, find Agatha, keep Theo safe.* I chanted it like a prayer. I grasped it like a lifeline.

The sun was warm over my chilled skin, and I let my aching eyes skip over the ship's deck. It was worse for wear. Large, jagged holes marred its sides. Some of the sails had torn and come free from their lines. Nemea's eel-stitched sail hung empty above me. Shame burned through me. Perhaps my mother could have guided a ship in this state alone, but I was not my mother.

I was something darker and plagued, something worse.

Bending was agony, but I scooped up my tunic, Nemea's crown and sword, and hobbled toward the edge of the ship.

Kill Eusia. Find Agatha. Keep Theo safe.

Keep Theo safe.

I clothed myself. I stared down blankly at the frothing water.

Keep him safe. Safe from me. For I had become his greatest threat.

Sea mist settled over me, and I set my plan. I would find Halla and take her with me. I would let her meet her beloved saint before she helped me end her. I'd bring Agatha to safety. The command I sent to the sea was crystalline: *Guide me to Varya one last time.*

I stepped off the edge of the ship, and the water swallowed me whole. It hauled me up and held me, so I floated on its surface like an old corpse.

In the cool, in the salt, my dream flashed to my mind.

The faceless woman, floating over the waves. No eyes. No hair. Adrift. While a dark, lurking presence combed through the depths below.

Starved.

Searching.

It finally found me.

ACKNOWLEDGMENTS

Writing a book is far from a solitary endeavor. And while I am the one who put the words on the page, I was only able to do so because of the support of the following people.

To Doug. It's because of you that I write love stories. Thank you for holding me and our little family up. Thank you for celebrating me, for believing in me. You are steady and bright, and our life together is my greatest joy.

To my mom, Lynn Quinones. Thank you for your unwavering support. For happily watching my children so I could steal some writing time. You have always made me feel like my wildest dreams were not so wild, after all. In large part, it's because of you that I've reached them.

To my agent, Sheyla Knigge. You are a brilliant partner, and I am grateful every day for your keen story sense, for your passion, and for your reminders to get off Goodreads. How thankful I am that you saw the potential in me and this book. It's been a hell of a year and a half. So happy to have shared it with you.

To my editor, Julia DeVarti. You understood my story from the start. I don't think there's a better feeling in the world than having a creative partner who loves your work for the same reasons you do. Thank you for your generosity, and your sharp feedback.

To the rest of my team at Little, Brown and Company. I am

overwhelmed by all the support, excitement, and expertise that every one of you poured into this book. Sally Kim, Gabby Leporati, Danielle Finnegan, Kirin Diemont, Linda Arends, and Amy J. Schneider, thank you, thank you. And huge thanks to my team at Gollancz and my editor, Millie Prestidge.

To my writing wife, Rachel Gillig. I am convinced there is no surviving this job without you. And if I could, I wouldn't want to. Thank you for your heart, your wit, your Greg-like sensibilities, your understanding, your commiseration. Your friendship is one of the greatest parts of this journey and I am so much better in every way for it.

To Caitlin Poole and Ginger Swan Lindsey. For years, you have gotten your hands dirty with me. You have combed through ideas and plot holes with me. You have celebrated successes and mourned losses with me. I feel eternally lucky that I found you both.

To Nirmaliz Colon Acosta, April Chandler, Marissa Young, Ellie Burke, and all the other writing friends who read, gave feedback, cheered me, and guided me. In some way, at some time, you impacted this story's path, and mine, and I'm so grateful.

To Allison Saft. Thank you for your truly endless generosity and insight on this book. Your constant belief and feedback helped grow this story, and me, in so many ways. I'm forever thankful to call you a friend.

To Hannah Teachout. Thank you for your expertise and steady support. To Skyler Wry, thank you for believing in me and telling me to just *start* when I said I wanted to write a book all those years ago.

To my family and friends, near and far, your love, enthusiasm, and support have meant the world to me. To every reader who picks up this book, thank you from the bottom of my heart.

ABOUT THE AUTHOR

Kalie Cassidy was born and raised in Southern California and spent over a decade working in Los Angeles as a professional theater actor, coach, and acting teacher. She now lives in the Midwest with her family and rambunctious golden retriever.

If you enjoyed

IN THE VEINS
OF THE DROWNING

look out for

IN THE WAKE
OF THE RUINED

BOOK TWO OF THE SIREN MAGE

by

KALIE CASSIDY

1

I crawled out of the sea like some graceless water creature, unused to the air and hard sand.

In one fist, I gripped Nemea's sword. On the opposite arm, looped around it like an overlarge shackle, was his crown. I'd been delirious with pain and exhaustion, floating over the sea's surface and through the remnants of the battle, slipping in and out of consciousness for the whole of the night. There had been no deciphering between dream and reality as bits of soldiers' bodies bobbed on the water beside me. Ship flotsam mingled with the blood-laced foam.

It had been a strain to keep my power focused, as that spell seemed to have reduced me to almost nothing. The taste of it still sat on my tongue, an incessant hunger for more pulsing through me with each thump of my sore heart. My senses had been dulled by the fierce, terrible pain in my middle, and yet, I'd managed to force the sea to ferry me across its surface. All the while, I'd clung to the sword and crown like the dented pieces of metal were what kept me afloat. They were imbued now, anointed with Nemea's blood. When I touched them, I remembered that I had slain a monster.

I remembered that I could do it again.

Shaking, and on all fours, I paused at the edge of the waves and looked up the dune.

The white sand rolled gently, creased by the wind, and I realized the sea had spat me out onto the very beach where Halla had performed her offering to Eusia. Where I had choked on the draught that had severed my bond to Theodore. I could make out the stairs that led to the flower garden, where the pain had brought me to my knees and blotted out my vision. The pale walls and turrets of Genevreer Palace loomed beyond in an endless, mocking sprawl.

I lay slowly onto my side and let out a sob at the flare of pain in my stomach. I could hardly stand, let alone reach the palace, traverse its halls.

"Your house is too big, Theo," I mumbled to myself, sounding half dead.

Perhaps I was.

The moldering, sea-filled hole in my middle throbbed like a heartbeat, carrying pain from my tender scalp to my wet toes. It pounded in my lips, in my fingers, and all I wanted was to sleep on the warm sand. I closed my eyes, only to have my thoughts flicker and distort like images from a violent fever-dream. I imagined the empress on her swaying ship, and Eusia in her little pool of dark water, and Halla, warm and safe with Theodore in the palace above me. I imagined Agatha's halo of dark curls, her wide, shining brown eyes, and there was fear in them.

A thin whimper filled my throat. Agatha, who never seemed to fear or fumble. Who was made of steely resolve. Agatha, who had given me years and years of stalwart care and friendship. Who'd done so much to ensure I would never be alone or afraid.

"Get up," I said, the words sharp air through my teeth, "get up, get up, get up."

With pain licking at me like wildfire, I pushed myself back up onto all fours. I knew, even as I dragged myself — and my damned sword and crown — over the sand, toward the garden stairs, that I wouldn't be welcomed back on palace grounds. I'd threatened the safety of the Varian kingdom in more ways than one. I'd gleefully choked Chancellor Eftan in farewell. But I was too unwell to enact my plan alone, and there was only one person in the palace who cared for Agatha the way that I did.

The sun beat against my back, and still, my skin stippled from a deep, penetrating cold. I reached the base of the stairs. Though my arms shook, I lifted Nemea's sword, and brought it down against the wooden treads with a loud *clang*. I did it again. And again. Tears slid down my cheeks, over my pinched lips, but finally a gold-armored soldier appeared at the top landing.

He squinted down at me. "Oy! You all right?"

In answer, the sword clattered from my hold. I collapsed fully against the wood. "I need Commander Mela." The words were hardly loud enough to reach him.

His boots thudded his descent. Once on the tread that my head rested upon, he squatted to inspect me, then reared back with recognition — with fear. "Ahh shit."

"I won't hurt you." My voice rasped, ugly and thin.

He reached out and plucked Nemea's sword from where it had fallen. Then, he slipped the crown from its place around my limp arm. My resistance was delayed — a weak jerk and a curl of my lip.

A grave note colored his voice. "Right, but I won't be takin' you at your word." He coughed in discomfort. "Sorry, Your Majesty."

There came the rattling of a chain. Fingers gripped my forearm. The biting cold of metal enveloped my wrists and squeezed and squeezed.

The sun shone behind him, and I squinted, trying to see him better. I'd not expected to be welcomed, but a nick of surprise cut through me anyway. I couldn't ignore its sting, nor the question that accompanied it: *Did Theodore order this?*

I opened my mouth to ask, but the guard rose and started back up the stairs with my sword and crown in his fist. An incoherent protest shook up my throat. My arms wobbled as I tried to push myself up, to crawl to the next stair, but pain spread through my stomach in a shocking burst. My limbs gave out. I laid my cheek once more on the warm, smooth wood, and the afternoon light dimmed to black.

I woke to the sound of more boots. Boots, and clanging armor, and murmuring voices. My senses rushed with the cutting sun rays, with the warm air perfumed with the scent of Theodore's flowering vines. The stairs I lay upon ached against my body, and my wrists were heavy with the manacles that guard had locked around them.

"Lachlan," I said on a jagged, searching sob. My head sat in a fog. My vision was bleary. "I need to see Commander Mela. Please. Not the king. I need Lach —"

Something bit into my shoulder. I squinted up at a handful of armored soldiers, swords drawn and poised on me. One of them spoke, though I was too beset to decipher which. "We're ordered to run you through without trial if you use your power."

My heart struck my ribs. "Who ordered tha —"

"She's supposed to go straight to the prison tower, isn't she?" asked another soldier, cutting me off.

"No. Please," I managed, "I need . . . I need to tell Lachlan about his wife."

"Mela doesn't have a wife."

My mind, my tongue, could not find and form words quickly enough. Chain rattling, I tried to twist, to sit myself up straighter, but a guard pinned me still by pressing a boot to my hip bone. "Uh-uh," he grunted.

A piercing screech tore up my throat. Some of the guards jolted and swore at the sound. I couldn't comprehend how that pressure alone was enough to ignite a blaze of agony through the whole of my body. It sent panic through me. I was weaker, tremulous, when all I'd previously known was a body that had felt sturdy and capable.

You will only find relief in your king. The words Eusia had spoken to me scraped through my head, a provocation and a warning made one. *Only the king will do.*

The guard yanked his boot from me, more from fear, I guessed, than remorse or pity. Perhaps he thought whatever vile thing coursed through me might seep from my skin and creep into him. Then the group of soldiers was straightening, clearing their throats, making themselves look well disciplined and alert as descending footsteps sounded above me.

"Found her at the base of the stairs," one of the guards said. "Do we carry ahead as usual? Not sure if royalty is treated differently from commoners in something like this, Commander."

I lifted my head just in time to watch Lachlan lower himself to kneel beside me. Our gazes locked.

His mossy eyes were cold, his mouth sat at an unfriendly slant. He looked empty and worn. "Queen, commoner, and Goddess alike," he said, voice bereft of its usual mischievous tone, "are all equal when it comes to the law."

Fucking bastard. I let out an angry breath and fought to hold up my manacled wrists. "Unchain me."

He ignored my words. "You look like a living corpse, Imogen."

"Lach." His name came out as a squeak. "What are you doing?"

"My job." At my look, he stood and loomed. "You've been proscribed."

I didn't know that word or its implication. I shook my head, frantically scanning the half dozen swords that were still trained on me.

Lachlan spoke to me slow and clear. "You've been condemned and banned from Varya for crimes of entrapment, treason, endangerment, and murder..." He cleared his throat. "Your Majesty."

"Who did I entrap—"

"The *king.*"

"That's not—Lachlan, you were there. You know the truth..."

His lips twitched. "Help her stand," he said to the two guards nearest me. As they hauled me up with hard hands, another cry shredded my throat. Lachlan scowled, and I searched for any concern in his flattened gaze. When I didn't find it, my chest hollowed out. "We have testimony that you ordered the murder of the captain of the *Hercule*, that you stowed away and endangered a Varian warship in the midst of battle."

A plummeting sensation took me as I remembered that captain's death. The deep, gurgling wound in his gut, the putrid lures that I'd cast into his killers. Lures I couldn't control. I used the soldiers' hold on me to keep myself up. "I didn't...I sank Serafi ships—I helped you win that battle." I groaned through my clamped teeth. "I killed Nemea. His crown is mine."

Lachlan's eyes went round with the impact of my confession, but he said not a word.

"Who proscribed me?" I finally whispered, unable to keep the wobble of hurt from my voice. "Was it Theo? Or did you and Eftan force his hand?"

His throat moved as he swallowed. The moment stretched, thin and taut as a string. When he finally answered me, it was with a choked voice. "The king and his council are one and the same."

I could only hold his unfeeling gaze, hoping to elicit some shame or remorse in him. Quickly, he flicked his eyes toward the top of the stairs, and the guards that held me turned me roughly. I spun like a cloth doll, loose and lolling, as they hauled me up to the flower garden. With each jostle I whimpered, barely able to keep my legs moving in step with theirs. At the top, they released me, and I fell to the soft grass in a tremoring heap.

Slowly, as the guards all filed in, and Lachlan came to stand before me, I sat myself back on my haunches. I went still, quiet. For a desperate moment, I thought to search for my power beneath the heavy shroud of pain. To send out a slew of lures at once and unchain myself.

The tinny scrape of a dagger torn from its sheath pulled me from my mind. Lachlan shook his head. "I see your wheels turning." He stooped to pick up the chain that hung between my cuffs. "Use your power" — he pointed the dagger directly at me — "and I'll have no choice but to use this."

I locked my gaze onto its silver point. "You wouldn't have the chance." Then, I studied his dark-rimmed eyes, resolute and grim, and could see no scheming in them. It set me off-balance, how we had gone from a warm, if awkward, farewell just yesterday to this.

His lips twisted. "Two of my guards are Siren-bound, Imogen. They'll kill you before you can beg. And I've told you before, I have no desire to see you dead."

I'd known Lachlan's fears over how I might set Varya toward ruin from the first. He'd threatened and scolded me and made his dislike clear. Our discord had sat between us like a reared-back weapon, but I never once thought he would bring it crashing down so violently.

He raised his brows in unhappy irony and gave my chain a tug. "Rise, Your Majesty."

Not long ago, the Mage Seer had given me guidance: *Take what you want.* I wanted to curse and gnash. I wanted to scream and be heeded and see all these guards on their knees. But I also wished, for better or worse, to live.

I stood with my clamped teeth bared.

Lachlan led me by the chain — my crown and sword in his other fist — with two of his guards trailing us. Slowly, painfully, we wove through riotous beds of orange and yellow and red blooms. We passed the glittering fountain that cradled three proud Siren statues in its center. With each step my throat grew thicker.

I'd returned to this place, and all its beauty, with the purpose of ending a threat, but as I moved closer to the palace, glowing pure white in the afternoon sun, I remembered that I was the danger cutting through its grounds. I was the terror encroaching.

As we crossed under a sun-dappled tunnel of vines, its white blooms yawning and plentiful, I stumbled over my own feet. My pain thrummed. It set sparks off in my vision. I closed my eyes, tried to focus on the warm rays of light, how they kissed my cheekbones, and I thought of Theodore.

As intemperate and corrupted as I was, I could never risk his safety, even for Agatha. Not with the dark and terrifying yearning that flooded me at the very thought of him. It came on like a fever, heat storming through me. My mouth watered with a hunger that needed sating. I yearned for his blood, for his flesh between my teeth. For his soft lips against mine.

I stopped hard in my tracks, pulling my chain taut. My eyes flew open. I could hardly delineate between my own care and desire, and the way Eusia wanted to consume him.

Lachlan spun, brow knit as he glared at me over his pauldron.

"Don't..." I whispered to him, struggling to keep my eyes from welling. "Don't let him near me."

Unlike Theodore, Lachlan's face was readily sculpted by his emotions. Sympathy softened his stern brow. But on its heels came a flash of suspicion. There was a question he wanted answered, a wariness he needed soothed. I held his glare and tried to will his trust, ignoring entirely whether or not I deserved it. His mouth firmed, he gave a brisk nod, then his gaze cut to the soldiers behind me. "You're dismissed. I have her from here."

"Sir, we'll take her," one of them objected. "You're not safe with her alone."

Not safe. How strange to have lived so long ruled by my own fears, only to become the source of it for others.

Lachlan started back down the path, toward the palace. A high whimper split my lips at the sudden movement. "You've been given your orders," he said.

Good. Now we would be free to speak, and I could try to pull him to my side.

The guards lingered behind us for a moment, and as I waited, I studied the rigid line of Lachlan's shoulders, the determined yet vacant way he seemed to move, as if a vital piece of him had been carved away and it was now sheer force of will that animated him. It was so unlike him — even in his anger he'd been effusive, glinting with mischief.

Finally, we reached the empty palace terrace. I tried to slow my steps. "Lach, wait." He tugged, and I cried out, but he kept our pace, pressing onward toward the glass door. "Gods damn it, you asshole," I hissed. "It's about Agatha."

His steps hitched. I'd found the crack in his armor, and I knew how tender the flesh was beneath. My words were a well-honed blade. "I know where she is."

But my attempt didn't pierce. Lachlan carried on, doggedly as before, and led me through the door. "Did you hear me?" We were in the Garden Room, crossing over its gleaming floors, past its bloom-painted walls. "Lachlan, are you actually going — "

"Quiet." He took me toward the entry hall, but I'd heard worry in the word.

"We're running out of time," I said, voice loud and shaking. "The empress might have — "

He stopped and whirled, eyes wide with a horrific look. "The *empress?*"

I nodded and took in his stricken face. His neck strained, eyes widening as he composed himself. He gave me a warning glance, then tucked us into the shadows of the eastern stairs before we could be noticed. He scanned the entry hall. A few soldiers milled. Some servants cleared away decorations.

Awareness prickled over my skin, and I finally took in the space myself. When I'd left — just yesterday — it was being set for a wedding. Flowering vines had been woven through the black marble banisters, where they looped around the ankles of the Great Gods' statues. Obelian sigils had hung beside Varian ones, a mingling of deep blues and greens. Now, all of it was half undone. Before the statue of Ligea, who stood beneath the western stairs, two maids worked together to fold a deep green and gold banner, making crisp creases. They tucked it neatly into a basket at their feet.

"What happened?" My voice was a shaking whisper. "Did he call it off?"

Lachlan's shadowed brow bent, a wary look in his gaze before eyeing the paneled wall at the base of the western stairs. "Keep moving."

I dug in my heels. "Did he call it off?"

"*Please*, be quiet, Imogen." He scanned the room once more, and whispered, "No."

"Then what — "

"Not here." He started us toward the far wall, and the narrow door hidden there. Each step had me feeling like I might crumble. He took my arm when my knees started to give. Hinges squealed, and I hobbled into a small, windowless room. An armory. There was a narrow hearth, a handful of lit torches in their holders. Maces, flails, and battle-axes hung on the dark wood walls. An old table and chairs took up the center of the space.

Lachlan clicked the lock over and stared at me. His even mask fell away, replaced by dire intensity. "Where did the empress take her?"

An awful cold crackled through me. "To Anthemoessa," I said. "Where Eusia is."

His color drained, his skin looking suddenly waxen. With a horror-struck look in his eyes, he seemed to sort through battering thoughts.

"Tell me what's happened with the wedding." I spoke too strongly, making pain flare deep in my middle. "Yesterday, when I left —"

Lachlan gave a sharp shake. "Yesterday?" The word broke in his throat. He shook his head again. "It's been two days, Imogen. Two fucking days since you left."

I sucked in a breath as I tried to comprehend. I could not wrap my mind around it — that I'd spent two whole days on the water, fighting toward land in a spell-sick stupor, clinging to my meager, inactionable plan, while Agatha sailed nearer and nearer to danger. By now, she might have reached it.

"How far is Anthemoessa?" My voice was small and frantic.

"Just over three days." Wood scraped as he pulled the nearest chair from the table and collapsed into it. He clutched his short hair in his fingers. "But it's near impossible to get there."

I gaped at him, willing my pain, and shock, and anger, to solidify into something violent enough to sustain me. "Stand up, you ass." His head snapped up, wet eyes to mine. "You have pined for her for a lifetime and *now* you collapse? When she needs you most?"

His fist slammed the table. "What can we do? You've been proscribed —"

"No thanks to you —"

"It *wasn't* me. The council put it to a vote at Eftan's insistence." His look was severe. "Everyone in the palace knows who you are and that you are to be imprisoned until trial. Admitting to regicide, like you just did in the garden, won't help you either."

"Tell Theodore to pardon me."

He shook his head. "He's not here."

A new pain tangled in my chest. I took a small step back, as if I could escape what he would tell me next.

"The wedding has been moved to Theo's ship." He spoke in starts and stops, like it took effort to form the words. "After that battle, after you went missing, Theo snapped . . . He altered all the wedding contracts. They set off for the docks a couple hours ago. They're headed to Obelia so Halla can have a proper wedding celebration with her own people."

I had to play the words over again in my head, had to fight to keep my stumbling heart intact. I needed Halla. I needed to get to Agatha. And foolish and dangerous as it was, I couldn't snuff out the insatiable *want* I felt for Theo.

For a long moment, our gazes held. I could nearly feel the charged air between us slowly transmute our sorrow and terror into an unmapped, awful idea.

"Lachlan." Despite how it ratcheted my hideous pain, I forced in a deep breath. I clung to the table's edges to keep myself still. "We need to get to that ship."